Also by
SUZANNE ENOCH

Some Like It Scot

SUZANNE ENOCH

St. Martin's Paperbacks

This is a work of fiction. All of the characters, organizations, and events portrayed in this novel are either products of the author's imagination or are used fictitiously.

SOME LIKE IT SCOT

Copyright © 2015 by Suzanne Enoch.

All rights reserved.

For information address St. Martin's Press, 175 Fifth Avenue, New York, NY 10010.

ISBN: 978-1-250-04163-0

Printed in the United States of America

St. Martin's Paperbacks edition / October 2015

St. Martin's Paperbacks are published by St. Martin's Press, 175 Fifth Avenue, New York, NY 10010.

10 9 8 7 6 5 4 3 2 1

Chapter One

L ord Munro MacLawry crept forward and down, his
bare knees digging into the soft, mossy ground beneath him. The chill breeze lifted the black hair off his
brow; he'd hiked halfway around the valley to keep the
wind in his face. The black and white and red plaid of
his kilt had been worn and muted even before he'd taken
to crawling through the mud and brambles, because he
wasn't fool enough to wear his dress kilt on a hunt.

Of course he might've worn trousers and had something covering his knees, but he wasn't a damned Englishman. He wasn't hunting for sport, and he wasn't
trying to show off for any damned Sassanach lords and
ladies who thought working up a sweat was gauche. He
wanted some bloody venison for dinner, and with the
current chaos at Glengask Castle, the simplest way to
get it would be to bring it to the table himself.

As he crested the low rise he paused, stretching out
flat to listen to the wind in the pines, the loons calling
from the reeds on the west bank of Loch Shinaig a
half mile to his right. The rain had held off for most of
the morning, but with the clouds piling up against the

mountains he'd be in for it any time now. It was a lovely morning, all in all—not the calm, clear days the Sassannach south of Hadrian's Wall preferred, but a cold, wet, wild Highlands come-hither morning.

Whether the rain held off or not he likely only had another hour or two to remain in the valley. After that, the Marquis of Glengask would be turning out half the household to track down his youngest brother. That was even more certain than the coming storm.

Simply by going out alone he'd violated at least half a dozen of his brother Ranulf's—and thereby clan MacLawry's—rules. Munro allowed himself a grim smile. Hell, aside from being out in the wilds alone, he hadn't bothered to tell anyone else where he was going, he hadn't brought a groom or one of Ranulf's deerhounds with him, he hadn't worn a warm coat, he hadn't stayed within sight of Glengask Castle, and . . . He counted on his fingers. Well, at least five violations, anyway. This had the makings of a grand morning, whatever the weather.

Too many damned rules, and as far as he was concerned, too many people willing to follow them without question. Aye, he understood the reasoning behind them—rivalries with other clans, bandits, poachers, the unpredictability of the Highlands terrain and weather—but at twenty-seven years of age he'd put himself through much worse. Intentionally. Bedding two sisters beneath the same roof, tossing tree trunks that weighed nearly as much as he did, and participating in some rather ungodly brawls didn't even scratch the surface.

With a slight grin that left the taste of dirt in his mouth, Munro edged forward again, creeping below the level of the tumbled boulders and low, wind-bent bushes until he caught sight of the red deer he'd been pursuing since daybreak. A lone stag; from the size of his rack the lad looked to be a year or two past his prime. Likely he'd been overthrown by some younger buck and now decided he preferred the bachelor life, anyway.

Well, Munro could certainly sympathize with that. Over the past year and a half both of his older brothers and his younger sister had gone and married, leaving him the sole unattached MacLawry sibling. It was all sugar and roses enough to rot his teeth, and then seven months after the first marriage the tide of bairns had begun to arrive. One each, with another due in a few weeks and—unless he was mistaken, a fifth was getting itself ready to debut in the spring. Evidently his generation of MacLawrys was extremely fertile.

And he was happy for the lot of them. More than happy. But while he had nothing against being Uncle Munro and having babies leak all over him, that was as close as he wanted to get to being a parent—because of what that meant. One lass only, for the rest of his life? What sort of nonsense was that? Keeping low despite his height, he edged within rifle range of the stag.

For Saint Andrew's sake, he was the youngest of three lads, with one male heir already born to the marquis. He had no bloodline for which he was responsible, no need to produce a son to keep his title, and whatever his siblings might have begun hinting, he meant to continue enjoying himself until his important parts wore out and fell off.

Munro eased his rifle into position, closing one eye to gaze down the iron sights. He was perfectly happy spending his nights with whomever he wished and his days doing whatever he pleased. For the buck, though, not having a herd to help him watch for enemies meant ending up as a tasty roast on a MacLawry banquet table.

The deer lowered its head to graze, and Munro let out his breath, then curled his finger around the trigger.

Sharp as thunder the shot echoed down the length of the valley and back again. For a moment it sounded like an entire regiment of lobsterbacks had opened fire. The buck dropped where it stood.

It was a damned fine shot—but he hadn't made it. His rifle still held ready, Munro opened both eyes to follow the thin, white trail of gun smoke back to the tumble of rough rocks on his left. For a long moment nothing moved, and if not for the dead buck in the clearing he could almost think he'd imagined the shot, that it had been thunder to join the deepening drizzle.

As still as he held himself, his heart pounded. Another few seconds and it might have been him down in the clearing, ripe for a shot between the shoulder blades. Both he and his middle brother, Arran, had been shot before, and it wasn't an experience he cared to repeat on someone else's whim.

Finally, one of the boulders shifted, becoming a gray blanket that stayed low to the ground and edged forward. The end of a musket protruded from beneath the wool, but if not for an occasional glimpse of boot or hand, it might have been a wild Highlands spirit gliding among the trees and rocks.

Down in England a commoner who killed a deer on a lord's land could be thrown into prison for poaching. Up here he might lose a hand for it. But in MacLawry territory his brother Ranulf, the Marquis of Glengask, generally allowed anyone who lived on his vast lands to hunt for food.

At the same time, this end of the valley was well known to be the MacLawry siblings' favorite hunting grounds. And it was too damned close to the castle for anyone but the immediate family to be shooting at things. The most unusual thing about Munro being there this morning was that he'd come alone. But he'd done it before and never encountered anyone. Hell, after eighteen months of a truce with the Campbells, a man should be able to go hunting on his own—whether Ranulf approved of the idea or not.

As a MacLawry he would be within his rights to claim the stag for himself, but that seemed supremely unsporting. From the glimpses he had of the gun, it was a muzzle-loader—which meant that if the lad had missed, he wouldn't have had time to reload before the deer fled. That had definitely been a shot worthy of a Highlander.

The blanket sank down again beside the animal, and Munro started to his feet, ready to call out both his approval and a warning not to shoot. When the lad rolled up the blanket and shoved it into a satchel, though, Munro frowned and dropped to the ground again.

The hunter wore rough trousers and a plain white shirt, work boots, and a wool coat that had definitely seen better days, topped off by a ragged straw hat that drooped on both sides. But that wasn't what caught Munro's attention. Rather, it was the long red hair pulled back into a wild mare's tail that trailed down between the poacher's shoulders, and a glimpse of a pale, delicate-looking cheek. The lad was a lass.

Quickly and efficiently, she butchered the deer, and between the ragged coat and the meat slung over her shoulder Munro couldn't make out any more details of physique. But now that she was out from under the blanket, watching her walk, seeing how she shifted her weight to carry the musket and satchel, she couldn't be anything but a she.

Munro rose to a crouch again as the lass headed toward the west end of the valley and the rugged gorge beyond. His brother Arran, set between himself and Ranulf in age, had several times accused him of being uninterested in puzzles and mysteries unless he could put the result on a plate and eat it. A crack shot, trousers, long red hair, and tits, though, added up to a puzzle that interested him.

Keeping well back and under cover, he followed the oddly clothed lass out of the valley. Aye, he was a big man, tall and broad-shouldered as a mountain and all muscle if he said so himself, but he damned well knew how to move quietly when the circumstances called for it. Any stranger who thought it a bonny idea to hunt in MacLawry territory—nearly within rifle-shot range of Glengask Castle—well, that was a circumstance in itself, without adding a lass to the equation.

The MacLawrys had been taking in the cotters of other clans for years, practically since the damned Highland Clearances had begun, but as a matter of safety he or one of his brothers had either met each of the refugees and shaken hands or had arranged for a trusted MacLawry chieftain to do so—and to make certain a fisherman was a fisherman, and not some assassin from clan Campbell or Buchanan or Fraser or elsewhere. It wouldn't do to have any troublemakers looking for a way to slip in close to the family and begin another clan war.

Most frequently over the past eighteen months, arranging the greetings and seeing the newcomers settled in had fallen to him, alone; Ranulf and Arran had been otherwise occupied with going to London, falling in love, and marrying. He didn't recall meeting or even hearing about a woman in trousers, though, and he was fairly certain he wouldn't have forgotten such a thing.

As for the local lasses, he was well acquainted with most of them. Very well acquainted. There were a handful of redheads, but she wasn't one of them. It behooved him, then, for the sake of his family's safety, to figure out who she was and from where. He'd already seen the evidence that she was a dead shot with a musket.

Big, heavy plops of rain had him soaked to the skin by the time they reached the narrowing, higher end of Gleann Tàirnich, and amid the thick trees and house-sized boulders along the side of the valley he had to close the distance between them to keep her in sight. He expected her to continue on to one of the small clusters of cotters' huts that had sprung up between the foothills and the river. Instead, though, she headed toward the center of the canyon, winding her way along what he realized had once been a road. Now it was barely more than a rutted carpet of wet leaves and fallen branches. Abruptly even that ended, and with no visible effort she hopped over a low stone wall and vanished.

As Munro reached the broken wall he stopped, crouching to gaze beyond the tumbled, moss-covered stones at the ruins beyond. Haldane Abbey had stood at the head of Gleann Tàirnich for nearly four hundred years, and it hadn't been occupied for the past hundred or so. It sat empty because a hard winter's snow had collapsed the entire back of the building, and the rest of it hadn't been worth the expense of renovating.

Regardless of that, it seemed that Haldane wasn't empty any longer. Leaking, dreary, dangerously unstable, and reputedly haunted by at least three former residents and a hound, Haldane remained free of the influx of refugees from the Campbells, the MacDonalds, and the Gerdens and Stuarts. In fact, none had even been tempted to settle within its sight.

The redhead could be one of the specters, he supposed, except that as far as he knew spirits didn't kill and butcher deer, nor did the female ghosties wear trousers. Haldane was a MacLawry house on MacLawry land, and if he wanted to he could simply march up and demand to know who was trespassing. That was how he normally would proceed; hell, his siblings didn't call him Bear just because of his broad shoulders. Unless he cared to spend the rest of his day staring at tumbled walls, though, he needed either to advance or retreat.

Metal clicked behind him. Halfway to his feet, Munro froze. *Damnation.*

"This is my place." A female brogue came low and steady from behind the weapon. "No one was here, and I claimed it. So ye go away, big man, and save yerself some trouble."

And there he was, like a boy caught with his kilt up. His brothers would be laughing their arses off. "I'll agree ye're a fine shot, lass, but do ye ken ye can handle me all by yer lonesome? And I didnae see ye reload."

"Then make yer move and we'll discover how observant ye are," she returned. "I said I dunnae want trouble. I left ye near half the stag, so walk back doon the way ye came and go claim it before the rats and wildcats and foxes take it from ye."

Shooting a charging man was nothing like taking down a buck unawares—and that was if she'd even managed to stuff a ball down the old muzzle-loader while she made her way up the valley. At the same time, it was a bit disconcerting that she'd known precisely where he was since she'd brought down the deer. He hadn't suspected that anyone was within a mile of him until she'd fired. Slowly he rose, straightening his knees and keeping the rifle in his right hand pointed toward the ground. Neither this moment nor a quarter of a deer was worth either of them dying over.

"I'll go," he agreed, taking two long steps away from her. Then he stopped, took a breath, and turned around to face her.

He could count the number of men who'd bested him in hunting or battle on one finger—well, on no fingers, because no man had ever done so. As of this morning, he could no longer make that claim about females. His gaze was somewhat obscured by the musket aimed steadily at the center of his chest and by the ancient hat pulled low over her eyes, but he could see enough that he would know her again. Wet scarlet hair hung across her face and escaped from the long mare's tail draped over one shoulder. A straight nose, cheeks streaked with dirt and rainwater, lips that might have been full and sensuous if they weren't clenched together hard enough to blanch any color from them, she looked to be in her early twenties, if that.

"That's enough gawking fer ye, *àluinn*. Away with ye. Dunnae come back. I reckon there's enough ground in the Highlands that ye can avoid this wee bit of it."

And she continued to dictate terms to him, even if she *had* called him handsome. Hm. "I reckon I could avoid ye," he agreed, keeping a careful eye on her as he resumed his retreat. "Whether I will or nae, well, that's another question, isnae?"

"Aye. Come test me again, big man. I'll nae be so polite next time."

If this was her being polite, seeing her rude would be quite the spectacle. He continued backing away,

moving slowly enough that she would hopefully understand that he damned well wasn't frightened of her.
This merely happened to be one of the few occasions
where it seemed preferable to avoid bloodshed. He was
out here on his own, after all.

Even so, he was tempted. How difficult would it be
to circle around behind the estate and show the redhead
just what it meant to turn a weapon on a MacLawry?
She wouldn't boast about besting him after that, he reckoned. Munro paused at the bend of the rutted path, then
took a breath and continued away from the pile. Aye, he
could scare the wits out of her, make a few threats, but
for once he decided on restraint. She'd truly surprised
him, and if anything, that deserved more of a response
than some fist shaking. It would never do if she ran off
before he figured out who she was.

Once he'd put Haldane out of sight behind him, he
turned his back on the place and retraced his steps to
the stag. With the rain only a lone fox had found the carcass, and that wee beastie fled at the sight of him. It
was about time something showed him the damned respect he was due.

After he finished the butchering work she'd begun,
Munro slung the deer over his shoulder and made his
way to Loch Shinaig and then north along its west bank
until Glengask came into view beyond the meadow at
the top of the rise. Trudging around the side of the
sprawl to the kitchen entrance, he kicked at the door
until Timothy, one of the footmen, pulled it open.

"I've brought supper," Munro said, grunting as he
shoved past the servant and stalked into the kitchen. The
cook, Mrs. Forrest, hurriedly cleared off a table and
he dropped the animal onto it.

"Where's the back half?"

The middle MacLawry brother, Arran, stepped down into the kitchen. *Wonderful.* If Arran was there, then his wife, Mary, and their bairn, Mòrag, would be, as well. Generally he was pleased to see the lot of them, but today he would have preferred a few damned minutes to himself. "I got hungry," he returned.

"Ye must've, if ye're eating venison straight off the hoof."

With a snort Munro moved around his brother to wash up in the large kitchen sink and then head for the main part of the house. He would damned well tie himself to a stake and set fire to it before he would admit that a lass had outshot him with a fifty-year-old musket and then ambushed him. He'd never hear the end of it. Ever.

Arran, who could scent trouble better than a hound, followed him. "Ye didnae go oot alone, did ye, Bear? Ye know ye shouldnae."

"If I'd wanted company I would've taken one of the dogs. Owen, bath. Hot," he said, as the head footman emerged from the morning room.

"Aye, Laird Bear. I'll see to yer rifle fer ye."

Munro handed it over, keeping the muzzle pointed well down. "It's loaded," he cautioned.

"So ye *clubbed* the deer to death before ye ate it?" Arran pursued.

"Ye keep telling me it's dangerous oot of doors, so I reloaded. And if ye must know, I crossed paths with an old lass and her three grandbabies. I gave them a good supper." Munro halted to face his brother. "Is there anything else ye want to know aboot my morning?"

Arran lifted both palms in a gesture of surrender.

"Nae. I dunnae want my head knocked off my shoulders. Come play billiards with me and Lachlan when ye've washed the blood off ye."

"Lach's here, as well? And Winnie, I suppose. And wee Colin."

"Aye. And my Mary and Mòrag. Is that a problem fer ye, *bràthair*?"

Munro shook himself. "Nae. If I'd known the Mac-Lawry army was here, I would've killed a bigger buck."

"Or nae have eaten half of it on the way home." Arran chuckled, clapping him on the shoulder.

"Aye. Go away. I'll be down in a bit."

He'd grown up in a large, loud household, and the only difference two wee lads and a lass, his nephews and niece, had made was that the MacLawrys—and in Lachlan and Winnie's case, the MacTiers—could now see a future that a few years ago they hadn't truly been able to imagine.

"Comb yer damned mane while ye're at it. Get yerself civilized so ye dunnae frighten the wee ones."

And *that* was the rub. Today with the rain and blood soaking into his shirt, with a mysterious lass leveling a musket at him, returning to bairns and wives at Glengask all seemed so . . . domestic. Two years ago the MacLawrys had been the strongest, fiercest, most progress-minded clan in the Highlands. This morning, though, he could swear he'd heard Ranulf singing to his seven-month-old son and heir, William. Ranulf, whose glare had caused more than one man to piss himself.

At least Munro had been able to go out hunting, however poorly that had ended. The rest of them, though, were definitely not about to frighten any stray Gerdenses or Campbells into surrendering. Not any longer. Not with bairns tucked against their breasts, wives on their arms, and lullabies on their lips.

After he'd bathed and changed into a clean kilt and shirt and his old boots, he went and tracked down Ranulf. The head of clan MacLawry leaned against the door frame of the nursery, gazing at the loud, crawling chaos of babies and their mamas inside. And damn it all, he was smiling.

"Ran?"

The marquis straightened, turning to face him. "That was good of ye, to give over half the buck to the widow woman. They've more need of it than we do."

Of course Ranulf would have heard the tale already. There wasn't much that happened in the Highlands without his knowledge. "I—"

"And the next time ye go off by yerself to hunt, I'll set my hounds after ye." He indicated the two large deer-hounds lying close to the wall in the hallway and likely attempting to escape the notice of the babies. "Peace with the Campbells or nae, ye'd still be a prize kill fer some."

Munro nodded. He could argue the point, but he would lose. It was easier to simply agree and then ignore the warning. "I went by Haldane Abbey," he said, instead of conceding. "The whole south wing's gone now."

"I havenae even thought aboot the abbey fer years." The marquis tilted his head. "What sent ye that far south on foot?"

"Ye didnae give it over to anyone, did ye? Some cotter and his kin? I thought I saw footprints aboot it. Old ones, but it made me curious."

"Nae. I'd nae risk anyone there, even fer a single night." Ranulf gazed at him. "Do ye ken it means trouble?"

Bloody wonderful. The last thing he wanted was to send lads out there to hear from the trouser lass that she'd already leveled a gun on him. "I think it's more likely some of the village lads looking fer spirits over the summer. We used to do it." He shrugged. "The next time I head oot that way I'll take a closer look to be certain."

"The next time ye head oot that way with Debny or some of the other lads to keep ye company," Ranulf amended, squatting to pick up a black-haired bairn crawling for the dogs. "Dunnae take unnecessary risks, *bràthair.* I'm nae jesting with ye."

For a moment Munro divided his attention between the Marquis of Glengask and his seven-month-old son. The next marquis, the next head of clan MacLawry, presently trying to eat his father's fine white shirt. "It seems to me, *bràthair,*" he returned, reaching out to run a forefinger carefully along the wee bairn's ear, "that I'm the only MacLawry who *can* take risks, these days. And ye need a man who can."

"Bear, ye—"

"Ye ken that's true, Ran. Ye may be civilized now, but the Highlands arenae. I dunnae mean to fling myself off a cliff, but I'm nae domesticated. And if I choose to go oot hunting from time to time, I'm seven-and-twenty. I reckon that's old enough to be able to decide fer myself what I'm willing to risk."

The marquis eyed him. "Then perhaps it's time I find ye a wife to settle ye doon."

"Hm." Tired with being threatened today, Munro turned on his heel. "I suggest ye dunnae, if ye ever want to see me again. If I want a wife, I'll find one fer my-self."

"Havenae ye already bedded every unmarried lass in the Highlands?" his brother asked. "Nae a one's caught yer attention?"

"I've bedded barely three quarters of 'em." And that wasn't even counting the redhead in the trousers. "A night's fun, aye, but a lifetime? Ye're giving me the shivers."

"Times are changing, Bear. Ye need to change, as well, or ye'll find yerself left behind."

Given the alternative, being left behind didn't sound so terrible. At any rate, not having a wife and bairns left him free to scout Haldane Abbey again. The trouser lass had called it *her* place, which said to him that she'd set-tled in there. He therefore had a fair suspicion he'd be seeing her again, and that the next time he did so, he wouldn't be the one caught unawares.

Chapter Two

E lizabeth, it's me," Catriona MacColl announced in a low voice, making her way over a fallen doorway archway in the long hallway, down an uneven trio of stairs, and into the one solid room remaining in the old fortress.

Or relatively solid, rather. She could see the sky in one corner, and rain trickled down the wall to gather in a growing pool creeping outward with spidery tentacles. Mostly because of the existence of several old work-tables and a dented teapot she'd decided this room had once been the kitchen.

At any rate, the old ruin had never had a proper stove that she could tell. Its last occupancy had been too long ago for such an innovation. Instead, a chest-high fire-place fitted with iron shelves and a turning rack squat-ted against the middle of the longest wall. The room was large and windowless, and in the days when it had been fashionable for nobles to eat food cooked on a hearth, the rack would have been turned by a servant boy or even a dog in a wheel.

Since she had neither of those, she nudged the pile

of blankets beside the hearth with the toe of her boot. "Elizabeth. Did ye put the water on to boil?" she asked, even though she could clearly see that no pot hung over the fire.

The blankets stirred. "The water had a cricket in it." Hazel eyes with long, straight lashes blinked beneath a neat coif of dark blond hair.

"So ye scooped it out and put on the water, aye?" Catriona dragged a heavy, three-legged table nearer the light of the fire and set down the venison to slice it into strips and then cubes with her boot knife. She needed to sharpen the damned thing; it was nearly like sawing with a spoon.

"I hope we haven't yet sunk to something that barbaric," Elizabeth MacColl returned in her proper London tones. "I dumped it out in our pond, there."

Catriona stifled a sigh and sawed harder. "Then ye went out and fetched another pot of water, I assume."

The blankets stood. "You told me not to go outside. And I'm certainly not going to use the stuff running down the walls."

"Boiling it would've killed the cricket, ye know."

"But not my memory of it being there, paddling across the surface." Elizabeth shuddered. "Honestly, Cat, why couldn't we stay at an inn? You said this was MacLawry land. They take in refugees. And an inn would have been warmer and drier than this. *And* you wouldn't have to hunt our dinner. Or cook it."

"I reckon this is safer," Catriona returned. "And it's nothing I'm nae accustomed to. Now. Will ye cut up the wild onions while I fetch more water?"

"Yes, of course." Elizabeth shrugged out of the blankets. She wore a pretty yellow muslin beneath a wool mauve-colored spencer jacket, fit for the fanciest drawing rooms in London. "I am trying to be helpful, you know. If you need anything sewn or embroidered, you'll be happy I'm here."

"I'm happy now, ye goose." Catriona straightened to hug her younger sister with the arm that wasn't streaked with deer blood.

"I don't know why." Taking the knife gingerly, Elizabeth began tentatively smashing the onions to bits. "I didn't mean for my first letter to you in five years to be a request for aid. I meant to stay in touch with you, as I promised."

"I could've sent ye a missive or two, myself. We were both too busy, I suppose." Cutting ties had also made for less conflict within the two households, but they both knew that.

Elizabeth sniffed, though Catriona wasn't certain whether it was from the onions or her sentiments. "When I saw you on my doorstep, Cat, I . . ." She grimaced. "I should have scooped out the cricket."

Catriona kissed the top of her sister's—half sister's—hair. "I'm wet through, anyway. Another stroll through the rain'll be refreshing."

As if to counter her optimism, thunder rumbled in the distance. But today the weather concerned her less than did one of the Highlands's other hazards. She'd hardly expected a six-and-a-half-foot man to come creeping through the trees like a great, silent, black-haired lion. He'd likely tracked the buck for some time, given the sad state of his clothes, but she'd been crouched there for three damned hours, waiting for a deer to stroll by and not daring to stray farther away from where she'd placed her sister.

Aye, she likely should have let him have the kill, but he hadn't looked nearly as hungry as she felt. When he'd let her take her share of the meat and go, she'd thought herself safe—a fellow poacher wasn't likely to cause a stir over something as plentiful here as red deer. Aside from that, she was no unsuspecting buck out for a stroll, and he was as big as a wall. But for Saint Bridget's sake, he was quiet. Thank goodness she'd kept to her habit of looking back after she'd jumped the wall, or he might have remained undiscovered on her trail until he'd suddenly appeared in the kitchen. She stifled a shiver, not wanting to have to relate this latest bit of trouble to Elizabeth.

Retrieving the pot they'd acquired, she slipped back up the hallway to stop just inside what remained of the front doors. The wind had picked up, but she couldn't detect anything out of place—and no sign of the giant. It wouldn't remain that way, though. As happy as she'd been to find this place in the middle of the wilds, they couldn't stay now. The big man would return with his laird, no doubt, and drive the MacColl sisters out. Or worse.

Yes, she was fairly certain they'd found themselves on MacLawry land, but the MacLawrys were a fairy tale, as far as she was concerned. Lord Glengask, the stories said, welcomed both his own people and those fleeing from other clans as their lairds turned their farms and cottages and shacks into grazing land for damned Cheviot sheep.

She scowled. Glengask would have no reason or cause to welcome either her or Elizabeth, regardless, and several fine reasons to turn them away. If she'd been alone, she would have finished packing her things and disappeared deeper into the wilderness by now. But she wasn't alone, and she didn't know how much more wild living Elizabeth had left in her.

As cold and full of leaks and holes as this old fortress

was, it remained a definite improvement over most of
the other places they'd lately found themselves. In London, people—or those marginal citizens whose paths
she'd crossed in the late hours—noticed her attire. Out
here, however, no one looked askance at her. Well, no
one but Elizabeth, of course.

She squatted by the small stream running behind the
ruins and filled the pot with fresh, cold water. Taking
the moment to wash her hands and wipe her palms on
her trousers, she smiled at how uncivilized and unfashionable she must have looked to Anne Derby-MacColl
when she'd arrived in London—what had it been?—five
weeks ago, now. The combination of loathing and I-told-
you-so satisfaction on her stepmother's face had nearly
made her laugh. Well, Mrs. Derby-MacColl wasn't
laughing now, she'd wager. In fact, Catriona was surprised they couldn't hear her throwing one of her tantrums all the way up into the Highlands.

No, the trousers she wore both fit her and kept her
warm, but she'd learned a long time ago that they definitely made her more noticeable. And today she had
been noticed. She needed to solve this new problem, not
dwell on old ones.

Very well, then. She would pack up their belongings,
such as they were, and shift them into the shallow cave
she'd discovered halfway up the valley. She and Elizabeth would stay in the ruins, because, well, the nineteen-
year-old couldn't even put up her own hair. The mere
idea of sleeping in a cave would send her into a faint.

That way she and Elizabeth would only need to get
themselves somewhere safe if the big man reappeared.
If Catriona saw no sign of him over the next few
days, she would bring their things back into the ruin
again. As wrecked as the old building was, it felt safer

than moving about in another clan's territory. And with winter edging ever closer, she needed somewhere with at least a partial roof over them.

Uneasiness shivered down her spine. The Highlands loved winter; deep and brutal and long, the two seemed reluctant to part company for the other three seasons. And the chill had her giving the one heavy blanket they had over to Elizabeth already. In a few weeks a drafty old ruin like that could become nearly as deadly as being caught out of doors. Frowning, Catriona returned as swiftly as she could to the house.

Elizabeth had moved on to finish cubing the venison, and with a short smile Catriona hung the pot over the fire. Her sister might have no idea how to live in the Highlands, but she was making an attempt, anyway. That left it to her to make the experience as safe and livable as possible. She sent an assessing look around the room. The old kitchen remained fairly intact, except for that west corner of the roof, and the wall below it that had partly collapsed into the neighboring room. If they meant to winter here, she had some repairs to make. Old Tom and his simple son Connor would have had it seen to in a week, but Old Tom was better than a hundred miles away, and she wouldn't send for him even if she could. No, this was *her* task, and she needed to figure out how to make their temporary home secure against intruders and the weather.

If that mountainous lad hunted here, perhaps a village lay closer than she'd realized. Hm. It would be risky, but she needed a hammer and a saw, and a selection of other items while she was at it. Of course none of her potential thievery would matter if the giant came calling again, but it seemed well past time they found some luck.

Once the water boiled, the smoke from the fireplace hopefully blending into the rain and clouds, she dumped in the onions and venison, and a sprinkling of the salt she'd taken from the last inn they'd passed through. As far as cooking went it was beyond simple, but at least the contents were plentiful.

"Your clothes are steaming, you know," Elizabeth pointed out. "If you catch pneumonia I'd . . . Well, I don't know what I would do. And that's the trouble, isn't it?"

"This isnae my first rainstorm, Elizabeth," Catriona countered, but she went over to their bags and found a fresh shirt and trousers, anyway. Half the lads between London and the Highlands were missing clothes after she passed through, but she'd left a bit of coin where she could. That would have to do. "Better?"

"Yes. Thank you."

Catriona used the moment to stuff hairbrushes and a shawl and other incidentals back into their sacks and satchels, trying her best to make it look as if she'd merely felt the need to tidy up. With any luck, Elizabeth wouldn't even realize anything had changed.

"What are you doing?" her sister asked on the tail of that thought.

"I . . . may have caught sight of someone," Catriona admitted, keeping her voice cool and level. "If we need to move, I dunnae want us delayed."

Elizabeth knelt beside her. "Cat, all of this trouble is my fault. You don't need to hide things from me. Especially danger."

"It isnae yer fault. It's yer mother's fault, and all ye did was have the courage to say nae to it. As for the rest, I'd appreciate if ye'd allow me to be the older sister and do the worrying for the both of us."

"You *are* worried, then."

"I'm cautious," Catriona amended, and handed over a deck of playing cards from her pack. "A game of piquet while we wait for stew?"

Her sister grinned. "Yes, please."

Two hours later Catriona sat cross-legged on the floor to eat, while Elizabeth took the house's single chair. Trousers, hunting, and eating with her fingers—she imagined her own mother would faint from embarrassment at the mere thought of it, though from her father's stories, Caitir MacColl had been eminently practical. Perhaps she would have approved, after all—if not of the circumstances, then of her only child's consequent actions. As for her father, well, if Randall MacColl hadn't gone and caught the fever, then none of this would be happening. If he'd been alive, a great many things would be different right now. Of that she was certain.

"I wish we had more books," Elizabeth said into the silence, startling her a little. "We could read to each other in the evenings, instead of imagining what must be going on in London. Or thinking about what we'll do once winter settles in."

Whether Catriona had ever spared a thought for the goings-on in London or not, she needed to remind herself that as young and sheltered as Elizabeth was, her sister wasn't an idiot. "I think with a few minor repairs this place would do us quite well for the winter. As for London, ye'll see it again. And ye'll have a few fine stories to tell aboot yer time away." She patted her sister's foot. "I'm sorry ye had to leave yer books behind. They were too heavy to carry. But I'll find ye a tome or two."

She'd left her own books behind, as well. Whether her bedchamber remained as she'd left it or not, however, was another question entirely. From the way her cousin Morna had been eyeing her view out to the harbor and the ships docked there, she doubted it remained hers. Not that that mattered. She didn't intend to return. The three books she'd brought with her—her favorite three—were in the bottom of a river somewhere in the Midlands, where no one who might be looking for Elizabeth would ever find them.

Catriona shoved the rest of her things into a beat-up portmanteau and a potato sack. She'd begun with even more than the books—a small, delicate carving of a fox made of antler, an old rune stone for luck, a few ribbons for her unruly hair—they'd seemed important when she'd set off to the south, but on the way north with Elizabeth they'd been more of a nuisance than anything else, an extra weight that only slowed them down. She'd given them away without a second thought. Elizabeth needed some of her pretty things about her. Catriona did not.

"We're staying here?" her sister said, giving the hole in the corner of the ceiling a dubious look.

"Aye. We have fire, plentiful game, water close by, and most of a roof. I reckon I can figure out how to patch it before first snow."

"I'll help you," Elizabeth stated, squaring her shoulders.

All of her plans depended, of course, on whether the big man in the white, black, and red kilt went and tattled on her to the local laird or clan chieftain. Perhaps she should have shot him instead of the buck. That would certainly have simplified matters. If she began murdering people for inconveniencing her, though, well, she would have begun with her uncle and the Duke of Visford and her own stepmother—and then she would deserve whatever misery came her way.

Oh, they should just leave. The building was awful and rotted, after all, with just enough remains of old paintings and bed sheets and broken knickknacks to be unsettling. The next valley over might well hold a hunter's cottage abandoned for the winter—a place with a window or two, a solid ceiling, and even some nuts or grains she could snatch before the vermin got to them. They wouldn't have to shift their blankets every time it rained, and no muscular giant of a man would know where they slept.

Why was she even thinking of him? Yes, he'd been reasonably pleasant featured—or at least that had been her impression. She'd only seen him from the back until that last moment when he'd turned around to say he would likely return. "Stupid giant," she muttered, shoving her cleaned knife back into her boot.

"What was that?"

"Just cursing the weather. It's a Highlands tradition."

Elizabeth chuckled. "I think I remember that."

Perhaps she'd dealt the big man a blow to his pride, but he was the one who'd followed her and refused to lose her trail. And she'd only told him to leave her be, for heaven's sake. Men never listened to reason when their manliness was called into question, but what choice had she had? She couldn't very well hide in the shadows while he discovered Elizabeth or looted their things for what little they possessed. Or worse, allow him to assault one of them simply because they happened to be females on their own.

It would likely make more sense to sleep in the cave along with their things, but that would be the point where she began to wonder if she was actually helping Elizabeth out of her troubles or creating a whole new set of them. "I'm going to shift some of our things, just in case," she said, rising and slinging a satchel over her shoulder. "I'll be back within the hour. I'm leaving ye the musket, but dunnae try to use it unless ye have no other choice."

"It's getting dark."

"I ken where I'm going. Dunnae worry. With this rain no one'll be out and about."

"Except you."

"Well, I'm a bit of a madwoman, if I recall yer mother's greeting correctly." And that of countless other people she'd met over the years. Flashing a grin at her forlorn-looking sister, she dug into one pack and pulled out the single book she'd kept with her. "Occupy yerself with this."

"Oh, Byron's poetry! You never said!"

"I was saving it for a rainy day." She grinned again. "Which is today, I reckon."

By the time she returned, Elizabeth was asleep in her pile of blankets, the fire was down to glowing embers, and the rain had begun to taper off. Catriona threw another branch onto the fire, stripped off her clothes to lay them on the hearth, and carefully slipped her book from beneath her sister's fingers. Settling in with her own blanket, she tried to read. In the quiet, though, her mind kept drifting to a very annoying giant with very fit-looking thigh muscles beneath that kilt and a head of shaggy black hair almost down to his shoulders.

Grumbling, she shifted again, sitting as close to the fire as she could, the heat making her skin feel dry and tight. She read until her eyes refused to stay open. If the big man reappeared, this would likely be the last dry, warm sleep either of them could expect for the next few days, until she found them another place to hide. And thoughts of the giant were not going to keep her from it.

"Hello the house!"

Ice slammed down Catriona's spine. Sitting straight upright from the thin blanket before the hearth, she dove for the musket beside her even as she noted the wan sunlight drifting in through the hole in the corner of the ceiling. "Stay here," she hissed as her sister struggled upright, grabbing for her clothes, throwing them on, and then bolting from the kitchen. She knew that voice already. She'd let him go once when he'd blundered after her; this time he was a threat, and she wouldn't be so charitable.

"Red! I know ye're in there! The chimney's smoking."

Next would come the torches and the flames—the usual way Scottish lairds rid themselves of villagers they no longer wanted about. How many were with him? Was Glengask himself outside with a dozen rifles aimed at the old pile? Catriona scrambled up the half-collapsed wood and stone stairs to peer out one of the many cracks in the upstairs walls. Only silent, damp forest appeared to her view. She'd overslept, blast it all; rays of sunlight broke through the heavy clouds low in the eastern sky. With a muttered curse she hurried to the next opening, a misshapen, glassless window. Still nothing.

Had he called out and then ducked into hiding again? Was he trying to lure her into the open? *Damnation.* She shifted to the next window—and then spotted the giant. He had a huge gray deerhound at his side, its head level with his waist, but she couldn't see anyone else. Surely he wasn't daft enough to appear with only a dog to support him.

"I told ye to stay away," she called out, ducking into the shadows before she spoke. "I'll nae warn ye again."

When she next peeked out, he was scanning his gaze across the second-floor windows, clearly looking for her.

He was younger than she'd realized yesterday, the scruff of his beard in the scattered sunlight making his face look lean and dashed handsome. "It's nae safe up there, ye ken. That whole floor could give way in a stiff breeze."

"It's nae safe oot there for ye, giant," she returned, shifting her position yet again. "I'll give ye to the count of five to clear away from here. If I still see yer arse after that, I'll put a ball in it."

He didn't move. "Be reasonable, Red. I only brought ye some bread and a blanket. I reckon old Haldane Abbey was drafty even before it collapsed."

She edged sideways, gazing at him through the broken casement. "Ye expect me to believe that, ye big lunk?"

His rather fine brow furrowed. "I go by Bear. I prefer that to 'giant' or 'lunk,' if ye dunnae mind."

"So ye think we're neighbors now, do ye? Leave the satchel and go. And dunnae come back."

This time she could swear a smile touched his mouth. "Nae. I reckon I'll bring it inside," he countered. "The dog is Fergus. He'll nae harm ye, if ye behave yerself. And neither will I."

Ha. She would never give him the opportunity to do such a thing. On the other hand, unless she *did* mean to shoot him, she was going to have to permit him into the building. He wasn't a coward, and that was damned certain, but that information didn't precisely do her any good. She was a Highlands lass and could pass for one, but one word spoken by Elizabeth and he would know she was English—or at least that she'd been raised that way. She couldn't risk that.

Before she could consider her strategy he started around to the front of the house. *Damn it all.* She picked her way back down the fallen staircase as swiftly as she could, taking only a second to be thankful once again that she wore trousers. This crumbled house was no place for a woman in skirts to be crawling about. Or a man in a kilt, likely. Or she could hope so, at least.

And he wore a kilt again today, along with heavy boots, a plain white shirt, and a black wool coat. Why that mattered she had no idea, but she'd noticed his appearance with a clarity that surprised her a little. Perhaps she'd finally taken to heart the proverb about knowing thy enemy. It was too late to learn the lesson, really—or maybe it wasn't, since she and Elizabeth were still free.

Catriona made her way through the tumbled ruins to the doorless front entry and leveled her musket at the opening as the so-called Bear hopped over a pile of stones and strolled inside. "I dunnae recall inviting ye in," she snapped.

"I dunnae recall asking fer an invitation," he returned, giving a short whistle. The hound leaped through the opening to stand again at his side.

Now that they were on the same footing both man and beast seemed even more massive, and she couldn't decide which was the more dangerous. And then the hound took a step forward, its hackles lifting, and bared its teeth in a growl that sent the hairs on the back of her own neck pricking.

"Fergus is advising ye to lower the musket," the big man commented easily, shifting the satchel he carried slung over one shoulder. "I suggest ye pay attention."

"Neither of ye frightens me. If ye feel the need to give me charity, leave the blanket and bread and go. Otherwise someone's likely to get shot."

The hound crouched, edging another step forward. Uneasiness clenched into Catriona's spine. Scottish hounds had been bred to take down deer; she would hardly be a challenge. This was a chess match, though. The musket was her weapon, and the dog, his. Who would fire first? Or who would blink?

Light green eyes gazed at her for a long moment, more subtle and contemplative than she expected. Then with a visible sigh he snapped his fingers. "Fergus, off. Down."

With what sounded like a disgusted humph the dog sat, then lay down with his large gray head on his paws.

"That's good, then," she said, pushing her sudden relief aside. She was nowhere near being safe, yet. "Now ye, big man. Off."

"Bear, I told ye."

"Bear, then. Put down the satchel and be off with ye."

Moving slowly, keeping his gaze on her, he complied. "Ye dunnae need to fear me, lass. And ye're welcome to stay on here. Glengask welcomes all Highlanders, as long as they dunnae make trouble."

She snorted. "So ye speak fer the mighty Lord Glengask, do ye? Forgive me fer nae giving ye a curtsy."

"In those trousers? I'd like to see that."

For a moment she felt self-conscious, but that wasn't disdain with which he was eyeing her. The realization made her feel . . . prickly on the inside. It was a sensation she wasn't certain she liked. "Not if ye were the Bruce himself," she shot back.

Not just her words remained defiant. The musket didn't waver, either, and Munro didn't bother to hide his scowl. For Saint Andrew's sake, he'd called off the dog *and* brought her gifts it looked like she could definitely use. And his presence still offended her. Him, the man who'd been voted the May King by the village lasses for four years running. The man who'd bedded both Bethia and Flora Peterkin in the same night without either of them being the wiser—or any less satisfied with his efforts.

Of course he spoke for Glengask, but he had the feeling that admitting to being the marquis's brother wouldn't gain him any favors. It might earn him a ball in the chest, in fact.

This redheaded lass was quite the puzzle, really. In addition to her general hostility and skill with firearms, she didn't seem to be the least bit charmed by him. And he'd never until now encountered a lass who didn't find him charming—or at the least, desirable. Of course she didn't know who he was, but he'd always thought that being a MacLawry was merely the second—or third—most interesting thing about him. For a man of nearly seven inches above six feet and all of it lean, fit Highlander sinew and muscle, well, he showed fairly well if he said so himself.

The damnedest thing of it was that while he didn't seem to be making an impression with her, she'd obviously done so with him. Otherwise he wouldn't be standing there with a gun pointed at his heart. He didn't know quite what to do with that fact. Arran had always teased that if he couldn't eat something, bed it, or punch it, he had no use for it. Well, he wanted to bed her, so he supposed this all made some sense, at least.

"I'll go, then," he finally said, taking a half step backward when he would much rather have been moving forward. "I'm nae afraid of ye, Red, but I'll respect yer wishes. And ye need nae fear me, either. I've nae told a soul that ye're here."

She tilted her head, dark brown eyes regarding him. "I dunnae fear a thing in this world, Bear," she retorted. "If I did, telling me there's nae a soul but ye to put me in danger might cause me to pull the trigger and end the annoyance ye've caused me."

Very well, he could concede that admitting he'd kept her presence secret likely wasn't the most brilliant thing he'd ever done. That would teach him to try comforting a female who didn't need or want comforting. "That would be unneighborly of ye," he said aloud.

For a heartbeat he could have sworn the corners of her mouth lifted, but he wasn't about to wager his life on that. Nor could he afford to take the time to note that her lips looked soft and supremely kissable, or that the brown of her eyes was so deep a man could find himself lost inside them. That was not the sort of thing a man contemplated while a woman was threatening to kill him.

"Ye said ye were going," she reminded him after a moment. "So go."

Munro didn't feel ready for the meeting to end, but pushing her further this morning would be risky at best. And taking the gun out of her hands, while it would end the danger to him and likely surprise the devil out of her, wouldn't make them friends. "Aye," he agreed, and slowly turned for the gaping hole where the front door had once stood. "Just keep in mind that I'm a neighborly lad, and there's no reason fer ye to flee on my account." After this, he didn't want to come by again and find nothing but cold ashes in the hearth. "Or to shoot me."

"I suppose that's my concern, and none of yers," she said coolly, the musket turning to match his retreat.

"And ye're welcome fer the bread and blanket, Red," he commented over his shoulder. "I'd say a prayer fer yer safety in church if I knew yer name. Or I could just ask Saint Andrew to look after the mad, redheaded lass with a musket and no manners presently resting her head at old, haunted Haldane Abbey. That'd suffice, I suppose. There are those who've told me I have something of a booming voice, but I'll try a manly whisper."

He could almost feel the heat of her annoyance and frustration against his spine. The odds were fairly even that the next sound he heard would be a ball carving through his backside, after all. Eventually perhaps he'd come up against a challenge he didn't care to meet, but today wasn't that day. Then he heard her slow breath, in and out. "Cat," she said, so quietly he almost didn't catch the word.

"Beg pardon?"

"Ye heard me, ye big lunk. Ye may say a prayer fer Cat, if ye've a mind to. But dunnae come back here to tell me aboot it."

"Cat it is, then. Is there anything else ye might have need of while ye're staying here, Cat?"

She snorted. "Aye. Some Shakespeare and smoked pork would be dandy. A whetting stone and a silver spoon fer my porridge. But ye're nae to return, so I reckon I'll do without."

He made a mental note of her requests. Clearly she thought him a poor cotter, more than likely a poacher, and for both their sakes it might be wise not to correct her misapprehension. Not yet, anyway.

Cat. That was something, anyway. He'd heard of a cat-and-mouse game. This one would evidently be a game of cat and bear. Because whatever she thought she wanted, he wasn't about to leave her be.

Chapter Three

B ear."

Stifling a curse, Munro hefted the sack he carried from one hand to the other and paused on the main stairway landing to let Ranulf catch up to him. "Did ye see it's raining again?" he asked, before the marquis could begin a topic of conversation. "If this keeps up, I fear we're in for the devil of a winter. I'm off to see Lachlan and Winnie. Do ye reckon Lach still kens how to hunt after being domestified fer a year?"

Ranulf lifted an eyebrow. "Firstly, I dunnae think 'domestified' is a word. Secondly, I reckon Lach'll manage. Ye've hunted with him before now. I doubt today will find him nae knowing which end of a gun is the dangerous one."

"Aye. I reckon ye've the right of it. I'm off, then."

"Ye ken we have a gamekeeper, *bràthair*. Ye dunnae need to keep the house in meat fer the winter all on yer own."

Munro forced a laugh and continued his descent. "The house has more mouths than it used to, these days. I reckon Earcharn could use some help." In the foyer he shrugged into his heavy sealskin coat and donned a wide-brimmed hat. "Aside from that, I'm nae a domestified—domesticated—lad. I cannae sit aboot the house smiling and cooing over my bride and my wee bairn, because I have nae such things keeping me here." Cooper, Glengask's butler, pulled open the front door for him, and he stepped out into the wind-driven rain. "I'll spend my days out of doors while I can, before the snow comes to stay fer the winter, if ye dunnae mind."

The footsteps trailing him stopped in the doorway. Inwardly wincing, Munro squared his shoulders and continued forward. No, he wasn't clever-tongued like Arran. In fact, he generally made a point of speaking his mind; it made for less confusion later. And no, he wasn't as half-witted as his family generally assumed, but the impression made things easier on all of them. Even so, if he'd insulted Ranulf this time, it hadn't been intentional.

"Bear."

He paused, but didn't turn around. "Aye?"

"Take Fergus with ye."

Relief curved his lips. "Thank ye," he said, continuing up the slope toward the stable. He whistled, and a moment later the larger of Ranulf's two deerhounds padded up beside him. "I hope ye behave yerself today, lad. Nae frightening the Cat." Though truthfully, she hadn't looked all that frightened.

The dog wumphed, hopefully in agreement. Running across Ranulf and concocting that damned story about hunting had changed his plans; now that he'd invented a hunting excursion with his brother-in-law, Lord Gray, he would have to follow through with it. Ranulf had an unnerving tendency to detect falsehoods and pursue them until he had the truth. He could stand a word or

two with his closest friend, anyway. It had been a while
since they'd discussed anything but how old a bairn had
to be before he could learn to ride a horse.

While it likely didn't matter that a lass had taken up
residence at Haldane, Munro knew Ranulf wouldn't like
the idea of a stranger—especially one who could shoot
the face off a shilling—squatting so close to the main
house. And he had a fairly good idea what his brothers
would have to say if they learned that he'd been driven
off by a lass wielding a musket—twice now.

He tied the sack to his saddle, and then swung up on
his waiting gray gelding, Saturn. Gray House wasn't
precisely in the opposite direction of where he'd intended to go, but it was a good two miles out of his
way. It meant a quick trip to Haldane, but that might well
be for the best. The lass had warned him not to come
by again, but she couldn't shoot him if she didn't see
him. Hopefully.

After walking into the bowels of Gray House so many
times over the years that he practically thought it an ex-
tension of his own territory, he was startled into a halt
by the sight of Dodge the butler blocking the foyer.
"Where's Lach?" Munro asked, rubbing his fingers
against Fergus's stiff ears.

"In the library, m'laird," the heavyset Highlander returned in a hushed voice.

"Is someaught amiss?"

"Nae, m'laird. It's just that . . . Well, young Laird
Colin has been a wee bit fussy, and he's only just now
quieted doon. Lady MacTier is asleep in the morning
room, and—"

"I'll keep my voice doon," Munro whispered, unwilling to listen to a recital of how many hours Lachlan
and Rowena's bairn had kept the house awake. His sister

Rowena had been a yowler as an infant, too—and to an eight-year-old lad the sound had been like a cat's screeching.

"Thank ye, m'laird. We all appreciate yer understanding."

And his unwillingness to hear more baby squawking. For Saint Andrew's sake, he heard it almost every day with Ranulf and Charlotte's son, William. With a nod he headed up the stairs and down the western hallway. The library door stood half open, and he slipped inside to close it behind him—then froze.

The trap sprang closed before he'd realized he'd been caught. Lachlan MacTier, Viscount Gray, stood before one of the room's tall, narrow windows and rocked backward and forward on his toes and heels like an escaped Bedlamite. In his arms he held a tumble of blankets, from which one tiny, clenched fist emerged to stretch skyward.

Generally cynical green eyes widened as the viscount spied Munro. "Dunnae ye dare speak in more than a whisper," he whispered, turning half away as if to shield his seven-month-old son from the blast of sound his uncle was poised to emit. "Or ye either, Fergus."

The hound promptly lay down as close to the door as he could get. "Yer damned butler already muzzled me," Munro muttered back, diving into a chair by the fireplace. The liquor tantalus stood by the back wall, living up to its namesake, but in the presence of a bairn and at scarcely nine o'clock in the morning, he couldn't quite justify a glass of whisky.

"Good." Lachlan, still bouncing on his toes, walked gingerly closer. "What are ye doing here?"

"I came to take ye hunting. I hadnae realized ye've turned into a lass." The insult lost a bit of its sharpness with both of them whispering at each other, but from the way Lach narrowed his eyes, he'd heard it well enough.

"My bride's getting her first hour of sleep in nearly twenty," the viscount murmured, "as is my lad. If ye're thinking that being married makes ye soft, then ye keep yer damned temper fer an entire day while everyone aboot ye is wailing."

"I—"

"Colin fell asleep in my arms, and I reckon I'll keep rocking him until either my arms fall off or he wakes with a smile. Do ye have any difficulty with that?"

Munro shook his head. "I'll admit ye dunnae sound like a lass," he returned, "but ye're still rocking a bairn in yer arms when ye could be oot huntin'. Or riding. Or playing cards or billiards."

The wee fingers of the wee fist stretched out, then curled again. "Go away, Bear," Lachlan whispered. "I cannae explain what it is to have a lass and a son ye'd die fer. Nae while I'm trying to keep them both asleep."

So no one wanted him about today. And how odd was it, that after knowing Lachlan his entire life, at this moment he felt like he had more in common with the wildcat hiding in Haldane Abbey? "Of course ye cannae have me aboot where quiet and subtlety is required," he retorted, mostly remembering to keep his voice down. "I'm nae but the loud brute of a man ye send in to scare people." Munro stalked to the door as Fergus rose again.

"Bear, I ken ye dunnae like the idea of being domesticated, but—"

"I dunnae like the idea of being taken fer granted. I dunnae like the idea that ye find me in the wrong because I dunnae want what ye have. So go rock yer bairn and sing yer lullabies. I'll go find someaught large to shove at."

As much as he wanted to slam the door behind him, that would only prove that he was the ham-fisted, small-brained oaf his family seemed to think him. So instead he left it open, padded down the stairs, and settled for a nod to the butler as Dodge handed him his raincoat and hat and pulled open the front door.

Damnation. With two brothers, Lachlan, and a younger sister, he'd grown up accustomed to having someone with whom to chat or compete or drink. And now they'd all gone and found other people—and left him feeling more . . . set into his role than ever. The only difference was that he now had more people to protect, had to be bigger and still louder to keep the attention of any envious eyes trained squarely on him. He didn't mind it. He approved of it, actually. It was only that both he and his family had come to believe that the loud, brawl-happy Highlander wasn't just who he was, but all he was.

In fact, the only person in the Highlands who only knew of him what he chose to show her was the red-headed wildcat. He wondered if she'd found the gift he'd left on her doorstep, and whether it was too soon to go ask her in person.

"I don't have scissors," Elizabeth muttered, scowling. "Might I use your knife?"

Catriona wiped the blade on her sleeve and then handed it over. Her sister cut the thread and then straightened to examine her handiwork. The knee of the trousers definitely looked patched; neither of them could have disguised that even if they'd cared to do so. But the rectangle of cotton was neat and tightly stitched, likely with more skill than the rest of the garment. "That's nicely done," she commented.

Her sister dimpled. "Thank you. The next time we should remember to bring scissors, though. One good pair would make things so much easier."

Aye, the next time they felt the need to flee hearth and home for the wilds of the Highlands, she would try to be more prepared. And more . . . ruthless. No being amused, even briefly, by giants carting fresh bread about.

She picked up a piece of the bread Bear had brought her—them—yesterday. He'd provided a small cup of butter, as well, and both she and Elizabeth had made good use of it. Even in this chill weather neither treat would last them long, anyway. Until recently she'd thought bread was bread, and one loaf would do as well as any other. Traveling by mail coach and hay cart and purchasing food at whatever inn happened to be the most out of the way, though, had given her a slightly broader frame of reference. And the bread she held now happened to be exceptional. No grit from the millstones for her to pick from between her teeth, no burned crust or underbaked middle.

Rich man's bread. Or at least well-off-man's bread. And that made her exceedingly curious about where and how Bear had come by it. He dressed like a cotter or a poacher and moved with the stealth and grace of a hunter, despite his height and broad shoulders. Had he stolen it? Had he obtained it from his master's kitchen? She supposed he might well be the gamekeeper for Glengask, though that put him far too near noblemen's ears for her comfort.

Something deep inside the building groaned creak-ily, and she caught sight of Elizabeth wrapping her new blanket more closely around her slender shoulders. The place had a name now, which she appreciated, but then he'd gone and said that Haldane Abbey was haunted— and Elizabeth had heard him say it. Any ghosties had best stay clear of both of them, as far as she was concerned. She had enough earthbound troubles to keep her quite occupied.

"Did you hear that?" her sister whispered.

"Aye. The loose boards up by the stairs, I reckon," she decided. "If they fall, it'll save me the trouble of pulling 'em out to repair the roof."

Blast the giant for saying such a thing, anyway, especially in the same sentence where he'd said she was welcome to stay there. Had he hoped she would faint or throw herself into his manly arms? Ha. A few spirits wouldn't make her run to or from any damned thing. She practically slept with one eye open, anyway, and if she shivered from a little more than a chill breeze, she would never admit it aloud.

Donning her damp, patched trousers again, she stomped into her boots. There. Trousers and boots felt more capable, she supposed it was. "I'm off to get more water," she said, tucking in her shirt and pulling the rattiest of the blankets over her shoulders. "And I'm fairly sure I spotted some late raspberries up at the edge of the meadow."

"Can't I go with you?"

"Elizabeth."

"I know, I know, I need to stay hidden. But I'm not a child, Cat. I'm nineteen, and all this . . . danger you've put yourself in is because of me. Aside from that, it's raining, and that giant man hasn't come back. And I'm going mad in here, even with Byron for company."

The giant hadn't come back since yesterday morning,

anyway. "I'm nae certain Byron's good company for a lass going mad," she admitted, hiding her frown. "Very well. Just stay close, and do precisely as I say."

"I will." Elizabeth wrapped her blanket around her shoulders and then slipped it up around her face. It wouldn't do much to keep her dry or warm, but the stream and the meadow were only a few minutes away.

Catriona took up her musket and led the way outside Haldane Abbey. Elizabeth carrying the pot did make the task a bit easier, but it also made her twice as wary about venturing into the open. She knew about risks, and her father had taught her how to take care of herself. Since she'd left her home on the Isle of Islay she'd felt far older than twenty-four, and a far greater age difference than the five years that actually separated her from Elizabeth. And the one thing she'd realized immediately was that she needed to take care of her sister, protect her, watch out for her. Kittens in the Highlands rarely lasted long on their own.

The stream was hardly more than a moss-edged trickle where it emerged from the rocks a few hundred feet from the old building, but the water was fresh and cold and clean. The access to nearby water had made this location even more appealing than it had been merely by virtue of its isolation. "Set the pot here and let it fill," she said softly, unwilling to disturb the soft rustle of wet leaves with conversation.

That done, they continued up the narrow, steep end of the gorge to where it opened on a green and purple meadow. Cattle grazed on the far side, but an old fence kept them from the gorge and the treacherous footing below. If they were indeed able to remain here for the winter, one of those cows might just find its way onto their table, though that would be even riskier than poaching deer from Laird Glengask.

They tromped through the wet, knee-high grass to the fence. A pair of scraggly raspberry bushes leaned there, just out of reach of hungry cow tongues. Most of the berries were well past being edible, but a handful toward the bottom of the bush looked at least passable.

Elizabeth straightened as she popped one into her mouth. "I don't know why Mother refused to return to the Highlands even for a visit," she mused, gazing at the rugged, fog-draped mountains around them. "It's so lovely here. And the letters you used to write me, about the MacDonald clan gatherings and the fairs—I wish I'd been old enough to remember more of it."

"Well, after ye've turned one-and-twenty ye can come up here whenever ye wish." Catriona forced a chuckle, declining to mention that she wouldn't be anywhere close by there, herself. "Though after hiding up here all winter, ye may never wish to set eyes on Scotland again."

"I will, because you'll be here." Her sister bundled the berries into a handkerchief. "The only good thing about this nonsense is that we're together again. Out of everyone I know, everyone who used to invite me to soirees and country parties and say what dear friends we were, you're the one who came to aid me when I asked for help."

Eventually, one day, Catriona would tell Elizabeth just how splendid the timing of her letter had been. For now, though, she nodded and helped herself to a berry. "Of course I came. We may have different mothers, but Randall MacColl was father to us both, and that makes us sisters." She took a breath. "Now come along, before we both catch our death."

They had enough venison left for another two days, and then she would have to go hunting again. With salt she could preserve the meat longer, or with a smokehouse she could see that they had enough to last them the winter. But she had neither of those things. Perhaps if the giant didn't return she could turn the small storage room at the very back of the east wing into a room where she could salt and cure meat. Not for the first time she wished she'd spent more time with the village butcher and learned how to do some of these things. She had an idea, of course—her father had made certain of that—but she doubted he'd ever had this particular scenario in mind for her future.

As they reached the low stone wall, she helped her sister over the tumble, then hopped the barrier herself. And then she stopped. To one side of the half caved-in entryway lay a heavy-looking sack. Her heart thumping, Catriona put out one hand to stop her sister from advancing. "Wait here," she instructed, setting down the pot and unslinging her musket. The woods still dripped emptily around her, the only sound other than the wind in the treetops. Had it been there earlier? Blast it, she hadn't been looking for burlap sacks tucked into holes, so she had no idea. After a long moment spent searching for any sign of movement, she squatted down and opened the sack with her free hand.

Several parcels wrapped in heavy paper tumbled out. With a curse she shoved them back in and lifted the sack. "Can ye get the water?" she asked.

"Yes. Is that from your friendly giant?" Elizabeth returned, carefully hefting the pot and following her inside.

"He's nae my anything." Catriona led the way into the kitchen, checking every shadow and alcove as she went. They hadn't been gone that long, but it would only take a moment for a man, however broad-shouldered, to find himself a hiding place in the ruins. *Her* giant. Ha. She handed her boot knife to her sister. "I'm going to check the rest of the abbey," she said, heading up the hallway again. "Yell if ye hear someaught."

She supposed the sack itself might have been the trap; if no one moved it, he could assume she'd left the area. Leaving it there for anyone to see, for anyone to become curious about Haldane Abbey, though, made her even more nervous than taking unasked-for gifts—if that was what it contained—from a man who owed her no loyalty and who couldn't possibly represent anything but more trouble.

No giants lurked amid the tumbled stones, though, and Catriona made her way back into the kitchen. The scent of fresh bread touched her, making her mouth water. Elizabeth sat at their worktable, the contents of the sack spread out before her. For a bare moment Catriona frowned, but she quickly willed away the expression. The sack wasn't anything she'd asked for, and she claimed no ownership of it. Just the opposite.

"Oh, honey," her sister exclaimed, waving a small jar at her. She set it aside as Catriona approached, and pulled a larger bundle out of the wet burlap. "This feels like—oh, it is! A book!" Swiftly she pulled the paper off the tome. *"The Complete Shakespeare,"* she read. "We can read the plays to each other!"

Hm. What cotter or poacher owned Shakespeare? Unless he'd stolen it. In that case, its owners might well blame her for the theft, if they caught her with it. He was certainly not doing them any favors, damn it all. And she wasn't at all touched by the happy note in her younger sister's voice. Blowing out her breath, she picked up the largest and heaviest of the packages, untied the twine, and opened it. Her mouth twitched.

"What is it?" Elizabeth asked, as she dove back into the sack for yet another package and produced a whetting stone, as well.

"Smoked pork." Enough to last them a fortnight, if they were careful with it. In this part of the Highlands, smoked pork that looked and smelled this fine was nearly worth its weight in gold. Yet he'd managed both it and the Shakespeare, *and* honey, within a day.

"We seem to have acquired a benefactor," her sister commented, showing Catriona a large sack of salt and a sealskin slicker. "You won't get soaked to the skin if you have to go out in the rain."

As her sister shook open the slicker, a small, shiny object fell to the table with a sharp, hard clatter. Catriona's heart stammered, then began pounding. A silver spoon.

Damnation. Yes, she'd asked for just such a thing, but first of all she'd been jesting, and second of all, well, she'd never expected him to actually deliver one to her. She picked it up and turned it in the firelight. On the front of the handle a capital *G* in lovely cursive formed part of a rose. "Damnation," she said aloud, dropping it again.

"What's amiss?"

"That spoon belongs to the Marquis of Glengask. Or his household, at the least."

"Do you think this Bear person stole it?"

"He either stole it, or he came by it legitimately," she returned. "What I mean to say is, look at all this. No poacher or cotter could afford such fine bread, and that doesnae even take into account the honey or the pork, or the slicker. If he's a thief, he may well lead Glengask's men to come looking here. If he's part of the household, he may tell Glengask aboot us, anyway. We need to go."

"But he said we were welcome to stay."

"And the Duke of Visford said ye were welcome to be his new bride. Do ye think that was oot of the kindness of his heart?"

She immediately regretted the comparison as Elizabeth shuddered, clutching her blanket more tightly around her shoulders. Closing her mouth, she hugged her sister. Whatever she knew, whatever she might have said to someone older or less . . . delicate, she supposed it was, Elizabeth was who she was. And above everything else, Elizabeth needed to be both protected and looked after.

"That was a poor comparison," she said slowly. "This Bear hasnae done anything threatening. My only concern is that he knows where we're laying our heads. Or where *I* am, anyway. I dunnae think he knows about ye. I would prefer that no one at all knew what we were about, or had any idea of where we might be found."

"If you assume everyone in the world means us harm, then does it even make a difference if you keep me away from London until I reach my majority?" her sister countered. "By your way of thinking, I'll never be out of danger, and we should live like hermits for the remainder of our lives, huddled and frightened in some cave or something."

And she'd been about to suggest they spend the night in the cave where she'd hidden their supplies. Even so, she found it hard to believe that she was being too distrustful. "Perhaps he's merely a kindhearted giant," she said after a moment, "and perhaps he's trying to keep us here while he inquires about whether any females have gone missing and if there might be a reward for their return. I dunnae ken which one it is, but I think it'd be foolish to completely ignore one possibility in favor of the other simply because it's easier to do so."

Elizabeth picked up the discarded spoon. "And no doubt Mother *has* offered a reward for my return." She sighed. "It's only that this"—and she gestured at the peeling walls around them—"is the wildest place I've ever been. If you think it doesn't keep us hidden enough, of course we should go. But when do we reach the point where we're someplace so wretched that surrendering begins to sound like the better alternative?"

Never. But that was her, accustomed to a rougher life, taught to shoot when she'd barely been big enough to hold a gun, shown how to live off the land because that was what her fierce, independent ancestors had done. And because she'd been raised by a father who had no use for frilly gowns and fine china. Or females in general, really. For a long moment she gazed at her sister's profile. Far more than five years of age divided them.

"We'll stay here, then." She interrupted her sister's relieved exclamation with a fist against the tabletop. "For the time being. If the giant gives any sign of doing more than leaving us bread and honey, or if he brings anyone else along with him, we *will* be leaving. Agreed?"

Elizabeth nodded. "Agreed."

As if to emphasize the wisdom of that decision thunder rumbled through the rooms, the boom rattling the walls and sending several stones tumbling out in the hallway. On the tail of that, rain began pouring down the chimney so hard it sent the fire hissing and sputtering.

Then the hail began, striking the floor above the

kitchen like miniballs from a cannon. Well. That settled that. She refused to believe in divine intervention—the time when that might have been useful to either her or Elizabeth had passed several weeks ago—but she wouldn't risk their lives to flee during a hailstorm.

Whatever her apparently generous neighbor thought to accomplish by leaving treats on her doorstep, though, she had her own plans. And they did not involve remaining here at Haldane Abbey long enough for him to cause her more trouble. She had enough to worry over without adding Bear to the mix.

The cook scowled when Munro strolled into the kitchen. "Nae again, Laird Bear," she said, clucking at him.

"Nae what?" Munro returned, eyeing the large cooking spoon she waggled in his direction.

"Ye cannae possibly be hungry. I swear ye ate half a cow fer breakfast."

"I'm still a growing lad, Mrs. Forrest," he said, and scooped a full tray of fresh sugar biscuits into a cloth.

The spoon rapped him across the knuckles. "Those are fer the bairns and their mamas!"

Wincing, he flexed his fingers. "Get away, ye madwoman. I can see ye've another tray in the oven. The bairns willnae starve. They dunnae even have teeth, most of 'em."

"Their mamas do."

Ignoring the cook still batting at him and her helpers busily trying not to let her see them laughing, he opened a likely looking canister, only to step back at the abrupt, pungent odor. "What the blessed hell is that?"

"Dried bay leaves. Leave them be!"

He set the lid back on. "Seems to me ye should have a care where ye keep yer poisons, Mrs. Forrest."

"It's nae a poison. Go away, ye big brute of a man, before ye curdle the milk!"

"Fine. I'll go, if ye make me up a hot porridge to take oot fishing. And a loaf of bread." Munro sent another look about the large, warm kitchen. "And that roasted game hen."

"The whole hen?"

"Aye. I cannae get enough of yer fine cooking, lass."

The rotund lass flushed. "That's what ye said two days ago when ye emptied the larder. I was nae flattered then, and I'm nae flattered now."

This was going to be troublesome if it continued much longer. Even his legendary appetite could only explain so much. Stifling his annoyance at being delayed from doing something to which he'd already set his mind, Munro favored her with his most charming smile. "I cannae help myself," he drawled. "Whenever I set eyes upon ye a mighty hunger comes over me." Taking her ample waist in his hands, he drew her up against him. "I'll either have ye, or I'll have yer cooking."

The other kitchen maids were howling with laughter, and finally with a guffaw Mrs. Forrest shoved at his chest. "Och, ye naughty lad. Go and fetch a basket, Willa, so we can make up a proper picnic luncheon fer Laird Bear."

A basket. Definitely more presentable than a sack, but he would have to make up a tale later when he didn't return with it. If this kept up much longer—and he hoped it would—he would have to begin purchasing food items from the village. Ranulf and the family would only believe so many stories about chance encounters with widow women and their hungry grandbabies, and why he was apparently now eating at least double what he generally consumed.

Debny the head groom had already tied a fishing pole to Saturn's saddle, and Munro secured the large, cumbersome picnic basket himself. The big gray had been bred from generations of warhorses, animals who had both the stamina and strength to bear knights wearing full armor into battle. A fishing pole and luncheon basket were hardly a challenge, but from the way Saturn turned his head to eye his burdens, he thought them well beneath his dignity.

"I put an apple in my pocket fer ye, so dunnae complain," Munro said, swinging up into the saddle.

The groom emerged from the stable. "M'laird, yer brother the marquis said I was to make certain ye didnae go off alone," he called, hurrying forward to catch Saturn's bridle.

Munro blew out his breath. "Fetch Fergus or Una fer me then, will ye?"

"The hounds went with Lord and Lady Glengask doon to An Soadh," the head groom returned, naming the nearer of the two sizable villages on MacLawry land.

"Well, then, I dunnae suppose the fish can do me much harm." With a nudge of his boot Munro backed the horse a few steps, then headed them south toward Loch Shinaig.

A moment later a horse pounded up behind him. "I reckon I'm nae a hound," Peter Gilling said, the footman slowing to a trot as he drew even with Saturn, "but I do follow the MacLawry's orders."

"I dunnae require a nanny, Peter." Munro favored the footman with a raised eyebrow. He felt more like growling, but Gilling would know that an offer—or order—of company on a fishing expedition should not cause him that much annoyance. The clouds and drizzle had finally fled late last night, though, and after two days of miserable weather and no excuse to go outside he found himself both restless and exceedingly curious to see if the Cat had fled Haldane.

Leaving the last sack of supplies on the doorstep had been a gamble, but after seeing the wild redhead and then a second lass head out to pick raspberries, he'd decided a face-to-face confrontation would rouse more hostility than it would gratitude. He could tell just from the inappropriately dainty gown the taller lass wore that she wasn't from anywhere nearby—or anywhere this far north.

The temptation to follow them had pulled at him, but the Cat had been carrying that damned ancient musket in her right hand, and he'd already bellowed that he was going hunting with Lach—as poorly as that had turned out. At least now he knew what she was protecting. Why or from what eluded him, but he would figure it out. Saint Bridget's tits, he couldn't seem to think about anything else, anyway. Even asleep, dreams of a lithe, red-haired lass with long, trouser-covered legs had him restless and frustrated.

"The loch would be in that direction, m'laird," Peter Gilling said, pointing over to the left.

Munro drew up Saturn. "I need yer oath aboot someaught, Peter," he stated, turning in the saddle to face the former soldier.

"I'll nae give it to ye blindly, Laird Bear," the footman returned. "The last time I gave a blind oath, I ended up helping yer *bràthair* Arran kidnap a Campbell. And I had to wear a damned dress."

"I saw that. Ye werenae a pretty lass." Munro took a breath. "I found someaught, and I gave my word that no one else would hear of it. So I reckon ye can either take the same oath, or I'll tie ye to a tree to keep ye from following me."

The stout man scowled. "I dunnae want to be tied to a tree."

"And I dunnae want to have to tie ye to one. I reckon ye'd give me a fight, and ye might get hurt. I'm assuming, though, that ye willnae just turn around and go home."

"I willnae. I'm protecting ye with my life."

"Then it's yer oath, or the tree."

Peter Gilling took a deep breath. "I give ye my oath. As long as whatever yer secret is, if it doesnae cause harm to ye or the rest of the MacLawrys, I'll keep my gobber shut aboot it."

"And I'll hold ye to that." Munro nudged Saturn in the ribs, and they started off again. "We're nae going fishing. And the luncheon basket isnae fer us. Ye're nae to converse with anyone, and ye'd best call me Bear."

The servant narrowed his eyes. "This is sounding very familiar," he grumbled. "Ye arenae hiding a Campbell or a MacDonald lass from her family, are ye? Because I dunnae relish the thought of fleeing to the Colonies with ye. I said I'd go with Laird Arran if it came to that, but it's nae a thing a man decides on a whim."

"It isnae like that," Munro returned, though he didn't precisely know who the Cat was or what she *was* hiding herself and the other lass from. But they *were* hiding; he knew that as well as he knew his own face.

"Well, that sounds like the right words, but I reckon I'll keep my two peepers open, anyway."

He wouldn't get a better answer than that. The idea of bringing another soul with him to Haldane Abbey still didn't sit well, but if Ranulf suspected he was up to something, slipping away anywhere on his own would become next to impossible. Peter Gilling was the least of several complications he could imagine.

They rode up the long, shallow valley, its deep greens turning to gold and orange with the crisp autumn weather. A large herd of red deer pounded across a rain-swollen stream to his right and vanished into the thick stand of trees beyond. He made no effort to be stealthy; the Cat would likely hear or see them approaching, any-way, and trying to remain unseen would get him or Peter Gilling shot.

"Haldane Abbey's ahead," the footman commented, and spat over his left shoulder.

"Aye. Keep yer opinion aboot it to yerself."

"It's nae an opinion, m'lai—Bear. That place is haunted."

"Then stay here. Just remember ye swore an oath."

"I knew this was a poor idea. Why do I nae listen to myself?"

"Because ye have more adventures if ye dunnae." Munro took a breath as the old ruin came into sight. "Hello the house!" he called.

The two women could be gone, of course. That would return everything to normal—to preparations for win-ter, to the daily routine of siblings and bairns and with him feeling the deepening need both to protect them all and to flee to where things could be as they were again—the MacLawrys and the Campells one murder away from open war, he and his two older brothers standing shoulder to shoulder to shoulder, feared and respected and damned ferocious Highlanders.

But that was the past. He couldn't begrudge Ranulf the happiness and peace the marquis and chief of their clan had found in his wife and son, even if Charlotte was a delicate Sassenach. Damned Arran had started out well, kidnapping Mary Campbell out from under half of clan Campbell and defying the Duke of Alkirk—the Campbell, himself. That had turned domestic, as well; Mary was a MacLawry now, and only a few weeks away from giving Arran his second bairn. His sister, Ro—

A musket ball shredded a branch two feet from his head, the loud report sounding a heartbeat later.

Well, she was still in residence. Peter Gilling threw himself out of the saddle, using the horse for cover and freeing his formidable blunderbuss in the same moment. Munro, though, raised both of his hands in surrender and nudged Saturn with his knees into a slow walk.

"Stop!" the sharp female voice he already recognized commanded.

"Dunnae shoot, Peter," Munro muttered, then sat straighter in the saddle. "I'm surrendering to ye, lass!" She likely had no idea that he'd never uttered those words before, but the fact that she didn't know that about him was . . . thrilling, almost.

"It's nae surrendering if ye dunnae do as I tell ye," she returned. "I dunnae want to shoot ye, Bear, but dunnae mistake reluctance for lack of conviction."

"And dunnae mistake my good humor fer stupidity," he countered, even as it occurred to him that wild, uncivilized lasses didn't use words like "reluctance" or "conviction." Perhaps the dainty lass had taught them to her, though. "I gave ye my word that no harm would come to ye here."

"Ye also swore that ye'd nae tell another soul about me. Unless that's a spirit behind ye, I'd say yer word isnae worth shite."

Civilized lasses didn't say "shite." This Cat had interested him from the moment he'd set eyes on her. Given his general dislike of puzzles he'd put his intrigue to lust, but the more contradictions to her, the better he liked it. He didn't even mind that she had a musket pointed at him. None of this made any damned sense at all. And even if the rampaging, larger-than-life Bear was mostly for show, he did like for things to make sense.

"M'lai—Bear, I'm thinking ye should reverse yer course, there." Gilling's unamused voice came from behind him.

"This is Peter," Munro said, knowing he had no intention of retreating. "We . . . hunt together from time to time, and I didnae want him coming across ye by accident."

"So ye brought him by on purpose? Would ye like me to set out some tea and biscuits, then?" came her sarcastic reply. "I can dig two holes in the ground as easy as one large enough to fit ye. Now fer the last damned time, go away."

"I dunnae think I will. In fact, I intend to untie this basket and walk it through the front door. So if ye think I mean harm to ye, ye'd best put a ball through me." With that he swung down from Saturn.

Peter made a wheezing sound. "Bear, please dunnae do this. If ye get yerself killed, yer brother'll see my bones scattered across the Highlands fer the crows to dine on."

"Ye and yer bones stay here, Peter." Munro untied the heavy basket and slung it over his left forearm. "I've been shot before, and I'm still standing."

"But—"

"Aside from that, I think the lass likes me. She'll nae shoot." Intentionally leaving his rifle behind with the fishing pole, he started forward. Tree branches obscured the upper level of the structure, but she seemed to have found a good vantage point. Dangerous as the footing was up there, that was where he would be. Especially if he had someone else to protect.

Setting the basket on the low wall, he clambered over. A musket ball slammed into the stone just where his hand had been a heartbeat earlier. Mortar and stone chips blasted outward, biting into his cheek. Damn, she was a fine shot—unless she'd meant to hit him just then. Without bothering to brush the dust and rocks off him, he picked up the basket and continued forward, to the front door. At the same time, he counted off in his head—a seasoned soldier could reload and fire a musket in fifteen seconds.

Fifteen plus two seconds later, the door frame directly by his head disintegrated. And he decided he'd damned well been patient enough.

Dropping the basket, he charged for the half-collapsed stairs and scrambled up them. She'd have to reload again, and this time he wasn't being some lunk with a target painted on his skull. She would have to be in the northeast corner and leaning halfway out the window to get off that last shot, and he leaped over a tumble of wall and furniture that blocked his path. Whether she would actually shoot him the next time or not, he didn't mean to stand there and make it easy for her. He might be attempting some patience, but he wasn't weak-hearted.

An unhinged door looked like it had been wedged closed. Munro put his foot to it and shoved. The old oak slammed onto the floor, dust and plaster filling the air like snow. And there she was, dropping the ramrod and lifting the muzzle in his direction.

Dark brown eyes widened, a curse crossing her lips. He saw it all with startling clarity even as he roared and threw himself forward. Munro grabbed the weapon away from her with one hand and caught up the material at her throat with the other, dragging her up against him before she could flee or, more likely, punch or kick him.

"That is enough shooting," he growled.

"Let go!" she yelled back at him, leveling a kick at his man parts.

Munro lifted her off her feet before the blow could connect. "How many bloody times do I have to swear I dunnae mean ye harm, ye wildcat?" he returned, his gaze lowering to her cursing mouth.

Not certain whether he was about to make things better or worse, only knowing that simply grabbing her by the shirt wasn't enough to satisfy him, he bent his head and took her mouth with his. It wasn't gentle, or subtle, but her lips were warm and softer than he expected, and she immediately stopped trying to thrash him.

"Ye damned heathen," she spat, wiping at her mouth.

"Aye, and dunnae ye ferget that, next time."

He set her down and took a step backward before he turned on his heel. "Now," he said, hefting her musket in his left hand, "let's go meet the other lass and ye can tell me yer troubles over some porridge and roast game hen."

Chapter Four

He knew about Elizabeth.

For a moment that thought kept Catriona frozen where he'd set her feet back on the uneven floor. She'd been—or thought she'd been—so cautious. Elizabeth had only been out of doors once in the past week. It must have been when he left that last sack of food. Had he watched them the entire time?

At the landing he stopped and turned around to face her. "I dunnae think ye want me barging in on the lass withoot ye giving her warning," he said, motioning her to precede him.

"I dunnae want ye barging in on her at all," Catriona returned, scowling. Short of trying to knock him down the stairs, though, she had no idea how she would prevent it.

And it was her own damned fault. She could have shot him thrice, and each time she hadn't been able to make herself do it. He had another man with him now, and she could tell herself that it would have been too difficult to do away with both the giant and the stout fellow with the blunderbuss, but attempting to fool herself seemed both useless and dangerous. Something had made her hesitate, and she needed to discover what. And why.

He grabbed her forearm as they reached the main floor, and towed her along while he retrieved his pretty picnic basket. "So ye think this is an outing, do ye?" she snapped, wrenching her arm free and striding down the uneven hallway ahead of him. "Is that why ye kissed me? Because now ye've brought a basket and I'm to fall for yer gentlemanly ways?"

"I'm nae a gentleman," he returned from close behind her. "I *am* tired of being shot at, and I reckoned kissing ye might stopper the unladylike curses ye were spewing at me."

"And once again I have to put that back on ye, as I would have nae reason to curse if ye did as I asked."

"Good God, woman, I'm trying to help ye. Do ye never relent?"

"Nae." With that she whipped around, coiled her fist, and swung as hard as she could at his jaw.

At the last second he ducked backward, catching the punch on his shoulder. The momentum sent her forward, and before she could catch her balance he grabbed her around the waist and heaved her up into the air—over his shoulder. Like a sack of potatoes.

"Put me down, damn yer eyes," she growled, punching at his back and kicking at his chest.

"I warned ye, wildcat. More times than I generally warn anyone."

Her musket lay on the ground where he'd dropped it, but he squatted to retrieve the picnic basket and then straightened again. Her weight seemed no more significant to him than the porridge and roast chicken he claimed to be toting. And he didn't seem willing to put her down as he strode, with her arse first over his shoulder, toward the kitchen.

"Ye wouldnae have surrendered, I'll wager," she said, trying to keep her breath.

She swore she could feel him chuckling beneath her. "That is the truth," he admitted. "And if ye hadnae bunched yer arm up before ye turned around, ye might have landed a blow."

So now he wanted to criticize her fighting technique. "If ye werenae eight feet tall, I would almost call the fight fair," she retorted. "Now put me down."

"That would make me a damned fool, wouldnae? I think I'll keep ye right where ye are."

Instead of kicking at his chest, she bent her knee and aimed her boot heel at his skull. The blow didn't connect; his arms wrapped around her legs so tightly she could barely move.

"If ye're thinking of pulling my hair next," he muttered, "think again. Ye're a lass, but that willnae stop me from giving yer arse a wallop. And this isnae encouraging me to put ye doon. Now give me yer word that ye'll behave yerself."

She wanted to screech at him that no one—*no one*—spanked her, but that would likely only serve to encourage him to do just that. Surrender wasn't in her vocabulary, but as she squeezed in another breath Catriona decided that perhaps a truce would be acceptable. "Fine," she snapped. "Ye have my word. I'll nae try to pummel ye for . . . the next five minutes. Put me down so I can keep us both from getting shot when ye turn the corner."

That, at least, gave him pause, and after far too long a moment of him standing there holding on to her, he dipped a bit and set her feet on the ground. Before she could even regain her balance, though, much less aim a boot at his man parts, he wrapped iron fingers around her elbow. "Ye're doon. Now behave, wildcat."

The exasperation in his tone actually made her feel just a little satisfied—she wasn't the only one out of sorts. "I only said I wouldnae try to pummel ye. And I dunnae recall asking for yer help, or for ye to bully me into doing as ye say. Whatever's driving ye, it has naught to do with me."

"It has everything to do with ye, Cat."

Those words from him ricocheted and rattled about in her mind, clanking and loud and shoving aside other thoughts that would have been much more practical and useful. Did this have to do with the kiss? Or did he know something else? And now she didn't know which path she preferred.

"Nae reply to that?" he said, amusement touching his voice. "Do ye become mute when ye cannae talk with yer musket or yer fists?"

"Ye have me outnumbered, ye brute," she retorted. "And I'd be a fool nae to acknowledge that ye're stronger than I am. And meaner."

"I dunnae ken which of us is meaner."

Clearly it was him, but arguing over that wouldn't gain her anything but an aching head. "I suppose I've nae choice but to see what sort of trouble ye mean to make before I comment on anything else."

She heard his intake of breath, and waited for him to protest—again—that he meant her no harm. As if she'd never been injured by someone with good intentions. And those people had supposedly been friends and allies, and hadn't slung her over their shoulders with no apparent effort. Bear had no reason to do anything but serve his own best interests, and that could be very bad for Elizabeth and her.

As she turned into the kitchen ahead of him, for a moment she thought Elizabeth had fled. It would mark the second time her sister had actually done something to save herself—though the thought of an English-raised debutante alone in the Highlands sent her heart pounding in alarm.

Then she caught sight of an edging of blue material behind the overturned cabinet they'd shoved against one wall. Elizabeth would have heard the shouting and shooting, and for once she'd kept her wits about her. "As ye can see," she said, turning around to face Bear and doing her best to block his view of the cabinet, "I'm the only lass here. I'll be gone from here by sunset, and ye can go find some other lass to rescue or bother or whatever it is ye spend yer days doing."

"Mm-hm. So the lass behind the cabinet there is imaginary, I presume." He nudged her sideways. "Ye've nae need to fear me, lass. I'd guess by yer skirts that ye're English," he continued, setting the basket on the hearth. "As I told Cat, here, I only mean to see that the two of ye are safe and well."

Slowly, her hands visibly shaking, Elizabeth straightened and stepped over the corner of the cabinet. "You have blood on your cheek, sir," she observed, with that one sentence confirming that she was both English raised and a lady.

Catriona stifled a sigh. "He's bleeding because he stepped where he wasnae wanted."

"You shouldn't be so prickly, Cat," her sister returned. "He brought us bread, after all." She offered her hand to the big man. "I'm Elizabeth. Thank you for your kindness."

Bear wiped his hand on his kilt, then took Elizabeth's fingers like he worried he might break them. "Bear. I'm glad to see at least one of ye doesnae see a wolf behind every tree."

"Wolf? I hope you're being allegorical, sir." She shivered again, moving closer to her sister. "There aren't wolves here, are there, Cat? You go out alone all the time."

"There arenae wolves in the Highlands. Nae for years and years. There arenae bears, either, except for this stupid one." Wonderful. More things for Elizabeth to worry over. Catriona favored Bear with a glare, to find him gazing at her.

Men didn't look at her. Not with that expression in their eyes. Not with lovely, refined Elizabeth standing there. And he'd kissed her, though she'd thought that had been more to shock her into surrendering than anything else. But what if it hadn't been?

"Aye," he said after a moment, blinking eyes which she for some reason decided were the color of spring leaves before he turned to face Elizabeth again. "It's only an expression. Ye'll nae find any fierce beasties aboot bigger than wildcats or foxes."

"Well, thank goodness. With a name like Bear, I thought you might have been named after one. I would faint if an actual bear strolled into the kitchen here."

Their unwanted guest grinned, the expression very attractive and exceedingly disarming. "Bear's only a nickname my *athair*—my father—gave me when I was a bairn. He reckoned I'd grow up to be the size of one. My given name's Munro."

Well, wasn't this friendly? Elizabeth hadn't seen him hauling her sister about like a bale of hay, however. "So now ye've met us, Munro. Just two lasses making our own way in the world. We've nae riches for ye to take, and all we ask is to be left alone."

Instead of replying, he turned back to the hearth and opened the picnic basket. Without ceremony he unwrapped a beautifully roasted game hen set on a platter. Squatting beside it, he pulled the thin knife from his boot and flipped it in his hand, no doubt to demonstrate that he knew precisely how to use it. With another glance in her direction he deftly sliced off a drumstick.

"I didnae bring plates or forks," he said, and handed the delicious-smelling piece up to Elizabeth.

Her sister dragged over the chair and sat. "I'll manage," she said with a smile. Apparently anyone who claimed to offer help was a knight in shining armor as far as Elizabeth was concerned. "It's lovely to have something other than rabbit and venison to eat. And to have someone else with whom to converse."

Was Elizabeth flirting? *Good heavens.* That was damned well enough of that. After all they—she—had been through over the past weeks, Catriona did not intend to allow them to be caught because of a chicken leg and an admittedly handsome face. "Munro, why did ye bother to promise ye'd nae tell a soul about us if ye had nae intention of keeping yer word?"

He handed her the second drumstick. If it had been larger she would have brained him with it, but he likely wouldn't even feel the blow. And it did smell very good.

"We make do with what's handed us," he said after a moment. "I couldnae shake Peter this morning. All he knows is that a lass shot at me thrice, and that he's nae to speak a word of it."

"And ye trust him, do ye? He's obligated to do as ye say?"

Bear's jaw clenched. "Aye. He is."

That was certainly interesting. "So ye have someone ye can order about? Are ye the lord and master of the valley, then, here to decide our fate?" The idea that he'd merely been playing, toying with her—them—made her angry, but she did already have a suspicion or two about him. Especially after hearing his given name. As she waited for him to answer, she glanced again at her knife on the hearth, newly sharpened thanks to his gift of that whetting stone. With the right distraction this could be her chance—though his speed had already surprised her twice today.

"He's my uncle," the giant finally bit out. "Uncle Peter. I told him I was going fishing, and he begged to come along. It's rare to find him this far from the loch. I might've stayed away from ye, I suppose, but I thought it a shame to allow this fine game hen and porridge to go to waste."

"Oh, porridge?" Elizabeth broke in.

"Aye. And fer that I brought bowls and spoons."

"More silver spoons, I assume?" Her sister might be ready to trust someone simply because he brought a tasty dish or two, but Catriona was not.

Bear handed the cloth-wrapped canister to Elizabeth before he rose again. For heaven's sake he was tall. He seemed to fill the entire room, and his muscular frame and broad shoulders made him both unmissable and formidable—and that wasn't even taking into account his stealth or speed.

He stalked to the door, pausing only to glance back at her over his shoulder. And then he was gone. Catriona stared at the doorway, which abruptly seemed smaller without him occupying it. *What the devil?*

"Why were you so mean to him?" Elizabeth demanded. "He's the first friendly face we've seen since we left the mail coach!"

"He brought us food," she snapped back. "That doesnae make him friendly. It only means he hasnae yet gotten what he wants from us in return for his gifts. And given that we have naught to hand, I can only imagine what his price might be. He already threatened to spank me. Do ye ken, Elizabeth?"

Her sister's eyes widened. "He did what?"

"Ye heard me." It was all his fault, but her cheeks warmed, anyway.

"I think you must have misunderstood him. You are far too cynical, Catriona."

"And ye're too trusting." She took the porridge from her sister's hands, but couldn't quite bring herself to dump it on the fire. "How well has that served ye so far?"

"That isn't fair."

"Mayhap it isnae, *piuthar,* but if people were as trustworthy as we hoped, neither of us would be in the kitchen of a broken-down, haunted old house in the middle of the Highlands. And if we cannae trust our own family, what in the world makes ye think we can trust a complete stranger?"

"Because he's a stranger," Elizabeth answered, lifting her chin. "What could he possibly want from us that he couldn't already have gotten by force?"

"Ye—I . . ." Catriona trailed off. Scowling, she marched to the doorway and back again.

A month and a half ago, the morning after she'd received Elizabeth's letter, she had purchased passage on a boat leaving her home on the Isle of Islay and sailing over to Ayr on the main coast of Scotland. From there it had been hay carts, mail coaches, whatever she could find that would get her to London with the fewest delays. While she hadn't seen any pursuers coming or going, she *knew* they were about, searching at the least for word of Elizabeth's whereabouts. They were undoubtedly looking for her, as well, but it was . . . easier to tell herself that this was for her sister's sake.

"All he needs to do is tell the wrong person about us, and ye'll be back on yer way to London, thrown into a white gown, and shoved down the aisle with the Duke of Visford. Wife number five, ye told me in that letter. And ye forty-two years his junior."

Elizabeth shuddered. "You don't have to remind me, for heaven's sake. But that doesn't have anything to do with Bear. Munro. Whatever he chooses to call himself. He gave his word that he wouldn't tell anyone else about us. And he's brought us blankets, and you a warm coat, and food." She poked Catriona in the shoulder. "And considering how large and full of muscles he is, it might be wiser for us to be friendly than for you to bark at him until he *does* tire of us and do something we'll regret."

"Ye should listen to yer friend there, wildcat," his low brogue came, from only a foot or two behind her. She whipped around to see him gazing down at her, arms folded over his broad chest, and the other man, his supposed uncle, standing behind him and carrying her musket. The two of them looked nothing alike. *Wonderful.*

"She's my sister," Elizabeth corrected. "Half sister, actually."

Catriona wanted to scream and pound her fist against something. Did no one else understand what secrecy meant? This was her rescue, her plan, and now everyone wanted to step in and ruin things without even knowing the entire story. It was ridiculous. Intolerable.

"Interesting," he drawled, gesturing at the older man.

"This is Peter. Uncle Peter, this is Elizabeth, and that is her half sister Cat."

Uncle Peter nodded, tugging on the front of his brimless wool tam. "Lasses."

"Peter, why dunnae ye look aboot here with Miss Elizabeth and let me know what else they might be needing?"

"Aye, I—Bear. Nephew."

"We dunnae need anything from ye," Catriona stated, putting her fists on her hips, "except for yer absence."

He faced her again. "And ye, wildcat, are going fer a stroll with me."

Uneasiness snapped her spine straight. "Nae. I willnae."

Bear took a slow step closer. "Aye. Ye will."

She had to lift her chin just to keep her gaze on his face. The threat was clear; she could go on her own two feet, or he would sling her over his shoulder again. The benefit to doing as he said, she supposed, would be putting distance between him and Elizabeth. At the same time, she hadn't brought them all this way to leave her sister in the company of some grizzled Highlander—even one with an innocuous name like "Uncle Peter."

Seeming to sense the reason for her hesitation, Bear glanced at his uncle. "We'll nae go far," he said. "If someaught frightens ye, Peter, ye call oot, and we'll be back in a heartbeat." With that he gestured her toward the doorway.

Damnation. Taking an exaggerated breath, she stomped out of the kitchen. At least she could make it look as if she had a choice, whether she actually did or not. "Damned bully," she muttered.

"Ye ken yer sister has the right of it," he said coolly, staying on her heels. "I *could* have gone doon to the tavern at An Soadh and told every man I saw that two lovely lasses have settled into the ruins of Haldane Abbey all by themselves."

"Ye gave yer word that ye wouldnae. Though I dunnae ken ye take yer word very seriously."

"My point being," he continued, "that I've known yer whereabouts fer a week." He moved past her to hop up on the rough wall that ringed the front half of the house. "I have kept my word, though me nae being a complete idiot, I *did* tell someone I trust where I'd be. That way if ye shot me in the noggin I'd have someone to see me buried."

He offered her a hand, but she ignored it, jumping up on her own to sit beside him. Not too close beside him, though; the idea that she . . . owed him something for not wagging his tongue didn't sit well with her at all. "Ye might try seeing things from where I stand, ye great brute. I'll nae thank ye for simply doing the decent thing and not getting my sister and me murdered. I didnae ask ye for a damned thing, and ye still shoved yer way into my affairs. If ye'd done as I asked a week ago and stayed away, we'd both be happier."

"I didnae say I wasnae happy, lass." His mouth curved in one of those maddening, astoundingly attractive smiles he seemed able to assume at will. "Ye have a way of bringing fire to a cold day. And whether ye want it to be so or nae, I did run across ye, and now I'm obligated to look after ye."

Catriona opened her mouth to tell him precisely how ridiculous he sounded, but then she closed it again. How many times had she heard something similar? She'd been born in the Highlands, after all. Of course the clan looked out for its members, protected them—or that was how the words went, anyway. In actual practice she'd found matters to be somewhat less . . . straightforward. And that one man's idea of a lass's best interest might not be her own. But Bear seemed utterly serious. "I'm nae yer clan, Munro. Ye've nae such obligation to me."

He tilted his head, a lock of his shaggy black hair falling across one green eye. "Ye're a lass who's hiding. That—"

"How do ye know I'm hiding?" she broke in. "I'm showing my friend—my sister, I mean—the Highlands."

"And trying to keep the fact that ye're related a secret," he stated. "I knew ye were sisters; ye have the same nose."

"Please. We dunnae look a thing alike."

Where Elizabeth was all long, elegant lines, straight golden hair, and rich hazel eyes with those thick lashes, she was short and curvy with her mother's red hair and her father's brown eyes. It was possible, she supposed, that their noses were similar; she had never compared them that closely.

"What clan are ye?" he asked.

"What clan are *ye*?"

"I told ye I was clan MacLawry. Ye're in the middle of MacLawry land, ye ken."

"I'm a MacLawry as well, now," she commented. It made for a fairly bold lie, but clan MacLawry was huge and growing every day as Lord Glengask welcomed refugees from other clans. So the stories went, anyway. She could be one of the newcomers. Bear wouldn't know the difference.

"Are ye, then?" he asked, lifting a curved eyebrow.

"Aye. The MacLawry himself gave us use of Haldane

Abbey. He said we could stay as long as we liked, and that we would be left alone here."

"Ah. A generous man, is the MacLawry."

"Very generous."

"He might have found ye a place where the roof isnae caved in, though."

Bear gazed at the large manor sprawled before them, and she took it in all over again, herself. When she'd first come upon it she'd nearly passed it by—the top floor was little more than outer walls holed by broken windows open to the sky, while the collapsed roof had broken through half of the second level. Vines and weeds slowly pried the cracks farther apart, while tree roots broke through the drive and abandoned pathways.

Belatedly it had occurred to her that a place so clearly ruined and abandoned might be perfect. Once she'd made her way inside to find the nearly intact kitchen, she'd felt . . . relieved, and hopeful, for the first time in weeks. And then, not ten days later, Bear had stumbled across them.

"I imagine as long as I'm pleased with the lodgings, then that's all that matters," she returned finally, deciding she needed to say something.

Munro pulled an apple from his pocket and offered it to her. Aye, he'd promised it to Saturn, but for Saint Bridget's sake this lass was more skittish than any wild pony. In fact, he half expected to get his hand bitten for his trouble, or at the least an apple thrown at his head. Instead, though, and after another suspicious glare from her, she lifted it out of his palm, polished it against her coat sleeve, and took a big, crunching bite.

Munro had a knack with animals—because he was barely more than one himself, according to his siblings—and for some other mysterious reason, a marked popularity with females. He happened to be made up of the various parts a lass favored, what with his height and large . . . muscles, a face they told him was handsome, and a plump purse. He could have his pick. And he did, frequently.

But this wild redhead didn't want anything to do with him. The sister seemed pleasant enough, if a tad too delicate and refined, and he had noted that she possessed a fine figure and a pretty face. Somewhat to his own surprise he had no interest in Miss Elizabeth, though. No, he wanted the lass with the fiery hair and the curves that those shirts and trousers she wore only accentuated. He wanted the wildcat.

"So if I were to go away, that would prove ye could trust me, aye?" he said, yanking a long stalk of grass from the base of the wall and sticking it between his teeth.

"Aye. It would."

"Except ye'd keep looking fer me to come back with a crowd of drunken lads or someaught. Which to me says ye'd nae trust my absence, either."

"I'd manage."

He chuckled, blowing out his breath. "Ye're a hard-hearted lass, Cat." How the devil was he supposed to convince her to trust him? With a horse, he gave it an apple and then he rode it. A lass might require flowers or a pretty bauble, but the principle was generally the same.

"I'm nae hard-hearted," she said unexpectedly. "I dunnae want ye about because I have a plan. Ye're nae a part of that plan. In fact, ye're making things worse."

"I'm making things worse fer ye?" Munro furrowed his brow. "Mayhap ye didnae plan fer a handsome, manly lad such as myself to cross yer path, but if ye say that me bringing ye food and blankets is hurting ye, I'll call ye a liar to yer face." Especially after the damned effort he'd gone through to get her those things.

She made a growling sound. For a heartbeat he thought he might take an apple to the ear after all, but instead she heaved it over his head and into the underbrush beyond. "Why do ye insist on coming about here where ye're nae wanted? Why?"

"I'm stubborn," he answered promptly, somewhat mollified that he wasn't the only one frustrated by this game of chess, or whatever it was. "And I'm accustomed to getting my way. A fellow—or lass—generally doesnae risk standing toe-to-toe with me." Except for her, in fact.

"Then I'm a good lesson in disappointment for ye."

"Or I'm a good lesson fer *ye*." He wanted to edge closer to her, take her hand, ensure that he had her attention, but that would likely see her fleeing or fighting again. She'd kept from trying to hit him for better than five minutes now, and he didn't want to end that streak of good fortune. "I'm nae going away, Cat. So I suggest ye make use of me."

"To what, hold the walls up with yer great muscles?"

She had a sense of humor, anyway. "I know this land, fer instance," he offered. "If ye mean to stay on here, I can see to it ye've nae unwanted visitors, and that ye have enough food and warm clothes and blankets." It didn't seem like much when he said it aloud, but he had a good idea if he offered to shower her with gifts and assistance the wildcat would turn him down flat.

"And how do ye mean to afford this, Munro?" she countered. "Even if I had nae objection to a man, a stranger, keeping us in food and clothes, surely ye've a better use for yer blunt. Yer own family, for example. Ye've an uncle; is there anyone else?"

Lying to her about his relationship to Peter had kept him from having to admit that he went about with servants and bodyguards. And hell, Peter *was* practically his uncle. But the more lies he told, the more he'd have to remember later, and the more he'd have to make amends for later. Because this wasn't just a bump in his road. This was a new road, altogether. The certainty with which he knew that startled him a little.

"I'm nae married, if that's what ye're asking," he said aloud.

Her cheeks darkened. "That is *nae* what I'm asking. Why should I care, except that ye mauled my face?"

Well, that wasn't at all flattering. "I didnae maul ye. That was a damned fine kiss. It's nae my fault if ye dunnae ken a good kiss when ye get one."

She made a scoffing sound. "Ha. I imagine I can outthink ye, outshoot ye, *and* outkiss ye, Bear."

Not only did that sound like a fine wager despite the blatant insult, but it could also give him cause to stay about. "Let's set us some targets, then," he drawled, hopping down from the wall and intentionally leaving her to make her own way to the ground. She wasn't one for being coddled, and that was damned certain.

"I dunnae—"

"If *I* win," he interrupted, "I'll do fer ye as I see fit, and ye'll nae protest aboot it. If *ye* win, I'll do fer ye as *ye* see fit—as long as it doesnae include me leaving ye here on yer own. Because that I willnae do."

Cat slid to the ground, pausing to dust off her curvy backside before she looked up at him. "All of that seems tilted in yer favor."

"Only if ye ken I've nae better to do than tote dead, roasted birds fer ye and yer *piuthar*."

"For all I ken, ye dunnae. I've nae idea who ye are or what ye do. Other than come by far too often and step into my affairs, that is."

With her chin up, her dark brown eyes meeting his with a fearlessness that was both rare and intriguing, he very nearly caught her up in his arms and kissed her again. But they'd managed a semicivil conversation, and he didn't care to retreat to the trying-to-shoot-him part of their relationship. "Ye tell me someaught, and I'll tell ye someaught."

"I could tell ye anything then, Bear."

"Aye, ye could. And so could I, I reckon. Do as ye will."

As he spoke, it occurred to him that he was going to a great deal of effort for no discernible reward. With most lasses, he didn't even have to bother with bringing posies. They were Highlands lasses, born and bred to live in this rough, wild land. Some of them used their beauty or their skills at seduction. Some were clever or cunning, and others relied on their wealth or breeding. They were all part of a clan, close and interdependent and, despite being scattered into small towns and villages and grand houses, never quite alone.

This—she—was different. Self-sufficient, alone but for a delicate younger sister, and apparently quite content to be so. Determined to be so, even. Whatever her reasons, he found her . . . fascinating. He wanted to know about her. And considering that she didn't seem a lass he could bed for one or a handful of nights and then walk away, he might well have lost his bloody mind.

"Ye've a very serious frown on ye," she noted. "I hope it's because ye're regretting threatening to spank me."

Munro started. How long had he been standing there, staring at her? "Nae. I had to do someaught to get ye to stop thrashing aboot. It's only that thinking too hard's likely to catch my hair on fire. Or so I've been told." By his brother, Arran, and on numerous occasions, actually.

She snorted. "Since ye clearly willnae go away, put up the damned targets." Cat jabbed a finger into his chest. "But I warn ye, ye'll nae like what I have in mind for ye when I win."

"I'll risk it." Because whether she'd realized it or not, the moment she'd agreed to participate in the contest he'd already won. She'd given her permission for him to continue to come calling whenever he chose. Their tales were intertwined, now. Just the way he wanted it. Not as clever as his brothers, ha.

He led the way back inside the ruins to find Peter standing over Elizabeth's shoulder while the lass wrote out a short list of items. Several times Rowena and Arran and even some of the other servants had attempted to teach Gilling to read and write, but the footman seemed to view his illiteracy as a badge of honor—or at least of stubbornness.

"Ye've made some progress, then?" he asked, noting that the musket stood against the rickety old table. Well, he'd have to trust Cat not to shoot him, eventually. Now seemed as good a time as any. He shifted sideways, intentionally leaving the path open between the lass and her weapon.

"Aye," Peter returned. "Nae lass should have to go withoot a proper teapot."

"Well, we dunnae have tea, so it's nae so difficult," Cat put in, as Munro tried to decide whether Gilling was being sarcastic or not. The footman grumbled so regularly that it was sometimes difficult to tell.

"Uncle, go set up a few shooting targets, will ye? The lass and I have a wager to settle."

The footman lifted a thick eyebrow. "Ye're shooting against a lass? *Ye?*"

"Aye. Me. Go see to it," Munro countered, before Peter could mention the clan gatherings and country fairs where Laird Bear MacLawry had defeated all comers and had the wee ribbons to prove it. If the wildcat decided the wager wasn't fair, they would all have to go back to the beginning again.

With a quick nod Peter left the kitchen, and Munro perused the list Elizabeth handed up to him. She actually had written "teapot" in neatly scripted pencil, along with a pair of cups and saucers to go with it, tea leaves, some hair ribbons, and an oil lamp, with the word "tarp" at the bottom as if it had been an afterthought. Or more likely, a suggestion from the eminently practical Gilling.

The list told him a couple of things. Elizabeth had never lived in anything but comfort previous to this. She had no idea how to live . . . here. And while she was likely the reason for this flight into the Highlands, she was not the captain of the expedition. That title went to the mad redhead currently digging through the picnic basket and making involuntary happy sounds as she discovered the bowl of sugar and the small sack of salt he'd managed to liberate from under Mrs. Forrest's disapproving nose.

"May I, lass?" he asked, gesturing for the stub of a pencil.

Elizabeth put it into his hand, this time the brush of her fingers against his unmistakably intentional. "Your uncle scoffed at being able to read my 'frilly scribbles,' as he called it," she said, with a breathy chuckle. "I'm glad to see you don't share his disdain for reading and writing."

Saint Bridget, the delicate flower was flirting with him. Aye, she stood a handful of inches taller than her sister, but with her dainty speech and impractical clothes she seemed far more breakable than the wildcat. "As long as I'm nae expected to produce poetry, I reckon I can manage," he said aloud, not certain he liked the way he so easily fell into his old thickheaded persona. Perhaps he'd been wearing it for so long that he *had* become that half-wit. "That Shakespeare book yer sister asked for. That was fer ye, I assume?"

"Both of us, really. We practically have Cat's book of Byron's poetry memorized, and I never liked *Childe Harold's Pilgrimage* much to begin with."

Well, that was interesting. Clearly he needed to do some more chatting with young Elizabeth if he wanted answers about who these lasses belonged to and what they were doing in the middle of clan MacLawry territory. He caught sight of the salt sack vanishing into a leather satchel. Why did questioning Elizabeth feel like cheating? If one lass would talk and the other wouldn't, logic said he should get some answers from the chatty one. Even if he'd rather pry them out of the other one.

Munro glanced over at Cat as she straightened from the satchel and took a moment to tuck a straying strand of hair behind one ear. As far as he was concerned, she was the lass to pursue. Her sister seemed barely more than a child, and a man didn't want a child in his bed. A man wanted—*he* wanted—a lass with steel in her spine. At least this time he did. He didnae bed children, but he'd had his share of flirty, flighty lasses. More than his share. Or that was how it abruptly felt, anyway.

"M'la—loving nephew," Peter said from the doorway,

making Munro wince. "I've set up a half-dozen targets fer ye and the lass. And I fetched yer rifle from Saturn."

"Saturn?" Cat took up, nearly succeeding in slipping a biscuit into her trouser pocket without him noticing.

"My horse. Now that I consider, it doesnae seem fair fer me to pit a rifle against a musket. Why dunnae ye choose whichever one ye prefer, and we'll both use it?"

"Fine. My musket."

"Ye do ken a rifle's generally twice as accur—"

"I chose," she interrupted. "Elizabeth, would ye come out with us? I reckon the odds of some other stranger bullying his way into the house are fairly small, but then Munro may have told any number of his other relatives about us."

All it would take was telling one particular relative, and she'd likely find whatever plans she had overturned and stomped into the mud. But this wasn't any of Ranulf's business, and Munro meant to see that it stayed well away from his oldest brother's notice. "Nae," he said aloud. "But I'll take another witness so ye cannae dispute the results later."

And because he'd already decided that whichever of these lasses he wanted in his bed, he hadn't been lying about one thing: now that he'd met them, he had an obligation to keep them safe. That held true even if part of him did hope that Cat would try to pummel him again so he'd have an excuse to sling her over his shoulder. Trousers or not, when she wriggled she was all lass. And he liked the way that felt.

Chapter Five

Ranulf glanced over at the empty chair to his left, then returned to his breakfast of blood pudding and tattie scones. Since the platter of scones on the sideboard was still fairly full, he would hazard a guess that Bear hadn't yet risen. Potato scones didn't survive long when Bear was about.

After another few minutes of unexpected and unusual quiet, he turned in his chair to face the redheaded butler standing behind him. "Did ye ferget someaught, Cooper?"

"M'laird?"

"The newspaper, Cooper. I ken it's nearly a week old by the time it gets here, but I do like to know what's afoot south of Hadrian's Wall." He shouldn't have had to explain it; after all, he'd been reading the London *Times* every morning for better than the past decade.

"I couldnae find it this morning, m'laird," the butler returned, his jaw clenching. "I'm certain it arrived last evening with the post, but this morning when I went to look fer it, well, it had gone."

"Is Arran here?" His younger brother made for the

most likely suspect, but Arran lived a half mile away at Fen Darach with Mary and young Mòrag and another bairn due just after Christmas. Arran also received his own copy of the newspaper, the absence of which Ranulf only minded in that it disrupted one of the few orderly things in his day.

"Nae, m'laird. Shall I send someone into the village to find ye another copy?"

"Aye. We cannae have the rest of the family knowing things I dunnae."

"I'll see to it right away, then." Cooper gestured at Owen, the head footman, and the stout Highlander strode out of the room to begin bellowing for a groom and a horse.

"Is something wrong?" Charlotte, Lady Glengask, asked in her proper English tones as she strolled into the morning room.

Immediately Ranulf stood, his heart speeding just a little at the sight of his honey-haired wife. "Aye. My newspaper's run off. We're aboot to send oot the hounds." Taking her hand, he leaned down to catch her mouth in a slow, lingering kiss.

Her free hand slid around his shoulders as she kissed him back. "What was that for?" she murmured, her fingers flexing in his. "I saw you just twenty minutes ago."

"I liked what we were up to. Thought we might do it again," he returned in the same tone. "After ye eat, of course. Cannae have ye wasting away."

Charlotte laughed, her cheeks darkening prettily. "I'm meeting Winnie and Mary in the village for luncheon," she stated, giving him a last kiss before she resumed her way to the laden sideboard, "but I believe my morning is free."

That was a good thing; he was fairly certain he would

combust if she'd had plans that didn't include being naked with him. "Cooper. Send word to Father Dyce that I cannae meet with him this morning," Ranulf instructed. "I'll ride by the church this afternoon."

"Aye, m'laird. Ian, go see if ye can catch Owen."

As the second footman fled the room, Charlotte took the seat at Ranulf's elbow. Two years ago breakfasts had been a mad affair, with Arran and Bear and Rowena, and more than likely Lachlan MacTier, all stumbling in with the two hounds and friends and whatever tales or stragglers they'd picked up the night before. Now Bear was the only sibling still to be found at Glengask, and over the past fortnight even he'd been absent from breakfast more often than he'd appeared.

With Munro's grumbling about all the domesticity suffocating him and then the growling he'd reportedly done at Lachlan when Lord Gray declined to go hunting with him, Ranulf had to wonder if his brother was actually feeling jealous. Or lonely, or left out. The past months had been so occupied with marriages and pregnancies and bairns that perhaps he hadn't paid as much attention as he should have. That would have to change.

If he dug into Bear's troubles this morning, though, he was likely to lose both the time and the . . . desire presently coursing through him for the Sassannach lass currently drinking tea with her pinkie delicately lifted in the air. Ranulf took a breath. Aye, his family came first. Always. But Bear could come first this afternoon just as easily as he could this morning. He took a breath. "Cooper, let Bear know I'd like a word with him today, if ye please."

"I'll see to it, m'laird."

"In fact, I'll meet him at noon at the Bonny Bruce." That should suffice; luncheon at the tavern would make

Munro happy, and a meeting where they would both have to keep their tempers pleased *him*.

"I'll have Ian inform him as soon as the lad returns."

When Charlotte chuckled, he looked over at her. "What's so amusing, *leannan*?"

"I was just thinking that Cooper likely wishes you had your newspaper."

He snorted. "This is a quiet morning, lass. Nae brawls last night, nae cattle gone missing, nae a lass storming the hoose armed with a broadsword and looking for Bear."

"It was a shovel; not a broadsword. And as I recall it worked out well—for Bear, anyway."

Ranulf lifted an eyebrow at her coy smile. "Ye, my dear, are wicked," he drawled. "I recall when ye were a proper English lass."

Charlotte leaned across the corner of the table and kissed him soft and slow. "That was before I met a scandalous Highland laird," she murmured, and nipped his bottom lip.

Standing, Ranulf moved behind her, helped her to her feet, then swung her into his arms. "Hang breakfast. Ye and I are going back to bed." And whoever had his newspaper, he hoped they were enjoying it.

"Ye see?" Munro said, flipping the pages of the newspaper he'd set on the ratty table of the tumbledown kitchen at the center of Haldane Abbey. "There's nae mention of any lass missing from London."

Cat slammed her hand down on an article about the overspending of Prince George, preventing him from turning the last few pages. "I'll look for myself, if ye dunnae mind, giant. And even if they dunnae have a wee story about Elizabeth, that doesnae mean anyone's stopped looking. It only means they arenae talking aboot it."

The woman refused to give even an inch. And while it did leave him frustrated and annoyed, her stubbornness also aroused him. Why, he had no idea, because she was a damned spitfire and the top of her head barely reached his shoulders, but there it was. "Mayhap ye could give me a bit more information aboot ye, then, and I could be of more help."

Dark brown eyes lifted to meet his. "I won yer silly shooting contest, and I asked ye for a newspaper. Here's a newspaper. And ye moved the boards out of the hallway so I dunnae have to climb over them any longer. That's as much help as I need from ye today. Ye may go."

Munro straightened, beginning to wish he'd taken the outcome of that contest a bit more seriously. Aye, he'd arranged it so he would be at Haldane, one way or the other, but Cat enjoyed ordering him about just a little too much. "As I recall, ye also wished for a door ye could bolt against me. I happen to have just such a door outside. Are ye still done with me, woman?"

Those brown eyes blinked, and for a brief moment genuine surprise touched her expression. Then she visibly squared her shoulders, and he girded his loins for further combat. The lass likely ate any bouquet of flowers a poor, unfortunate beau might give her.

"Ye cannae put a new door on the front of this wreck without any passersby knowing someone's in residence." She didn't say anything else aloud, but her tone implied a "ye fool" at the end of the sentence.

"It's nae a front door; it's a door fer the kitchen. And I didnae say it was new."

Silence. "Oh. All right, then. I suppose that'll do."

"Thank ye, ye stubborn lass." With that he marched

back down the hallway and outside to where Peter Gilling sat eating an apple on the seat of a well-laden wagon.
"Let's get to it, shall we?" Munro said crisply, and with
a grunt heaved the heavy door onto his shoulder.

"Am I still yer uncle, m'l—"

"Aye," Munro interrupted, before the footman could
finish speaking. The lass had made her first concession,
and he wasn't about to set her back up again by letting
her overhear that not only was he not a gamekeeper, but
he was the MacLawry's own brother.

"Then, nephew, have ye lost yer damned mind? Dunnae ye think someone at Glengask'll miss a door?"

"Nae," he decided, stepping up into the house again.
Glengask Castle had more than fifty rooms and probably better than a hundred doors. The unused linen
closet at the back of an unused room in the corner of
the east wing hadn't been opened for at least five years.
Now it didn't need to be, because the door was about
to be put to much better use elsewhere. Getting it out of
Glengask without anyone seeing him had been a tale
all by itself.

Cat stood in the kitchen doorway as he approached,
her gaze traveling up and down the length of him in a
way that made him feel distinctly warm. Aye, he was a
strong, fit man to be carrying a door about on his shoulder, and it was about time she noticed that.

He set the door down and leaned it against the wall.
"Yer door, Cat."

"The opening's too big for it."

"That's why I also brought wood and bricks and mortar. And unless ye ken how to hang a door, ye'd best
stay well back."

Her sister immediately returned to mending a shawl

by the fireplace. Cat, though, stood her ground. "I reckon I can use a shovel or a hammer as well as any man."

Peter walked up and handed her a satchel of tools. "That's bonny, because I dunnae ken how my nephew and I can do it alone."

That wasn't at all helpful, but at the same time Munro had no objection to keeping her close by him all day. "Let's get the frame measured up, then," he said, heading back outside for a stack of lumber.

"I thought ye were Glengask's gamekeeper."

She'd followed him. "In the Highlands a man does what's needed," he returned, ignoring the unexpected thrill that ran through him at her pursuit, instead pulling the boards out of the cart and then crouching to heave them up on his shoulder. "And what's yer complaint aboot me being a handy fellow, what with ye being a lass who wears trousers and shoots dead-on with a musket?"

"I've nae complaint." She hesitated, then lifted a trio of bricks in her arms, cradling them against her chest as she fell in behind him. "I cannae help but wonder what ye expect in return for this door, Munro."

He sent back a glance at her. "Just a wee bit of trust, lass. That's all I ask." For the moment, anyway. Suggesting that he'd like to—that he intended to—bed her, would only get him a brick thrown at his skull now.

"Ye give me a door, first. Then I'll consider."

Her gaze skimmed him again as she turned away. She at least seemed aware now that he was male—or more likely, she'd decided his muscles could be useful. He wondered again which clan she claimed, or if she even had one. Given the obvious culture of her sister, he guessed that she *did* have a clan, and that she was no fringe hanger-on. If that were so, however, what had happened to send the two lasses fleeing into the wilds? And why *was* there no mention of an ongoing search for a missing Society lady in the newspaper?

"Tell me someaught," he said, pulling a hinged measuring stick from Peter's satchel and unfolding it. "Is this yer last resort?"

"What do ye mean, 'last resort'?" she returned, from closer behind than he expected. "Having ye give me a door?"

"Nae. Being here at Haldane Abbey. Was coming to MacLawry territory yer first choice or yer last one?"

He heard her take a breath, but when she didn't immediately tell him to mind his own affairs he busied himself with measuring the uneven opening. If she'd decided to at least consider answering him, he could call that a victory.

"It wasnae my first choice," she finally answered, her voice pitched low enough that her sister halfway across the room likely couldn't hear a word of it. "I originally thought somewhere less . . . isolated would do, but Elizabeth cannae even pretend to be a Scot."

"Ye mean her pretty ways make ye too noticeable." As opposed to Cat's wearing trousers—which any red-blooded man would have to be blind not to notice.

Another hesitation. "Aye. And that's all I'm saying about it."

"Did I *ask* ye anything else?"

"Ye—"

"Excuse me, lass." Peter edged by them to set another pile of bricks against the wall.

Both Munro and Cat jumped. *Damnation.* He, at least, knew better than to forget his surroundings. Out in the middle of nowhere could be the most dangerous place for a MacLawry sibling to be. "Do ye reckon we have enough mortar and plaster, uncle?" he asked, mostly to remind the footman yet again of their charade.

"Aye, unless ye decide to patch the corner of the ceiling," Gilling returned, gesturing at the spot where sunlight glinted through the roof. "We dunnae have the tarp yet, though."

Oh, they would be repairing the roof. Just not today. "Help me mark the lumber, will ye?"

The lads generally hired to make repairs and build cottages in An Soadh had been eager to sell him supplies, even after he'd awakened them at four o'clock in the morning by pounding on their door. Both men, though, had asked where he was headed and whether he needed more assistance, so he and Peter had actually left the village westbound before circling around to the south and east. Little as he knew about these sisters, he was quite aware that he'd been supremely serious when he'd said he would protect them—protect her—whether they wanted his assistance or not. And that meant even from the curious of his own clan.

"Tell *me* someaught," Cat said after a moment, crouching to hold a plank steady as he marked it. "With all the time ye've spent here, hasnae his lordship noticed ye shirking yer duties? Are ye nae worried ye'll be sacked?"

"His lordship's table doesnae lack fer meat," he returned truthfully. "I reckon as long as that's so, whatever else I choose to do with my time is my own affair." He straightened. If they were circling back around to questions about the MacLawrys, he needed to change the subject. "In fact, I've some beef in the wagon fer ye. Uncle?"

Gilling sank down against the wall. "I reckon ye'll

have to fetch it yerself, nephew," he said, sending his employer an uncertain glance. "My back's near broken."

Well, he'd made the footman his uncle, so he supposed he'd have to live with the consequences of that—until they returned to Glengask, anyway. And it would give him a moment to consider how much more lying he wanted to do. "Then take a rest, old man. I'll be back in a minute."

From the look Bear sent her, he clearly expected Catriona to tag along after him. Instead, she plunked herself down next to his so-called uncle. The giant had proven himself adept at avoiding her questions, but Peter Gilling didn't seem nearly as glib—and she had some suspicions for which she needed some answers. The moment Munro turned down the hallway, she sighed.

"Bear's helping us isnae going to cause him trouble, is it?" she said with a frown. "I know Lord Glengask has two brothers and a sister, the lot of them all married over the past two years. That's a great many mouths, when ye add in the bairns and the servants."

"Lord Arran has his own house at Fen Darach, and Lady Winnie lives with Lord Gray at the MacTier hoose," the grizzled fellow returned. "It's only Glengask and his lady and their wee bairn William at the castle now, along with L—the youngest brother. He isnae wed yet."

"And what's his name?"

Gilling's eyes widened, and then he abruptly began coughing. "Och," he managed, between bouts of hacking, "a bit of . . . water . . . lass."

Elizabeth hurried over with a handleless mug, and he gulped the contents down ferociously. Then he needed more water. By then Catriona was fairly certain of the reason behind his abrupt ailment. *Good heavens.* She'd wanted a place where she and Elizabeth could disappear, or at least remain anonymous. If her suspicions were true, Bear was the very last person with whom she wanted to be acquainted.

When he strolled back in, she rose to poke a finger into his hard chest. "So yer uncle seems to have forgotten the name of the youngest MacLawry lad. Since this laird lives with the marquis at Glengask Castle, I reckon ye ken who he is. Why dunnae ye tell me, then?"

Bear looked from her to the abruptly silent older man. "Didnae I tell ye to keep yer gobber shut, Peter?"

"Aye. She tricked me, though."

And doing so had been much easier than she'd expected. But she wasn't about to give Bear time to think up some other lie or excuse or to drop dead of the plague or something. She poked him again. "What is his name?" she demanded, jabbing her finger in time with her words.

He took an audible breath. "Munro," he said slowly. "Though he goes by Bear, mostly."

Catriona had expected to hear exactly that, but it still stunned her for a moment. For God's sake, she'd . . . Thank goodness she hadn't begun to like him, because that would have hurt. "Ye bloody liar," she snapped, refusing to acknowledge anything more than her anger.

"Of course I lied," he retorted, his green eyes narrowed. "Nearly the first thing oot of yer mouth when we met was that ye expected Lord Glengask to ride in and burn ye oot. I wanted to help ye. I still want to help ye. What the devil does it matter who my brother is?"

She wanted to pummel him, but he probably wouldn't even feel it. "It matters! Ye should have told me!"

"Nae. I should've done exactly what I did, so that now ye can bellow at me but nae fear I'll harm ye."

Catriona realized she had both hands clenched into fists. He made a good point, and she took a hard breath as she glared at him. Of course he might be attempting to avoid her wrath by making his deception her fault, but then perhaps it was. Partly, anyway. "Ye cannae blame me for being wary."

"I dunnae blame ye. But then ye cannae blame me fer being cautious." He took a long step closer to her. "And ye'd best keep in mind that ye still have a secret or two yerself before ye decide how much growling ye want to do now, ye mysterious lass."

That stopped her retort. Aye, he'd lied to her. But he was correct; she'd lied—or at least omitted the truth—to him, as well. Of course she had a better reason for her caution, because she wasn't about to feel guilty for keeping Elizabeth and herself as safe as possible. "So ye're a good man despite yer blue blood, are ye?"

He shook his shaggy head at her. "Nae. I'm a man. And that's the sum of it. Where I lay my damned head has naught to do with my character."

"Ye say that now because I caught ye in a lie."

His brows lowered, jamming together. "I said it before. I'm only reminding ye it's still true."

Damn it all, she'd suspected almost from the beginning that he wasn't a gamekeeper, though never in a hundred years would she have guessed he was the youngest brother of the MacLawry. One thing she *did* know, however, was that when—if—she told him the tale she carried, he would throw whatever response she made now right back at her. And the oddest part of it all was that she had the feeling that she *would* be telling him. As if over the past days their lives had become intertwined despite her best efforts to remain unentangled.

"Ye still should have told me," she said finally, wondering why she wasn't as angry as she likely should have been, and deciding to leave answering that question for later. "Yer being here will attract attention. I dunnae want attention."

"I gave ye my word, lass," he said after a moment, before he picked up a saw and returned to his work. "I mean to keep ye—and yer sister—safe."

From the last glance he sent her, Munro had also expected her to kick up more of a fuss. Blast it, she wanted to. And she could tell herself that her calm had nothing to do with how very fine he looked in his coarse cotton shirt and black and white and red kilt and those scuffed leather work boots, and everything to do with what would happen if he learned anything else about her.

Squaring her shoulders, she turned her back on the two men and strode into the depths of the kitchen. She had a rabbit to spit and put over the fire. And she wanted a closer look at the newspaper he'd brought. The news was nearly a week old now, but it seemed like there should have been . . . something. Some sign that the Duke of Visford was displeased to find his betrothed gone, that her stepmother Anne Derby-MacColl had offered a reward for her only child's safe return.

"He's the Marquis of Glengask's brother?" her sister whispered, leaning over the table beside her as she finally gave up on scouring the newspaper. "He doesn't look like a lord."

That made her smile. Half Scottish or not, her sister was so very English. "What does he look like to ye, then?"

"I don't know. One of those men who teaches aristocrats how to box, or perhaps a stable boy or something. I mean, he's very fit."

That, he was. "At least we know the truth of it, now."

"Yes." Elizabeth clutched her sister's hand. "I was glad when he and his uncle found us. I mean, I love you, but they were someone to talk to. Now, though—what if they know Visford? What if the marquis has already told him that I'm here?"

Catriona squeezed Elizabeth's fingers as they began to shake. "Hush. He doesnae know who ye are. If he did, we'd have seen Lord Glengask already. And I promised ye that I'd keep ye safe, *piuthar*. No matter what."

"I believe you, Cat. I wouldn't be here if I . . . Oh, my," she breathed, her cheeks darkening.

Her heart pounding in abrupt alarm, Catriona turned around. Had someone followed Munro after all? Then she caught sight of what had attracted her sister's attention, and her pulse sped even faster. "Oh, my," indeed.

Munro MacLawry had removed his shirt. His back to them, he sawed at one of the planks while muscles played beneath his skin and a slow trail of sweat meandered down his spine to the belt around his hips and the kilt beneath. One thing was clear; he was a magnificent specimen of the male figure.

And he *was* magnificent. All six and a half feet of him. When he straightened and turned around she caught a glimpse of a flat, well-muscled abdomen before she quickly averted her gaze. It would never do for him to catch her ogling him. He was just a rude, annoying, meddling, lying giant, after all. *But my, what a giant*.

The warmth shivering through her middle felt so . . . odd. At her father's estate she'd spent most of her days in the company of men. Hunting, sheep shearing, fishing, riding—all the things a father would want a son to know. And that son, for all intents and purposes, had been her. Or it had been, until two years ago.

But none of that explained why she couldn't stop looking at Munro. The flex of his muscles, the occasional glimpse of roped thighs as he crouched to set boards in place, the sweaty hair clinging to his brow and temples—it pulled at her, made her want to run her hands across his bare skin, made her feel . . . unsettled, but not in an unpleasant way.

The other fellow, Peter, who was more than likely *not* Munro's uncle, had removed his shirt as well. When she glanced over at him, though, she felt nothing. And she didn't like it—or rather, she didn't like that she did like this feeling.

Cursing under her breath, she went to skin the rabbit. A moment later warmth pushed at her from behind, and she turned her head to see a broad chest. Catriona lifted her gaze to meet amused green eyes looking back at her. Could he see on her face the lust she felt? *Damnation.* "What do ye want?" she snapped, sharper than she intended.

He reached past her, close enough to touch, and retrieved another of the mugs he'd brought along the day before. "Just a swallow of water, lass," he drawled with a slight, engaging grin, and tilted his head back to drink. His Adam's apple bobbed, and rivulets of water ran down his chin and throat to trail down the light scattering of hair on his chest.

"Ye're doing that on purpose," she stated, moving so she was no longer between him and the table. The position made her feel vulnerable, and she didn't like it.

"Doing what? Drinking? Aye. A man builds up a

thirst." He emptied the mug and set it down again with a clank. "Come and see if ye agree with what we've built ye so far."

Built her? They all knew full well now that this property was much closer to being his than hers. He certainly had no reason to continue wearing his gamekeeper mask any longer. And yet, both he and Peter Gilling continued to work to put up a door and repair the walls that would not only help keep her and Elizabeth safer, but enable her to bar the door against him. It made no sense.

Of course she already knew precisely how much they'd accomplished this morning, because she'd been sneaking looks every time she could manage to do so without him noticing. Even so, she made a show of walking over to the doorway while he followed close behind.

They had the opening framed to the size of the new door, and had also nailed up planks on either side to both shore up the wall and provide a skeleton for the bricks and mortar that would follow. A clan chief's brother or not, Munro knew how to use his hands. Another flutter shivered through her gut. "Ye've made it very sturdy," she said aloud, wrapping one hand around a timber and tugging at it. The two-inch oak didn't budge.

"We cannae have it falling doon with the next gust of wind. And with winter close by, the winds will come. This'll keep ye warm and safe inside."

"Ye expect us to be here when the snow arrives then, do ye?"

Green eyes studied her face. "Aye. I do. Did ye have another plan?"

She'd had oh, so many plans, and they'd all crumbled into dust. This truly was the only one she had left. "I suppose ye'll have to wait and see," she returned, heading back to the table.

A hand closed over her shoulder and spun her around again with an ease that left her a little breathless. Men didn't put their hands on her. Not when she was the daughter of Randall MacColl. And not when she dressed like one of them. "Do ye have another plan?" he repeated, his voice lowering to a soft rumble.

"Ye're building me—us—a door. That doesnae gain ye a place at my table. I'll nae share my counsel with ye, Laird Munro MacLawry."

"You shouldn't be so mean to him, Catriona," Elizabeth broke in, even as Bear narrowed his eyes. "He's only ever been helpful."

"And why is that, do ye think, Elizabeth?" she countered, reaching for the annoyance and anger she'd had so ready to hand just a few days ago.

"Because we are ladies in distress, and he is a gentleman," her sister said, as if that explained everything. As if the world was that simple. With a flounce of her pretty green and blue muslin skirts, Elizabeth swept up another mug of water and carried it to the doorway and Peter. "There doesn't have to be any other reason but that."

"Ye should listen to yer sister, bonny lass," Munro said, releasing her before she could even think to jerk out of his grip. "And ye'll tell me yer tale, wildcat. I can be patient."

He didn't look patient. More perceptive than she'd expected, yes, but not patient. Yet there he was, carrying a bucket outside to fetch water so they could mix the mortar. And however many times she'd told him to go away, he kept returning. Perhaps he *was* more patient than she'd realized. The only question was, why?

"Dunnae call me a wildcat," she ordered belatedly, striding after him to remain in earshot.

"That's yer best retort? Ye're getting soft, Catriona."

She nearly stumbled, not at the insult, but at hearing him say her full name in his deep brogue. Nothing should be allowed to sound that warm and enticing.

"I amnae. That's merely the most recent annoying thing ye've said to me."

He slowed. "Is that so?"

"Aye. It is. And dunnae think ye can glare at me and make me cower. Ye're a big man, Bear, but I'm nae afraid of ye. Nae fer a single damned minute."

Moving with that deceptive speed and grace of his, Bear swung around, pushed her backward against the stone wall, and took her mouth in a deep, hot kiss. The empty bucket dropped to the floor with a clatter that sounded far more distant than it was. Splaying his big hands against the wall on either side of her face, he leaned in, demanding with his lips and tongue and teeth. His touch didn't feel so much like a kiss as it did a full-on assault of her senses.

With his body hard against hers, she could feel the iron of him through her thin man's shirt, unyielding and velvet all at the same time. She had to stand on her toes and lift her chin to meet him, heat cascading through her as abrupt and burning as a bonfire.

"S . . . stop," she finally managed, shoving at his bare chest with both palms.

"Nae." He kissed her again, the pull of his mouth nearly making her eyes roll back in her head. This was the very thing that could make a lass faint, she decided. Not her, of course, but any other lass would surely swoon into his manly arms.

"Stop!" she repeated, more forcefully.

Munro lifted his head an inch or so from hers. "Ask me nicely."

As if she could say anything at all with his mouth doing those things. For God's sake, she could barely conjure a coherent thought, and that was only a single word—"more." "Please release me."

The words came out as hardly more than a mumble, but a moment later he took a long, single step backward. "I'll release ye, Catriona," he rumbled, something sharp and compelling at the edge of his words, "but I willnae let ye go. Nae just yet."

"That doesnae even make any sense."

"Then why are ye still standing there?" he returned.

Dammit all, she *was* still standing there, her back to the wall and her palms flat against his warm chest. And then he had the nerve to grin down at her. With another curse she didn't care if he heard, she snagged the bucket and stomped outside. *Good heavens. Good heavens.*

This man was going to be a problem.

Staying on at Haldane Abbey had seemed the best solution both for her and for Elizabeth, but now she wasn't so certain. And not because Munro MacLawry had kissed her—deliciously kissed her—again, but because she'd kissed him back. And that would never do.

At the rivulet beyond the back of the abbey she clambered down to jam the bucket beneath the miniature waterfall. Saint Bridget and Robert the Bruce. Munro was the brother of the MacLawry. He was *Lord* Munro. People noticed him. How could they not? He stood at least six-and-a-half-feet tall, had eyes the green of a spring meadow, and a face that would make even a grandmother sigh.

She didn't wish to be noticed. That had been the point of coming here. Well, partly. Catriona frowned. Perhaps she needed to admit, to herself at least, that she would have ended up somewhere deep in the Highlands even if Elizabeth hadn't needed rescuing. That she had needed rescuing, as well, and in the absence of any assistance she'd decided to rescue herself.

"Move over," Munro said, and squatted down beside her to lift the full bucket out of the water.

"Ye're nae a polite man, are ye?" she commented, standing when he did.

"I've noticed that ye prefer direct talk to a pretty turn of phrase, lass. Or am I wrong aboot that?"

No, he wasn't wrong. "Why do ye care what sort of speech I prefer?" she asked anyway, because his reasoning felt . . . significant.

That attractive smile touched his face again. "I'm a man people fear, Catriona. Whatever might be inside my skull, I'm built to be a brute. People dunnae insult me to my face, and they dunnae tell me things I dunnae wish to hear. I like ye. I like that ye stand toe-to-toe with me, that when ye say someaught ye expect me to answer ye back. I like that ye look me in the eye when ye've a disagreement with me."

I like ye. The rest of what he said seemed honest and genuinely complimentary, but it was those three words that sent bats rattling around inside her rib cage. Men didn't like her. She was too abrupt, mannerless, mannish, better than they were at the things on which they prided themselves, and she didn't hide that fact. They didn't pursue her, because her father hadn't permitted it. But Munro didn't know who her father had been, who her uncle was. He didn't even know her family name or her clan.

"Naught to say aboot that?" he prompted, heading

back to the house without her. "Dunnae tell me ye're shy now, wildcat. Ye tried to shoot me just a few days ago."

"All ye've done is prove ye're a madman, Bear Mac-Lawry," she mustered. "If ye only like someone who'll disagree with ye and call ye names, get yerself a Sassannach."

An abrupt laugh rumbled from his chest. "That's more like it, lass," he returned, still chuckling. "Ye've yer wits, and that's fer damned certain. And ye make me use mine." He narrowed one eye. "I didnae think I'd have much use fer a lass who used her gobber fer chatting, but ye've a way aboot ye."

For him, that likely sufficed as a compliment. Oddly enough, she did feel flattered. Or perhaps she hadn't eaten enough today. "Do ye reckon ye'll finish the door today?" she asked, mostly because believing a man's compliments—and especially those of a man who knew even a little about her—would only see her in more trouble. And she bloody well had enough of that all on her own.

"Nae. We'll brick up the wall and leave it to set. Hanging the door can keep until tomorrow or the next day." She felt rather than saw his glance. "Ye cannae wait to bar it closed and keep everyone away from ye, I wager."

"Ye and yer so-called uncle are the only everyone I've seen since we arrived, so aye."

"Ah, lass. Ye wound me. Ye'd bar the door on yer own allies? And what if I felt the need to kiss ye again?"

They were far too close to the kitchen for him to be saying that in that rumbling, carrying voice of his. "Hush. I dunnae want to have to explain yer mauling me to Elizabeth."

"Or to yerself."

He'd managed to speak that very quietly, and when she shot him a glare he only gazed back at her innocently. As if she would conjure those words in her own mind—and in his voice to boot. Annoying, aggravating, attractive man. If he would just stop kissing her . . . Except that she didn't wish him to stop. Not just yet, anyway.

Chapter Six

B ear!"
     Munro snapped his eyes open, diving for the dagger he'd set on a stool beside the big brass bathtub. A heartbeat later he realized Ranulf stood in the doorway, and he sank back into the warm water. "Ye nearly scared me oot of my own skin."

"Where were ye today?" the marquis demanded, shutting the door behind him and leaning back against it, his arms crossed over his chest.

"Oot."

"That's nae good enough."

Munro frowned. Evidently he'd had a better day than his oldest brother. "I had Peter with me, as ye ordered. We went fishing."

"And where's yer catch? There in the bath with ye?"

"Even I dunnae always catch someaught. What's got yer kilt in a twist?"

"Ye went fishing yesterday, too. And the day before, if I recall. And ye've nae brought home a single trout or pike in all that time. So I ask ye again—where were ye today?"

Munro pushed to his feet, water dripping down him back into the tub and on the floor around him. The air immediately began cooling his skin, but a damned Highlander didn't mind a wee bit of cold. More important than that, he had no intention of being towered over by anyone. Even his oldest brother. "First ye tell me I cannae go aboot on my own, and now ye dunnae like the way I fish. I'm thinking *ye're* the one with the problem, Glengask."

His brother picked up a towel and threw it at him. "Ye and I have some things to discuss. In my office. In ten minutes." With that Ranulf left the bedchamber again, closing the door hard behind him.

Well, that was dandy. A full day of toting rocks and doors and lumber, and now Ranulf wanted to yell— evidently because he wasn't catching enough fish. True, he hadn't been spending much time at Glengask, but he didn't imagine he'd actually been named the gamekeeper in his absence. They had peace in the valley now, so he wasn't needed to loom over enemies at the moment, either.

Grumbling, he pulled on a clean shirt, stomped into his boots, and wrapped a freshly pleated kilt about his hips. These days both of his brothers and even his brother-in-law Lachlan generally wore trousers, but that Sassannach attire wasn't for him. It never had been. Aside from kilts being one of the oldest of the Highlands traditions, he liked the idea that the moment anyone saw him coming, they knew he was a MacLawry. Arran said he lacked subtlety, but to him that sounded like a compliment. Subtlety was for diplomats, and he wasn't a damned diplomat.

Tempted as he was to linger in his private rooms simply because of the marquis's order that he appear at once, he'd yet to shrink from, or make any effort to avoid, trouble. And so he grabbed a coat off the back of a chair and left his bedchamber, shrugging into the wool garment as he walked. Only one thing mattered: no one could know about the two lasses hiding out at Haldane. He'd given his word.

When he walked into Ranulf's spare office his brother already stood at the window, his back to the room and his arms crossed again over his chest. The two deerhounds were curled beneath the desk, either not sensing or not concerned with their master's mood. Other than not catching any fish and being away from the castle for most of the past three days, Munro had no idea what he'd done to incur the MacLawry's censure. Hell's bells, he'd been spending most of his spare time away from Glengask for weeks, since well before he'd met the wildcat.

"I sent Ian to look fer ye this morning," Ranulf said, as he returned to the window. "Ye werenae to be found."

Munro shrugged, sitting. "I told ye I was with Gilling. As ye ordered. And I left early this morning to go fishing, because I'd nae been having any luck. Is there someaught else ye want to know?"

"Ye were supposed to meet me at the Bonny Bruce fer luncheon today."

"Ye should've told me last night, then, because fer the last damned time, I wasnae here!"

The marquis faced him. "And that's my point. Ye've been spending too much time away from here. I rely on ye, Bear."

"I meet with every cotter and peat cutter who stumbles into the valleys, making certain none of 'em are here to make trouble. Ye've made peace with the Campbells, and so we've nae had so many refugees lately.

And winter is coming, so those in search of a haven have likely already found a place to hunker doon until spring. Either way, it's hardly a task that takes all my time."

"Ye being bored isnae an excuse fer ye to go missing. From now on, ye will tell *me* where ye're off to, and when ye expect to return. I'm busy enough that I dunnae have the time to go searching fer ye every damned day."

So that was what this was coming to now? Him being just another task on his brother's schedule? "Nae," he said aloud.

Ranulf's jaw clenched. "It wasnae a request."

Both dogs' heads lifted, and one by one they emerged from beneath the desk to stand on either side of Ranulf. Fergus had been part of the family for six years, and smaller Una for just over five. As little as Munro believed one of the hounds would take a bite out of him, they did make for something else he needed to keep an eye on.

"I dunnae care what it was," he said anyway. "I'm nae some bairn ye can push aboot. I'm seven-and-twenty now. Ye cannae ootfight me, and I'm nae scared of ye, either. I've nae intention of telling ye where I am every damned second, any more than I tell ye when I take a shite or when I put some lass on her back."

For a long moment the marquis gazed at him, his expression flat and unreadable and his blue eyes icy. After all, no one defied the MacLawry's commands. Except for him, apparently, and all because of a few kisses shared with a redheaded spitfire lass so desperate to escape something that she couldn't trust anyone.

"Do ye want to remain beneath this roof, Munro?" Ranulf finally asked, his voice clipped. Fergus began a low growl, only quieting when the marquis put a hand on his head.

So they'd reached threats already. "I stay here to watch over ye and Charlotte and wee William through the night," he returned, trying hard to keep a rein on his own temper. "Ye've men aplenty to protect ye during the day. And I dunnae care to be surrounded by cooing lasses and wailing bairns. Ye be as civilized as ye like, Glengask. But dunnae try to put a leash on me to ease yer own mind."

"If I meant to ease my own mind, *bràthair*," Ranulf retorted, his voice rising, "I'd send fer Lady Eithne Boyd and see ye wed. That would give me an alliance with the Stewarts, and fer once ye'd be useful."

" 'Fer once,' is it?" Munro snapped, shoving to his feet again. "If that's yer only use fer me, then ye can find a way to mend old Ailpen Mackle's roof fer him withoot denting his pride. And ye can see to the squatters at the south end of Glen Carrog withoot letting 'em know that we know they're spying fer the MacDougalls. And dunnae ferget to call on Miss Malvina Sorlie and make certain she's nae convinced herself again that ye've lobsterbacks hidden in the attic here and they need to be burned oot. Ye—"

"That's enough, Munro."

Both dogs were growling now. Ranulf had raised them to be absolute protectors of the family, but the fact remained that *he* had raised them. "Nae, it isnae. Ye bring Lady Eithne here, and I'll pound her skinny brother into paste. Then see if ye can make yer alliance."

Very seldom did anyone—much less one of his own siblings—push Ranulf as far as Munro just had. The marquis's face paled, his jaw clenched so tightly Munro was fairly certain he could hear his brother's teeth grinding. "Have ye had yer say then, little brother? Have ye explained to me how very hard ye work to do yer duty? Then ye'll stay in the damned hoose until I decide what to do with ye. And that's the beginning, middle, and end of it."

Staying in the house meant breaking his word to Catriona. And leaving would now mean breaking the MacLawry's law. All because he didn't care to become the civilized, bowing, cooing fellow Ranulf decided he should be. "I dunnae give a damn what ye decide," he rumbled. "If ye think ye can make me do what ye want fer no damned good reason but yer own pride, ye're welcome to try."

With that he turned around and yanked open the door so hard it slammed into the wall. A vase in the hallway crashed to the stone floor and shattered. Munro stepped over it and kept walking. Keep him in the house like some disobedient hound. *Ha*. It would take Ranulf, Arran, Lach, and half the household lads to even slow him down.

And that was Ranulf's solution to him wandering about like the free man he was? To marry him off to some wall-eyed Stewart lass? Even if he wasn't intent on stalking a very different prey at the moment, he would throw himself off the top of Ben Nevis before he'd lay his mouth or any other body part on Eithne Boyd.

Not quite certain what he meant to do beyond leaving the damned house, he retrieved his rifle, stuffed his antler-hilted *sgian-dubh* into his right boot, and pounded down the stairs again. He more than half expected Ranulf or his deerhounds to come charging after him, but other than the usual bustle at Glengask and his own racketing about, he couldn't hear anything.

Then Charlotte stepped into the hallway in front of him. With a curse he stopped before he could crash into his sister-in-law and knock her to the floor. "Charlotte. I've nae time fer chatting."

"Follow me, Bear," she said, in her usual calm, practical tone, and vanished back into the downstairs sitting room.

Stifling an annoyed sigh, he trod after her. "I'm in a hurry, *piuthar*. What is it ye want?"

The nanny, Rose or Daisy or some other flower, sat on the deep couch with seven-month-old William on her lap. With a murmured word Charlotte lifted her son into her arms, and the nanny glided out of the room and closed the door behind her. "Sit," the marchioness instructed, sinking down on the couch.

If this had been Glengask issuing commands, Munro would have known precisely how to respond. A lass, though, wife to his brother and a sister now to him—that was much more complicated. With a hard breath, trying to ease his temper before he let loose and snapped at her, too, he sat beside her. "I'm sitting. Now what?"

She shifted William onto his lap, and the bairn immediately reached for the rifle he'd propped against the couch. Alarm stinging through him, Munro lifted the weapon and dropped it behind the couch with far less care than he generally took. Christ. He'd learned to shoot at five or six, but the boy was only seven months old, and Ranulf's son. His own nephew. No harm was allowed to come to William, his mother, or her husband. No matter how angry he was, that fact never changed.

But he wasn't about to change, either. "Ye can hand me all the bairns ye like, Charlotte. They dunnae make me a civilized man. They dunnae make me yearn fer a wife and little ones of my own." He gave over his fingers to the lad, who decided they were handholds to get him up the back of the couch.

"Ranulf only wants what's best for you."

"Ranulf wants what's best fer the clan."

"Why can't that be the same thing?" she pursued. "Surely you have no objection to meeting the right lass and being happy."

Arguing with a female was much trickier than straight-out fighting a man. Particularly when the lass was gentle and kind and thoughtful and a civilized Sassannach, and he was none of those things. "I'm happy now," he said, realizing at the same moment that "happy" wasn't the correct word. That, however, was his own business to decipher. "And have ye ever set yer peepers on Lady Eithne Boyd?"

"No, we've never met, but—"

"Her eyes look in two different directions, neither of them being directly at ye. She's skinny as a pole, and a breeze would likely break her in two—if it didn't lift her up and carry her away to Skye."

Charlotte's abrupt cough sounded closer to a laugh. "Very well. Perhaps Lady Eithne is not the woman for you. But she's not the only female in the Highlands."

Unbidden, his mind went to the wild redhead hidden in a valley two miles away. She was becoming an obsession, but she was *his* obsession. One he was not willing to share. "Ye're assuming I'd rather be shackled to one lass than have any of them I wish, whenever I choose. That's done me well, as I recall."

"But what about children?"

He untangled William from the cushions and handed the black-haired bairn back to his mother. "I like yers well enough. And Arran's and Winnie's. I'd die fer 'em.

But dunnae take that to mean that I yearn fer my own. Or fer any one woman. Or fer anyone who thinks they have the right to tell me what to do." With that he stood, retrieved his rifle, and headed back to the hallway. "And ye can tell Glengask I meant what I said. I'll nae be kept a prisoner here, and I'll start a war with the Stewarts before I marry a one of 'em."

As he strode outside and across the clearing to the stable he could practically hear the ruckus he'd likely begun inside the house. "Debny," he barked as he stepped through the stable's open double doors, and the head groom appeared from one of the rooms at the back of the building.

"Aye, m'laird?"

"I'm taking Saturn oot again."

The servant nodded, stepping over to fetch a saddle and tack. "I'll have ye and Gilling ready to go in a snap."

"Just Saturn." He caught the groom's involuntary glance toward the house proper. "Now, if ye please."

With a grimace, Debny resumed saddling the big gray gelding. He would likely report to the house the second Munro rode out of sight, but that didn't trouble him a whit. He had no intention of being caged, or of giving the impression that he could be—even for a moment.

The only thing that troubled him was Peter Gilling. Aye, the servant had given his word to keep the lass's location and existence secret, but Munro had seen grown men piss themselves when confronted with Glengask's full wrath. Hopefully once the footman sensed trouble, he would make himself scarce to avoid betraying anyone.

And domesticated as they were, his brothers were welcome to try to track him down. They didn't spend

nearly as much time out of doors hunting and fishing
and patrolling their land as they once had. As he still did.

As he swung into the saddle it occurred to him that
he'd decided where he was headed even without thinking about it. Catriona would likely try to shoot him again
for appearing twice in one day, but for his part, he looked
forward to seeing her once more. He'd enjoyed just being Bear, without the weight of MacLawry dragging behind him. And other than a few biting comments about
his lying tongue, Cat hadn't treated him any differently
once she'd learned the truth. No lifting her skirts—or
taking down her trousers, in her case—in hopes that
bedding him would cause him to fall hopelessly in love
with her, making her part of the most powerful family
in the Highlands. No altering her responses to avoid annoying him. Hell, knowing the truth merely annoyed
her more.

Perhaps that was the lure. She didn't give a damn
that he was a brother to the MacLawry, and conversely
he wanted to know precisely who she was and from
where she'd come. The more she refused to tell him,
the more he wanted to know. Now that he considered it,
he might have decided he enjoyed puzzles after all, if
they were all curvy females wrapped in men's clothing
and topped with a mane of deep red hair that he wanted
to tangle his fingers through.

He knew himself to be a man who liked women and
drink and the hard Highlands life. The wildcat spun him
about, when he had a reputation for punching or avoiding things and people who didn't fit with the life he'd
made for himself. With her, however, kissing and a long,
heated string of thoughts about her naked and moaning
beneath him beat down every other thought in his head.

Shaking himself, he rode Saturn out of the stable,

then circled around to the back of the building. There he kicked a barrel aside and leaned down to grab the cloth sack hidden beneath it. It would never do to have a maid discover him hoarding hair clips and spyglasses in his bedchamber.

Forty minutes later he tethered Saturn behind a deadfall with both grass and water within easy reach, then hiked the last quarter mile to the abbey. If he'd taken the direct route he might have been there in half the time, but defying Glengask had consequences. And that meant taking precautions—especially with his promise to a certain lass at stake.

He reached the broken front door without anyone trying to put a ball through his chest. For a moment he debated whether to call out, but he wanted to see her without her knowing he was there. Without the walls and pits she spread around herself to keep everyone else at bay. To himself he could admit that he wanted to see her smile, even if it wasn't at him.

Walking as softly as he could in his heavy boots, he edged along the hallway toward the half-finished kitchen door. Female muttering caught his attention, and he stopped to listen. He'd already told Cat he wasn't a gentleman, and so he refused to feel a damned ounce of guilt for sneaking about. Sneaking was practically a way of life in the Highlands, anyway.

". . . think he would turn us out?" Elizabeth said in her cultured English tones. "He's been nothing but kind from the moment we met."

"Kindness isnae the problem," Cat returned, her brogue pretty as sunlight. "If anyone finds us here, they'll send ye packing back to London, likely with an armed escort. Ye said yerself that the Duke of Visford's nae a man to trifle with. And if Bear discovers ye're the fat old bastard's betrothed, well, Highlanders dunnae care to stir up the wrath of the Sassannach."

That was a cartload of shite. He couldn't think of one true Highlander who wouldn't relish the chance to spite the English. Actually doing so, though, took more than courage. It took the backing of a clan that had power and strength enough to make even the Sassannach pause. Ranulf had made most of his reputation by generally ignoring English law and doing what best benefited clan MacLawry. That made him the exception to the rule. Catriona had to know that. Why, then, was she lying to her sister about the help they could receive? What did she have to gain by staying on in the wilds?

"I love that you called His Grace a fat old bastard," Elizabeth returned with a giggle. Munro could almost see her blushing. "If I'd been able to say that to his face, perhaps he would have refused me outright, or Mama would have changed her mind about pushing for a wedding. We could be in London right now, sipping tea and shopping. Oh, I would purchase you so many pretty gowns, Cat. You would be swimming in silk, and all the young men would bring you posies."

"The last time I wore a gown I tripped over the hem," Catriona commented, her tone rueful—and unless Munro was mistaken, a little wistful. "I'm nae suited for such things."

"Nonsense. With that hair of yours, I'll wager you're the loveliest lass on Islay." She paused. "But now you can't go home, can you? Because you came to help me."

"Dunnae worry yerself about that. For the Bruce's sake. Ye're my *piuthar;* I will always come when ye need me." She sighed, the soft sound making Munro's cock jump. "Aside from that, Islay's nae the same now. With our papa gone, I've nae real wish to return."

"But you're the oldest. Daughter or not, you were—"

"I'm nothing, Elizabeth. Uncle Robert is chieftain now. And he and I dunnae . . . see eye to eye."

Daughter and now niece to the chieftain of Islay. That damned well made her part of clan MacDonald. Carefully avoiding the rubble and stacks of new masonry, Munro moved back up the hallway toward the front door. Christ in a kilt.

The MacDonalds—or the southernmost half of them, anyway—ruled the Isle of Islay. MacDonalds and Mac-Lawrys didn't mix. They weren't at war, though at one time or another they had been. Over the years that warfare had more or less evolved into an agreement to avoid each other.

From what he could piece together from that snippet of conversation, their mutual father had been a clan MacDonald chieftain. He'd died, and now their uncle claimed the title. Aye, he'd also heard the bit about Elizabeth running away from some fat duke or other, but he set that aside. Sassannach affairs were none of his.

Catriona was a damned MacDonald, in the middle of MacLawry territory. With them tangled in some marriage scandal atop all that, he was doubly glad Ranulf didn't know about them. The marquis had married an English lass, and now had English relations and English allies. If Ranulf thought sending Elizabeth back south would somehow benefit the clan, Munro wouldn't put it past him.

His rifle in one hand and the sack of silly gifts in the other, he backtracked well out of sight of Haldane Abbey and then hiked back to where he'd left Saturn. The house would be turned out by now, with every available man hunting for him. And if Ranulf did get Peter Gilling to flap his gums about where they'd spent the last handful of days . . .

"Damnation," he muttered, tying down the sack again and swinging up on the gray. MacDonalds. He'd been willing to risk discovery while they'd been a pair of lasses needing rescue, because he could protect two stray lasses even from his own. But Cat and Elizabeth weren't just strays. They were daughters of a dead MacDonald chieftain.

And yet he still wanted to protect her. Them, rather, whether she would ever admit to needing his aid or not. In order to do that, though, he needed a plan. No doubt his brothers would expect something ham-fisted from him, like standing at the door of Haldane and swinging a sword at anyone who dared approach, but luckily for everyone concerned he did own an ounce of subtlety. No one but he believed that, but there it was. And for once he had a reason to use his skull for something other than butting heads with other people.

Once he reached the west shore of Loch Shinaig he turned Saturn north. At the old tumbled stones where he and Arran and Lachlan had once played at Highlanders versus lobsterbacks he swung down again and stuffed the sack into the hole where toy Sassannach redcoats had regularly met their doom. He damned well didn't want to have to explain why he was toting hair clips about.

Only after he'd hidden his treasure did he join the trail that circled the loch. Slowing to a canter, he continued north toward Glengask castle in as obvious a fashion as he could. He was only angry after all, not hiding lasses from his own clan.

"Bear!"

He looked up to see Arran galloping toward him

on his lean black Thoroughbred, Duffy, and stifled another curse. Arran was clever; he'd seen evidence of his brother's keen wit and quick mind on more occasions than he could even recall. A servant would have asked fewer questions—which would have been handy considering he hadn't yet decided what he was willing to do for a lass who'd shot at him three times.

Arran drew even with him and turned Duffy around to face north. "Ye headed home?"

Munro glanced sideways at his brother, this time thankful for the reputation he'd earned over the years, even if it frequently made him uncomfortable. People generally tried to avoid making him angry. "Aye."

"Good. Do ye mind if I ride along with ye?"

"Nae."

They rode on in silence. Perhaps he would be able to get by without making up a tale, after all. Because if there was one thing he hated more than being ordered about, it was lying to his own family. Lying about a lass who could possibly be an enemy didn't sit well with him at all.

"I hear ye havenae had much luck at fishing, lately," Arran finally offered.

"Nae. I havenae. And that's a fine reason to order me locked away like a bairn or a lunatic."

"I've a bairn who's walking now, with a bit of help; lunatic isnae a poor description. But when her wee hand wraps aboot one of yer fingers so she can keep her balance, it's . . . miraculous. Ye ken?"

So they were determined to make this fight about marriage and bairns. So be it, then. At least it kept them looking away from Haldane Abbey and its new residents. "Ranulf was supposed to marry a Stewart," he said, slowing to a trot. "Or a MacDougall at the worst.

He married a Sassannach. Winnie was supposed to marry a Buchanan, and she went and wed one of our own chieftains. *Ye* were practically engaged to Deirdre Stewart, and ye ran off with a Campbell, of all things. If Ran thinks he can make one of his alliances through me just because I'm the last MacLawry withoot leg shackles, he can go f—"

"I doubt he'd try to force ye into anything, Bear," his brother interrupted. "He's . . . concerned ye arenae happy. That ye feel left oot. Or left behind."

He doubted Ranulf would have phrased it so diplomatically. "Ye only heard his side of the argument, then," he commented. "Lach gave me the same speech. I think *ye* are the ones who dunnae know what to do with *me.* But that isnae *my* problem. It's yers. And if ye dunnae leave me be—the lot of ye—ye'll nae like what happens next."

Arran scowled. "I'm nae threatening ye, Bear. So dunnae threaten me."

Bah. This was why he preferred leaving diplomacy to his silver-tongued brothers. Whether it was because of his size or the ham-fisted demeanor he favored, nearly every statement he made ended up sounding threatening. "Dunnae be an idiot, Arran," he said aloud. "I'd nae harm a one of ye, and ye know that."

"Then what—"

"Just leave me be, will ye? I'm nae one of yer bairns; I can feed myself. If I want someaught, I can damned well get it fer myself." He wasn't surprised that his words prompted an image of Catriona. What *did* surprise him was that he continued to lie to his family over a lass. A lass who belonged to a rival clan, yet.

"I cannae speak fer Ranulf, but that all sounds fairly reasonable to me," Arran said, clearly not hearing his brother's thoughts, because Munro knew damned well that what he wanted wasn't logical or reasonable at all.

He could pace about the house for a few days, then, and all of this finding-him-a-wife nonsense would hopefully go away. At the same time, the idea of not returning to Haldane Abbey tomorrow made him feel ill. And therefore he would find a way to see her tomorrow, because he simply couldn't imagine a circumstance, a world, where he wouldn't do so. What that meant to a man unaccustomed to wanting one particular lass, to looking forward to conversing with any lass, he had no idea. But evidently he meant to find out.

"What were ye aboot?" Arran pursued. "Riding in a circle until Saturn fell oot from beneath ye?"

"Aye. And then I'd carry him fer a bit," Munro returned absently. He'd been playing this part for so long that it didn't require conscious thought any longer. Before Catriona, it hadn't bothered him as much. Now, though, he abruptly wondered whether Arran would fall out of the saddle if he began a conversation comparing his brother's romance with Mary Campbell to that of Romeo and Juliet. He could carry it off, he presumed, even if he really didn't see the need for it.

His family had enough clever thinkers. With things as they had been over the past few years, they needed his brawn. Up until now he'd wished they'd realized he did know how to read, that he did read, and that he had actual thoughts and opinions from time to time. As he glanced sideways at Arran's amused expression, though, he decided that being taken for a buffoon finally had its advantages. As long as Cat never saw him that way.

Chapter Seven

"S top trying to shake it loose," Elizabeth said, leaning as far away from the fire as she could while she tentatively stirred the pot of rabbit stew they were heating up for breakfast.

Catriona gave the new frame for the kitchen door a last shove. "I'm nae trying to shake it loose; I'm making certain it'll stand."

"Against what? An angry bull?"

"Nae. An angry bear."

Her sister laughed, but Catriona didn't join in. She and Elizabeth might have an ally for the moment, but given those rather spectacular kisses of his, he was not helping them out of the goodness of his heart. He wanted something—wanted *her*—and the idea of being in the big man's arms sent heat shooting from her chest down between her legs.

Damnation. She and Elizabeth might have escaped London and the MacDonalds, but that didn't make them safe. Given the unexpected aid they'd received from Bear, a friendly face when she'd never expected to find one, trusting him felt easy. It even felt right, given the

MacLawrys' reputation for taking in refugees. If that had been the end of it, she likely would have been relieved to have a little help. But she felt things now. Soft, fluffy, warm things that a lass in her circumstance couldn't afford to feel. And not just for her sake, but for his, as well.

As it was, she was fairly certain he'd been drawing out this door frame construction far longer than the task required. First they'd needed better lumber. Then more bricks. Then Peter had evidently added too much water to the mortar, so they'd had to pull out half the bricks and place them over again. And let the mortar set a second time. For five days in a row now he'd come by daily, and damn it all, she'd begun looking forward to seeing him.

If she'd genuinely been some cotter's daughter and he a lord's gamekeeper, then she would have been able to admit that she liked when he visited, and that she looked forward to the next time he would steal a kiss from her. She might even have kissed *him*—that . . . arousal was a fairly new experience for her, after all, and she liked the way it felt. Very much. But that wasn't who they were, and she couldn't afford to engage in daydreams. They both carried the weight of their clans on their shoulders, even if he didn't yet know that about her.

She looked at Elizabeth again. Even though her sister was half Scottish, clan didn't play much of a role at all in her life. Elizabeth was a younger daughter, for one thing, and for another she'd had such limited contact with the MacDonalds since she and her mother left Islay for London that mostly she'd been forgotten. That was why once their father died, her mother could put her into the hands of a four-times-married duke three times her age and no one bothered to protest.

For Elizabeth, even doing something as outlandish as putting on MacLawry plaid likely wouldn't stir a single MacDonald eyebrow, and that was even with everyone knowing the MacLawrys had the largest standing army in the Highlands. She didn't have the same luxury. Back in her clan, she was noticed, whether she wanted to be or not. Whether she'd tried to go unnoticed or not.

"What is it?" Elizabeth asked, frowning.

Catriona shook herself. Thinking in theory that the MacLawrys could protect Elizabeth even from the Duke of Visford was one thing. Actually navigating all the twists and turns required to see something so complicated through was another game entirely. And it would have to involve matching Elizabeth with Bear, which she didn't at all like, anyway. He hadn't kissed Elizabeth. He'd kissed *her*. It made sense as a plan, but sometimes she had as little use for logic as it seemed to have for her.

"Cat? You're making me nervous."

Blast. "It's nothing. I was just wishing ye could see the Highlands from a more comfortable place, instead of scrambling for food and a warm blanket with winter creeping in."

"Oh, pish." Elizabeth flipped a hand at her. "I was eight when Mama decided she couldn't survive another moment with those kilt-wearing heathens." She grinned. "You see? I even remember her exact words. And I remember the smell of fresh heather, and the wind coming off the sea, and the sound of bagpipes at every birth and death and marriage. And I remember chasing you across the meadow and Mama yelling at us to behave like ladies. I wanted to wear trousers too, you know."

"That was why yer mother decided to leave Islay with ye. She didnae want a daughter who acted like a son, and Father wanted another of those." That *was* precisely what her father had wanted—or rather, he'd wanted a son and decided to make do with her. And Elizabeth would have been next, if not for Anne Derby-MacColl. "If it was my fault ye had to leave, I'm sorry, Elizabeth."

Setting the spoon aside, Elizabeth walked over and wrapped her arms around Catriona in a hard hug. "Don't you dare apologize, Cat. I had a great many friends in London, both men and women, but I only have one sister. Whatever idiocy happened in between, I'm glad we're together again."

Catriona hugged her sister back. "So am I, *piuthar.*" Even if Elizabeth kept imagining extravagant shopping expeditions where they both ended up swimming in gowns and frilly hats, she'd never called Catriona mad or mannish—which raised her well above the rest of the family and clan on Islay.

All of that—the sideways glances, the comments about a lass uncivilized even by Highlands standards, the men whom she might have liked but who made her feel awkward and far out of her depth when they weren't making fun of her behind her back—came rushing back in on her like a cold, icy rain. Stepping out of her sister's embrace, Catriona walked over to retrieve her oversized coat and musket.

"If ye can stir the stew once in a while for the next hour or so, I'm going to see if I can find some mushrooms for tonight's fish."

Elizabeth sighed. "Yes, I can do that."

Aye, she should stay and do more hugging and chat about fashion and perhaps even finally tell her sister just why she'd been so eager to leave Islay for London and then on to a remote ruin as far away from clan

MacDonald as she could get. Those were her troubles, though, and Elizabeth had enough of her own.

As soon as she had open sky above her, Catriona slowed and took a deep, cleansing breath. The scent of a coming rain touched her, crisp and chill. It wouldn't be long before snow fell. That would complicate things, because while it would discourage potential visitors from wandering through the valley, it would also make her own tracks that much easier to follow.

Snow would also make simply moving about more of a challenge, but winter had never stopped her before. Of course previously she hadn't been trying to hide from anything but the deer and rabbits and birds. Now she had two lasses to keep hidden away.

Of course she also had some unexpected and unasked-for help. Aye, Munro aggravated her with his assumptions that he could provide things for their stay that she couldn't, but in truth the simple fact was that he could. He could bring them blankets and bread, make them more secure in a place where she hadn't expected to be stopping—but was now rather . . . pleased that she had.

The south end of the valley where Haldane sat remained bathed in early morning sunlight, while the widening northern slopes were already obscured by lowering clouds. The breeze had dropped to almost nothing, leaving the autumn day oddly and heavily silent but for the few birds that hadn't flown south. They were likely in for a long, deep soaking once the weather reached them. When she returned to Haldane she would have to move their supplies well away from the puddle in the back corner of the kitchen, and hope it didn't swell into a lake.

Once she'd climbed to the top of one of the myriad rocky outcroppings she crouched down on her haunches and took a moment just to gaze at the view all around her. Leaves of deep yellow and orange shivered in the slow breeze, the colors softening to a dense green toward the valley floor. If she could paint she still didn't think she could capture the wild beauty of this place. Yes, she'd wanted somewhere to hide, but she hadn't expected to be enchanted by it. Or by her would-be rescuer.

Movement to one side of the old road caught her attention. Her heart rate accelerating, she scrambled down the rocks and edged closer so she could get a better look. A few weeks ago the idea of anyone approaching her refuge would have terrified and angered her. Today, as she made out the big gray gelding and a black, shaggy head of hair beside the horse, a smile touched her mouth before she could catch it back again.

Munro and Peter Gilling left their mounts half a mile from Haldane and well off the main trail. At least he knew how to hide his tracks, and he took care to do so. That caution had to be for her sake, she knew. With a deeper grin, telling herself that the satisfaction running beneath her skin came from the idea that she meant to surprise him rather than from something more intimate and primitive, Catriona slipped down the hillside. Using the rough terrain as cover, she moved in behind the two men, edging closer with each step they took and using their own conversation to hide her movements.

"Well, that's fine fer ye," Gilling was saying in a low voice. "Ye got to have a pleasant ride across the countryside. I spent nearly three hours hiding inside a wardrobe."

Bear snorted. "I've apologized fer the past five days fer nae warning ye, Peter," he returned in the deep rumble that seemed to resonate through her. "Even though the first time ye told yer story ye spent an hour inside a storage room. Fer the last time, I didnae know Glengask decided that was the day to announce I should be paired off with a damned Stewart. If he hadnae ambushed me, I would have sent ye off to An Soadh before the bellowing began." He clapped the older man on one shoulder. "But thank ye fer hiding. Truly. We dunnae need Ranulf butting his head into my affairs. And the lass—lasses—dunnae need it, either."

Catriona missed a step and nearly crashed into the big man from behind. It was difficult enough to match his long stride without hearing that the MacLawry had apparently nearly found out about her and Elizabeth, and that Bear hadn't mentioned a word about it to her. Or that he was supposed to marry a Stewart. Though why that should matter, she had no idea. It would get him out of her way, certainly, and that should have been a good thing. But it didn't feel like one. She could tell herself it was because she'd nearly decided to match him with Elizabeth, which couldn't happen if he wed someone else, but trying to fool herself didn't make much sense.

"I'm thinking I'll be sleeping in that wardrobe until ye're done with this nonsense at Haldane," Gilling returned. "Just to be sure yer *bràthair* doesnae come to ask me questions while I'm all unawares."

"It's nae nonsense, Peter," Bear retorted. "I may nae ken exactly what it is I'm doing, but it's nae nonsense."

"I've nae wish to get my nose bloodied, m'laird, so I'll nae argue with ye."

Catriona took a last, closing step to put herself directly behind Bear. "If yer brother thinks ye're spending too much time at Haldane," she said smoothly, "then I'd suggest ye keep yer distance from it."

"Well, I'm nae going to listen to ye on that count, now am I?" he returned in the same easy tone.

Blast it. He'd known she was there, then. "Ye dunnae listen to anything else I say, so I sup—"

Before she could finish her sentence, Munro whipped around, pulled the musket from her hands, and grabbed the material beneath her throat to lift her clear off her feet. "And dunnae startle a man like that, unless ye want yer gizzard on the ground."

"Ha! I *did* surprise ye, then." And there she'd been, ready—or so she'd thought—for him, and she'd still ended up dangling in the air and without a weapon. The youngest MacLawry brother had a reputation for being dangerous, and despite his generally affable demeanor toward her and Elizabeth, she abruptly saw why he was considered deadly.

"Aye, ye did." He continued gazing at her, drawing her just a breath closer. "Quieter than a hunting owl, ye are."

"Put me down, giant, and then ye can give me a compliment," she returned, very aware that if anyone else in the entire world had just manhandled her like that, she would be swinging for his straight, perfect nose.

He set her back on the ground. "Ye smell like fresh pine."

"Is that a compliment?" she queried, unable to keep a smile from touching her mouth.

"Aye. Give me a moment if ye want a prettier one."

"Nae, that'll do." Catriona took a breath. "If yer brother is suspicious aboot someaught," she pressed, trying to keep her attention on the conversation, "ye shouldnae be here. With the amount of time ye've been spending on that door, ye couldnae be surprised he's noticed yer absence, giant."

His curved brows furrowing, he handed her back the musket. "I'm finishing yer door before I decide anything else," he returned, and resumed his easy stride toward the abbey. "And Ran's only wondering if I'm staying away from Glengask because I'm jealous of all the newlywed nonsense and yowling bairns there. None of it has a thing to do with ye or Haldane."

At some unseen signal Peter had moved into the lead, leaving her to walk beside Bear. "And are ye?" she asked, trying not to like the way he'd matter-of-factly handed back her heavy musket. It was hers; she should be the one carrying it.

"Am I what?"

"Jealous of all the newlywed nonsense and yowling bairns."

For a moment he gazed off into the woods. "Nae."

"If ye wish me to believe ye, ye're going to have to make a wee bit more of an effort than 'nae,'" she returned, attempting to imitate his guttural response.

Green eyes caught hers, humor and quite possibly exasperation dancing in their depths. She'd become accustomed to seeing the latter expression in the faces of her kin. This time, though, it wasn't about her choice of dress or her lack of . . . finesse. And that felt refreshing.

"It's nearer to rotting my teeth than making me jealous," he went on after a moment. "They're happy, my brothers and my sister. That's nae a thing to make a man jealous. I'm annoyed that they cannae believe what I just told ye. Glengask, especially, cannae accept that I leave the hoose fer the peace and quiet, as if he likes hearing his bairn bawling before dawn and that setting the hounds to howling."

He frowned again. "Dunnae misunderstand. I've two nephews and a niece now, and the lot of 'em are more precious than the air to me. But I dunnae have a sudden urge to marry the first lass Glengask shoves in my direction so I can make a handful of my own."

"Ye dunnae need what they have in order to feel happy for them," she supplied, wondering again who this pushy lass was that his brother had tried to set on him.

Bear snapped his fingers. "That's it, exactly. If I said it that pretty way they'd nae believe it came from me, but I may have to try it, anyway." He took her free hand in his.

Abruptly she had trouble remembering anything she'd said previously. "Why wouldnae they believe ye?"

He shrugged his broad shoulders. "Ranulf's the calculating one, Arran's the clever one, and Rowena's the good-hearted one. I'm the hardheaded one who talks with my fists." He curled his free hand into a fist and jabbed it at the air. Even that gesture looked absolutely lethal.

"Do ye mean they think ye're . . ."

"Cork-brained? Aye. Most of the time, anyway. I dunnae mind, because they generally leave me be. But now they seem to think I dunnae have the wits to decide anything fer myself."

That was interesting. In the short time she'd known him, he hadn't had any difficulty at all making decisions. And she didn't know many other Highlands lords who could both rebuild a wall and door frame, and hang a door. Aye, he was large and stubborn, but she'd never even thought for a moment that he was unintelligent. Why would his own family think such a thing? "Who is this Stewart lass ye dunnae want about ye, anyway?" she asked into the silence.

"Lady Eithne Boyd. Ye ever heard of her?"

She shook her head. "Nae."

"She's so wall-eyed she can watch ye coming and going withoot turning her head."

A laugh burst from her chest. "That's cruel, giant."

"Then *ye* try talking face-to-face with her and figure oot which eye to look into."

He continued to hold her hand as they walked, chatting, and for once Catriona decided not to point out that she could keep her balance and find her way just fine without any help from him. His hands were big but long-fingered, with an elegance and gentleness to them she wouldn't previously have expected. A great deal about Munro MacLawry wasn't what she'd expected. And to herself she could admit that perhaps it wasn't such a terrible thing that the two of them had crossed paths.

"I brought some more hair ribbons and a mirror fer Elizabeth," he said after a moment. "And a pair of night rails. I didnae ken if ye wore one, but I reckoned it might come in handy when ye needed to wash yer things."

She *did* generally wear a night rail, the one female garment she'd insisted on having, though she'd left it behind at Islay. It had seemed an unnecessary thing to pack when speed had been so vital. "Thank ye."

"I also brought ye a heavy coat. It's likely a bit oversized, but I noticed ye've a patch or two on that one." With their joined hands he indicated the mismatched patch on her sleeve that Elizabeth had sewn for her.

"Ye dunnae think . . ." Catriona pushed the question away. Why was she asking for criticism when it so frequently found her all on its own? "We'll have rain by noon, aye?"

He glanced up at the slowly approaching clouds. "Aye. I reckon so. But that isnae what ye were going to ask me."

Drat. She already knew that he wasn't obtuse or unobservant. And what did she care what he thought of her, anyway? She resisted squaring her shoulders. "I've nae heard much commentary from ye about the way I dress, is all. Some of the lads I grew up with say I'm . . . mannish for wearing trousers." That was an extreme understatement, but it sufficed for the conversation.

Bear snorted. "If I wore a gown would ye say I looked girlish?"

"Nae. I might think ye looked a bit . . . absurd, though."

"And so I would." This time he chuckled. "With my great arms sticking oot from the lace and my feet jammed into those wee delicate slippers I'd be a sight to send the pipers jumping off the roof."

A tear leaked from her left eye, and with one hand in his and the other gripping her musket she had to wipe it away against her shoulder. "So that's me, then." She already knew it, of course, but to hear him agree when he'd never done anything but spoken his mind, well, at least it confirmed that she'd made the correct decision when she'd fled Islay.

"What?" He pulled her to a stop, swinging around so he faced her. "That's nae what I said."

"Ye said how absurd ye'd look in a lass's clothes. And here I am in—"

"Nae," he repeated, louder. "I said exactly what I said. That I'd look a sight in a gown. Ye . . . well, I dunnae quite ken how to describe how ye look to me withoot ye slapping me fer being too forward."

"I'll nae slap ye." Not unless he said something worse than what she was already imagining, anyway.

"Fine. Ye dunnae look like ye're in borrowed clothes. They fit ye, and ye move like . . . ye're graceful in 'em."

He cleared his throat, hauling on her hand to start them off toward the abbey again. "When a lass wears a gown, ye see her face and her arms and her neck, and ye get a good look at her bosom. The way it looks like it wants to escape, anyway. Then there's a ribbon beneath her ribs, and the rest is a mystery."

"And?" she prompted, deciding Elizabeth would already be scandalized at the conversation.

"Just remember, ye asked me to say this." With a frown he glanced at her and away again. "Then when—if— ye win the lass's favor, ye lift up her skirt and there it all is."

Good God. "I thought we were talking about what *I* wear."

"I'm getting to that, ye wildcat. Saint Andrew and all the angels. When I look at ye, ye arenae trying to impress me. Or anyone. I see yer eyes first, dark as chocolate and looking right back at me. I cannae see the skin of yer arms or yer bosom, but I see yer wrists, and the way the buttons . . . pull when ye stretch or turn, and I see how yer shirt tugs over yer breasts and how small yer waist is where yer trousers begin. And I see yer legs, lass, where they start and how long they are and the way yer arse curves . . . It's—well, ye put a tent in a man's kilt, Catriona."

She couldn't help glancing down at that, but his kilt looked as fine and smooth as it ever did. The place where *her* legs started began to feel rather warm and tight, though. "So I dunnae look absurd to ye," she managed, wishing she could keep her voice steady and failing badly at the attempt.

"Nae, ye dunnae look absurd. And if any man's said so to ye, he's either lying or he's jealous."

She didn't quite believe that, because he'd left out

how she appeared to other ladies and to the men of her family who'd wanted her to be . . . a lady, she supposed it was. Less difficult to explain. Easier to manage. Catriona cleared her throat. "I've nae had a conversation quite like this before," she admitted.

"Good."

"And why is it good?"

"Because I dunnae like the idea of some other lad talking aboot yer legs to ye. If ye dunnae believe that, lass, it'd be my pleasure to drag ye off behind the wall there and show ye just how desirable ye are to me."

And she was supposed to continue a normal conversation after this? Was he jealous of these other men who didn't actually exist? Her heart fluttered a little. "I appreciate ye speaking to me honestly," she said after a moment, "but ye have to admit what ye described doesnae sound very romantic. Mayhap I dunnae wear a gown, but I *am* a lass, ye ken."

"Ye didnae ask me to seduce ye," he returned without hesitation, stepping over the broken wall in front of the Haldane entry and then putting his big hands around her waist to lift her across as easily as if she'd been a wee lamb. "Ye asked if I thought yer garb absurd, and I dunnae. If ye want me to tell ye how yer hair shines like autumn leaves and ye make me think of long nights before a fire or someaught, well, I reckon that's a different conversation."

She swallowed. "I reckon so." Given the way she felt at this moment, if he had decided it was time for that conversation, she would likely be dragging *him* over the garden wall. And then she abruptly had to wonder just how many other lasses had lifted their skirts for him. "Why me, Bear?"

For a second she wasn't certain she'd spoken aloud,

and she more than half hoped she hadn't. But his hands remained about her waist, and he held her there until she had to look up at his face. He didn't look annoyed, or exasperated, as she'd expected, given her general ham-fistedness about . . . well, everything. Rather, his sensuous lips were straight, his expression as thoughtful as she'd ever seen it.

"Ye're nae a lass fer a tumble and a swift farewell, are ye, Cat?" he asked quietly, for once keeping his voice low.

If she said that she was, would he give her a tumble and then say farewell? That would solve several of her problems—the nagging lust for him that touched her every time she set eyes on him, his troublesome presence at Haldane Abbey. "Nae, I dunnae reckon I am," she answered after a moment. With only herself for two lasses to rely on, she couldn't afford to be stupid, however much the idea might presently tantalize her.

"And given that I already know that aboot ye, I imagine I'm still here, looking at ye, because I like what I've seen so far, and—"

"Ye've had other lasses, Bear, so dunnae pretend ye've stars in yer eyes where I'm concerned."

Finally his lips curved. "I think mayhap I do have stars in my eyes where ye're concerned, wildcat." He took a breath. "Do ye need an answer now? Or cannae we simply let the days unfold? Because this"—he released her waist to gesture between them—"isnae someaught I'm accustomed to."

Taking some time seemed a rather spectacular idea, she decided, especially when it meant she wasn't expected to know how she felt, either. Except that now she felt a little more at ease—if he didn't know what came next, she could hardly be expected to. "Very well."

He certainly seemed to know what he was talking about where females and sex and anatomy were concerned, and no man could be that self-confident unless he had a herd of brokenhearted, well-sated lasses trailing behind him. And yet . . . And yet he'd barely given Elizabeth a first glance, much less a second, and her sister had been the toast of London with at least a dozen beaux before Anne Derby-MacColl had decided a duke would best benefit the family.

As Bear helped Peter Gilling toss a newly fallen beam into a half-collapsed side room, Catriona snuck a longer look at the front of his kilt. No telltale tent jutted out from between his thighs, though they had been walking and talking for several minutes since he'd left her with that mental image. She knew what it meant, as well—that he lusted after her. Because she had legs, apparently.

No, that wasn't quite true. But deciphering the rest could wait until he wasn't standing ten feet away from her. If she was lucky, she might even procure a glass of whisky, first.

"Would you care for some rabbit stew, Bear?" Elizabeth asked, shaking Catriona loose from thoughts about what that particular Highlander had beneath his kilt.

"I'd nae take yer food, bonny lass," he returned, and stripped off his shirt despite the distinct chill in the air. "I did bring ye a bauble or two, in the sack there."

Hm. No sense getting a clean shirt all sweaty, Catriona supposed. She wanted to pull up a chair and watch him work, and while she did that she wouldn't have minded hearing him talk a bit more about how he found her desirable. He was what her uncle would call "direct," though when she spoke *her* mind the words he'd used to describe her were "unsophisticated" and "tactless."

But that was all gone. And the ill-fitting future he'd mapped for her—which he'd likely done mostly to be rid of her, now that she considered it—remained on Islay and at someplace called Torriden Hall far to the north. By spring hopefully they would decide she was dead or well out of their reach in the Colonies, and they'd make their plans without her.

"Lass, I reckon the door should open oot into the hallway," Munro said, hefting the heavy oak door sideways to demonstrate, "and it would be easier fer those inside to secure that way. If ye mean to pile furniture in front of it, though, I'd recommend it swing in, toward the kitchen."

He was teasing her. Lifting an eyebrow, she put her hands on her hips and strolled forward. "Could ye show me the other way again?" she asked, a hopefully contemplative expression on her face.

With a half grin he heaved the door around once more. "This way?"

"Hm. I'm nae certain."

"Make him do it again," Elizabeth whispered from beside her.

Oh, she wanted to. She wouldn't mind watching the flow and flex of those muscles of his all day. But she wanted it—him—to be all for her. Not for her sister. Not even to look. "Considering the lack of pileable furniture in here," she said after a moment, "I reckon yer first suggestion is sounder. The door should open oot, toward the hallway."

With a nod that sent wavy black hair across one eye, he set the door down again. Elizabeth's sigh was audible, but Catriona kept hers to herself. Likely every lass for a hundred miles admired his easy physicality. She wanted to be different, but she was a warm-blooded

Highlands female, after all, and he was a prime Highlands male. Of course she liked the look of him. But it wasn't just that, and all those other annoying, interfering feelings were more difficult to explain. And to explain away.

While she busied herself with scaling and gutting a pair of trout that had gotten themselves hooked on the lines she'd set overnight, Elizabeth sat at the table, delicately sipping at her bowl of stew, one pinkie lifted as she maneuvered her spoon with the skill of a champion duelist. And that was while she made a soft *O* with her mouth to blow on the hot mix and ogled the brawny man in the doorway all at the same time.

For Saint Andrew's sake. She had nothing with which to compete against pretty words and refinement and the lovely silk gowns that swished when Elizabeth walked—no, glided—across a room. Aye, Bear had said her man's attire aroused him, but underneath the clothes she had the same parts as any other female, and far less idea how to do the mysterious things that caused a man to write poetry or pick posies or any of those other things they did when they admired a lass. Or to want to marry a lass and make her a viscountess and expect her to be able to host parties and play the pianoforte and chat about Paris fashions and dance a waltz.

Bear might not know what he wanted of her, but sooner or later he was bound to realize that whatever it was, another lass, any other lass, would likely be better at providing it than she. She was accustomed to that, to being overlooked and passed over, of course, but he'd bothered to notice her first. That would only make it worse—whether she actually even liked him or not.

"Where are ye off to, lass?" Bear asked, as she shoved by him.

She hadn't even realized she'd stood up from the hearth. "I forgot mushrooms," she improvised, surprised there was enough air in the hallway for her to draw a breath.

"Take yer musket, then," he countered, putting his fingers around her wrist. "And yer coat."

Catriona jerked free. "Dunnae tell me what to do," she snapped, but turned back, slipped on the new wool coat he'd brought for her, grabbed up the weapon, and stalked out into the hallway again. There was pride, and there was foolishness. And she did try not to be foolish, despite what everyone else might think. Despite what she might be thinking at this very moment.

He hadn't tried to stop her, at least. Did that mean he knew she could take care of herself? Or that he was relieved to see her go so he could flex his muscles and say charming things to Elizabeth? Catriona shut her eyes for a moment. She *knew* it was the former. Why, then, had that other question even occurred to her?

Because she was stupid and mannish and naïve and didn't have any idea how to tell a lad she liked him. Not without being laughed at, anyway. Not even after he'd more or less said that he liked her. She moved slowly along the floor of the valley, looking for thick patches of trees and fern where the largest mushrooms would have found a dark place to root. She didn't hold out much hope that the resident animals had left anything edible behind, but at least it had gotten her away from Haldane for the moment.

Simply avoiding the entire mess of men and courtship was much, much simpler. And smarter, too. She hadn't ventured into the middle of MacLawry territory to find a man. She'd done it to avoid one. And the—

Leaves crunched on the old roadway just below and

to her right. Immediately she crouched, stilling. It could be deer; they'd been foraging throughout the valley since she and Elizabeth had arrived there. Another crunch. It sounded heavier than a deer, and less tentative—which made it one of three things in the Highlands: a cow, a horse, or a man.

Very slowly, her heart pounding, she touched the ferns blocking her view and drew them aside. Black, shiny hide, muscles playing beneath. A stirrup, and a man's boot. And then a gray hound's head, swiveling in her direction, sniffing as if he recognized her, and then facing forward again. Was it Fergus? The hound that belonged to the MacLawry?

Catriona took in a slow breath, holding it until the horse and rider passed. Then came a second, and a third. A glimpse of black and white plaid, a thick band of red threaded through it like blood. MacLawry colors, but not Bear or Peter Gilling, because they were still inside Haldane. And so was Elizabeth.

Willing herself not to shake, she waited motionless until the fifth and last horse passed by. Then she scrambled up the low rise to the far side, cutting across the stream there and heading at a dead run back toward the ruins. *No, no, no.* This was exactly what wasn't supposed to happen. Thank God Munro was there, and Elizabeth wasn't alone. Damnation, she should never have left her sister's side.

The horses moved at a walk, but they had the more direct path. She had to circle around toward the collapsed rear half of Haldane, and she had to be quiet about it.

"Bear!"

A low baritone voice broke through the quiet, and she skidded to a stop against the backside of the low wall that had once encircled and protected Haldane Abbey. Someone, at least, knew Munro. Had he tricked her after all? Did he know who she and Elizabeth were?

"Hello the abbey! I know ye're in there, Bear! We found Saturn, and Fergus led us directly here when I put him on yer trail."

He hadn't brought them here at least. Not intentionally. At the moment it shouldn't have mattered, because a representative of the Marquis of Glengask, if not the MacLawry himself, sat on a horse twenty-five feet from the front of the ruin where she'd hid her sister. But it did matter. Catriona clenched her musket, but she didn't lift it. Not yet. A few weeks ago she would have fired by now, but since then her already complicated life had become even more muddled. And so first she needed to know what, precisely, the MacLawrys were doing on her doorstep.

"Bear!"

"I heard ye," Munro's deep, familiar brogue answered, and she risked a glance around the broken section of the wall beside her. The big man stepped out of the open entryway, but remained on the off-kilter top step. "Is someaught amiss, Ranulf?"

This *was* the MacLawry, then. Lord Glengask. She wished she could see what the marquis looked like, to see if he resembled his youngest brother, but if she could see him then he might well be able to see her. Instead she held on to her musket and cursed silently. Munro had brought her complications, just as she'd known he would. But until this moment she'd begun to think befriending him, or at least allowing him to befriend her, was worth the risk.

"Ye ask an interesting question, *bràthair*," the marquis returned. "I dunnae suppose ye know anything aboot a good portion of the kitchen pantry supplies going missing, along with a dozen blankets, one of my wool jackets, some of the good silverware, and a storage room door, do ye?"

"Nae, I dunnae."

The bald-faced lie surprised Catriona, and she risked another look at Munro MacLawry. He'd donned his shirt again, but it hung untucked over the top of his kilt, and he held a hammer in one hand. He did not look like someone a sane man would cross.

"Are ye certain that's the answer ye care to give me, Munro? I'm here to decipher a puzzle. That's all. I've nae wish to fight with ye, but I *will* figure oot what's afoot here."

Chapter Eight

H is jaw clenched, Munro took a half step forward. This was *not* how he'd intended the morning to go. Particularly not after his very interesting conversation with the scarlet-haired wildcat. In fact, for once his family had been the last thing on his mind.

If Catriona stumbled across this little meeting, someone would get hurt. And given her quick temper and the musket she carried, it might be her. *Damnation.* If she'd trusted him just a little more, she might have told him the things he'd discovered yesterday when he'd eavesdropped on her. And those things would come in handy just now in a conversation with Ranulf. If he had to use them without her admitting to them first, she would undoubtedly find out. That wouldn't bode well for him getting her to take those trousers off.

If she'd been alone in the Highlands, she might have run at the sight of the crowd at her temporary front door. She wouldn't, though, because Elizabeth remained inside. His best guess about her whereabouts was that she was somewhere very close by. Close enough to hear every word he said. He clenched his jaw, a dozen curses vying to be the first one he let fly. The best he could hope for was that Catriona didn't shoot anyone before he could solve this little problem.

"Bear?"

"I'm trying to decide whether or not I have a disagreement with ye." Movement to his left caught his attention, and he glanced in that direction. If Ranulf had sent someone to flank him, that changed the equation. Instead, though, he met a furious dark brown gaze, and took an abrupt breath. "Give me a damned minute, will ye?" he continued aloud, hoping she realized that statement was also meant for her.

"Aye. Take yer minute," Ranulf returned.

The marquis was actually being generous. Glengask didn't tolerate subterfuge or lies, particularly where his own family was concerned. Like everyone else, though, Ranulf had a healthy respect for his youngest brother's strength and his temper. Munro could use that to his advantage, but it would be a tricky proposition. And it would require that Catriona trust both him and the clan MacLawry. While he was at it, he might as well wish for a dragon to come by and fly him away.

Facing the mounted Ranulf again, he subtly gestured with the fingers of his left hand for Cat to stay where she was. Later he could question why he'd just decided to lie to his brother in favor of a wild-hearted Mac-Donald lass. Now, he just needed to make it believable.

"I reckon I've decided," he announced, flipping the hammer in his right hand.

"And what have ye decided, then?"

Ranulf was the only one of his party who'd spoken, despite the fact that the more diplomatic Arran and even Lachlan MacTier waited behind him, along with two grooms. They'd come ready to use brute force, Munro realized, even though they had no idea what the brawl might be about.

"I've decided to tell ye what's afoot here. And I've decided the lot of ye are going to be reasonable aboot it."

"I'm certain we will be," Arran put in abruptly, before Ranulf could respond to that.

Good. "It's a bit of a story, so ye'll listen to it all before ye set foot in this hoose."

"Bear, I willnae be dicta—"

"Tell yer story, then." This time it was Lachlan, one of Glengask's own chieftains, who interrupted their laird. Munro and Lach had practically grown up in each other's pockets, which was likely why he wasn't anxious to begin a brawl he hadn't won since they'd both turned ten. They all knew something had been troubling him, Munro realized. Had they come out here to help him, though? Or to make certain whatever he was about didn't cause trouble for the MacLawrys?

"Thank ye, Lach," he said aloud. "I will." He took another breath, mentally crossing his fingers both for luck and against the lies he would tell. "A week or two ago I stumbled across a lass while I was oot hunting." It took every bit of willpower he possessed not to look over at where Cat was hiding; he could practically hear her teeth grinding.

"A lass," Arran repeated, lifting an eyebrow.

"Aye. A lass. The daughter of Randall MacColl, laird and chieftain of the Isle of Islay, as it turns oot."

"Clan MacDonald," Ranulf bit out, his expression settling into one even grimmer than usual.

"She was raised English, by her mama. It seems when old Randall died a short time ago, his widow decided to marry their daughter off to a Sassannach duke. Young

Elizabeth didnae like this idea, and so she fled to the Highlands. This is as far as she got."

"Which Sassannach duke?" the marquis asked flatly.

"Villferd or Vinfer or someaught. He's aboot a hundred years old, and he's already buried a dozen wives."

"Visford?" Arran supplied, as Munro had expected.

"Aye, that's it. Visford."

"If I recall, he's past sixty, and four times a widower."

"To a lass nae yet twenty, I dunnae ken the exact numbers matter." Munro flipped the hammer again. "I dunnae hold with anyone, lad or lass, being shoved into a match they cannae stomach," he continued, favoring his oldest brother with a pointed look for effect, "so I gave her my word she'd be safe here. And I gave her some food and blankets and a door to keep the cold oot while I decided on how best to approach ye aboot this." He paused. "Now, since I reckon ye've given me yer word to be polite and nae to hand Lady Elizabeth a single fright, I'll invite ye in to make her acquaintance."

For the first time he realized why he'd grinned and laughed and agreed with his family every time they'd called him thick-skulled and direct and incapable of subtlety. It had been for this exact moment, when he needed them to believe everything he said. And he hoped to God it would be worth it.

"Where's Gilling in all this mess?" Ranulf asked, stiff-backed and clearly not amused, but not suspicious over the tale, either.

"Dunnae blame Peter. Ye told me I couldnae go aboot alone, and I told him to keep his damned gobber shut about the abbey. He's inside keeping watch over the lass while I'm here flapping my gums with ye. Now are ye

going to be civil, or are ye going to turn aboot and leave?
Those are yer two choices. I'm nae joking aboot."

Slowly Ranulf swung out of the saddle and stepped
onto the weed-broken gravel, the rest of the men with
him immediately following suit. "I can see that. Introduce me to the MacDonald lass, then."

Inside, Munro itched to dive over the wall and grab
hold of Cat, so he could explain to her what he planned
before she either fled into the wilds again or decided to
put a hole in him. Whether she realized it or not, the
entire subterfuge had been for her sake. Her sister's
quandary barely qualified as interesting, by clan standards. He knew far less about what troubled Catriona,
but her very skittishness told him clan MacDonald
figured into it. Until she trusted him with her tale, he
would protect her. And at the moment that meant keeping her away from both her clan and his.

Putting himself between Ranulf and where Cat remained crouched, Munro gestured his brother through
the open entryway. Once they were all safely inside, he
angled his head toward the low wall. "Stay there," he
murmured. "I gave ye both my word. I mean to keep it."

"Ye'd better, giant," drifted back to him almost
soundlessly. "I'm watching the lot of ye."

Before he could convince himself it would absolutely
not be suspicious for him to linger outside, he turned
around and walked down the wrecked hallway toward
the old kitchen. With less than a minute's warning, he
had more hope than confidence that his hastily thrown-
together plan would satisfy his crafty brothers. "Trust
me" and "we've nae heard of Cat" had sounded like bold
enough instructions, but now he needed a nineteen-year-
old wide-eyed lass and a stubborn, set-in-his-ways
footman to stand straight before the chief of clan Mac-

Lawry and lie. It was a feat few attempted and even fewer managed.

He pushed his way to the front of the Highlanders as they reached the half-finished kitchen doorway. "We're coming in, Peter," he called out. "Dunnae blast a hole in anyone."

"As ye say, m'laird," the former soldier returned in his heavy, gruff brogue.

"This isnae a war," Ranulf stated. "Stop yer growling and stomping." With that the marquis stepped around him and into the kitchen.

Damnation. Munro followed; he needed to keep control of the situation, keep Glengask from asking too many questions and discovering that a second, more troublesome sister lurked just outside.

The young, honey-haired lass stood halfway behind Gilling, her hazel-eyed gaze fixed on Ranulf as if she expected the man to spew fire from his fingertips. Evidently even the Sassannach feared the MacLawry now, though given the mayhem that had transpired during Ranulf and Arran's visit to London, it wasn't that surprising.

"Elizabeth," he drawled, moving to a point where he could intercept either her or his brother, "this is the Marquis of Glengask, my oldest brother. Ranulf, Lady Elizabeth MacColl. My guest."

He said that last bit very deliberately, and caught Ranulf's responding sideways glance. As his guest, Elizabeth was under his protection. She clearly meant a great deal to Cat, and for no other reason than that he would see that the wild lass's sister remained safe.

She curtsied prettily. "My lord. Thank you for letting . . . me stay here."

Munro heard the hesitation, but hopefully Ranulf had

not. With the blankets folded up and stacked in a dry
corner and cups and plates scattered across the table and
hearth, determining how many people were residing
there wouldn't be simple, and they had to give Ranulf
no reason to suspect there might be more than one lass
at Haldane Abbey.

The marquis inclined his head. "Lady Elizabeth. Ye
claim clan MacDonald, aye?"

"Clan . . . Yes. I suppose I do, anyway. My father was
a MacDonald chieftain. My mother . . . didn't care for
clan politics or the Isle of Islay. This is the first time I've
seen Scotland in eleven years."

"And why are ye here now, lass?"

Munro frowned. "I told ye why she was here. Because she didnae want to marry a man forty years—"

"I asked the lass, Bear," Ranulf snapped, cutting him
off. "I'd appreciate if she answered me, herself."

He would have to hope that she'd heard enough to realize she should tell the truth. Munro gave her a slight
smile and an encouraging nod. "Tell him aboot yer
mother's plan fer ye then, lass."

She swallowed, taking a moment to look at the group
of tall, formidable men now ranged in front of her. "Of
course. I assume my father always hoped I would marry
a Highlander," she said in her cultured English tones.
"He died nearly two years ago before anything came of
it, and that was when my mother decided we—she and
I—would be better served if I married a wealthy English
lord."

As she spoke her voice flattened, as if she'd become
so accustomed to feeling angry and frustrated that it
infused all the parts of the tale even now that it had
been more or less resolved to her satisfaction. A lass
more than likely raised to disdain her Scots relations

and who'd still turned to one of those relations for help. Except that Elizabeth couldn't tell that part of the story. Munro readied himself to interrupt again if need be, before she could let the actual Cat out of the proverbial bag.

"I had several proposals, but they were all younger brothers or minor titles. And then the Duke of Visford came calling, and offered to purchase my mother a new coach and a new house in London in exchange for my hand. She agreed before I'd even met him." Elizabeth took a breath. "I don't know if you're acquainted with His Grace, but he's . . . not a pleasant man. And he's sixty-one years old and has had four wives already. The rumor is that the last one jumped out a window." A tear ran down her cheek, and she frowned as she brushed it away.

"Dunnae weep, lass," Munro said, stepping over to put a hand on her shoulder. "Ye made yer way here. And ye dunnae have to go back."

When he glanced up, Ranulf was eyeing not Elizabeth, but him. "Aye," the marquis said after a moment. "Ye're safe here. How did ye end up in MacLawry territory, though, instead of yer own MacDonalds?"

"I'm not certain. I took the wrong mail coach, and then I . . . I stole a cart, but I got turned around, and it rained, and—the—"

"Hush, lass." Munro made a show of guiding her to the room's one chair and helping her sit. As he faced away from his brothers he flashed her an appreciative smile, which she returned. "Cat's hiding outside," he breathed. "She's safe."

Elizabeth nodded. "Am I?"

"Aye. Ye are. I gave ye both my word. I dunnae think Cat wants to be caught, though."

"No, she doesn't. I only wish she would tell me why."

"That makes two of us, then."

So Elizabeth didn't know, either. That was interesting. But he couldn't take the time to figure it out now. Now he had to convince Ranulf and the rest of them to ride away from Haldane Abbey because they'd seen all there was to see, and Cat could come back inside before the rain began.

"Ye and Peter have done a fair job with this door," Arran said, tugging on one of the uprights.

"It's a beginning." He gestured at the hole in the far corner of the roof. "That's next."

"I'd be happy to lend ye a hand," Lachlan took up.

"Nae." He'd spoken too sharply and answered too quickly, but the idea of more men wandering about the estate, married and MacLawrys or not, wouldn't sit well with Catriona. And it damned well didn't sit well with him, either. Perhaps he was generally a generous fellow, but not today. He had to share knowledge of Catriona with her sister, and to a lesser degree with Peter Gilling, but no one else was invited. Or welcome. "I reckon I'll see to Haldane on my own."

Ranulf put out a hand. "If ye want this old wreck, Bear, ye can have it. But it's nae a place fer a proper English lass to lay her head."

"That isnae up to ye, Glengask." Munro straightened to his full height. Apparently it was time for him to remind his brothers of his reputation. "The lot of ye are aboot to overstay yer welcome."

"What I mean to say, *bràthair*, is that Lady Elizabeth would be welcome to stay at Glengask. Ye cannae want her to sleep on the floor when we've soft beds aplenty. And that doesnae take into account all the MacLawry men we have aboot, to keep any Sassannach dukes well away from the lass. I'm nae acquainted with this Visford, but I reckon he cannae stand against clan MacLawry."

Munro stared at his brother. Of all the directions he'd thought the conversation might turn, Ranulf inviting Elizabeth to stay up at the castle hadn't been one of them. He'd expected anger at the idea of a MacLawry stepping into the middle of Sassannach affairs, and fury that someone might well be stirring up trouble with the MacDonalds. At the least he'd anticipated ending up bloodied and bruised for lying about the entire thing.

Before Munro could conjure a response that wouldn't undo all the lies he'd just told, Ranulf walked up to Elizabeth. "What do ye say, lass? Shall I send fer a wagon and have yer things brought up to a guest bedchamber at Glengask? Do ye reckon ye can make do with a bit of comfort?"

She looked from Munro to Ranulf. "May I have a word with Bear, first?" she finally asked, her voice a touch breathy.

"Of course, lass. I need a word or two with Peter Gilling, anyway."

The footman cursed under his breath, but joined Ranulf and his men by the door. Hopefully Peter had figured out the game by now, and wouldn't say anything to stir suspicions about a second lass staying here. As Munro tried to glare a hole through the servant, Elizabeth wrapped her dainty fingers around his arm and tugged him toward the hearth.

"Is your brother being truthful?" she whispered. "Can he—will he—keep Visford or my mother from dragging me back to London?"

"Aye," he returned, nodding, and attempting to remind

himself that for her, this wasn't simply a distraction. "He'd nae give his word unless he means to honor it."

"Then I think perhaps I should go."

He blinked, more . . . disappointed than surprised. "What aboot yer sister?"

"Whatever she's hiding from isn't about me. And I can't help thinking she'd have an easier time of it if I wasn't here to be such a nodcock about everything. And if your brother can protect me, well, that's all I require. Cat couldn't very well complain about it, either."

"Yer sister'll miss ye, lass." Nor would she like it. And she'd likely blame him, damn it all.

"And I'll miss her. But since she won't trust me, I have to rely on what I think will help her—and me— the most. If I stay here now, your brother *will* send men to either watch me or look after me, and they'll find Cat. If I leave, no one has any reason to return here." She tightened her grip on his arm. "Except for you, yes? She shouldn't be alone in the wilderness."

He took a breath. Elizabeth made sense, and whether he wanted to admit it or not, the moment Ranulf had ridden into view the MacColl sisters' stay here had been put in jeopardy. This was merely the least objectionable of all possible outcomes. "She'll nae be alone. And neither will ye. Whether ye're here or at Glengask, ye're still under my protection."

The wee, slender thing smiled up at him. It was odd that she was taller than Catriona, because it didn't seem like it would be that way. Catriona not only had some delightful curves to her, but in his mind the way she stood up to him, argued with him, matched him, made her seem closer to his own height. A few weeks ago, before he'd met the wildcat, aye, he might have welcomed Elizabeth in his bed. But now he'd been struck—the only question was whether it had been by Cupid's arrow, or some spoiled venison.

"I think ending up here is the best thing that could have happened to the MacColl sisters, Bear," Elizabeth was saying, "thanks to you."

"Dunnae thank me yet. I still have to tell yer sister ye've decided to go to Glengask. And ye still have to keep her presence here a secret."

"I can do that."

And with that, he dismissed her again from his thoughts. Yes, he needed to find a way to explain to Catriona what was afoot, hopefully before anyone tried to remove Elizabeth from Haldane. Even more than that, though, he wanted to know the reason Cat had looked so . . . lost, and even panicked, when she'd fled the kitchen earlier—an odd reaction to a conversation about which way a door should swing.

His own reaction had surprised him, as well. Rather than the usual lust that coursed through him whenever he set eyes on her, he'd fought the abrupt urge to pull her into his arms and simply comfort her. Tell her she needn't worry over anything because he would never let anything happen to her. That big as he was, the idea of making her cry, of upsetting her, scalded him.

"What have ye decided, Lady Elizabeth?" Ranulf asked, shaking Munro out of his reverie and making him wonder why his brother was being so bloody polite. The Marquis of Glengask did not treat kindly anyone who attempted to mislead or trick him.

"If you're certain my troubles won't be a burden to you, Lord Glengask," she said prettily, "I gratefully accept your offer."

"I'll send fer a wagon, then. Owen?"

"Oh, that's not necessary, my lord. If two of you can take the bags with my necessaries, I require nothing else." She gestured at the tumbledown kitchen. "Most of this I . . . acquired along the way. I think it would be rather out of place at Glengask Castle."

"I'll fetch Saturn and Gilroy," Munro announced, naming Peter's mount. "Ye'll ride oot with me, lass." And he would take those few moments outside to have a word with her wildcat of a sister.

"We brought the horses up with us," Lachlan said, before Munro could even make it to the doorway.

Damnation. What was he supposed to do now to gain a blasted second or two outside, claim he needed to take a piss? It would sound like the excuse it was. "Let's get yer things then, lass."

"I havenae been here in ages," Ranulf mused, strolling over to the fallen corner. "I think I'll take a look aboot the grounds while ye pack up."

"And I think ye've stepped far enough into my business today, Glengask," Munro said quickly. The last thing he wanted for either Ranulf or Catriona was for one to stumble across the other.

His brother stopped mid-step. "Are ye certain ye wouldnae care to rephrase that, Munro?"

So the marquis meant to be polite to the lass, but not to his own brother. Munro squared off. Perhaps this was where the brawling would happen. For Saint Andrew's sake, he felt frustrated enough to enjoy tossing a few lads about. That was what he did, anyway. Brawl. Everyone knew it. They likely expected it.

He hesitated for a bare moment. They *would* expect it, and that could work in his favor. "Didnae ye just give me this pile five minutes ago?" he retorted. "I've a mind to make some repairs. Ye can see the damned place when it's finished. Ye cannae see it now, when ye only rode oot here because ye dunnae trust me."

"I didnae trust ye," Ranulf agreed. "And dunnae expect an apology fer that when ye've been hiding a lass here. Ye certainly didnae trust *me,* now did ye?" Ranulf returned in the flat, low voice that had once caused a would-be assassin to wet himself.

"I reckon that makes us even. It doesnae make me feel inclined to lead a tour. Or to allow one." The best thing he could hope for was to make the argument about himself and Ranulf, and not about him keeping an additional secret his brother needed to uncover.

Ranulf gazed at him for a long moment, his blue eyes cool and assessing. "I did give it to ye. And I suppose we can discuss what ye mean to do with it later. And elsewhere."

Finally Munro let out his breath. "Aye. We can do that. Put oot the fire then, will ye, Arran? And let's head oot. I dunnae want Elizabeth caught by the rain."

Within five minutes the men had all of Elizabeth's things—and most of Catriona's—bundled into a battered portmanteau and a pair of frayed gunny sacks. Accustomed as Munro was to action, to acting on his impulses, he knew the best way to aid Cat at this moment was to do precisely nothing. And so he clenched his jaw, offered his arm, and escorted Elizabeth outside to the waiting horses.

He managed a glance or two in the direction he'd last seen Catriona, but only weeds and crumbling stone wall met his gaze. Aye, she had the stealth to remain unseen if she wanted to do so, but *he* wanted to see that she was safe and doing as he'd asked and not planning to shove the building over on his brothers before they could make off with Elizabeth.

"Ye'll like Glengask, lass," he said a little louder than necessary, as he released the nineteen-year-old to swing up on Saturn. "And as my brother says, ye'll be protected there. It would take an entire English army to breach the castle; I doubt this Visford Sassannach would dare attempt such an idiotic thing."

"I believe you," Elizabeth returned, facing Peter so the footman could lift her up sideways in front of Munro. "It's splendid that Lord Glengask gave you Haldane Abbey. As much of a wreck as it is now, I think you could make it lovely again."

She spoke in a carrying tone, as well. Hopefully between the two of them they'd managed to inform Cat that her sister wasn't being taken anywhere against her will, and that *he* would return to Haldane as soon as he could. Whether she wanted to see him or not was another question entirely.

Forty minutes later Glengask came into view beyond the loch and the edge of the trees, and he relaxed a little. The entire way he'd kept half his attention on the wilds around them, watching for the glint of a musket barrel, a glimpse of a shapely leg in men's trousers, shrouded sunlight on deep red hair. Nothing. Nothing but lowering clouds and a stiffening breeze.

At best she'd returned to the Haldane kitchen, where she would have a roof at least, but no blankets, a drowned fire, and a very small quantity of cold rabbit stew. At worst—as far as he was concerned, anyway—she'd seen that her sister was safe and she'd struck off deeper into the Highlands where he'd never set eyes on her again.

And here he was, trapped and forced into being civilized so he could keep his word to one sister while he broke his promise to the other. In addition, he'd made Elizabeth his charge. Escaping Glengask for Haldane had just become even more problematic.

"Your brothers are very gallant," Elizabeth murmured as she sat across his thighs, the golden curls at her temple tickling his nose as they approached the grand front of the house. "From what you and Cat said, I expected them to try to lop off my head."

They *were* being pleasant. Munro glared over at Ranulf, to find his oldest brother riding beside Arran and deep in conversation about something. As he watched, the marquis glanced back at him and away again. Even the thug he frequently pretended to be would know that something was afoot. More than once Arran had accused him of not seeing the entire forest in his eagerness to knock down a few trees, and he'd rather liked the metaphor. That didn't mean it actually applied to him. Not entirely, anyway.

"I hadn't come out yet when they were in London," Elizabeth went on cheerily, apparently and thankfully not needing him to contribute to the conversation, "but I heard the stories. They were in the newspaper nearly every day."

"The MacLawrys like to make a stir," he contributed, edging Saturn up closer beside his brothers.

"My mother was a guest at one of the parties they attended. She said she'd never seen such a fierce, bloody fight in a proper household."

If he hadn't been more concerned with where Catriona was and what his brothers were discussing, he likely would have found Elizabeth's conversation more interesting. He'd read the newspapers too, and he'd had letters from Arran and Winnie, but hearing the impression the MacLawrys made on Sassannach aristocrats who had no stake on the outcome—that seemed like it could be significant. Or at least entertaining.

He didn't have to be rude, though, especially when he needed to show his brothers that they'd best do as they promised where Elizabeth's safety was concerned. "Yer mama lived on Islay, though, aye?" he offered. "Ye said ye didnae leave until ye turned eight."

"Yes. She married Papa two years before I was born. Cat was . . . five, I think, when I came along. But I don't remember a party ever being held at MacColl House. I know Papa went to soirees, but Mama never went with him. She always said she had nothing in common with barbarians." She visibly winced. "*She* said that. I always found Highlanders fascinating. Especially the ones with those huge, bushy beards."

He laughed. "I grew one of those once. When I saw my first whisker I refused to shave it off until I had a nice, bushy badger on my face."

"Why did you shave, then?"

"It only took one lass saying she wouldnae give me a kiss because my beard scratched her cheeks." That hadn't precisely been where Bethia Peterkin had complained about the scratching, but the tale would do for a proper lass like Elizabeth.

"Well, I'm glad you shave. You're . . . Well, you're quite handsome, you know."

"Thank ye fer saying so, lass." He nodded, but she continued to look at him expectantly. *Oh, right.* "Ye're a bonny lass yerself, Elizabeth."

She smiled, her cheeks darkening prettily. "Thank you, my lord." Tapping a finger on his sleeve, she looked up at him from beneath long eyelashes. "I would have been happy to remain, growing up in the Highlands. I had a sister here, even if our father treated her like a son. I thought I would be able to wear trousers too, and learn how to shoot and ride bareback."

Abruptly this conversation interested him a great deal. No wonder Cat moved so well in boots and trousers; she hadn't donned them out of necessity, but because she was more accustomed to them than she was gowns and dancing slippers. "Did yer *athair*—yer father—try to raise ye as a son, too?"

"I remember he came in with a kilt for me once. My mother threw it in the fire, because a lady never shows her knees in public." She frowned. "We left Scotland less than a month after that. It was my fault, I suppose."

It sounded to him like Viscount and Lady MacColl had their own troubles aplenty. "Nae," he said after a moment. "Ye were eight. That made Cat, what, thirteen? Yer mother had time aplenty to see what lay ahead. Ye may have been an excuse, but it wasnae yer fault."

"That's what Cat said." She flashed her bright smile again. "But I'm here now. And even more importantly, I'm not married to the Duke of Visford. You're certain your brother won't change his mind about having me here?"

"He willnae. It's aboot power, lass. We have someaught His Grace Visford wants, but he doesnae have a thing Glengask desires. Look as far as ye can see in any direction. It's all MacLawry land. The duke could send solicitors or soldiers after ye, but well, we can make a bit of a stir, ourselves." That was a damned understatement, but she didn't need to know the details.

"Thank goodness. I mean, Cat came and rescued me, but I thought she would bring me back to Islay. To our clan. When she didn't, I knew something was wrong. I didn't know if it was about her or about me, though. Whatever it was, the two of us were alone in the Highlands. This—you—feels . . . safer."

Safe? Him? Well, he supposed for a young English lass in the wilderness, anyone who could put food on the table and a roof over her head would feel safer than the idea of being on her own. "Thank ye," he said absently, maneuvering Saturn directly behind Arran and his mount, Duffy.

"Will you show me about Glengask? I've heard so much about it. I'm looking forward to seeing it. And to sleeping in a soft, warm bed."

Something in the undergrowth moved, catching his attention. Catriona? "Aye. I reckon I can do that," he said belatedly. A pair of rabbits bolted away from the trail, and he relaxed again. He wasn't looking for rabbits; he was after a wildcat. Ranulf had changed the rules, but the game remained. And he played to win.

Chapter Nine

I knew Lady MacColl," Charlotte said in a low voice, sliding her arms around Ranulf's ribs and resting her cheek against his shoulder blade. "I never met her daughter, though. And I always thought the viscountess was a widow."

"The lass is just nineteen," Ranulf returned, his hands on the balcony railing as he watched Bear showing Elizabeth the foyer and morning room, below. "She would be a year behind Rowena and yer sister, aye?"

"Aye." She remained behind him, watching around his shoulder for a moment as the lass crossed the doorway and out of sight again. "And this Elizabeth is the reason Bear's been spending so much time away from here?"

He shrugged against her cheek. "I reckon so. I wouldnae have thought such a . . . dainty, proper lass would catch his eye, but he was ready to take on the lot of us if we so much as looked at her sideways. It nearly came to a tussle."

"I've seen how you tussle." She released his ribs, edging up beside him so he could put an arm across her shoulders. Her warm hand slipped beneath his jacket and around his waist. "She did make it well into the Highlands on her own. That takes some courage."

"I'll agree with that. What concerns me is why she would settle into the middle of MacLawry territory when the MacDonalds would be more likely to step in and protect her from a Sassannach marriage she didnae want."

"She told you that she lost her way, you said. I can believe that. Especially if she's practically a stranger to the Highlands."

"Aye." It did make sense, and it explained some of Bear's actions as well as Lady Elizabeth's presence. "But why did he keep her a secret?"

"That's simple, my love. She's a MacDonald. Bear knows what nearly happened when Arran fell for Mary."

"Mayhap. This is exactly the sort of thing, though, that I need to know. Fer God's sake, I welcomed Mary Campbell into our clan. Into our family."

"Yes, you did. After you nearly banished Arran and then chased the two of them across the length of England."

Everyone remembered that bit. No one, though, seemed to recall that he'd gone against his own better judgment to make peace with the Campbells just so Arran could keep his bride—and live with her in safety. He had no love for the MacDonalds, but this Elizabeth MacColl seemed barely to qualify as Scottish. As a matter of courtesy he would have to inform the Mac-Donald that the lass had appeared on his doorstep. And aye, the Earl of Gorrie would likely make enough of a fuss to gain some money or territory or a share in MacLawry business dealings, but if she was who Bear wanted, he would arrange for it to happen.

As the pair emerged again from the morning room, Lachlan came through the front door with Rowena on his heels. Lord Gray must have galloped all the way home to be back so quickly with his wife, but of course the youngest MacLawry would want to meet the lass for whom her brother had fallen. Ranulf imagined Arran would be back with Mary within the hour as well, the two of them only slowed by Mary's pregnancy.

"Does Mrs. Forrest know we'll be a full house for dinner?" Charlotte whispered, taking his hand to tug him toward the stairs.

"Aye. I sent Owen to inform her the moment we returned. She's been cooking extra every night because of Bear's thievery, anyway."

"So ye were living at Haldane Abbey?" Rowena asked Elizabeth, giving the younger lass a sound hug.

"Yes, I was. I got caught in the rain, and there it was."

"I havenae been there for years," the only lass among the MacLawry siblings went on with a warm smile. "Bear and Lachlan always told me it was haunted."

"Oh, goodness," Elizabeth exclaimed, shuddering. "I'm glad I didn't know that when I found it. Bear mentioned it several days ago, and I barely slept after that. I never saw or heard anything—except for the creaks and groans of the house, but, well, I was very glad to see Bear every morning."

"Just the thought of it would've been enough to frighten me away."

Lachlan pulled his wife away from the lass to kiss her on the temple. "Ye hid in the dark in a Campbell escape tunnel, lass. I dunnae ken a ghostie could stand against ye."

"That sounds like quite the tale! You must tell me what happened, Lady Gray."

"Oh, pish. Ye must call me Winnie."

It seemed Elizabeth MacColl was practically part of the family already. Ranulf gazed at her again. She looked . . . perfect, her golden-blond hair coiled beneath clips with tendrils escaping to frame her face, the merest touch of color on her cheeks and lips. Her green-and-pink-flowered gown wouldn't be amiss in any London drawing room, and he glimpsed the toes of shoes that Charlotte and Rowena would say were meant for sedately walking through a tame London park.

That was what . . . not troubled him, precisely, but left him unsatisfied. Young Elizabeth looked like she'd just stepped out the door of a proper house in Mayfair. What she did not look like was someone who'd escaped in a hurry from London and had spent the last weeks making her way through some of the wildest parts of the Highlands only to settle into a ruined kitchen of a ruined house.

He supposed it was possible; Bear had been acting strangely for a fortnight and had been spending most days away from Glengask for weeks before that. The Haldane Abbey kitchen had been tidy—or as tidy as a room with one corner fallen in could be—and either she'd learned to hunt and cook somewhere, which wasn't likely in those shoes, or Bear had been providing everything for her. That did explain why he never returned from fishing with any fish.

Ranulf shook himself. Whether something about her felt amiss or not, Bear clearly wouldn't allow anyone to question her about it. Not yet, anyway. Before things progressed much further, though, he needed to know. If she was playing on Bear's tendency to protect the weak and delicate, if she was simply a lass after the power and wealth of the MacLawrys, he would have to put a stop to it. Even if that meant a knock-down, drag-out fight with Munro.

For the moment, though, they were all friends. And for all their sakes he would take his time observing Bear and this lass, and trying to decipher whether his very experienced, ramshackle brother had fallen for a very unexpected lass.

Catriona crouched on the remains of Haldane's first floor just above the hole in the kitchen ceiling. Whatever Bear had ordered her to do, she wasn't about to cower in some corner and wait to be found. Wait to have all her plans ruined. Especially when her sister was alone with seven large clan MacLawry males.

What she heard down below, though, surprised her. The marquis clearly had a healthy respect for his brother, and Bear seemed to be pushing to protect Elizabeth well past what she'd expected of him—which admittedly hadn't been much more than a few loaves of bread and some attractively flexing muscles. But they—he—someone—managed to leave her out of the tale entirely. Neither Elizabeth nor Bear could possibly know why she was so . . . skittish, but they'd decided to keep her presence a secret, anyway. Bear had lied to his own brother, to his clan chief, to keep her safe. Just the idea of that stunned her. No one had ever risked anything for her sake. To hear him do so sent her chest thudding warmly—which annoyed her greatly, considering the circumstances.

When the MacLawry suggested Elizabeth join them at Glengask she'd nearly panicked. Elizabeth, though, hadn't seemed troubled at all. Of course, a warm bed and a lady's maid probably sounded like paradise to her Society-raised half sister. And then both Munro and

Lord Glengask had discussed just how much comfort
and protection clan MacLawry could offer.

She'd never set eyes on the Duke of Visford, but she
couldn't imagine an old man who preyed on young
lasses whose family needed money would dare risk
himself or his pride by going up against the MacLawry.
It was a shame, really, that the Marquis of Glengask was
already wed. If Elizabeth married him, the nineteen-
year-old would never have to worry about Visford, or
about having to live anything less than a comfortable
life with a handsome, strong, and brave husband.

Once they'd bundled up Elizabeth's and her things,
Catriona shifted to one of the broken-out windows at
the front of the abbey. Munro looked toward the wall
where she'd been hiding before, then frowned. Well, of
course she wasn't going to be where anyone expected.
That happened to be the point of hiding. Nor did she
feel the least bit appeased at the brief look of concern
that crossed his handsome face. Intentionally or not,
he'd been the one to bring Glengask here.

Peter Gilling lifted Elizabeth to sit daintily in front
of Bear, and her sister promptly put an arm around the
big man's shoulder. For balance, presumably. Catriona
glared at the back of Munro's shaggy head, willing him
to look back for her again, but he never did. Instead the
men rode away from Haldane, all convinced they'd left
with everything of importance. Perhaps, though, they
had. The party rounded the overgrown curve in the road,
and a moment later they were gone even from earshot.

For a long time Catriona remained crouched in the
shadows, listening, waiting for any sign that the men
might return. Nothing but scattered birdsong and leaves
rustling in the breeze drifted up to her. She straightened,

stretching the tight muscles across her shoulders, then made her way back to the abbey's ground floor.

The kitchen door still leaned against the wall in the hallway, useless and too late to protect anyone from anything. An odd, creeping uneasiness she couldn't explain crawled up her spine as she stepped into the room where she'd been living for the past month.

It stood dark and cold now, the fire quenched and the low clouds outside keeping the sunlight from the open corner. The cheap mugs and a pot of cooling rabbit stew remained, but not much else. Neither Elizabeth nor Bear could likely have come up with a reason to leave half the blankets and clothing behind, but the loss abruptly struck her. She had nothing.

When she'd left Islay she'd brought very little with her, but the hairbrush, clean shirt, and floppy hat, for instance, had all been necessary. Now, other than the heavy coat she wore—the one Bear had apparently stolen from the marquis's wardrobe—and the musket with a small number of lead balls and a pouch of powder, she might as well have been naked.

For the first time she realized how much . . . life her sister's presence, her singing and chitchatting as they went about their daily routine, had brought to the kitchen. Without Elizabeth there, everything looked old and dull and lonely. It looked like her entire past, actually. And the keen loss she felt was because of Elizabeth, of course. The abbey's sudden emptiness had nothing to do with the absence of the man who'd filled her days and her thoughts over the past fortnight. The man who'd just ridden off with her sister.

Catriona sat in the chair. Alone. It wasn't as if the word was foreign to her, for heaven's sake. She'd been

alone before. After her eccentric, strong-willed father
had died, she'd felt alone even with clan and family all
around her. In some ways, their presence had left her
feeling worse than alone—their scorn at her attire, her
directness, her complete inability to be the lass they expected her to be, had only added salt to the wound.
She'd loved Randall MacColl, and she'd lived her life
to please him. And then all of his decisions, all of hers,
had become something to be ridiculed.

Warmth spilled down her cheeks. "Stop it," she
muttered at herself, swiping at her cheeks with one sleeve.
Those people couldn't hurt her or judge her any longer,
because she'd left them all behind.

She could sit there and wallow in her solitude, tell
herself she deserved to be left behind. Self-pity wouldn't
accomplish anything, however, and it wouldn't keep her
warm tonight. It did, however, feel much easier than
doing anything to keep herself alive here, or to resume
worrying whether Elizabeth's good fortune would remain precisely that.

With a deep breath she stood again, then sank onto
her knees on the hearth to pull the damp wood and ashes
out of the fireplace. That done, she set in the dry wood
the men had thankfully left untouched, shredded Bear's
list of necessities to use for tinder, and pulled the flint
from her musket. A dusting of gunpowder and a few
strikes of the flint later, and with a flash the tinder ig-
nited. Once the wood caught fire, she sat back. "There.
That's better."

The list of her own necessities hadn't changed, even if
it differed greatly from her sister's: shelter, warmth, water,
and food. Now she had them back, though without a
blanket she would be going through the small supply

of firewood more quickly. That meant she needed to collect more before the rain began.

No sense waiting about, then. Catriona buttoned up her coat and made her way outside to find enough dead-fall to at least keep her through the night. It felt odd that her own safety was now her only concern. Lord Glengask had promised to protect Elizabeth, mostly at Bear's insistence. And however annoyed she was that Munro and then the MacLawry had stepped in, as if she'd been . . . insufficient where caring for her sister was concerned, for the moment at least, the solution seemed almost ideal.

Someone else would now look after her sister, make certain she had food and a dry place to sleep. And some-one else would keep watch over her, and see to it that His Grace the Duke of Visford got nowhere near the lass. Providing for one person was so much easier than looking after two, especially when one of them had no idea how to live roughly.

At the same time, though, and however gallant Lord Glengask had sounded making his proclamation, he'd made it without considering the longer road ahead. In a week or a month or when spring arrived, when Sassannach dukes and solicitors and army officers came call-ing to threaten the clan or Glengask's family or his many businesses with fines and sanctions, he might not be so eager to protect an English-raised lass he'd taken in out of charity. Especially one from a rival clan.

She wouldn't be able to blame him for it, either. The MacLawrys had no connection to Elizabeth, no reason to continue to protect her. Unless they did. And since Lord Glengask was married, that left Bear.

Catriona flung a rock against the trunk of a tree, the

solid thunk satisfying. Of course it had to be Bear. The giant, muscular man that no one in his right mind would cross. The man who'd tracked her here and then refused to be frightened away even at the point of her musket. The man who'd insisted not only on returning, but on bringing food and silly things like hair clips. The man who seemed to think being direct was refreshing rather than gauche. The man who'd kissed her, but had ridden off with Elizabeth.

She closed her eyes, then forced herself to open them again to finish gathering up the firewood. Whether she liked the idea or not didn't matter. It didn't even matter that she'd had the same idea earlier and then rejected it for . . . reasons on which she didn't care to dwell. The solution made sense. Elizabeth needed aid more than she did, and not just for a week or a month. Her sister needed someone to look after her. And once Elizabeth married, Visford would never be able to touch her, literally or figuratively. In addition, the MacLawrys stayed in the Highlands. That alone would keep Elizabeth's mother away from her daughter; Anne Derby-MacColl detested the Highlands.

Even better for *her,* the MacLawrys had no dealings with the MacDonalds, so perhaps after a time she could even visit. Yes. Munro needed to marry Elizabeth. She would merely have to find a way to make that happen.

Crouching, she picked up another branch and added it to the pile in her arms. Elizabeth would be safe, and that would leave *her* free to travel or hide away as she saw fit until the MacDonalds completely gave up on locating her. Yes, she would be alone, but she didn't need any help. It was Elizabeth who would never survive on her own.

Bear and Elizabeth might not even need much convincing; she'd ridden away on his lap, after all. And he'd stepped between her and his own brother. Why didn't she feel more hopeful, then? Why wasn't she relieved at the prospect of finally seeing her sister safe? Why did the idea of Bear kissing Elizabeth and telling her sister she was a bonny lass make her feel ill? For heaven's sake, she didn't even like Munro MacLawry. Yes, he had eyes the color of spring grass, and yes, his smile did shivery things to her insides, as did just looking at him. But he annoyed her, and aggravated her, and he'd interfered where he wasn't wanted.

Oh, it didn't make any sense. Why was he the one she'd been watching when her unwanted guests—and her own sister—had left? "Ye're a fool, Cat," she stated, turning back for the abbey. It wasn't fate or the stars or Cupid that had brought them together. Because whichever other circumstances might change, one thing never would; if she felt unfit to wed one man because of his status and position, she was just as unfit to marry another whose very presence caught peoples' attention.

Aside from that, marrying her had to be the furthest thing from his mind. And from her mind, of course. For Saint Beatrice's sake, he'd only kissed her a few times. Very well, twice. Not that she was counting. No doubt he kissed any number of lasses. With his looks and his family connections, females likely stood in a queue to kiss him and share his bed.

She had merely been convenient, and more than likely amusing. Bear had his rough edges, certainly, but that meant he needed a lass who could civilize him, or at least provide a civilizing influence for him. And that, however she might occasionally daydream otherwise, perfectly described Elizabeth.

The rain began a good ten minutes before she reached

the relative shelter of the abbey, and she wrapped her
coat around the armful of wood. Soaking wet by the
time she reached the kitchen, she tossed another branch
into the large fireplace and set the remains of the rabbit
stew back onto the fire. It was going to be a long day,
and an even longer night, because the first step in saving Elizabeth was going to be convincing herself that
Bear MacLawry wasn't hers. No matter what she might,
for a moment or two, wish.

Boots in one hand, Munro gingerly pulled open his bedchamber door and leaned into the hallway. A single
lamp remained lit, the wick turned low, with heavy
darkness hanging at both ends of the long corridor. At
nearly three o'clock in the morning the generally bus-
tling house stood silent but for the patter of rain against
the windows and someone's distant cough.

Lachlan and Winnie had elected to spend the night,
which decision he had to put more to his sister's immediate liking for Elizabeth than to any fear of a light
rain. They'd even put the lass in the room directly beside theirs. That was good; she seemed happy to be
back in civilization—or what passed for it in the Highlands, anyway.

And it wasn't just Winnie who seemed thrilled to
have her there. Surprisingly enough, even Ranulf had
cracked a smile or two over dinner. Aye, Elizabeth was
well bred and could likely hold her own in any conversation about fabric and fashion the lasses cared to have,
but the MacLawry didn't welcome just anyone into his
household. Questioning her abrupt popularity, though,
would be counterproductive; at least the lass's being
charming meant he wouldn't have to spend all of his free
time entertaining her on his own.

There was another lass with whom he'd rather spend time, after all. And he'd promised to protect her, too. With the hallway empty, he reached back into the room for the heavy bundle he'd wrapped in sealskin to keep the rain out. His stomach rumbled at him as he tucked the sack beneath one arm and silently shut the door behind him, but he ignored it and the hunger that went with it. If putting most of his dinner into his sporran allowed him to replenish some of the food they'd taken away from Haldane today, he would do it.

Quietly he descended the main staircase, avoiding the two squeaky steps with the ease of long practice. Usually, though, this was the time of night he returned home after spending the evening in the company of some lass or another. Meeting Catriona MacColl had upended his life in more ways than one.

The floppy hat and raincoat he donned in the foyer kept his top half mostly dry, but his feet were already wet by the time he sat on the outside step to pull on his boots. The weather didn't matter; by Highlands standards the light drizzle was only one step removed from sunshine.

With the stable boys and grooms sleeping in the room at the rear of the stable, he led Saturn outside to saddle the big gray. Luckily the lad was accustomed to coming and going at odd hours, and he didn't do more than snort once at the rain.

"Thank ye, boy," Munro said, as he finished tying off the bundle and then climbed into the saddle. "It's extra oats fer ye when we get back."

At this hour and with the rain filling and covering any tracks they might make, he headed them directly toward what he'd come to think of as Cat's valley. If anyone discovered him missing, they'd likely figure out where he'd gone, anyway—which was even more of a problem now than it had been yesterday. Especially when he felt the need to venture to Haldane before dawn and with its one known resident—as far as Ranulf and the others were concerned—asleep at Glengask.

He didn't doubt Catriona had gotten the fire going again, but that kitchen wasn't anything close to cozy. All of the blankets and her one change of clothes had left with Elizabeth's things this morning. Cat's sister had even had to conjure a tale of how she'd been prepared to dress as a lad if it came to that, which seemed to have satisfied everyone's curiosity about the shirt several sizes too small for it to belong to him.

Even more than concern over Cat's comfort, he wanted to know that she remained at Haldane Abbey at all. If she felt satisfied enough that Elizabeth was now safe, and angry enough at him for allowing Ranulf to discover her hiding place, she might well have set off deeper into the Highlands.

No. He wouldn't accept that. Either she was still at Haldane, or he would find her and bring her back. Whatever it was he felt around her, they weren't finished. Their tale had barely begun, and he couldn't escape the . . . belief, he supposed it was, that Cat was somehow vital to him. To his future.

Anyone who knew him would laugh at the idea that he'd become obsessed with any one lass—much less one who wore trousers and carried a musket. Aye, she was that, but that wasn't all she was. Whatever had driven her this far from MacDonald territory still troubled her, and that troubled *him*.

At the low wall he dismounted and tried coaxing Saturn into the entryway and out of the rain, but the gelding wouldn't have any of it. "Fine, ye brute," he muttered. "Ye stay oot here."

He couldn't decide whether it would be wiser to slip down the hall and get the musket out of her reach before she realized he was there, or to announce his presence and hope she wasn't angry enough about his whisking her sister away to shoot him. If she was there at all.

"Cat?" he called. Stealth had never worked well for him where she was concerned, anyway. "I'm alone, lass! Dunnae shoot me!"

Silence. His chest tightening, he strode up the hallway to the half-repaired door. A low fire hissed in the fireplace, protesting the rain dripping down the inside of the chimney, and his insides unknotted a little. She had to be here, then. Somewhere.

"Catriona?"

Metal clicked cold and deadly behind him. "Ye've some nerve, Bear. I'll give ye that."

He whipped around toward the near corner of the room to see Catriona lowering her musket. Relief, joined by something sharper and more heated, sent his heart pounding. "Thank God," he breathed, brushing the weapon aside and capturing her face in his hands. He kissed her hard, teasing at her mouth until she opened to him, their tongues tangling.

This was what he'd been yearning for all day, and this . . . heady arousal was what he'd lately felt only in her presence. Women, physical pleasure, were one thing. When he looked at her, talked with her, he felt more . . . aware. More alive, more challenged, than he had with any other lass he'd ever met. It didn't make any sense, because she also frustrated him more than any lass he'd ever met, but there it was. Perhaps it was lust; for the devil's sake, he hadn't had a woman in over a fortnight. Not since two nights before they'd met, actually. There was only one way to find out if that would purge her from his thoughts—and he had no objection to making that discovery, at all.

"Stop trying to devour me," she finally rasped, and shoved at his chest. "I'm angry with ye."

"Ye arenae," he returned, ignoring the protest when her mouth molded against his kiss again.

"I am," she insisted a moment later, and shoved harder.

She might as well have been a wee dove, but he took a reluctant half step back, anyway. If she took a look at his kilt she would see that he wasn't finished with her, but her chocolate gaze lowered to his mouth before she turned her back on him and with a shove of her shoulder against his chest walked over to the hearth. Swinging a pot over the low fire, she grabbed a spoon and began stirring.

Of course she wouldn't starve on her own; she knew how to hunt and trap, quite possibly as well as he did. But every time she ventured outside, she risked being seen. He wanted her to be able to go out when she chose to, rather than when she had to. "I didnae plan fer Ranulf to follow me here. That is my fault, though, and I apologize to ye fer it."

"Ye told a good tale for Elizabeth. And ye got yer brother to give his word that he'd see her kept safe."

"Ye were listening, were ye?" From the roof, he'd wager.

"Of course I was." She sent him a pointed glance. "Though I dunnae recall telling ye about the Duke of Visford. Did ye have that conversation with Elizabeth?"

Munro shifted the musket a little farther away, then stepped over beside her to sit on the floor against the side of the chimney. "I overheard the two of ye talking one day when ye thought I was elsewhere. I figured to keep my gobber shut until ye trusted me enough to tell me to my face, but when Ran appeared I had to tell him someaught of the truth or he'd know it was all a lie."

She kept stirring. "That's underhanded of ye."

"Aye." He shrugged. "Even if I'd had time to think up a tale, it had to be someaught Elizabeth could carry on with. And someaught that didnae involve ye." For a moment he studied her profile, uncertain what he was looking for, but liking what he saw. "I still dunnae ken what yer secrets are, lass, but since ye stayed hidden I figured I had the right of at least one thing. Glengask doesnae have any idea ye're here."

She nodded, still refusing to look over at him. "It's better that way. For my sake and for ye and yer brother. And for Elizabeth."

"It's clan MacDonald business, aye?" he pressed, reaching over to tuck a damp strand of her fiery hair back into place.

Catriona shrugged him off. "Dunnae ye try to get cozy with me, giant. Tell me how my sister fares."

So she still wouldn't tell him what troubled her. Very well. He could be patient, even if it was something he didn't practice much. "I imagine she's sound asleep in a soft bed with a warming pan at her feet and a fire in the hearth. My sister, Winnie, and her husband, Lachlan, are staying the night to see that she settles in, and I ken Ranulf's wife, Charlotte, is happy to have another proper English-bred lass aboot."

"Good. Elizabeth showed more spleen than I had any right to ask of her, but she's nae one to be happy unless she has people about. I ken she brightened up whenever ye came calling here. And nae just because ye gave her yer solemn vow to keep her safe."

Munro frowned at her. "Ye dunnae need to remind me aboot the words that came oot of my own mouth. I havenae fergotten them."

"Good. Because ye're the only friend she has, now. I imagine she'll be relying on ye quite a bit." The spoon's swirling accelerated. "In fact, ye should likely get back to Glengask before she or anyone else misses ye."

In his mind as he'd lain awake for most of the night and then made his way to Haldane Abbey in the damp, predawn darkness, Cat had been alone and cold and worried. He'd damned well been worried for her, wondering if he would ever see her again. Ideally by now they would have been naked together on the blankets he'd brought her, and he would finally be satisfying the craving that had seized him almost from the moment they'd met.

Instead she stirred a day-old rabbit stew and suggested that he leave. "I brought ye blankets and some venison." Perhaps that would earn him some damned gratitude.

"I hope ye didnae do anything that would bring yer brother out here again, Bear."

"I took my own things, and my own dinner. Ye need-nae worry."

"Very well, then." She lifted the spoon to gesture at the large room, then returned to stirring. "As ye can see, I'm perfectly fine. And I'll be better if ye dunnae bring any MacLawrys back here to see what ye're about. So go home, Bear. Elizabeth needs ye. I dunnae."

That did it. Alone, nothing but a small fire and the rain for company, and she still wanted him to leave.

Whatever the devil troubled her, she could at least tell him the truth about one damned thing. Munro reached over and grabbed the spoon out of her hand. "Ye dunnae need me?" he retorted, and flung the utensil across the room. "Then why are ye stirring soup at three o'clock in the morning? Why are ye nae sleeping?"

"I *was* sleeping, ye giant, until ye woke me with trying to get a horse into the foyer."

As she spoke she faced him again, and he got a good look at her in the firelight. Tired circles beneath her eyes, her damp hair in a loose, careless tail, her delicate jaw clenched—if she'd been asleep, he was a bloody Irishman. "Dunnae lie to me, lass. Ye were sitting in that corner where ye surprised me," he stated, taking her by the shoulders and pulling her to her feet. "Ye had that damned musket across yer lap, waiting fer trouble to find ye. Tell me I'm wrong aboot that."

She lifted her face, her dark brown eyes meeting his squarely. "Fine. Aye. I've been awake, because I didnae have any idea who else might have spied ye visiting here and might decide to invade my house."

"Then ye do need me, bonny lass. Because this isnae yer hoose. It's mine." He tugged her closer. "And ye're mine."

Chapter Ten

D unnae ye try that tone with me, giant." Catriona blinked, something unexpected jabbing into her chest.

"Ye disagree then, that withoot me ye wouldnae have a place to stay?"

The idea that she couldn't have protected her sister without someone else's help, that she needed him for . . . well, for anything—her first instinct was to punch him in the nose and tell him to bugger off, because it was just his manly pride talking, and she could make do quite well on her own.

"I ken the abbey is yours. That isnae what I was objecting to."

At the back of her thoughts, she tried to concentrate on the idea that he had proven useful, rather than how he'd just tried to claim ownership of *her*. She had to remember how tired and worn down Elizabeth had been before they'd stumbled across Haldane, and how relieved she'd been to find at least one room with an intact fireplace and most of a roof, somewhere they could spend a night without worrying about the weather and the temperature and highwaymen. Somewhere she could close her eyes and not think about anything but what sort of game she would be roasting tomorrow.

Eyes narrowed, he regarded her. Then he took in a hard breath through his nose. "Stubborn lass," Bear muttered.

"I heard what yer brother told ye this morning," she finally said, trying to pull out of his grip and failing to budge him as much as an inch. "Aye, Haldane belongs to ye, Bear. Congratulations. But ye promised to keep my sister safe. And the best way for ye to do that is to marry her. So stop saying I belong to ye and go back to Glengask and propose to her. Leave me be."

He actually looked shocked. "The hell ye say."

"It makes sense, and ye know it. I'll go, and ye marry her. She likes ye well enough as it is. All ye have to do is let go of me, ye big ox."

Instead, he gripped her more tightly. "I dunnae want ye to leave, wildcat. Ye *are* the lass I should be with, and I have nae idea what the rest of that nonsense means—except that I'm nae going to marry yer delicate Sassannach of a sister."

Catriona hammered a fist against his hard chest. "Ye cannae be as thick-skulled as all that." For God's sake, if he would just let go of her and stop looking at her so intently, she could explain why her plan for him and Elizabeth made sense. More sense than him pursuing her and causing more trouble for both of them, certainly. No one pursued her. Ever.

"It seems I *am* that thick-skulled," he growled back at her, walking her backward until she had to sit in the chair. "So I'll stand here glaring at ye, and ye explain to me why I shouldnae be calling ye a Bedlamite."

If he did claim to have some . . . claim on her, he

might at least try using complimentary words and not
calling her mad. Catriona folded her arms over her chest.
"It's very simple," she announced, wishing he would see
the situation logically for once, because she wasn't entirely convinced, herself. "Ye promised to see Elizabeth
safe. She can rest easy at Glengask *now,* but she cannae
be a permanent guest."

"So ye say. I dunnae think ye ken what my brother
can do fer her up here in the Highlands."

"Hush. I'm nae finished. I reckon the only way to
keep Visford away from Elizabeth is for her to be married to someone else." She paused, but he only continued glaring at her.

"And?" he prompted, crossing his arms as she had,
clearly refusing to see reason.

Surely he'd had at least one passing romantic thought
about her sister. Until the duke had come along, Elizabeth's letters had been filled with stories of the handsome
young gentlemen who pursued her. "Oh, for heaven's
sake," she finally burst out. "Ye brought her home across
yer saddle."

His glare shifted into a frown. Abruptly his hands
dropped, and he backed away a step or two. "I was being polite," he growled.

"That's nae politeness. That's nearly a proposal.
Marry Elizabeth. It'll save her from the duke, and she'll
civilize ye some. As much as can be done with ye,
anyway."

He continued to stare at her for several hard beats of
her heart. Then, his hands and his jaw clenched, he
turned on his heel and strode out of the room. His heavy
bootsteps receded down the hallway until she could no
longer tell them from the rain.

"Bear?"

Well, that hadn't gone at all well. Or perhaps it had. If it stopped him from kissing her and making her wish she had some idea how to act like a female, then good. He needed to go kiss and chat with Elizabeth. As she'd told him, her sister knew how to act like a lady, and could very likely teach him how to be a gentleman.

"Ye're daft, Catriona," Bear's deep growl came from the doorway, making her jump. "My brother's been trying to marry me off to one lass or another fer nearly two years, and I told him what I'm telling ye now— dunnae try matching me up with some lass because it suits yer lunatic ideas of domesticity." He took two long strides forward into the room, his head low and his eyes narrow. "I like yer sister well enough, but I willnae be marrying her. I dunnae want her. I want *ye.*"

Her heart abruptly hammering, Catriona stood up and backed away from him. She'd heard his anger when he'd confronted his brother, but she'd never seen evidence of a temper so notorious that stories about it had reached even to the Isle of Islay. Until now. "Elizabeth makes more sense for ye," she said anyway. "For both of ye."

"Nae," he retorted, grabbing up the musket that still leaned against the table and tossing it across the room like a twig. "It makes sense fer *ye,* because it leaves ye oot of the equation, free to go off and do as pleases ye withoot any guilt. But ye're in *my* equation, wildcat. I'm nae going away."

"Then I will," she stated, lifting her chin and surprised at how difficult it was to say the words aloud. "My sister is safe; there's nae reason for me to stay on here. As ye said, Haldane Abbey is yer property. I amnae, however loud ye bellow it."

Two feet from her, so close she had to crane her neck to meet his gaze, he stopped his advance. "Ye willnae go anywhere, Catriona," he growled, reaching out and wrapping his fingers into the front of her coat, dragging her up against him. "Say what ye like, but we both ken ye're running from the MacDonalds. And nae Mac-Donald can touch ye here."

"I didnae say anything of the kind."

"Ye didnae have to, lass." He took a deep breath, looking at her so intently she didn't think she could have looked away if she'd wanted to. "And I swear to ye," he went on more quietly, "ye've naught to fear from me. Ye can trust me with all yer secrets."

She wanted to. Even if keeping well away from him was safer. Safer for her heart. "I dunnae know how to play this game, Munro," she blurted. "I say what I think, and I think ye and Elizabeth make a good match."

Before she could take a breath, he kissed her, his mouth soft and lingering and warm on hers. "Say it again, then," he murmured.

"Ye belong with Elizabeth."

He dipped his head again, his too long black hair brushing her cheek as he took her mouth. Her fingers itched to wrap into his coat, and she sternly restrained herself. "Ye want me kissing yer sister, do ye?" he asked softly.

No! she yelled to herself, but for him she wrinkled her brow in what she hoped was a scowl. "Ye'll keep her safe, giant."

"Do I feel safe to ye?" he returned, his kiss this time hotter and more intoxicating than a glass of whisky.

He didn't feel safe. At all. He felt . . . dangerous, to her head and to her heart. "Stop it," she ordered, wrapping her hands around his and trying to free her collar from his hard, unrelenting grip. "I may be a virgin, but I'm nae an idiot. A few fair kisses willnae convince me of anything but that ye ken how to kiss. Because of all yer practice, I assume."

With a muttered curse he released her again. "There are lasses who would already have all their clothes off if I kissed them like that, ye stubborn woman."

"Then go kiss them," she suggested, even though just the idea of it made her hands curl into fists.

"I dunnae want to kiss them. I want to kiss ye. And hit myself in the head with a hammer, all at the same time."

Well, she could sympathize with that—not that she would tell him so. "There's a hammer, right over there."

"Bah. I dunnae know what to say to convince ye of anything, Cat," he returned, and stalked over to retrieve the musket. With obvious care he inspected the weapon, emptied the shot, and reloaded it for her.

"So ye'll go find Elizabeth?" she finally ventured, not certain what she'd expected to happen but feeling oddly . . . disappointed at the same time. As if something extraordinary had run right up to her, given her a look, and then turned around and walked away.

Bear snorted. "Nae. Ye may have befuddled me, but I'm nae an idiot, either." He narrowed one eye. "Despite opinion to the contrary."

Later she would attempt to decipher why his refusal of Elizabeth, his destruction of her swiftly formed plans, didn't bother her much at all. "Ye'll at least leave me be, then."

"Aye. I'll leave ye be," he returned, handing her the weapon. "Use the damned blankets I brought ye. I'll nae have ye freezing to death on my account."

Abruptly she wanted to cry. He'd given up—precisely as she'd asked him to, and yet—he'd given up. On her. "I will. Thank ye."

"Ye're welcome. Do ye have a timepiece here?"

"What? Nae. What are ye—"

"Here." He pulled a pocket watch out of his coat and set it on the table. "Make yerself scarce aboot ten o'clock, but be close enough to hear me yell. I'll try to have only Peter with me, but one of my brothers or Lach might insist on coming along."

Catriona eyed him. Either she was too tired to follow the conversation, or Bear still meant to return to Haldane. "I thought—"

"Ye thought what?" he broke in, setting the bundle he'd dropped in the doorway close by the hearth. "That ye'd managed to be rid of me? I dunnae mean to make it as easy as that. I'll leave ye be tonight, because ye're tired and ye've had all yer plans turned rightside doon, and because if I kiss ye again I'll nae be able to stop myself. But I do mean to have ye, lass, and I reckon I'll seduce ye until ye can think of naught but the two of us rolling aboot naked on those blankets." He gestured at them.

Now she'd likely never be able to sleep in them at all. "But—"

"Aye, ye drive me dizzy, wildcat, spinning me aboot so I couldnae tell ye where to find the sky. But I do know two things: first, I'm nae going to wed yer sister just so ye can have one less thing to keep ye here. And second, I like ye. I've a fondness fer ye I cannae explain to yer satisfaction, obviously, but I'm nae finished with ye." He retrieved his rifle, hefting it like it weighed nothing. "Och, and there's a third thing, too. Ye like me. Ye'll nae admit it, because ye're more stubborn than a badger, but a lad knows when the lass he's kissed, kisses him back. And ye, wildcat, kissed me back."

She couldn't deny that. Not tonight, when the warmth and taste of his mouth still lingered on hers. Not when her heart had nearly pounded its traitorous way out of her chest when she'd first heard him in the hallway. "I see ye as a friend, Bear. One I didnae expect. But—"

He lifted a hand. "Nae. Ye stop right there. I'm nae yer friend. What I want to do to ye I dunnae do with my friends." The big man flashed her a warm smile that did even more heated things to her insides. "We can be friendly, I reckon, because that's a beginning."

With that he walked up, gave her a last, too brief kiss that had her leaning up toward him, then left the kitchen. Catriona sagged back into the chair. All her plans for seeing Elizabeth properly and permanently taken care of, for her escaping from the contemptuous, condescending looks of . . . well, of everyone who knew her, all stood as ruined as the building around her. But in the midst of all that, one thought swirled—Bear MacLawry liked her, refused to give up on her, and apparently meant to woo her.

Heaven help her, she wanted him to woo her. She wanted to do more than kiss him. She wanted to feel his warm skin beneath her hands and hear him tell her again that he liked her and wanted her, and not because he had to, because she was a MacDonald chieftain's daughter— or niece now, rather—but in spite of that. No man had ever just liked *her*. Or if one did, he'd never had the courage to approach her and tell her so.

Wishing endlessly for things, though, had never made them happen. Or it had never sufficed before, anyway. At this moment, unless she'd dreamed everything that had just happened, Bear *did* want her. Now she only needed to decide if giving in to what her body wanted would be worth the trouble it would cause. Was what might well be her one chance at happiness, even temporary happiness, worth a war?

She stood up again, going over to open the bundle he'd brought. Two heavy blankets, a sealskin wrap with a hood to keep a good portion of her dry when next she had to go out in the rain, and a cloth-wrapped meal of venison and three thick slices of buttered bread. Gathering it up, she sat against the warmth of the chimney, pulled one of the blankets up over her legs, and ate her predawn breakfast.

As she did so, she opened the last item Bear had smuggled out to her. A book. *Robinson Crusoe,* yet. She'd read it before, but not lately, and now she had to wonder if Munro thought of her as Crusoe. And if she was, was she a shipwrecked wretch alone in the wilderness? Or had her rescue already arrived, and she merely lacked the courage to stretch out her hand and accept it?

"Damnation."

Perhaps she should just let Bear ruin her. It was only her presence the MacDonalds required—not her virginity. And she had no intention of giving them either one. Once she . . . lay with Munro MacLawry, then she could stop thinking and wondering about him and make her plans based on logic rather than on frustrated lust. And perhaps that would satisfy him as well, and he would stop saying so many tempting, naughty things to her.

The more she thought about it, the more sense it made. In exchange for a night with him, the path before her would be clear. She wouldn't have to spare Munro— or any idiotic dreams of a might-have-been future—a second thought.

* * *

"Where's the lass?"

Ranulf turned away from the library window as his younger brother Arran strolled into the wood-paneled room. "Charlotte, Rowena, and yer Mary took her doon to An Soadh. Evidently she requires a new bonnet."

At his gesture, Arran closed the door. "Any more conversation with Bear? Has he said what he means to do with Lady Elizabeth?"

"Nae. He's up at Haldane again, fixing the door and the roof, I assume. This morning he sent Debny into the village with an order fer cut stone and lumber." Sitting at the worktable, Ranulf pulled a letter from his pocket and slid it across the mahogany surface to his brother. "Until I hear differently, I'm assuming our *bràthair* is making Haldane Abbey livable because he means to live there."

Arran grimaced. "Bear's nae been one to spend much time contemplating. And I dunnae want to be the one to try to talk him oot of anything. But do ye ken he's fallen fer the lass, or has he just gone and rescued her and now thinks he's obligated?"

With a shrug, Ranulf sat back against his chair. "By Sassannach standards, he *is* obligated now. He's been alone with her. And considering that Peter Gilling was the chaperone, well—Gilling chaperoned ye and Mary on yer way north. We all ken how effective that was."

"I cannae argue with that," Arran said with a grin. He unfolded the letter Ranulf had given him, then shot his older brother a quick look. "Ye truly mean to tell the MacDonald she's here?"

"Her father was a clan chieftain. Gorrie likely doesnae give a damn where she ends up, but I'm nae going to be the one who made the trouble, this time. I'll be courteous and gentlemanly and inform him that I'm removing Elizabeth MacColl from his clan." He gave a dark smile. "That sounds courteous, doesnae?"

"Fer ye? Aye. But what if the MacDonald wanted her wed to Visford fer some reason? Suppose he disagrees with ye aboot the lass's future?"

This was why Ranulf valued the middle MacLawry brother's opinion so much. Arran generally had a way of thinking an event through not only to its logical, but also to its likely, conclusion. In this instance, however, he'd spent most of last night pacing, his bairn William in his arms, following the threads of every possible scenario. "Nae informing Gorrie seems a bigger risk to me," he countered. "Munro's my *bràthair*. His marriage willnae be overlooked, even if hers is."

"Aye. I'll agree with that. And I assume ye're expecting Gorrie to want someaught in return fer giving this mostly English lass to the MacLawrys."

"What I know fer certain is that if the marriage happens before he hears aboot the match, he'll want more from us. When he gets angry that we tried to go past him withoot asking permission, we'll also end up with a herd of MacDonalds looking fer trouble crowding our borders. In my opinion, one MacDonald here is enough."

"I cannae argue against that." Arran finished reading the missive and handed it back. "Ye're a generous man, Ranulf. Especially since Elizabeth MacColl is too distant from her clan to bring us any advantage. And I'm fairly certain the Stewarts willnae be happy to lose their last chance at a MacLawry marriage."

"I'm nae aboot to try to force Bear into someaught if he's finally found a lass to keep his interest fer longer than one night." He grimaced. "And he threatened to break Conchar Boyd in half if I tried to marry him off to Boyd's sister."

Laughing, Arran drummed his hands against the tabletop. "I should've thought of threatening to damage a lass's family if I didnae like the look of her."

"Instead, ye nearly started a war." And Arran's pursuit of Mary Campbell had nearly fractured the MacLawry family, which was worse than any damned war as far as Ranulf was concerned. After the near mishap with Arran, he'd taken a step back. He might suggest or even threaten, but he wouldn't force Bear to marry someone the big man didn't want. Nor would he prevent his brother from claiming a half-Sassannach, English-raised lass if she was who he wanted. After all, the MacLawry siblings were half English, themselves.

"I still cannae help thinking that Bear's nuptials are a bit anticlimactic," Arran resumed. "Ye marry a Sassannach, I have a Campbell, Winnie and Lach nearly get murdered before they come to their senses—and then Bear marries a MacDonald lass and costs ye what, a hundred acres of grazing land?"

Ranulf returned the letter to his breast pocket. "I'll nae complain aboot that. I ken I'm still the devil to the English and to our rivals here, and I mean to keep it that way. Within our own family, though, I believe we've earned some peace and calm. Dunnae ye think?"

"Aye. That I do." Arran pushed away from the table and stood. "And now I think I might find myself in An Soadh in time to purchase the lasses some luncheon at the Bonny Bruce."

Once his brother left the house, Ranulf had the letter sent off by special messenger north to the MacDonald. Then he sent Owen out to deliver luncheon to Munro and Peter Gilling at Haldane Abbey. It wasn't much in the way of a peace offering, but for Bear, food counted double.

He had the feeling it would take more than sandwiches when he sat down with Munro in the next few days and asked for some answers about the lass and when he planned on marrying her, because however distant her relationship with the MacDonalds, at least a token number would expect invitations. And coordinating any meeting between clans took both time and some finesse.

In the meantime, the MacLawrys and MacTiers would be occupied with making young Lady Elizabeth MacColl feel like a welcome part of the family. Even if he didn't quite see what had drawn one of them to the other. Bear had made it clear that that was none of his affair, and so he would keep his distance as much as he could—as much as the head of the family, the chief of clan MacLawry, and a brother, could.

Something had changed. Catriona couldn't quite put her finger on it, and it wasn't anything obvious, but it hung there in the air like the scent of pine trees in the cold. "Ye're certain Elizabeth is safe?" she asked, over the stack of lumber she and Peter Gilling were wrestling up the fractured staircase. "Ye gave yer word, Bear."

Unkempt black hair above a devilish handsome face appeared over the railing. "If ye ask me that one more time I'm likely to start howling like a banshee. She's surrounded by a half-dozen burly MacLawry men and, if that isnae sufficient, she has my sister on one arm and Lady Glengask on the other, and Mary Campbell-MacLawry in the mix, as well. Those lasses would make me think twice before I made a ruckus." He reached down and lifted the armload of boards with no noticeable effort.

"But they didnae make a promise to her. Ye—"

"Aye. I made a promise to her. Peter, will ye fetch the tarp and the bucket of nails?"

"Dunnae throw each other off the roof while I'm away," the footman muttered, then flashed her a smile and headed back to the ground floor.

Munro reached down again. "I also made a promise to *ye*, wildcat. Since I cannae divide myself in two, I've seen yer *piuthar* looked after, and I'm here. Now give me yer hand and stop trying to order me aboot. I told ye I wasnae going anywhere."

With an exaggerated sigh she gripped his hand, and he half lifted her over the rubble of the fallen second floor. "So now ye expect me to climb about on the roof with ye?"

Instead of releasing her hand, he drew her slowly closer. She had to put her palm against his chest to keep from falling against him. Aggravating man and his cheeky, attractive smile—and those delicious, naughty kisses. "Do ye ever take yer hair doon?" he murmured, lifting his hand to run the back of his forefinger down one cheek.

Why the devil did his touch make her shiver all the way down her spine and between her legs? She didn't want any of this to happen. For a long moment she gazed up at his springtime eyes, and he looked back at her squarely, intently, as if he was trying to memorize her features.

They couldn't go on like this. And since she would have been willing to wager that he wasn't going to give in, perhaps she needed to do so. Then, when he had what he wanted and she had a night like the one she'd been dreaming of whenever she managed to close her eyes, they could . . . well, set things back the way they should be. She couldn't set him after Elizabeth again, not after she'd been with him, but his presence would stop troubling her so.

Aside from that, and heaven help her, she wanted him. His kisses curled her toes, and the sound of his deep, rolling brogue made her heart hum. For the first time in weeks she didn't have to worry about her sister, and instead of running from what she knew she didn't want, she could look at what—who—she *did* want. Even if it would only be for one night.

A holiday from her own life. Yes. A very handsome, very muscular holiday who seemed genuinely to find her interesting rather than odd. Then, when they'd both slaked their lust, or whatever it was she should be calling it, she could think logically about what she needed to do. About which path would best serve her and her future.

"I'll give ye every penny in my pockets fer yer thoughts, bonny lass," Bear said, tilting his head. A thick lock of his black hair fell across his temple. "Because ye're nae fighting me, and ye're nae trying to flee."

Catriona snorted. "Does that make ye nervous, giant?"

"Aye. Ye're clearly pondering someaught, and that's nae been good fer me up till now."

Before she could change her mind, she lifted up on her toes, tugged on his hair to lower his face to hers, and kissed him. His mouth was warm, and he tasted of American coffee and marmalade. This time he didn't grab at her or try to pin her against what was left of the wall, and she realized he meant to follow her lead.

The realization was heady, considering he could haul her about as easily as if she weighed no more than a feather. Freeing her hand from his, she slid her arms over his broad shoulders. Only then did he grip her waist, pulling her closer. If she'd had any doubt that he truly did want her, the growing hardness pressing against her hip answered it. She couldn't breathe, couldn't get close enough to him, couldn't—

"Hello, the house!" a gravelly voice called from below. "I've brought ye luncheon, Laird Bear, courtesy of Laird Glengask!"

Panting for breath, Catriona broke the kiss. "Who—"

"Owen," Munro growled, setting her away from him. "The head footman at Glengask. Stay up here a minute."

She nodded, trying to force her mind to work again. So that was what it felt like simply to give in and enjoy a kiss. *Good Saint Andrew and all the heavenly angels.* "The—the blankets are in the corner beside the chimney."

"I threw a sack over 'em already, just as a precaution."

And he continued to protect her, even if he didn't know why or from what. She started to thank him, then glanced down. A grin curved her mouth before she could catch it. "Bear, ye've a tent in yer kilt."

He chuckled, trying to push the stubborn thing down only to have it spring up again. "Ye're a saucy minx, ye are," he told her. "Now dunnae distract me. I have to think of ugly, warty old men fer a bit."

Somewhat relieved not to have to carry on a conversation, she turned half away only to watch from the corner of her eye, fascinated, as the tent slowly smoothed out again. Abruptly he caught her arm and pulled her around for a quick, hard kiss.

"I'd tell ye to stop driving me mad, wildcat, but ye do that just by breathing."

That was quite possibly the most romantic thing she'd ever heard, much less had spoken to her. Now she wanted to kiss him again, whether he claimed that she already belonged to him, or not. "Go," she whispered instead, pushing him toward the stairs. "Before he comes up here looking for ye."

"Aye. Dunnae go anywhere. I'm nae finished with ye, yet."

An unaccustomed giggle broke from her chest. "Go, ye brute."

He hopped over the fallen mound of ceiling. "I'm going, woman," he muttered back, and vanished down the staircase.

No, he didn't own her. No one owned her. She'd left her home to make certain of that. But she'd been around men before—even handsome men, if not as handsome as Munro—and she'd never felt like this. It was all trouble, but for once she thought a bit of trouble might be welcome.

Chapter Eleven

Catriona sat down on the stack of lumber, listening as Bear greeted the Owen fellow. If this footman was anything like Peter Gilling, he would be far more than a lad in livery expected to deliver tea on command. The male staff of a clan chief's household, if he held to the old ways as Glengask did, would be trained warriors, ready to lay down their lives to protect the family.

Munro was a trained warrior as well, lethal when he needed to be, and casually dangerous by virtue of his size and strength. For some reason she still couldn't quite grasp, he'd decided to use that power to aid her. And to seduce her. It all seemed fantastical enough that she couldn't resist the opportunity.

From what she could make out, he gave Peter and Owen—and himself—a sandwich, then sent both men on an errand to the village for plaster and mortar and more tarps. She knew precisely why he wanted the other men gone, and the thought of what would happen next both terrified and excited her.

To him, this would likely be a hopefully pleasant

interlude, just one of many. With his looks and his family connections, how could he not have lovers scattered all across the countryside? Experienced, pretty lasses who knew how to please a man. He'd as much as said he did. As for her, well, she knew how to take down a twelve-point buck from a hundred yards away. Being unclothed with a man, though, was an entirely new experience.

"Ye can come doon now, Cat," Munro called from the base of the stairs. "We've a beef stew and mutton sandwiches."

Rubbing her hands against her thighs, she stood up. At least if she made a mess of things, he would realize he'd made a mistake in kissing her, and he would leave her be. And she would know that fleeing Islay had been the absolute correct decision. She would make a terrible wife, a horrible excuse for a lady, and an abysmal peace offering. Squaring her shoulders, she clambered down the stairs and up the hallway—and stopped at the closed door. Her new door.

She smiled, touching it, then stepped sideways to look through the unfinished wall beside it. "This is bonny," she said, "but I think ye forgot someaught."

He appeared on the other side of the open wall. "Aye, it may have a few flaws. It's nae finished, though. After yesterday I figured ye should have a bit more protection. I dunnae like the idea of ye spending the night awake with a musket across yer lap."

Pushing open the door, she stepped into the kitchen. Rather grateful for the distraction, she swung the door back and forth and then latched it closed. "Even like this, it'll give me a bit more notice," she said. "Thank ye."

"After we get the tarp set over yer roof, I'll finish the wall here and get ye that bar ye can put across it."

Catriona faced him. "Ye dunnae have to do all this, Bear. Ye've already lied to yer own brother, yer clan chief, about me."

"Aye. So I have."

His direct, unreadable gaze unsettled her a little. "Because ye want to bed me."

Bear gave a slow smile. "That's part of it. Ye stay in my mind, whether my eyes are open or closed. Mostly I lied because I dunnae want ye fleeing into the wilds. Because ye're a puzzle to me, and I cannae seem to figure ye oot."

"Ye like puzzles, then." Perhaps she should simply tell him everything, and he would stop . . . tempting her so.

He shook his head. "Nae. I dunnae. A puzzle's akin to looking fer the most difficult way to find a simple answer."

Well, that didn't make any sense. "Then why—"

His mouth closed over hers. She expected him to be rough, to throw her to the floor and smother her. Instead, though, he teased at her lips, nipping at her, tasting her with his tongue. Before she'd even realized it she had her hands tangled into his thick, disheveled midnight hair, heat swirling through her.

"Show me what to do," she said huskily, the moment she could draw a breath.

"Do as pleases ye, my lass," he returned, lifting her around the waist to set her down on the edge of the table.

That was better, because her legs felt unsteady as a new fawn's. She knew they would be wiser to keep their distance from each other, but with one of his big hands gripping her waist and the other cupping the back of her neck, the specific reasons for that eluded her. "That isnae very helpful."

"Then stop thinking so hard. This isnae aboot thinking."

"Oh. That's good." Being reasonable and being kissed by Bear MacLawry simply didn't fit together. And at this moment she preferred being kissed to thinking.

"Is it?"

For a moment she wondered whether he was questioning her response to his statement, or her reaction to his moving his mouth along her throat. In either case, oh, it was very, very good. "Aye," she whispered.

With him standing between her knees she couldn't help becoming aware that the front of his kilt was tented again, and rather impressively so. Because he wanted her. Quick shivers darted through her, tingling between her thighs. She wanted to see him, but that seemed very bold, and not at all something a lady would admit to—much less do. Then again, she wasn't much of a lady.

Before she could change her mind, she reached around his waist to unfasten the buckles on his right side. She'd seen men wearing kilts for most of her life, even though the practice had become less common in everyday dress. Even on Islay, trousers had become the norm, with the traditional MacDonald tartan only appearing on holidays and for weddings and funerals. And that was a damned shame, as far as she was concerned. A man wearing a kilt—especially one who wore it as well as Bear did—was a sight to behold.

Unwrapping the aprons, she drew open the kilt and then let it go. The material fell to the floor, but abruptly she scarcely noticed. One couldn't grow up among Highlanders without an occasional glimpse of a cock and balls, but a fit, aroused giant was something new. And very, very impressive.

"Ye see what ye've done to me, Cat?" he murmured,

sliding his hands beneath the shoulders of her coat and then pulling it down her arms. A moment later it joined his kilt on the dirty slab floor.

"Ye're a magnificent lad, Bear," she returned, tentatively running a finger along the length of him. Warm, firm, and reactive to her touch, he was. Damp spread between her thighs.

"And ye leave me breathless, lass, with yer long legs and all those curves ye have on ye. I want to touch every inch of ye. I want to kiss every part of ye. And I want to be inside ye. So if ye're bound to change yer mind, do it now. Otherwise, kiss me again."

She leaned up and took his mouth, nibbling his lower lip as he'd done to her. At the same time she stroked him again, wrapping her fingers around his girth, exploring him the way she'd wanted to nearly since she'd met him.

With a low moan against her mouth he parted from her again. "Lift yer arms, wildcat; I reckon I'll have ye naked."

The idea made her nervous. For the devil's sake, she'd avoided wearing gowns for her entire life. Wearing even less, and in front of this magnificent giant of a man, terrified her. But she'd made her decision, and she'd already taken off half his clothes. Fair was fair.

Sighing unsteadily, she released his cock and did as he bade her. Munro pulled her shirt from her trousers, then took the bottom hem of the rough cotton and lifted, pulling it over her head and then dropping it somewhere behind her. "Well, now," he breathed, his gaze on her bare breasts.

"What? I'm nae a lass who goes aboot flaunting her bosom, ye ken."

Green eyes touched hers, and then lowered again.

"Then I'm honored, my lass, because the sight before me is damned marvelous."

Before she could respond to that, as if she had any idea how to do so, Munro put his hands beneath her breasts, as if testing the weight of them. Then his thumbs brushed across her nipples, lightly at first, then more firmly. The sharp, tight sensation had her arching her back, pressing harder against him.

With a slight grin he leaned in, replacing one hand with his mouth. He flicked his tongue across her, and she gasped. "Ye're a wicked man, Bear."

"Then tell me to stop, Cat," he returned. Without waiting for her to answer, he lifted her off the table and set her onto her back on the floor—where he'd already spread out her blankets. Of course he knew what he meant for them to be doing, but part of her wished he wasn't so . . . confident about it. It only demonstrated that he knew precisely what he was about, while she lay floundering like a fish trying to breathe air.

Kneeling beside her, Bear stripped off his shirt and dropped it. She'd seen his bare chest and abdomen before, but now, abruptly, she could touch him. Warm, soft skin, with hard muscle beneath—muscle that flexed beneath her touch. Did she affect him, then? Did her touch please him? She wanted to ask, but it seemed a supremely silly question, and one to which she should likely already know the answer.

"Sit up, lass," he said, grasping her hands and tugging. "I'm taking that ribbon oot of yer hair."

"I can do that."

"Nae," he countered, his voice more firm and quick than she expected. He took a breath. "I reckon I'll do it."

"Fine. Ye do it, then. It's naught but hair. Hair that never does what I wish it to."

Bear moved around behind her, and the gentle tug and pull of his fingers unknotting her hair ribbon made her shiver from her scalp to her toes. *Good heavens.*

"They say a redheaded lass has a temper," he murmured from behind her, his fingers still toying with the long, wavy mass. "They say she's too full of passion, and more than likely a witch."

"I've heard all that before," she returned. "And worse. Is it what ye think of me?"

"I think ye'd run wild if ye could, keeping yerself away from everyone and everything. Ye think there's someaught odd aboot yerself, because ye dunnae ken why other lasses act the way they do, and why ye're the one who's in the wrong." Draping a long lock of her hair over her shoulder, he moved around to sit on his backside half facing her. "Ye're unique, and I reckon that's nae an easy thing to be. And I'm honored ye trust me enough to be with ye."

She scowled, wiping at her abruptly damp cheek. "Stop saying nice things and bed me, ye brute. I didnae come downstairs for conversation." Even if it was the nicest thing anyone had ever said to her.

"Well, then. Yer wish, wildcat."

He pushed her flat again and went to work unfastening her trousers. No one had ever done that for her before, and certainly not a six-and-a-half-foot, very aroused Highland lord. When he fumbled at it she tried to push his hands away to see to it herself, but he only scowled at her and refused to budge.

When they finally came open, he flashed her a deep grin. "That's better. Now lift up. I've a yen to see ye naked."

That was only fair, since he was already nude but for his boots. She lifted her hips, and he pulled her trousers down past her thighs. When she settled again, he lifted her legs, running his palms down from her thighs to her calves, removing the material as he went. One by one he pulled off her boots, then stripped the garment the rest of the way over her feet. His own big boots followed.

Before she could wonder what she was supposed to do next, he twisted onto one hip and kissed her again, slowly and deeply. Luxuriously, almost. He'd told her to do as she pleased, so she ran her palms down his spine to his backside, felt his muscles clench and relax beneath her touch. When he lowered his face to her breasts, though, she couldn't seem to do anything but moan and drag her fingers through his thick hair. Nothing had ever felt this good, this sharply pleasurable, before.

When his fingers drifted down her stomach and then between her legs, she squeezed her knees together before she could command them to be still. "I'm sorry," she rasped, her breath so uneven she was surprised she hadn't fainted.

"Dunnae apologize to me," he returned, lifting his head briefly before returning his attention to her breasts. "I've nae a thing to complain aboot. Just try not to yank all my hair oot."

She snorted, loosening her hard grip on his lanky black hair. This time when both of his hands went to her knees, she made herself cooperate. How odd, that her insides wanted him so badly, but her body couldn't seem to figure out what in the world to do about it. Perhaps he was correct, and she needed to stop thinking so hard.

He brushed a finger up along her most intimate place, and she shut her eyes, moaning before she could stop herself. For a man with two hands and one mouth, he seemed to be touching her everywhere at the same time, each sensation more pleasurable than the last.

"Ye want me, lass," he murmured, parting her folds and slipping inside with one wicked finger. She bucked against him, moaning again.

"I do," she managed, "so stop teasing me and get to it."

"This is all part of the fun. But, if ye insist . . ." Munro shifted over her, keeping her knees apart with his own. Resting on his elbows, he brushed hair out of her face. "Look at me, lass."

Catriona opened her eyes again. "I dunnae need to see ye to know exactly where ye are."

He grinned. "Aye. But I've someaught to say to ye. I'm nae accustomed to having virgins, but I'll be as gentle with ye as I know how to be. It'll hurt ye, though. I'd give anything if it wouldnae, but that's the way of it. Nae fer long, but it'll hurt."

She met his gaze, his face a foot from hers, looking down at her with a combination of concern and lust that made her ache inside. "Do ye think me a lass who shies away from a bit of pain?"

"Nae. I'm only being gentlemanly and warning ye."

"Then I'm warned. Get on with it, giant."

"Say my true name, first."

She narrowed her eyes, but he was stubborn enough that he wouldn't relent until she did as he asked. "Munro," she uttered, too breathily.

"That's more like it."

Munro sank down over her, his cock pressing at her entrance and then slowly, ever so slowly, sliding inside of her until she felt pressure. He took a breath that she could feel against her own ribs, then canted his hips forward and pushed deeply. She squeezed one eye shut at the sharp pain of it, and he froze again.

"Tell me when ye want me to move, wildcat," he murmured, taking her mouth again.

Almost immediately the pain began to subside, and she became aware of the indescribable sensation of his big cock filling her, his hips against hers, the hard, controlled weight of him on her. The . . . intimacy of their connection felt both wicked and madly romantic, in a way that had never touched her before. And he was holding so still, as if he feared she might break beneath him.

She reached up to grip his shoulders. "I want ye to move."

He did so, pulling back, and then entering her so fully she couldn't do anything but hold on to him, arch her back and groan. Beginning slowly, he entered and retreated so that she could feel every inch of him moving inside her. The heated tightness across her abdomen suddenly shattered into spasms of pleasure.

"Christ, lass," he groaned, his pace increasing as she continued to shiver around him.

If that was the "little death" the poets wrote about, she could see why they seemed so obsessed with it. "More," she ordered breathlessly.

"Aye."

After that, she couldn't conjure a coherent thought to save her life. Instead all she could do was feel—feel him entering her again and again, hard, faster, his harsh breathing against her neck, his hands at her breasts, squeezing and tugging in rhythm with his lovemaking.

She spasmed again as he pushed deeply into her and held himself there, shuddering. Ecstasy. That was what it was. Pure ecstasy. He'd claimed her, as he'd said he would, and she'd claimed him. Munro kissed her once more, then lowered his head to her shoulder, his breath hot and quick against her skin.

Munro. Bear. Would he say they were joined, now? That they were bound together? Handfasted, even? She wanted him to say that, even if it was an impossible dream. From his reaction she hadn't done anything horribly wrong, and more than anything she wished to do it again. With him. In a bed, this time. But that couldn't happen, either.

In fact, she'd told herself that she'd allowed this because it was meant to cure her of her . . . need to be with him. That she could part from him now, and go forward with the plans she'd made for herself weeks ago. Years ago, really, when she'd first overheard some of the daughters of other MacDonald lords giggling about how odd she was, wondering if she took her meals in the hound kennels and if she peed standing up.

She didn't feel odd now, at this moment, but she would again. And however much new knowledge she'd just gained, another man wouldn't be as . . . circumspect as Bear was. He wouldn't find her enchanting, or unique. Not in a good way.

"Let me up," she snapped, pushing at his shoulders. "I cannae breathe."

Breathing hard himself, Munro rose onto his hands and knees, reluctantly pulling out of her. She looked half panicked, so he settled onto his backside and leaned against the stack of bricks behind him. A hundred years ago, he would have thought a lass with Catriona's wild and sensuous nature a selkie. If she were a creature of myth, that would certainly help to explain why his want for her had changed into a need, as if he could never have her enough, be close enough, be inside her long enough, to be satisfied.

On the blankets in front of him, she didn't seem to have any sort of the same emotional turmoil sprinting through her. Instead, she slipped her man's shirt back on over her head, hiding her delicious tits from his view. *Damn.* He wasn't finished looking at them. Or fondling them. Or tasting them. When she dragged over her trousers and began pulling them on, he frowned.

"Are ye tardy fer an appointment somewhere?" he asked, nudging one of her boots farther away from her with his bare toes.

"Yer two lads'll be back here any time now," she returned, tying her splendid, flame-colored hair back into its loose tail.

"Nae fer an hour or more. Ye cannae be scared of me *now.*"

"I never was scared of ye."

He tried to catch her gaze, but she seemed determined not to look at him. Another reason for her hurry occurred to him, and he reached out to catch hold of her wrist. "Did I hurt ye, Catriona?" he asked in a lower voice. "I ken my first claiming of ye caused ye some pain. That willnae happen again. But if I was too rough, or I did someaught ye didnae like, ye must tell me. Because I swear I'll nae hurt ye again. Body or soul."

Dark brown eyes finally lifted to meet his. "That's quite the claim, Bear," she said, and reached across his bare legs for her stray boot. "Nae. Ye didnae hurt me, any more than ye said would happen. I liked it. I like the way ye touch me."

Well, thank God for that, at least, even if it didn't help explain her hurry to dress. But now that he knew she'd enjoyed being with him, finding the reason for her determination to flee became even more vital. Lifting his knee, he sent her off balance. There was no sense being a big, strong man unless he could occasionally use his height and strength to his advantage. "Then what's yer damned hurry, lass?" Twisting her to face him, he caught her up in his lap.

"Let go," she ordered, digging a sharp elbow into his bare chest.

"Nae. I dunnae think I will."

"But ye're naked."

"Aye. So I am. And so were ye, five minutes ago. Ye'd best tell me what's amiss, because I'm nae a warlock who can hear yer thoughts." He risked getting punched in the head and kissed her, long and deeply. "And however much ye argued with me before, ye're mine now, fer certain. Ye're obligated to tell me what's troubling ye."

"Ye're a brute and a liar," she retorted, thudding a hand against his ear. "Let me go."

"Nae."

She fought him for the space of another dozen heartbeats. Just as he began to think that he truly was going to have to let her go before she could hurt herself against him, she subsided. "I told ye that I dunnae know how to play this game. I didnae agree to being owned. And I dunnae ken if I'm supposed to sit at yer feet and make moon eyes at ye, or if we're to pretend naught happened, or if—"

"Maddening," he muttered feelingly, and caught her face in his hands for a deep, plundering kiss. And to his relief and joy, she kissed him back with as much heat as he gave.

"That doesnae help," she growled back, digging the pads of her fingers into his shoulders and seeking his mouth again.

Munro didn't lift his head again until he ran out of

air. "I cannae give ye all the answers ye want, wildcat," he panted, nibbling at her jaw, "but I'll tell ye this. If ye gazed at me with moon eyes I'd think ye'd lost yer senses. As fer the rest, I mean to recall that someaught happened between us, as much as I mean fer it to happen again. What we are together I dunnae know, because ye havenae told me yer thoughts, or yer story. I reckon, though, that I'll stay close by ye while I figure it oot. And I dunnae mean to let another man put his hands on ye." He kissed her again. "Now. How does that sound to ye, my lass?"

It wasn't at all what he wanted to say to her, but clearly at this moment she needed to feel . . . safe. Telling her how tangled up in her he felt wouldn't reassure her. It didn't reassure *him*. In fact, if not for his sharp need to keep her close by, he would be having a bit of a panic, himself.

Hell's bells, he'd bedded his share of lasses, and yet he'd never felt this lingering, strengthening yearning to simply remain in the lass's company—to the point that he had repeatedly lied to his own clan chief. It wasn't simply lust, either. Touching her, chatting with her, gazing at her—all those things felt equally important. Vital, even. And seeing her trying to walk away confounded him utterly. Did she not feel the pull between them?

"I have some things to figure out, myself," she said slowly, shifting to run a fingertip down his breastbone. Responding goose bumps lifted on his skin. "But I do know that we—together—wouldn't end well. I told ye that before."

"Dunnae be such a pessimist." Taking his cue from the way she kept touching him, Munro pulled the tail of her shirt free from her trousers, running a hand up beneath the material to close over her left breast. "We ended well a few moments ago."

Her shivering moan made him hard. Having her once again seemed more vital than anything else he could conjure. Shoving her shirt up as far as he could, he bent his head and took a plump tit in his mouth. Sucking, flicking his tongue across her nipple, he pressed her arse against his cock so firmly he was somewhat surprised he didn't tear straight through the seat of her trousers to get at her.

He plunged a hand between her thighs, pressing up in rhythm with his sucking. Of course he was far stronger than she, and he had to keep that in mind always—but now he didn't have to be quite as patient, quite as gentle, or quite as slow.

"Bear, my heart's about to explode," she groaned, arching beneath his hand.

"I'll tend ye," he returned. Swiftly he unbuttoned her damned marvelous trousers again and yanked them down past her thighs. Then, putting his hands beneath her arse, he shifted her over him and settled her down over his reaching cock.

Tight, warm heat engulfed him. Bricks fell off the far side of the pile as he held down on his thighs and thrust up into her, hard and fast. With a keening wail she came, while he plunged up into her again and again. Abruptly with a roaring surge he climaxed, spilling into her.

Sweet Saint Bridget. He knew how to bed women, and he knew how to take precautions with them. If Ranulf had made one thing clear as they were growing up, it was that litters of MacLawry bastards would not aid in keeping the clan secure. Bastards meant resentments and tangled lines of succession and—at worst— wars and fractured alliances.

And there he was, holding a MacDonald lass as close to him as bones and skin would allow, and he'd done nothing to prevent a pregnancy. Just the opposite, in fact. Glengask would have his head—or some other body part, more likely—for it, if his oldest brother knew. Munro wasn't certain losing his head, at least, would make much difference, because he'd clearly already lost his mind.

"How much can we do that?" Cat muttered, still out of breath, her arms around his shoulders.

"I'm disinclined to give ye a number, because if we reach it ye might ask me to stop."

She sighed. "It's easier to be naked here with ye," she commented, her expression easing into a rueful smile, "but I do need to think about some things. And I cannae think sensibly with ye touching me and . . ."

"And being inside ye?" he prompted, shifting beneath her so she could feel him still filling her.

"Aye." She flexed her bottom, and this time he was the one who groaned. "I cannae make sense of anything with yer body here, and yer eyes gazing at me."

Munro chuckled. "Do my eyes offend ye, then?"

"Nae. They dunnae. Now release me, giant."

"I'll let ye stand up," he countered, helping her to her feet. "I'll nae release ye."

Her scowl both amused and troubled him. "Stop saying that," she ordered. "I'm taking a sandwich, and I'm going fer a walk. Dunnae follow me."

He stopped himself before he could announce that he would gladly follow her anywhere, or that he belonged to her as much as she belonged to him, because clearly she didn't want to hear it. Whatever had troubled her since the moment they'd met continued to dog her, and until she agreed to tell him about it, all he could do was stay close by her until she decided she could trust him.

It seemed a worthy goal, even if it would please him at least as much as it pleased her. If she would simply tell him about her damned dragon, he would smash it into wee bits and slay it for her. Until then, all he could do was repair her house—because it *was* hers, whatever anyone else said—and kiss her senseless until she fell for him as hard as he'd evidently fallen for her.

"Nae."

"Aye," Bear returned, folding his arms across his chest and having the gall to look amused.

"Ye said ye had to come stay the night with me because I wouldnae be safe alone," Catriona retorted. "Which is daft, because I'm the one who kept Elizabeth safe before ye ever knew we were in the Highlands, but me going into the village with ye? How is that safe?"

"Because I'll be with ye. And because ye've spent too much time alone."

That, she had. She could feel the silence sometimes, heavy and very, very large, closing in on her. His solution, however, seemed like it would create more problems than it could possibly solve. "If ye want to go to the tavern with yer friends, then go. I've nae said a word aboot how ye should spend yer evenings. Ye cannae want to spend them all here on the hard floor, anyway."

Instead of replying, he dug into the burlap sack he'd brought with him and produced her floppy straw hat. "I liberated this from Elizabeth's bedchamber. I'll help ye tuck up yer hair. In that heavy coat and this hat, with the rain outside, ye'll nae get a second glance. Drovers come through An Soadh to drink at the Bonny Bruce all the time. Ye're just a short drover with long eye-lashes."

Part of her wanted to go. The Lion's Paw, the tavern nearest MacColl House on Islay, had always been full of song and laughter. It had also been full of whispering when she and her father visited, most of the gossip aimed at her appearance. Here, though, no one knew who she was. If she could pass for a man, some stranger no one had any reason to suspect was anything other than who she—or he, rather—claimed, there couldn't be any harm in it. Could there? A mulled wine would be so nice on a cold night like this one.

"Give me the damned hat," she finally said, and went to pull on the heavy coat Bear had stolen from the Marquis of Glengask for her.

She pinned her heavy ponytail atop her head and jammed the hat over it. With no mirror she had to rely on Bear, but he seemed assured that she could pass for a lad. And because she already trusted him more than she likely should, already liked him more than she knew she should, she followed him out of the kitchen and into the rain where he'd left Saturn.

Before he swung onto the gelding he pulled a pistol from his pocket and stuffed it into hers. "Because I'm being cautious," he said, flipping up the front of her hat and bending to give her a warm, openmouthed kiss. "Dunnae shoot anyone if ye can avoid it."

Catriona swallowed, the warmth of his mouth and the cold of the rain on her face startlingly intoxicating. Perhaps a cold whisky would serve her better than a hot wine. He didn't seem to expect an answer, because he didn't wait for her to reply before he mounted the gray and held a hand to swing her up behind him.

She'd ridden astride for her entire life. That was nothing new. Far more interesting was the way she slid her arms around his hard waist and beneath his coat. It would keep her hands warmer that way, she decided. As did resting her cheek against his broad back. Going into An Soadh was of course a risk. But because it meant spending more time with him, she turned into a brainless, flighty lass and agreed to it.

It was nearly an hour later and somewhere past midnight when they pulled up beside a two-story structure made of stone and wood, the shutters closed over the windows and light and the sound of bagpipes leaking from beneath the door. Bear handed her down, and hopped to the muddy ground beside her. "Stay close, and try nae to talk."

"And from ye, nae kissing, and nae holding my hand," she countered. "I ken how to behave like a man, giant."

"Nae. I doubt ye've fooled anyone into thinking ye a man. But here, they'll all think ye a lad unless ye give 'em reason to believe otherwise." He tugged the brim of her hat forward just a shade, then turned and left her to follow him inside.

He had a point. Everyone on Islay knew she was a lass who dressed like a lad. She hadn't needed to fool anyone. Her heart stammered a little as she kept close pace on the big man's heels and entered the Bonny Bruce.

Immediately they were greeted with a chorus of "Laird Bear" in both male and female tones. Well, she knew he was charming. It made sense that she wasn't the only one to think so. In fact, from the drinks tilted in his direction and the eyelashes flitting at him, he was extremely popular. And in no need at all of additional companionship from someone as odd as her.

"Mulled rum cider fer me and this lad I found here," Bear rumbled, putting a hand on her shoulder.

"Were ye lost, lad?" a grizzled older man asked slurrily, over a glass half filled with whisky.

"Aye," she returned, in as low-pitched a voice as she could manage.

"Found him near half drowned in the rain," Bear took up. "What was yer name? Porter. Aye. Porter. Up from Fort William and looking for a herd to drive."

"Ye've come to the right place, Porter," another man commented. "The MacLawry herds are the fattest in the Highlands."

"More important than that, where've ye been, Laird Bear?" a female voice asked, and a hand coiled around one of his arms. "All the lasses in the valley've been wailing with missing ye."

Munro chuckled, slipping free of the very buxom woman's grip as he made a show of guiding his new "friend" Porter to a chair at a small table to one side of the room. "I havenae heard any such thing, Bethia Peterkin. And ye know I've been listening."

Sitting opposite him, Catriona curved her lips in what she hoped was a smile. The idea of a mulled cider didn't sound quite as bonny now that she knew how much the lasses of the valley missed Bear's company. Presumably in their beds. He sent her a glance, evidently reading her expression. "I've been where I want to be," he murmured.

A pretty young girl brought over their drinks, the Bethia woman on her heels. "Tell me ye've missed me, Bear," she cooed, and sat herself across his thighs. "Ye know I've missed ye."

"I've been occupied, Bethia," he returned, setting the

woman onto her feet again with no discernible effort on his part. "Dunnae tell me ye've let yerself be lonely."

The room laughed, and Bethia Peterkin blushed prettily. She was just the sort of lass who'd said the sharpest things about Cat, always behind her back of course. This time she at least received an assessing look. Evidently she was too short to interest the lady, because a moment later Bethia swept away to pull some other man into a dance by the fireplace.

"Did ye court her?" she asked, keeping her voice well below the level of chatting and singing around them.

"Bethia? We're acquainted," he admitted, tapping his mug against hers and sitting back to take a drink.

"Like ye and I are aquainted?"

"I'm nae a virgin, wildcat. And it's a wee pair of villages here on MacLawry land. I dunnae generally go aboot seducing women from rival clans, ye ken."

"I'm from a rival clan."

He grinned, the expression heating her insides. "That, ye are. I've nae looked at another woman since I set eyes on ye, and I reckon I never will." Munro leaned forward again, making a show of shoving her mug of cider closer to her. "Ye're nae my first. But ye'll be my last, Catriona."

"Ye're that certain, are ye?" she responded, unable to keep her voice from shaking just a little. No one said romantic things like that to her. Especially not men who looked like he did, men who knew her and inevitably found her odd and even a threat to their so-called manliness with her skill at shooting and tracking.

Green eyes held hers. "Aye. I'm that certain. I'll nae repeat what I said to ye before, because firstly ye nearly bit my head off, and secondly, I dunnae want cider dumped over my head. But ye and I are a pair." He

Chapter Twelve

B ear, wake up, ye slug."
   Munro opened his eyes in the near darkness to the sensation of Cat shoving at his shoulder. For a bare moment he couldn't quite place where he was, until the naked woman sitting up beside him pinched his ear. Hard. "Dammit, woman!" he said, swatting at her hand.

"The sun'll be up in an hour, Bear. Ye need to go."

Blinking, he sat up and slapped himself on the cheek. "Ye might have thought to wake me with a kiss, instead of trying to tear off my ear. Especially after ye had such a fine time in my company last night."

"I *did* kiss ye, ye brute," Catriona returned, taking the blanket to wrap around herself and leaving him in the cold as she padded over to stir the fire in the hearth back to life. "Ye said 'haggis,' and held yer arm up like ye were delivering a toast."

He had been dreaming about food, now that he thought about it. A great feast with his family around him, and Cat seated at his side. The cold, dark kitchen at Haldane Abbey seemed a poor substitute for a grand banquet hall, but at least he had her with him. It would do for now. The haggis and feasting could wait.

Shrugging into his shirt, he stood and retrieved his kilt. "Ye kissed me?" he repeated, snatching a kiss as he bent down for his boots.

"Nae," she returned. "I said that because I didnae want a giant like ye weeping about having his ear pinched."

"Very kind of ye, lass." He snorted.

"Aye. I'm a true lady."

"Ye'll nae hear an argument from me." Munro finished belting the plaid into place, then stretched his back. "I need to fetch ye a mattress, Cat. I've slept on bare dirt more comfortable than this damned stone floor."

"I dunnae need a mattress; ye're quite comfortable, and warm."

Taking her shoulder, he turned her to face him and gave her a soft, slow kiss. "Ye can call me yer mattress, lass, but dunnae ferget the poky bits."

She laughed as she kissed him back, the blanket sagging when she lifted her arm to tangle her fingers into his hair. "I like the poky bits." Then she pulled back on his hair, backing him away from her. "Now go."

"Ye've a hard heart, wildcat."

"And ye've a stubborn one. I told ye to stay home, Bear, just as I have for the past week. Ye cannae be getting more than three or four hours of sleep each night, and still ye persist in riding here every night." Dark eyes searched his. "If yer brother knew ye've been riding about alone in the middle of the night, he'd burn this place to the ground with me in it."

"I'll nae have ye oot here alone in the dark, Cat. I'm nae arguing with ye aboot it."

The idea that she was spending so much time alone anyway troubled him; the thought of what could happen at night with only a kitchen door and a musket between her and any danger terrified him. Since she wouldn't come to Glengask, he came to her. If that meant retreating to his bedchamber to wait for the house to go to sleep so he could ride out to Haldane every night, so be it. He wouldn't have been able to sleep in his own bed while he worried about her out in the wilds, anyway.

"Then stop kissing me and put on yer boots."

He did as she said, but only after a last kiss to show her that he didn't intend to be ordered about by anyone— even her. Slipping out at night to protect her, to be with her, would all be for nothing if he didn't manage to return to Glengask and his bed before the house rose for the day. "I'll be back by ten o'clock," he said, shrugging into his heavy, dark coat. "I'll bring ye some fresh eggs and more tea. Is there anything else ye desire?"

Her lips curved in a soft smile that made him want to shed his clothes and fall onto the blankets with her again, the future beyond these moments be damned. Whatever he'd thought about a night with her curing his obsession, he'd been dead wrong. If anything, the desire, the need, to be close by her overwhelmed even his sense of loyalty to his own family.

"Some paper and pencil. I'd like to send Elizabeth a note."

Guilt tugged at him. He'd barely spared a thought for Cat's sister in a week, despite seeing her daily. In his own defense he'd only given his word to see her safe— and she was definitely well protected. Beyond that, all of his attention remained on Catriona, whether he was at Haldane Abbey or Glengask Castle, awake or asleep.

"I'll fetch them fer ye, lass. Or, I *could* bring Elizabeth with me today."

Warm arms wrapped around his middle from behind to straighten his kilt. "Och, ye're an embarrassment," she commented, even though he was fairly certain he knew how to put on his own clothes. Whenever she approached him first, touched him first, his heart stuttered, even when she had an excuse for the contact.

This lass, who could survive on her own in the Highlands, find her own food, and keep her sister safe—this supremely capable lass continued to baffle him with her hesitancy. It was as if she couldn't believe he could want her. At least now after a week of being in his arms every night she could admit that she enjoyed being with him. Her touch felt like a triumph, and he reveled in it.

"I'd love to see her," she said, "but she's safer at Glengask."

"Dunnae ye mean to say that ye're safer with her at Glengask? She's nae precisely been a secret. The letter her mother sent, accusing us of being barbarians trying to sully her good name, made me wish she'd come up here in person so I could set her on her arse, but it was all bluster, ye ken."

"I ken. I'm just relieved that yer brother has even the Sassannach aristocracy terrified of him. I noticed she didnae threaten to send Visford up to fetch back his betrothed."

He sent her a rueful smile. "I'm nae acquainted with this Visford, but I reckon a rich duke with a reputation for taking young brides and then driving them to death doesnae want to go to the effort of fighting to get one of them to return. He'll go find another young lass whose family needs money."

"It makes me wish I'd paid him a wee visit before I left London with Elizabeth," she said coolly.

"What? Ye'd have murdered him?" He didn't believe it, but he understood the sentiment. As for him, if the Duke of Visford had ever come within a mile of his own sister, well, the law in London would still be looking for Visford's carcass—not that they would ever find it.

She shrugged. "I cannae answer that. I ken he would at least think I might murder him."

"Fair enough. What might a manly, well-muscled lad do to help ye, then?"

Her arms withdrew again, leaving him chilled both inside and outside. When he turned around, the set expression on her face didn't warm him any, either. "Ye cannae do a thing more than ye've already done, Bear."

"But ye're a mystery," he pressed. "I want to know why ye'd rather sleep on a cold stone floor than in a warm, soft bed."

She walked over to the table, her shoulders high and square. Tense. "I've done all I can to tell ye that we shouldnae be together, Bear. But I'll be damned before I'd tell ye someaught that might get ye hurt. So ye can decide: either go away and dunnae come back, or leave things as they are. I . . . This is fine enough, isnae? Just me and ye?"

Perhaps he was more cynical than she was, but he didn't think the world would keep its distance for much longer, no matter how much the idea of just the two of them, even on a hard stone floor, appealed to him. Given the prickle of worry at the back of his skull, trouble *was* coming. And he would feel better for both of them if he knew from what, precisely, she was hiding.

"I like the idea of just ye and me," he said aloud. "Kiss me good-bye, and I'll see if I can manage to bring yer *piuthar* here withoot a retinue of armed Highlanders."

Catriona sighed, evidently giving up on the argument. "Stubborn man." Sliding her arms around his shoulders, she kissed him softly on the mouth. "Are ye on my side, Munro? Nae matter what happens?"

"Aye," he returned immediately. "I dunnae lie to my family fer just anyone, ye ken. Only fer ye, Catriona."

"That doesnae make me feel better, you know. I dunnae want ye lying to yer clan chief. Yer own brother. I'm still accustomed to nae having an ally."

He put his hands on her shoulders. "I *am* yer ally. Bark at me if ye like, my fine lass; I've nae plans to go away from ye. And I reckon I'll do as I see fit, whether ye approve or nae."

When she returned to the fire he continued to watch her, her confident, graceful motions, her scarlet hair trailing lushly down her bare shoulders. She could be gentle, and kind, and sensitive, but she wasn't a delicate lass; the Highlands and the way she'd chosen to live in them made her strong and practical and fierce and stubborn as the devil all at the same time. He'd met rough lasses, and ones who looked like a stiff breeze could break them. Never had he met anyone like Catriona MacColl.

"I love ye," he breathed, unwilling to risk the trouble saying it more loudly would cause.

She turned around. "What was that?"

Blast it. "I said I'll find some gloves fer ye. We'll have snow before long."

"Thank ye, Bear."

As he went outside to saddle Saturn, he could tell himself that admitting aloud how he felt would only drive her to flee, but it wasn't only that. He was a big, loud brute of a man his brothers liked to bring along with them because his presence intimidated people. How often had he heard that he hadn't a poetic or a romantic bone in his body, that his only taste was in his mouth? He'd almost begun to believe it—until he'd stumbled across Cat. She was a lass to make a man think of poetry. Fierce, old, bloody poetry. And fires, and heat, and sin. And he had no intention of ever letting her go.

With the sky beginning to lighten in the east, he pushed Saturn to a gallop the moment they reached the main trail. He could call this an early morning ride if someone spied him now, but the farther from Haldane he could get, the better. If either Ranulf or Arran realized he was making midnight visits to the abbey, his brothers would demand an explanation that he wasn't going to give them.

As he reached the stable he let out his breath, dismounting to lead the big gray into the warm building. Weariness pulled at him; Cat's assessment that he was only getting three or four hours of sleep a night was fairly accurate. Unless he wanted to try dragging her away from Haldane, though, riding back and forth two or three times a day had become the best solution.

"I'll see to him, m'laird," a gravelly voice said from a few feet behind him.

Stifling a curse, Munro whipped around to see Debny, Glengask's head groom, wiping his hands on a cloth and eyeing him in the light of the single lantern illuminating the large building. "I didnae mean to wake ye," he said aloud. "I felt a bit restless this morning."

"Dunnae apologize, Laird Bear. I've a colicky mare I've been tending, anyway. By the by, some of the lads wanted me to tell ye, they'd be pleased to help ye with rebuilding old Haldane, even if it is haunted. Ye and Peter dunnae need to do it all yerselves."

"I appreciate that, Debny. Tell the lads I may take 'em up on their offer." He wouldn't, of course, as long as Cat remained skittish, but it was nice to know he would have help if he wanted it.

"I'll do that. Go get yerself some breakfast, m'laird. I'll fetch Saturn a nice bucket of oats."

Saturn had earned it, after a week of working both day and night. Nodding, Munro trudged up to the sprawling house. With the sun not quite up he was hungrier for sleep than for breakfast, unusual as that was, so he passed by the kitchen for the servants' stairs. None of the other bedchamber doors were open yet, and he slipped into his own and shut it quietly behind him. Then he collapsed onto the bed, boots and all, to squeeze out another hour or so of sleep—and to dream about food and the redheaded wildcat who'd captured his heart.

"Bear!" Sudden pounding reverberated around him.

Why the devil was everyone interrupting his damned sleep? Opening his eyes, Munro sat up and swung his booted feet around to the floor. "Come in, fer God's sake!"

His door opened, and Ranulf stepped into the room. A hundred thoughts tangled through his head at his brother's set expression—had Debny said something about his predawn ride? Had Visford decided to take issue with the removal of his betrothed after all? Had someone discovered Catriona? *Bloody hell.*

"Duncan Lenox is here," his brother announced. "He spotted—did ye sleep in yer clothes?"

Frowning, Munro smoothed his shirt. "Aye. Apparently I did. What did Duncan spot?"

Duncan Lenox was a MacLawry chieftain, living with his three younger sisters and his Sassannach bride three miles or so to the northeast. His property edged up to Campbell territory, and if he'd spied something, it likely wasn't anything good. And if trouble was on its way, he needed to get to Haldane. Catriona was on her own there.

"He isnae certain. A dozen riders surrounding a coach, and MacDonald colors on display. They'll be here any time now, and I want ye—"

"MacDonald?" Munro snapped back, his heart thudding. MacDonalds were the worst kind of trouble he could imagine. "Damnation."

"I gave ye my word, Bear," his brother returned. "Elizabeth MacColl is under my protection. We'll negotiate someaught acceptable to both parties, and the lass will be yers."

Munro stopped breathing. Perhaps he was still asleep after all. Ranulf knew? Aye, his brother had a reputation for being all-knowing, but he'd been so careful. But the marquis wasn't flaying him alive for keeping Cat hidden. Something didn't make sense.

Abruptly it occurred to him. Ranulf was talking about a match with Elizabeth. And his brother might have been surprised by the MacDonalds' timing, but he wasn't surprised they were coming. "Ye sent the MacDonald word that ye had Randall MacColl's daughter here."

"I didnae want them thinking we'd taken her against her will. She said she fled London with nae more than a note to her mama, but it wasnae the English that concerned me. I dunnae want any misunderstandings that could cause a fight."

"But ye didnae see fit to tell me what ye did?" Munro might not know precisely what the problem was between

Cat and the rest of the MacDonalds, but he *did* know she'd fled to escape them. And now—bloody hell, if she caught sight of them, she would be gone before he had a chance to tell her . . . anything.

"Ye've been a mite stubborn and closemouthed," his brother returned. "Ye'd have to approach the MacDonalds sooner or later. I'm making it easier on ye. I'll shake hands and be polite. Ye just have to show yerself."

"Ye're making it easier on me, are ye?" Munro wanted to punch something, and he wanted to get to Haldane immediately. And he couldn't do either one without causing even more problems. Hell, he couldn't even inform his brother that the family was trying to pair him with the wrong MacColl sister. "I dunnae recall asking fer yer assistance. With anything."

"Well, ye have it anyway. Are we going to brawl, or are ye going to put on someaught clean and meet the coach with me?"

He cursed under his breath. "Am I supposed to smile, or growl?"

"Just do what ye do best."

Munro stomped over to his wardrobe. "Ye have nae idea what I do best," he muttered. He caught Ranulf eyeing him suspiciously, and took a breath. He would have a bloody mountain of actions to answer for later, but not today. "Ye didnae send for the Duke of Visford as well, did ye?" he asked.

"Nae. I dunnae give a damn aboot Visford. Even the lass's mother barely managed a bluster. The Mac-Donalds, though, I find mildly interesting. They might even turn oot to be useful." The marquis backed up, catching the door handle in one hand. "Ye've twenty minutes or so. I suggest ye look fierce, but be reasonable."

"I'm always fierce," he answered automatically, having had this conversation a hundred times before. "If ye want reasonable, send fer Arran."

"This is fer yer lass, Bear. Keep that in mind." Ranulf pulled the door closed, leaving him alone with his thoughts, such as they were.

At some other moment he might have been amused that the MacLawrys and Catriona both thought Elizabeth MacColl would be a good match for him. But he'd only met one woman in his life who could match him, and he wasn't about to give her up even if he couldn't tell anyone else about her.

Be reasonable with the MacDonalds. He might, if he knew what they required in exchange for leaving Catriona alone. Since he didn't, the best he could wish for was that they would fall into the loch and drown. He felt like both hands were tied behind his back, and the only way to resolve his dilemma would be to talk to Cat.

If he meant to continue lying to his family, he wanted it to be for a reason—a reason he understood and with which he agreed. Unfortunately for him and for the MacDonalds, he was going to have to meet them without knowing if they were friends or enemies. *Her* friends or enemies, which made them his.

Swiftly he shaved off his stubble and cleaned his teeth, then donned a clean kilt and shirt. He set aside his work boots in favor of more proper stockings and gillie brogues. Shoving his sharp *sgian dubh* into his right stocking, he ran a comb through his too long, unruly hair and headed downstairs.

Elizabeth stood in the foyer already, her expression excited. He couldn't blame his suspicion of the MacDonalds on her if she kept chattering about how much she looked forward to meeting members of her own clan. And he couldn't warn her to be cautious about what she said to them, because Ranulf, Charlotte, and Arran waited there, as well. Evidently the marquis had taken his advice and sent for his more diplomatic sibling. Squaring his shoulders, Munro stepped into the group.

"What did Duncan see, exactly?" he asked.

"He was oot riding with his Julia when he saw a coach and outriders heading this way doon the main road. He said they were flying a MacDonald banner, but couldn't decide if it was a peace gesture, or if they were declaring war on us."

"So ye're going to step oot onto the drive and hope they dunnae shoot ye?" However much his attention centered around Cat, this wasn't just about her. If the Mac-Donalds meant trouble, he wasn't about to allow Ranulf to step into the middle of it.

"I'm a cautious lad," the marquis commented, lifting an eyebrow. "I have armed men standing at the front of the hoose, and up on the widow's walk. If the Mac-Donalds mean trouble, they willnae get very far with it."

"But they're my . . . cousins, or some such thing," Elizabeth broke in, her happy grin fading. "Why would they want to make trouble?"

"I dunnae think they will, lass," Arran put in, sending her an encouraging smile. "Anytime two clans meet when they've nae had dealings together before, we try to be . . . prepared."

"Oh. That makes sense then, I suppose."

"Ye and Charlotte stay inside until I decide everyone means to behave themselves. I anticipate a friendly chat and everyone leaving satisfied," the marquis continued, nodding. "After all, we've something of mutual benefit to discuss."

Or so the MacLawrys thought, anyway. The Mac-Donalds might be here to discuss his marriage with

Elizabeth, or they might not be. Munro looked at his gathered family members again. A lie about who he might be wooing was one thing. Protecting Cat from questions she didn't want to answer was one thing. Keeping information from his family that could put them in danger was something else entirely.

Damnation. This, he hadn't anticipated, and while he could blame the arrival of the MacDonalds on Ranulf, anything that happened next would land squarely on his shoulders. "Ran, I need a word with ye. In private."

His oldest brother frowned. "Ye've poor timing, Bear. Can it wait?"

"Nae. It'd best be now."

"Then come—"

The pipers on the roof began playing. He was too late. Now the best he could do was keep everyone else safe. Including the woman living two miles away who had no idea the MacDonalds were literally on her doorstep.

Ranulf sent a last glance at his youngest brother, tempted for a moment to have the MacDonalds wait outside regardless of the consequences. After all, he had invited a correspondence, not a visit. Something clearly troubled Bear, and he didn't think it was simply because he'd sent word to Elizabeth's distant family without receiving permission to do so. Firstly, he was the MacLawry, and he didn't need anyone's permission to do anything. Secondly, he'd done it to help both Bear and the clan MacLawry.

Making whoever the MacDonald had deigned to send south wait, though, could well cause the very trouble he'd been attempting to prevent. And so he nodded at Cooper, and the butler pulled open the double front doors.

He stepped outside first, as was his duty and his right. Generally Bear and Arran would flank him, but today his mountainous youngest brother moved directly to his side, his posture decidedly . . . unfriendly. Aye, he could read his brother's moods better than most, but a hostile Munro MacLawry would be difficult for anyone to miss. And considering he was about to meet his future in-laws, however distant they might be, his demeanor didn't make much sense.

"Easy, Bear," he muttered, as the coach, its green and blue and red MacDonald colors flying, drew to a halt in front of them. "The lass's disagreement is with a Sassannach duke, nae with the MacDonalds. Dunnae start trouble here fer no reason."

"I reckon I'll decide whether or nae to be friendly *after* I make their acquaintance and hear their terms," his brother returned.

"Ye'll be cautiously friendly until I tell ye otherwise," Ranulf countered.

Munro sent him a hard glance, his jaw clenched. "Aye," he grunted after a moment, rolling his shoulders. "Cautiously friendly."

The dozen outriders, half of them in MacDonald plaid, dismounted to gather about the coach door. Whoever happened to be inside, his guards, at least, had come prepared for trouble. None of them carried weapons other than the traditional daggers in boots and stockings, but Ranulf had seen for himself how much damage a well-placed *sgian dubh* could cause. Then again, he couldn't blame them for their caution. They had a six-and-a-half-foot granite tower of muscle staring them down.

Inwardly sighing at his less-than-cooperative brother, Ranulf stepped forward as the coach door opened. If they'd all been friends, Cooper and a footman would have approached the coach and helped the occupant or occupants to the ground, but when strangers known to be less than friendly arrived, they were on their own, and left out in the open until they made their purpose known.

From the capable-looking entourage he'd half expected the MacDonald himself to emerge, but the man who stepped to the ground was at least three decades younger than the Earl of Gorrie. The young man flashed a smile, brushed light brown hair from his forehead, and motioned his men away.

"Please, lads. The MacLawry isn't going to slaughter me before we've even said our good mornings," he drawled, his accent more English than Scots. "You are Lord Glengask, aye?"

"Aye."

"Splendid." He stuck out his hand. "Charles Beaton. Viscount Torriden."

Torriden. "Ye're one of the MacDonald's clan chieftains," Ranulf said, shaking hands with the fellow.

"I am. I apologize for not sending advance word that I was coming. The MacDonald intended to send you a return letter by messenger, but I volunteered to carry it, myself."

Ranulf studied his unexpected guest as the lad continued chatting about the state of the roads and the weather. Either Lord Torriden was supremely oblivious, or he was pretending to be so. At least a dozen rifles and muskets were pointed in his general direction, and he stood face-to-face with all three MacLawry brothers, but he continued to behave as if he sat in the drawing room of an old auntie or something.

"Lord Torriden, my brothers Arran and Munro."

Arran stepped forward readily enough, a bemused

expression on his lean face, to shake the viscount's hand. Bear, though, hesitated. Ranulf held his breath, hoping he hadn't made a mistake in notifying the MacDonalds about his brother's impending marriage. Finally Bear met Lord Torriden's outstretched hand and didn't tear it off, which Ranulf decided to take as a positive sign.

"Since I'm unexpected, please allow me to explain my presence," the viscount went on, in his smooth, cultured voice.

"Ye'd best make it a good story," Munro drawled, lowering his hand again.

When the MacLawrys met with someone, they were united. That was the rule, and that was the law. Privately they could disagree, but in public they spoke with one voice. That was why they were respected, feared, and unmatched in the Highlands. Whatever had Bear's kilt in a twist, he either needed to control his hostility or go elsewhere. Immediately.

Ranulf leaned closer to his brother. "Ye shut yer gobber, or I'll shut it fer ye," he whispered, keeping his expression cool and relaxed. "I'll nae warn ye again."

Bear closed his eyes for a moment. Finally he opened them again. "Then make certain he's an ally, and ye'll have naught to worry aboot."

Taking a breath, Ranulf moved Arran between Bear and their guest. "Watch him," he murmured.

"Aye. Shall I fetch a club?"

Hopefully Torriden didn't realize how much potential danger he was in. Ranulf inclined his head, gesturing toward the front door. "We're aboot to sit doon fer luncheon. Ye can tell us yer tale over steak-and-kidney pie."

"Thank you for your hospitality, my lord. I admit, I wasn't certain what sort of greeting I would receive here, especially coming unannounced as I have." He looked over at his gathered men. "We're all friends here, lads. No fights."

"Ye heard the viscount," Ranulf echoed, signaling his own men to stand down. "Show the lads to the kitchen."

As the mingled MacLawrys and MacDonalds trooped around the side of the house to the servants' entrance, Ranulf led the way into the foyer. "Laird Torriden, my wife, Lady Glengask, and our guest, Lady Elizabeth MacColl."

The wording was as deliberate as it had been when Bear had used it a week earlier, and against him. As a guest of the MacLawry, Elizabeth would be protected by the might of the clan. And that might was considerable. With her very distant connection to the Mac-Donalds, that protection should be unnecessary, but Bear was being hostile about something. Before he relaxed his own guard, he meant to know what it was.

The viscount immediately stepped forward to bow at Charlotte and take Elizabeth's hand. Kissing her knuckles, he favored the young lass with a bright smile. "Lady Elizabeth. You're the reason I've come all this way. I'm so pleased you're still here."

Hm. Perhaps Bear *did* have something to be concerned about, if Torriden was after Elizabeth himself for some reason. But her engagement to the Duke of Visford had been announced, because he'd checked the London newspapers himself to be certain. To his knowledge no MacDonald had protested it.

Elizabeth smiled, but retrieved her hand quickly. "I don't understand, my lord. I know we're both part of clan MacDonald, but I haven't seen my father's side of the family—or the Highlands—for years and years. Why are you looking for me?"

"The dining room's this way," Bear put in, gesturing. "Mayhap ye can tell the lot of us why ye've come here in such a hurry."

"Certainly." Torriden offered Elizabeth his arm as they all headed for the informal dining room. "I'd heard, of course, that you've been living in London. What I'm hoping is that you might have some information for me."

"What sort of information?" she asked, sitting beside him at the long table.

Ranulf took the chair at the head of the table, keeping Charlotte directly on his left, and Munro on his right. His brother's behavior continued to baffle him, and he wanted to be close enough to grab hold of him if that became necessary. With Elizabeth about to leave the MacDonalds for the MacLawrys, Bear should have been going out of his way to be welcoming to Torriden. And he should have tried to take the seat on Elizabeth's other side. And he should have disliked the immediate attention with which the viscount favored his nearly betrothed, not the man's presence itself.

None of it made much sense, and he disliked the feeling that he'd missed something. Up in the Highlands, missing things got people killed. "What can we do fer ye, Torriden?" he asked. "I figured to settle any negotiations between our clans by letter."

"Ah. Yes. I nearly forgot." The viscount pulled a letter from his breast pocket and handed it down the table. "My presence here isn't about Lady Elizabeth and your brother. Not directly."

"Nae? Then what—"

"I wanted to know, my lady, if you've had any contact with your half sister, Lady Catriona. She vanished a week or so before you fled London. We're to be married."

Chapter Thirteen

Elizabeth's surprised, half-panicked glance caught Munro as he willed her to keep her wits about her. All the while he had to work equally hard to keep his seat and not go smash pretty Lord Torriden in the face. Of all the damned things he'd speculated over, Cat being promised to another man hadn't been one of them.

"My sister?" Elizabeth stammered. "Cat? She's missing? What happened?"

Thank Saint Andrew. "I didnae ken ye had a sister, Elizabeth," he said aloud, putting a frown on his face.

"I do. My half sister, Catriona. She's five years older than I am." She took a swallow of tea, looking as though she wished it was something stronger, and faced the viscount. "I've corresponded with her over the years, but I have no idea where she might be. Please tell me what happened."

Munro wanted to hear that, himself. This would have been so much easier if Cat had trusted him enough to tell him that she was betrothed, and that for some reason she didn't want the marriage. Now he had to scramble to catch up, and hope that Elizabeth didn't unintentionally say something to give the game away.

He looked at Torriden all over again. Too pretty by half, he decided, and a year or two younger than himself. All manners and sticking out his pinkie when he drank from his cup of tea. What was it about him that Cat had disliked enough to flee her home and family for a broken-down ruin in the middle of a rival clan's territory? Whatever it was, the idea that this . . . dandy had a claim on *his* woman didn't sit well. At all.

The viscount downed a proper-sized mouthful of steak-and-kidney pie, then wiped the corner of his mouth with a napkin. "I don't know if you're aware or not, Lady Elizabeth, but the MacDonalds of the Isle of Islay have been estranged from those of us in Sutherland to the north. Your uncle Robert, the Earl of Islay, de—"

"I know who my uncle is. He took my father's title when Papa died."

"Aye. And my condolences on the loss of Randall. He was a . . . unique soul."

She nodded. "Thank you. And thank you for calling him unique rather than eccentric. I have heard some of the tales, you know." Elizabeth took a breath. "But what did Uncle Robert do?"

"He arranged for your sister to marry me. He and the MacDonald evidently thought it would go a long way to mending some fences. But then she vanished. In the middle of the night, from what I heard. I thought she might have eloped with some young man she favored, but your uncle doesn't seem to think that's the case." His smile looked more like a grimace. "I'd hoped she might have contacted you, since you both left your homes at approximately the same time."

"The lass said she didnae ken where her sister is," Munro interrupted, jabbing a fork into his luncheon. "Asking her the same question five times'll only get ye the same answer five times."

"Bear," Ranulf cautioned from his left shoulder. "Did ye think to look in London? Mayhap she went to find her sister, nae realizing Lady Elizabeth had come north."

"I have a number of relations in Town," the viscount returned, "but while they said a redheaded figure was rumored to have been seen in the vicinity of Derby House, they actually thought it might have been a secret beau of yours, my lady, sweeping you away to Gretna Green before you could be married off to awful old Visford." He cleared his throat. "I am assuming I may refer to him as awful, since you did flee London."

"You may refer to him as anything you wish," she stated, her voice a bit unsteady. "I intend to have nothing further to do with him."

"So there was no redheaded lad accompanying you?"

"No. That would have been horribly scandalous! And my sister isn't a lad, anyway, so I don't see how that would matter even if it was true."

Munro decided he needed to give Elizabeth a bit more respect. She certainly knew how to whip a polite conversation about to her advantage. That *was* the sort of thing a lady learned how to do in London, but she did it well, and for a damned good cause.

The viscount's cheeks colored. "I didn't mean to imply anything. I had heard that your sister . . ."

She faced him directly. "That she what?"

"That . . . she has red hair. I thought she might have donned a disguise. I see that is not the case, though."

Munro knew Cat hadn't just begun wearing trousers

when she'd found Haldane Abbey. She had a reputation for dressing as a man, and he had more than a suspicion that had prompted some of her concern about being seen as mannish and unsophisticated. The Sutherland MacDonalds apparently knew about her choice of wardrobe, as well, and bloody Torriden thought it would be insulting to come out and directly say that Catriona wore trousers. The buffoon. Any lass with legs as shapely as Cat's could wear any damned thing she pleased, as far as he was concerned. And he meant to be the only one to see them up close, anyway.

"No, it isn't the case," Elizabeth agreed. "I'm sorry you had to come all this way to hear I cannot help you."

"I am not sorry," the viscount countered with his charming smile. "At the worst, I've been able to meet my betrothed's sister. At best, perhaps she will find her way here, looking for you."

The big grandfather clock in the foyer began chiming, and Munro abruptly realized it was noon. *Damnation.* He'd told Cat he would be back at Haldane two hours ago. And he now had several reasons for wanting to see her again, first among them being why she'd decided it would be better for them both if he didn't know she'd already been promised to another man. She didn't seem to be playing at this, but he did have his own code of honor. He'd never bedded another man's woman—until now, apparently. And he didn't mean to stop, either.

Conjuring a grin that felt hard around the edges, he pushed to his feet. "Pretty as all this talk is, I reckon ye dunnae need me fer it. I've some work to see to." Not waiting for permission or denial, he walked around the table for the door and stepped into the hallway.

Ranulf couldn't very well stop him from escaping, because his brother had locked himself into being polite.

A polite host didn't leave the table in the middle of listening to the lamentations of a guest. Fortunately, Munro wasn't a polite fellow, and he'd never been expected to be one.

"Where's Gilling?" he asked, as one of the maids crossed the hallway.

"In the kitchen, with those MacDonald lads," she answered, stopping to dip a curtsy.

"I'll thank ye to go tell 'im to get his arse to the stable."

She grinned. "I shall do that, m'laird."

"Thank ye, Gormal. And tell him to fetch me a half-dozen eggs, while he's at it. And a sack of tea."

As he headed for the foyer the two deerhounds emerged from the morning room, where they'd apparently been banished upon the MacDonald company's arrival. He scratched Fergus and Una behind the ears, then glanced over his shoulder. A little disruption would serve that dandy Torriden right. Having one of the hounds take a nip out of his arse would certainly make *him* feel better.

"Go find Glengask," he said, sending them toward the dining room. With a pair of happy woofs they galloped off.

Cooper was occupied in the dining room, so Munro grabbed his own hat off the rack behind the front door, along with his heavy riding coat, and headed outside. He wasn't precisely dressed for laboring at the abbey, but he didn't think he'd be doing much in the way of repairs today. If Cat had gone into hiding only to delay what she considered an obligation to marry Torriden, today would be a day for smashing things. If this was a game after all, if this lass was somehow unknowingly repaying him for breaking hearts by breaking his . . . No. No more conjecture. Today he needed some bloody questions answered, once and for all.

Catriona shivered as she dunked the wet cloth into the spring again, wrung it out, and then ran it down her bare legs. For Elizabeth she would have toted water inside the abbey and warmed it on the fire, but this way was much faster and much less effort—except for the icy cold of the water, combined with the chill air of a Highlands autumn.

Something crunched on the rise to her left, and she ducked lower. It was bad enough to be caught in men's clothes by a stranger. Being stumbled upon naked would be both mortifying and dangerous. When a doe wandered across the top of the hill, she relaxed again.

Bear liked her legs. He liked her arms, and her breasts—he liked those a great deal—and all her other parts. He didn't find her awkward or mannish, and when she lay naked with him, she didn't *feel* awkward or mannish. She felt . . . pretty. Lovely, even. And powerful. As much as she found delight in him, it aroused her at least as much that *he,* a man who'd likely had more lovers than he could count, found *her* exciting and desirable.

When she'd finished washing she dried herself with the blanket she'd brought along, and then dressed in her shirt and trousers again. Lord Glengask had mentioned that one of his coats was missing, but he hadn't asked about it while they retrieved Elizabeth's things. She was glad of that today as she shrugged into the heavy, oversized wool.

The doe had been joined by an amorous buck, and the two of them utterly ignored her as she stood to gather

her things and make her way back around the abbey to the only accessible entrance. After a week of daily visits from Bear and Peter the hallway was nearly cleared of rubble, even if the ceiling did sag in several places. And now at the entrance to the kitchen she had solid walls and a door that she could bar.

No one could drop in on her through the ceiling, either, now that she and her two visitors had secured the open corner with tarps and lumber and some very heavy stones. Or someone could get in, rather, but not without a great deal of noise and effort. That was the main thing she liked about the door, as well; she would no longer be taken by surprise.

Shutting it behind her, she hung the cloth and the blanket in front of the fire to dry, set her musket beside her at the table, and opened *Robinson Crusoe* to read until Bear arrived. Before he'd discovered them she would have had to spend this time out hunting and foraging, but she'd snared a rabbit overnight and presently had it roasting over the fire, and Munro was bringing eggs. She still had the bread from yesterday, and the wild onions, too—which left her time to do . . . nothing. It was quite refreshing, actually.

If anything, reading again about the tribulations of Crusoe made her appreciate having iron pots and tin cups and her father's old musket. She'd managed quite well for herself, really, and her own Friday happened to be wild as the Highlands, and handsome, muscular, and very, very capable, as well.

Slowly she sat back, one hand over the open book, and ran the other through her curling red hair. What was this, when she could simply relax for a morning? When she didn't have to waste time wondering what would happen next, what someone else meant to do to upend her life? When she had to remind herself that humming or singing likely wasn't a wise idea—because she had the urge to burst into song at odd moments? Was this peace? Contentment?

Contentment didn't quite feel like the correct word, but it was close. Happiness sounded even better, but made less sense. After all, she had no idea how long she would be able to remain at Haldane. And winter was definitely approaching. But at this moment, this morning, after a night in Munro MacLawry's arms, she did feel happy. And something more, that she didn't quite feel ready to put into words, even inside her own head.

"Ye're daft, Cat," she muttered at herself, but couldn't help grinning. "Completely mad. And now ye're talking to yerself, ye half-wit."

Twenty minutes later she took the rabbit off the fire and began separating the meat from the bones to make a rabbit and onion soup for herself and her lads. Bear had said they would be at the abbey by ten o'clock, but they'd already missed that by nearly an hour. Hopefully he'd overslept; whatever he might say, she knew he had to be exhausted. She smiled again. Aye, she'd told him he didn't need to bother with staying overnight in her company, but she had no complaints about it, either.

She'd stated several times that he and she together didn't have a future, but she was beginning to wonder if she were wrong about that. They could certainly never marry; as a brother of the MacLawry his marriage would have weight and consequences, and it would definitely be noticed. And she would only remain free of her family's entanglements as long as she stayed hidden. But here she *was* hidden, and if everything could stay as it was now, if a hundred things went the way she wanted and not the way they were supposed to—

The heavy door rattled. "Cat!"

Jumping, she glanced at the open pocket watch beside her. Half past one. Had something happened? Pushing to her feet, she hurried to the door. "Bear? Are ye—"

"Open the damned door!" he interrupted, in an angry growl.

Catriona put her hand on the bar. "What's amiss?" she asked, her heart hammering.

"I'm nae telling ye again! Open the door!"

Taking a hard breath, she left her hand where it was. "I dunnae think I will," she answered. "Ye're a big man, and someaught's got ye angry. So I'll open the door when ye convince me ye're nae going to begin tossing my things—or me—aboot."

Silence, except for her heart pounding so loudly in her chest he could likely hear it. Then with a resounding boom something solid collided with the door. Hard. It happened again, accompanied by a string of curses in mixed English and Gaelic. So this was what happened when she began to daydream about a perfect life with a man who seemed to like her the way she was.

Moving away, she reached behind her for the musket. "I'm armed, Bear," she called out. "Ye'd best behave yerself, or go away!"

The thumping stopped. A minute or two later a more polite knock sounded. "It's Peter, Miss Cat," the servant said in his gravelly voice. "I'm to tell ye that Laird Bear's gone fer a stalk aboot the garden, and he'll be back in a moment. And he'll be civilized."

"Ye arenae lying to me, are ye, Peter? He's nae standing right there waiting for the door to open?"

Another delay. "Well, he isnae now. He's outside. I swear on my mother's hair, Miss Cat."

Rather than debate over what made the hair of Peter Gilling's mother so swearworthy, she lifted the bar over its braces and set it aside. "What the devil's happened?" she asked, half yanking the servant inside and shutting the door so she could bar it again. "He told me I could shut him oot of the kitchen, but I didnae think I'd need to do so."

"I'm nae to tell ye a thing," the footman said stoutly.

"Can ye tell me why ye're here so late today? Bear told me ten o'clock."

The servant lifted on his toes, then sank back again. "All I can say is that we had some visitors today. Unexpected ones."

That didn't sound promising. Not at all. "Is my sister well?"

"Oh, aye. It has naught to do with that old duke who's after her. Dunnae worry yerself over that."

"Well, that's something. But why is Munro so angry? At me, apparently?"

"Ye'll have to speak with him to find that oot."

"I'll nae speak to him while he's trying to break my door down."

He shrugged. "It's nae wise to tell Laird Bear what he should or shouldnae do, but he seems to listen to ye. Give him a minute. I'll go oot and see that he's civilized himself some. If I knock two times, then two more times, it's safe to let us in. If I knock three times, then three more times, then dunnae open the door."

That all seemed very complicated, but since Peter was at least willing to help, she settled for nodding. "Thank ye. Even if ye willnae tell me what's afoot."

Once she closed him out in the hallway again, she

leaned back against the door. A few weeks ago if Bear had approached her like that she would already have shot at him, been packed, and likely would have turned up the table so she could cut through the tarp in the corner and exit out to the roof. It might be wiser—and easier—to simply escape now, anyway.

But that would mean not seeing him again. Ever. And evidently for the opportunity to be with him again she was willing to risk his anger and her continued freedom. That didn't mean, however, she wouldn't be cautious about it.

She waited, her cheek pressed against the door. The hallway sounded empty, but they'd made the door solid for a reason. She'd just never thought it would actually be to keep Bear outside. What could have happened? Thank God the Duke of Visford hadn't come calling, but *something* had clearly set Munro off. And it had something to do with her.

Had it been her uncle? She felt the blood leave her face. Had Uncle Robert heard that Elizabeth was here and thought her mad sister might be somewhere nearby? Oh, goodness. *No, no, no.* Because that would mean that not just Bear, but his entire family, had heard how . . . odd she was, and how difficult it had been to find a match for her, and how much was at stake if they didn't return her.

Two knocks reverberated against her cheek. Then two more. That supposedly meant she was safe. In reality, though, she wasn't nearly as certain. Catriona shut her eyes for a long moment, then opened them and lifted the bar. Even a coward had to face up to her past eventually. And today might well be her day to do so.

She pulled open the door, lifting her chin as she did so. Peter Gilling was there somewhere, but her gaze, all her attention stayed fixed on the giant who filled the open space. His green eyes were narrowed, fury and something she couldn't put a name to blazing through them and through every inch of his six and a half feet. He looked magnificent, even apparently ready to strangle her.

"What happened?" she asked, keeping her voice level.

"May I come in?" he returned, his own tone clipped and hard and clearly reined in as tightly as he could hold it.

Catriona stepped back from the doorway. "Certainly."

"Peter, go away."

"M'laird, y—"

"Go away," he repeated, through clenched teeth.

"Dunnae fret, Peter," she took up, though she didn't dare look away from Munro. "I've made a rabbit and onion soup for luncheon. It'll be ready soon."

With a grunt that sounded reluctant, the footman retreated. Bear, though, advanced, stepping into the room and shutting the door behind him. When she'd last seen him, before dawn this morning, he'd been amused and affectionate. Now he looked ready to erupt.

"I've a question fer ye," he said after a moment, stopping short of the fireplace.

"I'm listening."

"Are ye mine?"

The question caught her by surprise. "What happened after you left here?" she asked, moving around behind the table to where she'd left the musket, just in case. It seemed . . . wiser to keep at least one piece of furniture between them at the moment.

"Answer my question, and I'll tell ye."

"I like being with ye, Bear," she said slowly, trying

to feel her way through what felt like a much more important question than it sounded. "I like ye, more than I want to admit to ye. And I've told ye before, I dunnae think we'll suit. I've nae lied to ye aboot that."

He gazed at her levelly. "Viscount Torriden. Do ye think ye belong to him?"

Oh no. Catriona's legs went ice-cold, and she sat heavily on the floor. "Is he here?" she whispered, clutching onto the table leg.

"Aye. He is. Dunnae ye think ye might have mentioned that ye were betrothed before we . . . before I—"

"*They* said I was betrothed," she snapped back, taking deep breaths and trying to pull herself back to her feet. She was *not* going to convince him, herself, or anyone else if she couldn't even stand. "I never agreed to any such thing!"

"Dammit." Bear strode forward, grabbed her beneath one arm, and half carried her around to the chair. As soon as she was seated he released her again, as if touching her burned him or something. "I had to sit there over luncheon," he ground out, "and listen to him telling Ranulf how ye'd gone missing, and how ye'd been promised to him."

He stalked to the wall and back again, while she twisted to keep him in sight. "Bear, I—"

"Elizabeth lied when he asked if she'd seen or heard from ye," he cut in. "But I dunnae think he's convinced that she would come to the Highlands withoot someone to lead her here. Ranulf'll be the next to start wondering why a lass who'd been away from the Highlands for eleven years would return now—and why she wouldnae head directly to the MacDonalds fer protection." He sighed. "Yer sister didnae think to be apprehensive when

Torriden drove up. She was excited to meet someone from her clan."

Catriona lowered her head. "Ye may as well keep pacing, Munro. I'll tell ye what I can, and it'll be easier if ye're nae looking at me."

Instead he pulled the table a few feet away and sat on it to face her. "I like looking at ye, Cat. I lied to ye aboot who I was when we first met, because I didnae want to frighten ye off. I've nae lied since. Now I want to know if ye've been lying to me all along. If ye were just . . . making use of a man to gain ye protection from another. Or if ye've been playing, when ye mean to go and do as yer family wants."

She wanted to protest that she'd never lied to him about how she felt. How he made her feel. But if she said it now, either before or after she told her story, she knew precisely how it would sound: as if she was playing on his sympathies, and *was* using him for protection. All she could do, then, was continue to be honest.

"I've nae told ye some things, Munro, but I've nae lied aboot them." Since he wanted to watch her, she lifted her gaze to meet his. "My father wanted a son. He wanted a basketful of sons, actually. My mother, though, gave him a daughter, and she died before they could try for another. Withoot her, he decided he would raise me as he wished."

She gestured at herself. "I grew up wearing this. I learned how to hunt, how to shoe a horse, how to forage for myself. He kept my hair short until I refused to let him cut it. The MacDonald began pushing at him to wed one of the lasses from the Sutherland branch of the clan, so being a stubborn Highlander he went and found a Sassannach lady with blue blood and a need fer a title, instead. Then she gave him a daughter, too."

"Elizabeth," he put in.

At least he was paying attention. He hadn't decided she wasn't worth listening to. "Aye," she returned, nodding. "At first Anne tried to put me in dresses and teach me how to walk and talk properly, but Papa wouldnae stand fer it. Neither of them liked Elizabeth and me playing together, and when Anne caught Papa with a wee kilt fer Elizabeth, she took my sister and went back to London."

"Ye corresponded, ye said."

"Aye. From time to time. Less and less as we got older. We had naught in common." Cat shrugged. At the time she'd been relieved to only have to think of pretty things about which to write once or twice a year. "As I got older, I started to notice . . . well, lads, but most of 'em didnae want to be anywhere around me. That's when I realized I'd become some odd monstrosity. My father was a chieftain, so people had to be respectful to my face. That didnae mean they were so behind my back. And I heard things, of course."

"That's when ye stopped cutting yer hair, aye?" His expression had softened a little. To her relief she didn't see pity in his eyes, but then he'd never seemed to view her as odd.

"Aye. In a way it made me feel a little more like a lass, but I didnae have anyone I trusted to show me anything to do with it, or how to dress differently even if I wanted to. Then Papa died two years ago, and my uncle Robert became the Earl of Islay. A year or so ago he and the MacDonald began meeting, to try to mend the bad blood between the two halves of the clan. They decided I should marry Viscount Torriden."

She couldn't help the tremor that ran down her spine. The dread, the certainty that she would both embarrass the clan and be a poor wife and a very poor viscountess, all came rushing back again. "I'd never met him," she made herself continue, "but I'd heard of him. Educated in London and Edinburgh, handsome, and very . . . sophisticated. Which ye may have noticed doesnae describe me."

"Nae. I hadnae," he returned.

With a swallow, she grimaced. "My uncle wanted to be rid of me, I'm certain. I reminded him of his brother, and I'd nae to offer by way of power or prestige except by my marriage. And one night I went to go talk to him, but I heard him talking to my other uncle, Ràild. He said the MacDonald had asked him to supply a bride whose bloodline would help mend the tear in the clan, but by the grace of God he'd become the laird of his own grand island.

"He liked it that way. Rejoining the rest of the Mac-Donalds would lower him to a minor chieftain forced to obey the dictates of the MacDonald. By sending me to them, he would satisfy his part of any peace accord, but they wouldnae be happy aboot it. I was his way to insult the MacDonald withoot spitting at him outright."

She heard his sharp intake of breath, but he didn't say anything aloud. She didn't know what she wanted him to say, anyway—that she wasn't an insult to anyone, that it had been cruel of her uncle, that Robert was a clever bastard—none of it would leave her feeling any better.

"I knew then that if I married—I couldnae marry Torriden. It was bad enough being alone and laughed at in my own land. To be set up as a parody of a viscountess in the north . . ." She shivered again. "I couldnae do it, Bear. I dunnae ken if ye understand, but I couldnae."

"So ye ran. What happened with Elizabeth, then? Was that all just a coincidence?"

"Ye mean to say, did she actually want to marry the duke, and I convinced her to run instead? Nae. She wrote me. I knew I couldnae stay on Islay, but I hadnae yet decided what to do. And then I received her letter. She was so afraid, and her mother Anne wouldnae listen to anything she said. That's when I decided to go down to London and rescue her, and then rescue both of us." She took another breath. "And here we are."

Listening to herself, she heard a coward, someone who'd put the well-being of her clan at risk because she feared looking and feeling like a fool, because someone else had called her one. Trying to explain further would likely only serve to dig her hole deeper. Instead she folded her hands together and lowered her gaze to study the stone floor.

"Ye didnae answer my question, lass," Bear commented after a long moment. "Are ye mine?"

A sob ripped out of her chest. A week or two ago the idea of ownership had annoyed her, but she didn't see it the same way any longer. "I want to be, Bear. But how can I be, when I'm promised to someone else? I cannae be with anyone, because if I am, that means I've decided to do someaught against my own clan's orders. As long as I'm just . . . running, then naught's been decided. Do ye ken?"

Bear stood, straightening to his full height. "Torriden's here because Ranulf wrote the MacDonald. My *bràthair* thinks I've got it in my head to marry Elizabeth, and he'll nae waste an opportunity to gain influence with another clan. The viscount brought his laird's letter of agreement, but wanted to ask yer sister face-to-face if she had an idea where ye might be, since ye're betrothed to him."

And she hadn't told Elizabeth anything about this.

How could she, when her sister had been faced with marriage to a monster, and she'd run from being laughed at? "I dunnae know what to say, Munro," she finally whispered. "I thought we'd be safe from the Mac-Donalds here. I never expected to meet ye. Even less to . . . to . . ." She shut her mouth before she could ruin everything, and wiped at the warm wet on her face.

"Finish yer sentence."

Catriona looked up at him. "What?"

"Ye never expected to meet me. Even less to . . . What? Finish it."

Springtime eyes held hers, mesmerizing, giving her no time to think of an alternative or a direction she could turn away. And she actually wanted to say it. Her largest fear, in fact, was that he didn't return the sentiment. "To fall in love with ye, ye brute," she muttered, lifting her chin. "Now how does that help anything?"

"It helps me some," he returned, moving toward her. He didn't stop until he threw his arms around her, bent her backward, and lowered his mouth over hers.

She kissed him back, hope and joy and even gratitude flowing through her. He hadn't laughed, hadn't turned away, and he hadn't agreed with her uncle's—or her own—assessment of her character. No, saying it aloud hadn't helped anything. Except that it had. It changed everything.

Chapter Fourteen

Much of what Cat said didn't surprise him. She'd spoken enough about being alone and being uncomfortable around other people that the particular facts only served to fill in names and dates. None of that mattered, though. Not any longer.

"I love ye, lass," Munro murmured, lifting his head from her just long enough to say the words. "I'll nae have anyone take ye from me."

Her fingers dug into his shoulders as if she was trying to climb inside him. "I should've told ye about Torriden," she managed, in between kisses. "I didnae know how to admit to being such a . . . poor excuse for a lass."

Well, that couldn't be allowed to stand. Munro took her shoulders and held her at arm's length. "I dunnae ever—*ever*—want to hear ye say such a thing again. Yer *athair* sent yer life in a direction I dunnae ken if ye wanted. But ye're yer own lass now. I love this." He yanked down the collar of her shirt and put his palm roughly over her heart. "How ye dress it doesnae matter to me."

"This is all I know," she returned, soft tears filling her dark eyes again.

He took a breath, wondering if they'd both lost their minds, and why he was so content to remain a madman if he could be with his wildcat. "I'm nae a dainty man," he stated, pulling her to him again, "but I've a younger sister I helped raise. If there's someaught ye want to know, I'll do my damnedest to show ye. But only if ye want to know; I think I've already told ye what I think of ye in trousers."

Finally he felt her chuckle against his chest, and he relaxed a little. He didn't want her to flee, but short of spending every moment at Haldane Abbey he couldn't do much physically to stop her. She had to want to stay. "I dunnae feel like a proper lady when I'm with ye," she murmured, "but I feel like a woman."

The catch in her voice made him clench his jaw. He wanted to call her father a fool for making her into something that no one else would accept, simply because he'd been dealt a daughter rather than a son. At the same time, if Cat hadn't felt so much an outcast, so unfit to represent either her sex or her clan, he would never have met her. She would likely be wed to Lord Torriden by now, and the two halves of clan Mac-Donald would be happily reunited. He would be . . . continuing on, trying to avoid being trapped inside a household with a wife simply because it was the thing to do.

"Whatever it was that brought ye here," he said aloud, choosing his words more carefully than he generally did, "I'm glad ye're in my arms now." Separating from her a little, he bent to lean his forehead against hers. "And I've nae intention of letting ye go."

She frowned. "I said I love ye, giant, but do ye have

any idea what trouble comes with me? And nae just from Torriden. I ken ye've other lasses ye've . . . been with. Choose one of them."

For a long moment he studied her expression, the faint laugh-kissed dimple in her cheeks, the light dusting of freckles across the bridge of her nose, those chocolate-brown eyes and that luscious scarlet hair. "They were convenient," he stated, willing her to understand. "Ye're nae convenient. Y—"

"Well, then," she interrupted, flushing. "I dunnae—"

"Shut up. I'm nae finished with my sentence. Ye're nae convenient. Ye take some effort. Ye drive me mad. And there's nae another lass in the wide world who would do fer me now. So dunnae ye fret aboot Torriden. Ye dunnae belong to him. Ye belong to me."

"Only if ye belong to me," she retorted, typically stubborn.

It was one concession he was happy to give her. "That, I do, lass. I swear it." He snuck in to catch another kiss from her. When she wrapped her hands into the lapels of his coat, he lifted her off her feet so he could kiss her more squarely. And he wondered if she realized what it meant, when a MacLawry claimed a lass. Because nothing would keep them apart now, no matter the cost.

"M'laird?" Gilling knocked at the barred kitchen door. "Lady Cat? It's too quiet in there. Ye're scaring an old man."

Munro blew out his breath and set Catriona onto the floor again. "I made ye a solid door, at least," he muttered, walking over to shove up the bar. "And we cannae have him running to Glengask fer help."

As Munro pulled open the door, the footman stayed where he was. Given the reputation of his temper, he wasn't surprised at Peter's hesitation, but he couldn't quite believe that anyone would think he would actually hurt Catriona. He'd sooner throw himself off the second floor of the abbey. "Ye're nae so old, Peter," he returned, motioning the man to enter. "Grizzled, aye. Old, nae."

"I dunnae ken if that was a compliment or an insult," the servant replied, sending an appraising look at Catriona, "but I'm glad to see ye smiling, my lady."

"Aye," Munro put in. "And it's my aim to make certain she keeps smiling. So I reckon we need to convince Lord Torriden there's naught fer him here, and see him on his way."

How he meant to do that would be slightly more complicated, but it had to be done. With the viscount at Glengask, anything might happen. And while he and the MacLawry were likely to be pulled into MacDonald politics regardless, it would likely be wiser if it didn't happen over the muzzle of a weapon. If it came to that, though, so be it.

Both Cat and Peter were looking at him, so he shook out his shoulders. "Let's finish patching up the ceiling," he said aloud, "and make the kitchen secure. And then I reckon we need to start tearing doon the back half of the abbey. We'll set aside the usable stone and brick and then start rebuilding it. Once we've the back done, we'll move ye there, wildcat, and we'll do the same to the front."

Gilling blinked. "Ye mean to say we're tearing this place doon and rebuilding it?"

"Aye. It's a bit too far gone fer a few plaster patches and some nails, dunnae ye think?"

"Just the two of us?"

"The three of us," Catriona amended, but her brow

furrowed. "That seems like a great deal of work, Bear. The kitchen has what I require."

"But not what I require fer ye. Ranulf thinks I'm repairing the abbey so Elizabeth and I can make a home here. He's half right. And patching a few holes willnae make this a place to live in. Right now it's a place to survive in. Ye deserve better than that, lass."

Tears shining in her eyes again, Cat walked up to him. "Peter Gilling, turn around," she ordered.

"I beg yer—"

"I'm going to kiss Laird Bear," she interrupted. "So turn around, if ye please."

Shaking his head despite the grin tugging at his mouth, Peter did as she asked. The servant likely wouldn't be smiling later, when he had time to consider what such a kiss meant for the future of two clans—but that was later. Cat's uncle had meant her to be an insult, a jest sent to the northern MacDonalds that they would have to accept but wouldn't approve. A life of humiliation and behind-hand comments following two decades of similar treatment from her own. Well, that was now ended. And no one would be making fun of her again. Not while he had any say in the matter. Which he would make certain he did.

None of that mattered, though, as Cat slid her arms over his shoulders and leaned up against him to favor him with a deep, soft kiss. Perhaps because she wasn't very sophisticated where kissing and sex were concerned, her kisses mirrored her moods. And this kiss left him deeply . . . satisfied. It wasn't about sex or even lust, but felt and tasted of possession and happiness. He'd never had a kiss like it. He would never forget it. And he wanted more of them.

"Ye said yer brother was half right in thinking ye were building a home for yerself and Elizabeth. Which half is right, and what's the other half?" she whispered, running her fingers down his cheek.

His heart hitched. He wanted to say it, wanted to ask her, but she'd taken great pains to vanish rather than stand up to her own clan. Even after she'd learned they considered her to be an insult to the MacDonald. Aye, he would ask her, but not until he'd fought and killed all her dragons. "I'm building a hoose fer myself, of course," he drawled, forcing a grin. "And my horse."

Cat chuckled. "If ye say so, Bear." She pushed against his chest, and he reluctantly let her slip out of his arms.

"There's one thing I dunnae understand," he commented, realizing that they would not be having sex while Peter stood in the corner. "If, as ye say, yer uncle meant ye to be an insult to the MacDonald, why did Torriden come all this way on the slight chance of finding ye?"

She shrugged. "All I can figure is that Torriden has something to gain from it. Mayhap the MacDonald promised him someaught to mend the alliance, regardless of who he has to wed."

"Stop that," he stated, frowning. "I told ye that I love ye, so now when ye claim there's someaught wrong with ye, ye're insulting *me*. And I'll nae stand fer being insulted."

Whether she took his words seriously or not, she did nod at him. For a lass as wild-hearted and striking as she was to feel so inferior—her father hadn't done her any damned favors at all. If she wanted to learn how to be more proper he would do his best to show her, even if propriety wasn't exactly his strong suit. For her, he'd make an effort. She at least deserved a choice in how she wanted to be perceived.

"Thank ye for saying that, Bear."

"Aye. If ye dunnae believe I was serious, try calling me a liar."

"I dunnae want to." She took a breath. "As manly as ye and Peter are," she said, walking over to pat the footman on the shoulder, "I cannae see the three of us tearing this place down and putting it back together by ourselves."

And there she went, changing the subject again. One day soon he was going to convince her just how attractive and desirable she truly was, but he couldn't do it until she was at least half ready to believe him. Instead he sat in the chair. "Aye. I could hire workers from the village, and half of Glengask would tote hammers if I nodded at 'em, but ye'd have to stay closed up in the kitchen while they were here."

"So now I'm keeping ye from making a house of yer own."

And he was keeping her for himself, keeping her away from other people—even if that happened to be precisely the opposite of what she needed. "What if ye put up yer hair and I bring ye one of my big, floppy hats? Ye'd have to keep some distance, maybe stay up on the roof with me and toss doon the rubble, but—"

"Everyone knows everyone here," she broke in, her brow furrowing. "Every villager would know I'm nae from here."

"Then ye're from the south. It's up to ye, lass." And up to how concerned she was that Torriden was about— at least until Munro could be rid of him. Which would be by nightfall, if he could manage it.

She looked from her new door to the patched hole in the ceiling. "I'd like to consider it, if it's up to me."

"I said it was." Resisting the urge to shake her, to order her to believe him when he said she was safe, he settled for rolling his shoulders. "I came in a bit of a hurry today," he said. "I didnae stop by the village fer the supplies I ordered."

"I did bring the eggs ye told me to fetch," Peter commented.

"We cannae use eggs fer mortar," Munro retorted. Unused to being this . . . frustrated, he headed for the door. Catriona's stubbornness, her refusal to believe that someone else might be at least as concerned with her well-being as with his own—he couldn't punch that, and he couldn't bellow at it or tromp over it. It would take patience and finesse, and those were muscles of his that would require some stretching. "If the two of ye will start clearing the old back garden so we'll have room to pile the timber and stones we want to keep, I'll head into the village fer the lumber I ordered, and see if I can figure oot how to contact an architect."

Damnation, this had been a long day already. And he still needed to decipher how to remove Lord Torriden from Glengask. Once he'd dealt with that, then perhaps Cat would allow him to start introducing her to clan MacLawry, beginning with the village workers. Wee, careful steps. He could take wee, careful steps, if the dance concluded with Catriona MacColl in his arms.

"Bear!"

He wheeled Saturn around as Cat ran out of the abbey. "Aye, lass?"

She stopped beside him, grabbing one of his boots in her fingers. "Aye."

The immediate hammering of his heart seemed to

be all out of proportion with hearing one simple word. But he knew what he'd been thinking, and that word played a very large part in it. He hadn't asked her yet, though—and in fact, he had no idea which question she might be answering. "I need a few more words than that, wildcat."

A quick, uncertain grin touched her mouth. "Aye, I'll pretend to be some odd lad ye brought in to help ye demolish Haldane. I'll nae stay in the kitchen while ye're getting sweaty and taking yer shirt off."

She'd taken a step toward him. Toward trust. Munro leaned out of the saddle and caught her mouth against his. "I'll bring ye a hat and someaught shabbier to wear, then."

Keeping hold of his boot, Cat gazed up at him, her smile softer and even more compelling now. "I owe Elizabeth an explanation, if ye can convince her to come by with ye."

He nodded. "I'll see to it. And dunnae ye fret, lass; I'll see to it that Torriden doesnae come anywhere around ye." Pretty Charles Beaton had best stay well away from Haldane Abbey and Cat. If the man wanted to keep breathing, anyway.

"And just between us, lass, withoot Lord Torriden in earshot, ye've nae seen yer sister lately?" Ranulf asked, keeping his tone curious rather than threatening. The lass would likely break down in tears or faint if he did so much as frown.

Elizabeth shook her head, her gaze on the cup of tea in her hands. "I wish I could help," she returned. "As I said, Cat and I corresponded occasionally, but I didn't have any idea she was betrothed, or anything else."

"So ye didnae come north to find her?"

"I only wanted to leave England and the Duke of Visford's reach. I didn't consider much beyond that, I'm afraid." She glanced up, then back at the tea again. "I'm very lucky Bear found me when he did."

"Aye. Winter's nearly here, and the Highlands isnae a place fer a lass to be on her own when the snows come. Especially an English-raised lass."

He watched her expression carefully, noting the tightening of her mouth and the slight shake of her fingers around the cup. She could be lying; under other circumstances he would have been convinced of it. But she could also be a lass worried over her sister's disappearance, and as ignorant as she claimed.

"And thank you again for taking me in," she said, with a smile that didn't reach her eyes. "You had no reason to do so, and I'm very grateful that you did."

"We had reason," he returned, noting honey-haired Charlotte's arrival in the morning room doorway. "Ye'll be part of the family soon. And the MacLawrys always look after their own."

Her cheeks darkened, and she abruptly set down the teacup. "Oh. Yes, of course. I . . . Thank you."

"Ranulf, I don't mean to interrupt, but Sir Alpin Peterkin is here to see you or Bear," Charlotte said, brushing her fingers against his arm as she walked past him to sit beside Elizabeth MacColl.

Just her touch made goose bumps lift on his arms. "Bear's nae back, I assume?"

She shook her head. "And Lord Torriden's playing billiards with Arran and Lachlan."

Elizabeth looked up again. "I enjoy watching billiards. Do you think I might join them without making myself a bother?"

"Certainly," Charlotte answered, motioning Ranulf to leave the room. "Finish your tea, and we'll go upstairs."

So his wife thought she might have more success in discovering whether Elizabeth was telling the truth or not. Very well; Charlotte knew London and its social intricacies much better than he did, and she was certainly kinder and more gentle.

Under most circumstances he wouldn't care about one of the MacDonalds losing a potential bride and failing to reunite the two less-than-friendly sides of that clan. But Elizabeth was here, and that had brought the trouble to his doorstep. And so he needed to know whether he should be concerned or not. He'd stated to all and sundry that she was under the protection of the MacLawrys. If she was lying, that reflected on him. And *he* didn't want to be responsible for any MacDonald troubles. Especially ones that didn't have anything to do with him.

Sir Alpin Peterkin stood in the foyer, his hat literally in his hands. Generally the only dealings with the Peterkin family were Bear's, and Ranulf could only hope that one or the other of Peterkin's daughters hadn't announced that she was pregnant. God, what a mess that would be, especially with a marriage to Elizabeth all but done. "Alpin," he said, offering his hand. "It's good to see ye up here. What might I do fer ye?"

The older man shook hands, shifting his proper beaver hat to his left hand to do so. "I've someaught, um, delicate to discuss with ye or Laird Bear." He gave a nervous laugh. "I'm relieved it's ye, actually, m'laird."

With the morning room occupied, Ranulf led the way to the library upstairs. He'd discovered some time ago that meeting people in his office tended to unnerve them. "How is Lady Peterkin?" he asked, as they climbed the stairs. "Mrs. Forrest heard from someone in An Soadh that she's been in bed with the fever."

"Oh, she's recovered now, m'laird. Thank ye fer asking." He stopped inside the library door. "Might I close this?"

Hm. That didn't bode well. "Certainly. Might I get ye a glass of someaught?"

"No, thank ye. I ken ye're a busy man, so I'll get right to it." Sir Alpin shut the door and seemed to feel it necessary to remain close by the exit, which didn't leave Ranulf feeling any better about what might be coming.

Bloody hell. He'd told his brothers over and over again to be careful. And while he wouldn't have argued against Bear marrying either Bethia or Flora Peterkin, the lasses didn't have a sackful of brains between them. Which, come to think of it, he'd considered to be Bear's sort of lass. Elizabeth MacColl seemed far too dainty, but perhaps that had been her appeal; she wasn't like most other lasses in the Highlands.

"I'm listening," he prompted, when despite his stated eagerness to talk, Sir Alpin continued to stand there, grimacing.

"Oh. Aye. Um. Well, I ken that ye're aware that yer brother, Lord Munro, has . . . been after my Bethia. For two years, now. She's a flighty lass, Bethia. Her sister, too."

Ranulf put his hands behind his back so he could clench his fists without frightening the man. He and Bear were going to have to have a discussion now, whether his brother was determined to avoid one or not. It would be wise to have Lachlan and Arran remain close by, as well, because if it came to a fight he could use the assistance. And Bear might listen to Lach, even if he wouldn't pay heed to his older brothers.

"Um, well, it seems that withoot bothering to tell me, her own papa, Bethia has gone and promised herself to young Sorley Landers."

Ranulf blinked. "Sholto Landers's son? The physician?"

"Aye. That's him. She has her heart set on him, and doesnae care aboot his profession." He sighed heavily. "I had my own heart set on Laird Bear, but I cannae tell that lass what to do. I did think it my duty to tell Laird Bear myself, but if he's nae aboot, then—"

"I'll tell him," Ranulf interrupted, hoping his keen relief didn't show on his face. Bear had gone far past pursuing both Bethia and her twin sister, Flora, but if one of them had found someone else he didn't think his brother would be overly troubled. Not with an almost-fiancée under his roof.

"Thank ye, Laird Glengask. That is one conversation I didnae care to be present fer. Do tell yer brother, though, that Flora isnae spoken fer. And she and Bethia—well, they *are* twins."

"I appreciate ye informing me," Ranulf returned, moving to open the door again. "And be certain ye let us know the date. We'd be pleased to help ye with the wedding feast."

Now Sir Alpin was beaming. "That's very kind of ye, Glengask. Very kind."

Well, that was one problem avoided. Now he needed to gently steer Lord Torriden away—perhaps all the way to the Isle of Islay or back to Sutherland—to minimize the MacDonald presence here, and then get Munro to propose and set a date for the wedding. And then, by

God, when all of his siblings were happily married and had finished with scandals and beginning clan wars, perhaps he could sit back and . . . relax. At least until their bairns grew old enough to make things interesting again. With a slight grin he went to go rescue his wife from proper chats and tea.

Halfway to the door, though, he stopped. Munro had practically eaten Lord Torriden alive on sight, but he hadn't had any additional objection when the viscount had seated himself beside Elizabeth. And Elizabeth, who seemed to be fascinated with her clan, hadn't gone to her clan when she'd fled London. In fact, she couldn't have put much more distance between herself and her clan and still be in the Highlands.

Why go to the Highlands at all if she didn't have any intention of seeking out the MacDonalds? In addition, how did a young lass who hadn't seen Scotland since her eighth year survive in the Highlands for a month, by herself, and still manage to be clean, well fed, and wearing a proper set of shoes and a blemish-free walking dress?

With a curse Ranulf turned around again. "Owen!" he bellowed, striding back down the stairs to the foyer. "Find me my damned brother!"

The footman skidded into view. "Which brother, m'laird?"

"Bear." Of course, Bear.

"What would ye be doing right now if Bear hadnae dragged ye out here to stack bricks?" Catriona asked, digging a shovel into the cold ground and loosening up the pile of stones that had settled into the old garden.

"Now?" Peter Gilling returned, straightening from the pile of lumber in front of him. "More than likely I'd be putting wee silver utensils on the proper dining table and pouring wine into a decanter. Glengask has guests, so then I'd have to polish up the candelabras and put on my gloves to serve the dinner."

"Do ye like it?"

"I like being at Glengask. After old Glengask died, young Ranulf found himself a few lads from the clan who'd served in the army and who knew their way around weapons. He hired me and Debny and Owen and Cooper and a half-dozen others to serve in the hoose. Mostly, though, he brought us in to watch over his sister and brothers."

"The old Glengask was killed, aye? There were rumors of that, anyway."

"Aye. And the new Glengask swore it wouldnae happen again. We work hard, we play hard, and we're treated fair. Better than fair. I'd give my life fer any Mac-Lawry, and I'm honored to help protect them." He grinned, wiping his forehead. "I may nae fold the napkins just right, and I ken I talk a bit straighter to my betters than I should, but then the MacLawrys arenae like any other family ye're likely to meet."

And hopefully her cowardice hadn't driven the youngest MacLawry brother so far away he wouldn't return. She jabbed the shovel into the dirt. In her perfect world—or at least the one she'd imagined a few weeks ago—she lived alone and safe at Haldane Abbey, with the world far away from her. More recently her imaginings had begun to include Bear, at first coming by to chat with her, but now visiting her at least once every day and staying all day long.

Even that, though, wasn't enough. It couldn't be enough. She couldn't be a hermit who allowed only one other person into her life. By doing that, she would be limiting both herself and Munro. And so she would try, until she either convinced herself she could be so-cial and not do something idiotic, or until Bear realized he'd fallen in love with the worst woman possible and did walk away for good.

He loved her. Just hearing him say it had given her some courage. Lord Torriden lurked only two miles away, looking for her, but that knife edge of terror and panic had dulled a little. Munro loved her. She wasn't alone. Unless he'd given up on her, that was. After all, he'd vanished almost three hours ago.

"I hate to say it," she offered after a moment of dig-ging in silence, "but I think we're going to be doing this same work all over again in the spring, after the snow melts."

"Aye," Gilling replied, "but keeping my hands busy is better than reminding myself that I let Laird Bear go off to the village withoot me. Again. He isnae supposed to do that."

"Go after him, then," she said, grimacing. "I was here before ye found me, and I'm here alone at night." At least as far as the servant knew, she was. Actually, she'd forgotten that Munro was supposed to have an escort with him at all times; he'd come to visit her by night for the past week without anyone else being aware, much less riding with him. The idea that coming to see her might leave him vulnerable to an enemy of the Mac-Lawrys made her shiver. Aye, he could take care of himself, but no man could stop a musket ball.

"I reckon I'll stay here," the footman commented, re-trieving more scraps of wood. "I have orders."

"Do ye, then?"

"Aye. 'As long as that MacDonald buffoon is aboot, ye and I willnae take our peepers off Lady Cat,' he said. Torriden seems too pretty to be much of a menace, though, if ye ask me. Fellows like that dunnae like to risk getting their noses broken."

She hid a grin. "But Bear is pretty." Or rather, devastatingly, devilishly handsome.

"I suppose so. But ye'll never see him wearing those collars so high they poke a man in the eye if he turns his head. Or one of those neck ties with more frills than a flower."

"I'll have to agree with ye about that. I cannae precisely imagine him wearing a dandy's clothes."

Peter chuckled. "Aye. It'd be akin to ye putting on a lace gown, I suppose."

Well, that hurt. Thunking the shovel against the bricks to cover her flinch, Catriona sent him a sideways glance. How did he see her? Of course she'd never worn anything but a shirt, jacket, trousers, and boots in his presence, because that was all she ever wore, and all she owned. But evidently even the idea of her putting on a gown was the stuff of hilarity.

She closed her eyes for a moment. That was the same uncertainty that had dogged her since she'd overheard Elizabeth's mother mocking her attire, which Anne had taken to doing after the viscountess's attempts to dress her properly had been rejected by the viscount.

"Sometimes I hate being correct."

For half a heartbeat Catriona thought Bear was speaking. The voice wasn't quite as low, though, and aside from that, she'd heard it before. With a shriek she lifted the shovel, whipping the sharp end around toward the well-dressed man standing in the shadow of the ruins. "Stay back!"

"Lass! There's nae need fer that," Peter Gilling broke in with a gasp. "Lower yer weapon! Ye cannae threaten the MacLawry on his own land."

She didn't want to threaten him. He was Munro's brother, for heaven's sake. "I only told him to keep his distance," she retorted aloud, abruptly realizing she was very much alone again. Aside from the two huge deerhounds flanking the marquis, Peter would never so much as counter anything his clan chief said. "And this land isnae his," she went on. "It belongs to Munro."

The Marquis of Glengask tilted his head in the way that reminded her of his youngest brother. His eyes, though, were a hard steel blue rather than Bear's crisp green. And those blue eyes continued to gaze at her levelly.

In fact, he seemed content not to say anything. Perhaps he was so startled by her presence—or her appearance—that he had no idea how to respond. Given what she knew about him, though, it seemed more likely that he meant to allow Peter and her to argue until he had all the information he required. His reputation had traveled to all corners of the kingdom—clever, hot-blooded, but with an ice-cold resolve.

Catriona lowered the tip of the shovel. The best strategy for her, then, would be to make him talk. "So ye've seen me," she said, managing to keep her voice mostly steady. "What do ye mean to do about it?" There. Hearing him say something—anything—would serve to give *her* a bit of information. And the more she had, the better.

"Considering ye're spoken fer by a MacDonald chieftain and that ye've brought the MacDonalds to my doorstep, I ken what I *should* do," he replied coolly. "But ye've tangled my brother into it now."

A scowl furrowed her brow before she could stop the expression. "I didnae tangle Bear into anything," she snapped. "I told him to go away and leave me—us—be. And then ye came and stole Elizabeth, and he felt obligated to . . . look in on me, because I was alone. That puts this on ye, I reckon." Whatever else happened, she wasn't about to trap Munro.

"We'll see aboot that, I suppose. In the meantime, if my brother's looking in on ye, where might I find him?"

"He rode into An Soadh, m'laird," Peter answered quickly. "He ordered me to stay here and protect the lass."

The marquis lifted an eyebrow. "And I recall that *I* ordered ye to protect Munro."

"I—"

"Go and fetch him. Now."

Catriona didn't turn around, but she heard Peter setting down that last stack of lumber and stripping off his gloves. A moment later the footman fled around the side of the abbey.

"Now," Glengask went on, finally moving forward and taking a seat on the bottom half of a broken cherub statue. "I've an offer fer ye."

"Do ye, then?" She kept the shovel in her hands, wishing the musket she'd leaned against a tree a few yards away was much closer. Glengask didn't feel . . . safe. Bear didn't either, but in a different way. Munro would never hurt her; of that she was absolutely certain. At the same time, he was a strong, dangerous man. Like a giant club or an axe. The marquis seemed more like a sword—sharp, well balanced, and fast.

"Aye. I've a thousand pounds in my pocket. It's yers. All ye need do is make yer way into Edinburgh and nae come back here. I'll tell Lord Torriden that my sources thought ye'd been spotted in Aberdeen, and ye're as free as ye ever were, with enough money to see ye in a nice hoose with a servant or two."

"And why would ye do that fer me?"

"Because the MacDonald wants ye wed to Torriden.

I dunnae care fer either one of them, but neither do I want the MacLawrys put into the middle of another clan's affairs." He looked her up and down, and she was abruptly very conscious again of her man's clothes and heavy work gloves.

Never mind that just the thought of living in a large town, having to wear a gown and pretend she knew how to manage as a single lady in proper Society made her want to scream and cast up her accounts. Glengask wanted her gone because she could cause trouble for his family and for his clan just by her presence.

Oh, fleeing would be much more simple than standing there to be looked at by someone who viewed her as an inconvenience, as an object to be shifted and maneuvered in the way that best suited his own ambitions. That was how her uncle had viewed her. And it was undoubtedly how Lord Torriden saw her. Not Bear, though. He saw . . . *her.* Giving him up would utterly break her inside.

"Thank ye fer yer kind offer," she said when she thought she could control her voice again, "but I must decline."

"That's very proper language fer a lass who dresses like a drover," he observed.

"Enough," Munro growled, striding into view, Peter on his heels.

Thank goodness. She didn't need him to fight her battles, but simply having him there meant she wasn't alone. Now, though, the problem became preventing the two brothers from coming to blows. "Bear, dunnae—"

"Did ye tell Torriden where to find her?" he demanded, skidding to a stop in front of the marquis.

Glengask kept his seat. "Nae. This isnae aboot him. It's aboot—"

"Dunnae ye tell me what it's aboot," Munro interrupted. "Ye'll nae say a word to Torriden, or I'll see to it he never leaves Glengask alive. And ye'll leave my Haldane Abbey. Now."

"Look at her, Bear. She can take care of herself. Ye dunnae need to take in every wounded, peculiar animal who crosses yer path. This is trouble. Trouble the Mac-Lawrys dunnae nee—"

Munro hit him. The marquis rolled backward, deflecting most of the blow to his shoulder and landing awkwardly on his feet. His expression looked more stunned than pained, as if he couldn't quite believe that his own brother would punch him. Catriona felt stunned, herself.

Bear lifted him up by the collar before Glengask could find his footing. "Leave!" he bellowed, shoving his brother backward, toward the front of the house.

The marquis spat on the ground, pausing only to gesture at the hounds to stay where they were before he strode forward. "Down, dogs," he snapped. "I'll see to this myself."

When Bear stalked forward again to meet him, Catriona dropped the shovel and rushed in, grabbing hold of his shoulder. "Stop it!" she yelled. "He's yer brother. He's yer clan chief."

Bear curled his big hands back into fists. "He insulted ye."

For him that seemed to be all that mattered. "For Saint Andrew's sake, Bear, I've been insulted before. I can bash someone as well as ye can if I feel the need to do so. Ye apologize."

He sent her a startled glance. "Beg yer pardon?"

"Aye, that'll do. But say it to Lord Glengask."

"Nae. I willnae apologize fer protecting ye, wildcat."

She shoved at him. It didn't budge him an inch, but he did lower his arm and open one closed fist. "For the last damned time, I dunnae need yer protection. Nor will I be the cause of a rift between ye and yer family. So ye make this right, or I'm going." A tear ran down her cheek as she spoke, but damnation, she was serious. He had a family he adored. She could not—would not—separate him from that. Not for anything.

"Ye arenae going," he muttered darkly.

"Today, that is up to ye, Munro MacLawry."

With a heavy breath he faced the MacLawry, who'd stopped his advance to watch the exchange intently. No doubt he was trying to decipher if she was manipulating his headstrong brother or not. She didn't think yelling at someone and ordering them to do the correct thing was manipulating them, but she had little experience with subterfuge.

"I apologize fer hitting ye, Ranulf," Bear stated, his jaw clenched. "Ye can pummel me back, if ye like." He took a half step forward. "But I'll nae have ye here. Nae if ye cannae talk to Catriona in a civil manner."

For a long moment the marquis looked from one of them to the other. Then he put a hand down on the larger deerhound's head. "Come along, Fergus. Una."

"And ye'll nae say a word to Torriden."

Lord Glengask's footsteps slowed. "I willnae. But the next time ye set foot in my hoose, Bear, ye'll have that lass with ye so we can resolve this mess, or she'll be gone from here and this mess will be removed from my lands. If ye need someaught, ye can send word through Peter Gilling." He faced them. "Do I make myself clear?"

Munro nodded. "Aye. We're in agreement."

Steel-blue eyes met Catriona's. "Aye. We're in agreement. Fer now."

Chapter Fifteen

Once Ranulf strode out of sight, Munro expected Catriona to sag to the ground or reach for him. Instead she bent down, picked up a clod of dirt, and threw it at him. Hard.

"What the devil, woman?" he muttered, taking the blow on his shoulder. He might have dodged it, but then she likely would only have thrown something heavier.

"Ye might have warned me that he knew I was here," she retorted, the color in her cheeks and the edge to her voice the only real indications that she was flustered.

"I didnae have any idea he suspected someaught." Reaching out, he grabbed her wrist before she could throw something else. "I wouldnae have left ye if I did."

Abruptly she seemed to deflate, her shoulders lowering as she put her free hand on his arm. "Ye struck yer clan chief, Bear," she said, looking up at him from beneath the brim of her old hat. "Yer own brother."

"Aye, I did. And ye made me apologize." Slowly it began to sink in that they were still together, that Ranulf hadn't arrived with half the clan in tow and escorted Cat forcibly off their land. The marquis hadn't brought

Torriden along to claim his bride, or even ordered the
two of them to stay clear of each other. It could have
been much, much worse.

"Did ye think that would help anything, ye brute?"

"Dunnae call me that," he retorted. "I saw ye aiming
a shovel at him."

"I was ready to protect myself. I'm nae accustomed
to . . . being caught unawares."

He lowered his head and kissed her. At this moment,
that seemed more important than anything else he could
conjure. "*I* was protecting ye," he murmured, closing his
eyes as she kissed him back. If a few weeks ago someone had told him he would find such ecstacy in a mere
kiss, he would have laughed. Now he felt . . . light
inside, as if his feet barely touched the ground.

After a long moment she let go of his hair and stepped
back. "Stop kissing me," she ordered, though her gaze
remained on his mouth. "Ye've been banished from yer
own home. Ye did hear that, aye?"

"I heard it. It saves me the effort of riding home and
then sneaking oot every night." The larger scope of it,
the idea that he couldn't return to Glengask at all, he
would contemplate later. Because however much he disliked anyone—even Ranulf—telling him what to do, his
oldest brother had done him a favor. The marquis had
granted him more time with Catriona.

"Ye did what?" Peter Gilling interjected, his own expression a mixture of stunned horror and disbelief—as
if he hoped he'd dreamed the entire incident.

"That doesnae signify now," Munro returned. "Peter,
I'll make ye up a list of things I need. If ye could fetch
'em tonight I'd be grateful."

"Munro, ye ken that ye do have another option." Cat

took his hand, twining her fingers with his as if she couldn't quite keep herself from touching him. "Glengask said ye could come home when I was gone."

"Stop that right there," he cut in. "I'll nae have ye telling yerself ye're doing me a favor by stomping off into the wilds. We're likely to have snow by the end of the week, if nae sooner. Aside from that, nae. Ye arenae leaving."

"So ye expect me to go there with ye and be handed over to Torriden? I'll nae do it. I dunnae want to leave ye, but I didnae come all this way on a whim. I'll nae be an insult and a joke."

Her voice shook as she spoke, and he wanted to pull her close again. That would likely begin another argument about how she'd looked after herself quite well before she'd met him, and she could do so again. He didn't want to hear that she could live without him, because he wasn't certain he could live without her. The idea of her vanishing sent a shiver through his muscles and tightened his chest.

"Mayhap it's good that he found me," she went on, her fingers still twined with his. "The longer we pretended we could continue like this, the harder it would be to stop. Now we have to figure out how we end."

All of the options she imagined, he realized, ended with her being a social outcast, ridiculed and miserable and alone. He didn't know why, but she couldn't seem to imagine herself in any other way. It didn't matter how he saw her. With a hard breath he tightened his fingers on hers and tugged her closer. She could try to kick him if she wanted to.

"Here's what I see in yer future, my lass," he said, putting his free hand beneath her chin so that she had to meet his gaze. "Ye arenae leaving. That means ye're staying. And *that* means ye'll be joining me when I return to Glengask."

She frowned, already shaking her head. "Bear, I—"

"I told ye that I'd show ye as best I can how to be civilized, if that's what ye want to know. There's no sense hiding ye now, except from Torriden, and there's nae a man likely to gossip to a MacDonald. That means I can hire men to help put Haldane back together. Which means that ye and I have a bit of time together, so I can prove to ye that ye should hold yer head high."

"And then what, ye give me away?" A tear started in her eye, and she wiped at it.

"I'll nae give ye away. Glengask is the one who informed the MacDonalds where to find yer sister. This is his mess." He grinned. "Mostly. But I like a good mess."

After a moment her lips curved. "That does explain some things, giant." She continued to eye him, the brief humor fading again from her expression. "Ye ken this could end with ye being sent away from here forever. Ye already hit Lord Glengask. How much more do ye think he'll tolerate from ye?"

Whether that question troubled him or not, was his own affair. For her, he shrugged. "I have what I want. Everything else is secondary. But ye have to agree, wildcat. And ye have to trust me."

"I trust ye."

"Then it's settled."

"I dunnae wish to sound like I'm complaining, Munro, but if what yer brother said was right, and ye felt the need to rescue me like ye would a stray dog, ye need to realize that before we do someaught . . . someaught that cannae be undone."

She'd avoided using the word "marriage," more than likely on purpose. "I ken what I'm saying. But I'll nae ask ye the words until I know ye'll agree to them."

Cat took a slow breath, her dark gaze meeting his. "I wouldnae be doing my part if I didnae ask ye once more if ye're certain—before ye ask any questions ye cannae take back."

Damnation. This wasn't just about him. She wasn't a burden to him. And he was going to have some work to do to convince her just what a rare, valuable, precious lass she was.

"Why dunnae ye join me in the kitchen to see if the stew needs stirring, and I'll try to explain myself to ye," he suggested.

Color rose in her cheeks. "Nae while Peter is here," she muttered.

Munro moved closer. "He's leaving as soon as I send him after clean shirts and a shaving razor. And ye ken that in some parts of the Highlands we've been hand-fasted since the first time I had ye. So ye decide which words ye care to use when ye think aboot the two of us, my lass, and I'll go find some paper."

As he made his way around the front of the house he decided that however much simpler it might make things, if Cat had been the sort of lass he could shake some sense into, he wouldn't have felt the way he did about her. She was damned stubborn, and she'd been seeing herself in a particular way for so long that a few weeks of one man singing her praises wasn't enough to alter her opinion. For once his size and strength counted for nothing; all he could give her was time, and love, and hope.

For the first time in his life, he was going to have to be patient, however poorly he generally managed that.

With a snort he walked into the kitchen and found a piece of paper and pencil, then took a few minutes to contemplate which things he needed to have with him. It was odd, because he already had the one thing he truly needed, and nothing else mattered.

Well, nothing mattered except for the fact that he wasn't certain Catriona was willing to go to the same extremes that he was. He knew damned well what Ranulf had meant—he was to give her up, either to Torriden, or by sending her away out of the range of MacLawry responsibility. Or rather, blame.

Being banished from Glengask was supposed to make him see what a mistake he would be making and how uncomfortable life would be without a clan and his brother the clan chief. Clearly Ranulf didn't know how attached he'd become to his wildcat. He paused in his writing. In fact, his brother had sounded fairly certain that Cat was there only because of his propensity to protect wee things. Hm.

That could be a benefit. Ranulf thought him tangled with Elizabeth—not Catriona. Therefore this was only about teaching him a lesson. If Glengask had realized that it wasn't merely a barely remembered clanswoman his brother wanted, that Munro meant to marry the lass selected by a MacDonald chieftain to likely begin a clan war, he wouldn't have ridden away and let them be. Aye, for once Ran had made a mistake. And Munro would use it to his own advantage.

"Bear?"

He turned to face Cat. "Nae. I dunnae want to hear ye tell me what I shouldnae be fee—"

"Shut yer gobber, giant. I'm talking," she snapped, putting her hands on her hips.

Well, that was promising. Perhaps. "Then talk, lass."

"Ye'd defy yer brother and yer clan to be with me, ye say. Are ye certain of that? Have ye truly thought about what it means?"

"Aye, I've thought aboot it. Ye're worth it to me," he replied.

"Clan MacDonald wants me wed to Lord Torriden. Would ye have them angry with ye, when ye've nae clan of yer own?"

"Do ye think me a lad who's scared of a fight?"

"Nae. But what if I dunnae want ye to fight?"

"Then I reckon there are places we could go where the MacDonalds and the MacLawrys cannae stir up trouble fer us. And aye, I'd go to any one of those places, with ye by my side."

He gazed at her expectantly as she dug her fingers into her hips, her eyes meeting his but her thoughts clearly far from here. Wherever she was going, he hoped he was there with her. Finally she blinked, taking a deep breath. "I dunnae want ye to have to leave yer kin, Munro. I dunnae want us to have to leave the Highlands just so we can be together. But if it comes to that, I'll do it. I want to be with ye. I love ye. Ye drive me mad, and I dunnae ken what ye see in me, but I love ye."

Thank God, he thought, then said it aloud. "Thank God." He grinned, relief flowing through him like the summer sun. "Now I'd fight the world fer ye, wildcat." Stepping forward, he caught her mouth with his, pressing her back against the door frame with the force of his kiss. She wanted him. She wanted to be with him. And for her to simply say it aloud—he knew it hadn't been an easy thing. "I love ye," he murmured against her mouth.

She put her hands on his shoulders and shoved. "So

ye mean to drag me to Glengask and say yer piece to
yer brother and to Lord Torriden, then?"

"Aye. I'm nae going to sneak away like a snake. I'm
a brawler, lass, and I'll have a fight before I'd walk
away."

Catriona nodded. "Then I dunnae want to be the
one to embarrass ye—or myself. Can ye help me with
that?"

He tilted his head. "Ye ken ye look very fine to me
as ye are, I hope."

Color touched her cheeks. "I ken. But for my sake,
I . . . I dunnae want anyone whispering about me be-
cause I'm odd. They can gossip about why ye'd want a
MacDonald, but nae about why ye'd want *this* Mac-
Donald."

Munro nodded. "By God, ye're a marvel. Aye, I'll
help ye. I've a few things to add to my list, then."

Swiftly he added a note to the bottom of his list of
necessities, then went to find Peter. The servant couldn't
read, which made things a bit more complicated, but he
thought he might have someone on his side. Or she
would have been, if he'd trusted anyone enough to con-
fide in her.

"I dunnae understand, m'laird," Peter said, taking the
note and shoving it into a pocket. "Ye dunnae want me
going back to Glengask?"

Munro shook his head. "Gray House. And ye're to
give this note to my sister only. Nae another soul but
Rowena. Into her hands. Do I have yer word?"

The footman scowled. "Of course ye do. Ye may have
noticed that I've known aboot yer lass fer weeks now,
and I havenae told a soul."

"I noticed, Peter. And I thank ye fer it. Gray House.
Stay the night there. We'll see ye in the morning."

"I dunnae think Lord Gray's shirts will fit ye, though."

"Winnie will see to it. She'll likely ride with ye to Glengask in the morning with her own list."

"As ye say, then. But I dunnae like the idea of leaving ye here with naught but a door between ye and trouble, Laird Bear."

Clapping the servant on the shoulder, Munro nudged him in the direction of the cart. "There's been naught but a door between me and trouble fer the past week, Peter. And if ye look at this mess closely, there's been naught between me and trouble at all."

"I'll go, then. Fer God and Saint Bridget's sake, dunnae get yerself killed, m'laird. I would consider it my fault."

"I wouldnae."

"But ye'd be dead, so with all respect, Laird Bear, yer opinion wouldnae signify." Gilling rolled his shoulders. "I saw yer brother all the way from London to Gretna Green with Campbells on our trail. That made me uneasy. This"—and he gestured from Munro to the ruins— "gives me the horrors. Ye're assuming that MacDonald doesnae have spies aboot here, waiting fer ye or the lass to be caught unawares."

"Peter, go. If a MacDonald comes fer me or my lass, it'll be the last thing he does."

With a final grimace and nod, the footman stepped onto the cart and clucked at the mare pulling it. He rumbled down the badly rutted drive, and in a moment the sound of the wheels vanished amid the moaning sound of the crisp evening wind. Munro took a last, careful look about the grounds, telling himself it was merely caution and not anything prompted by the servant's wild imaginings, and then returned to the warm kitchen and the warmer arms of his lass.

And she *was* his lass, whatever anyone else thought they could dictate. She'd stepped into the fray with both feet, and he wasn't about to let her down. Now or ever.

"I'm here," Arran said, stripping off his heavy coat as he stepped into the office. A blast of cold air followed him into the room. "What's amiss?" He scowled. "And why do ye have a black eye?"

Ranulf narrowed both of his eyes, ignoring the resulting ache in the left one. "Close the door."

His brother did as asked, while Ranulf continued to weigh what he wanted to say. Generally he had a fairly straightforward view of the path he meant to lead his clan along. The family had become decidedly more complicated of late, but by now he'd thought he had that under control, as well.

"I'm trying to decide who would have the balls to punch ye," Arran went on, walking to the window and back again, "and I'm having a wee bit of difficulty coming up with more than one name. So I'm guessing ye either ran into a door, or someaught happened between ye and Bear."

"I didnae run into a door."

Arran uttered a soft curse. "I ken he was even more unhappy to see Lord Torriden than we realized. Did ye nae accept the dowry offer fer Elizabeth?"

"I found the sister. Catriona MacColl."

This time his brother sank into a chair. "She's here? Elizabeth lied to us, then?"

"Aye." She had, and he hadn't even thought to approach her about any of this. In his own defense, any conversation with Bear's nearly betrothed would have to be a delicate one, and he didn't feel diplomatic at the moment. "She lied to us, and so did Bear."

"B— She's at Haldane, then?" The middle MacLawry brother swore again. "No wonder he keeps going oot there. Why's he hiding her, though? Did she spin some tale about Torriden? Bear never could resist a rescue. Or a pretty lass."

"I dunnae know what she told him. She's an . . . odd bird, though. Wears men's clothes. I caught her digging oot the old Haldane garden with a shovel. She threatened to run me through with it." He hadn't believed her, of course; her expression had been more startled and horrified than anything else. Not frightened, though. Not of him, anyway. Just of him seeing her.

"She threatened ye? And why did Bear hit ye?"

Ranulf clenched his jaw. The simplest, most honest answer was that Munro had punched him because he'd insulted the lass. That made Bear more of a gentleman than he was, though, and everyone knew how unlikely that was. "I told him that he either needed to bring the lass here to hand her over to Torriden, or get her as far oot of MacLawry territory as he could manage."

"That sounds . . . reasonable. We've had a year of peace. Risking it fer a mannish chit who's promised to a MacDonald isnae someaught I'd like to see."

"Well, arenae ye civilized now?" Ranulf said dryly.

"I'm a father, Glengask. As ye are." He sat forward. "Where is Bear? I'll go see if I can talk some sense into him. Torriden seems pleasant enough. I dunnae see how the Lady Catriona lass could object to him."

"He's still at Haldane. After he walloped me, I told him he wasnae welcome back at Glengask until he dealt with the lass. He lied to me, and that has consequences."

Arran blinked. "Ye . . . Torriden was raised English, Ranulf. If he finds oot ye ordered yer brother to remain in her company . . . She'll be ruined. I cannae think the MacDonald will like that."

"Aye. That's why I sent fer ye. I didnae handle him as well as I should have. I ken that's my fault. He hauled me off my damned feet." He decided that Arran's responding snort was out of annoyance and not amusement. "I'm asking ye to go see him in the morning and see if ye can convince him to be more reasonable. This shouldnae have a thing to do with us. I'll nae have Bear drag us into the middle of another clan's business just because he's stubborn and thinks a lass needs a rescue."

His brother nodded. "I'll chat with him. And remind him that Elizabeth is here withoot him." He glanced toward the curtained window. "Aside from that, I'd nae be surprised if we have snow tomorrow. Haldane Abbey's no place to be when the weather turns."

Hopefully Bear wasn't stubborn enough to risk that. It was bad enough that he wanted to marry a proper, dainty lass who looked like she'd blow over in a stiff wind. If he dug in his heels about a lass meant for a chieftain of another clan just because his brother had told him to be rid of her . . . *Damnation.* Ranulf had learned over the years that simply bellowing orders didn't always suffice. But Bear had always been the hard fist behind his commands—not the one countering them.

"Ranulf?"

He looked up again. "Aye?"

"It may take some blunt to fix this. If I know Bear, he'll nae abandon a lass. Especially one who might have batted her eyes at him and asked fer his help."

"I offered her a thousand pounds already. She turned me doon."

"Perhaps she figures Bear could see her with more."

Arran thought for a moment. "With two or three thousand quid she'd be able to rent her own coach and find herself a cottage in Aberdeen fer the rest of her life, if she wanted. With that, Bear would see that she doesnae require his rescue. Maybe I can make him see that she'd actually be safer withoot him attracting everyone's attention."

Ranulf nodded. "Make it three thousand, then. Ye can tell him aboot her safety, but offer her the blunt oot of Bear's hearing. See if ye can convince her there willnae be any more, and that I willnae have my brother tangled into this mess."

"I can do that."

It all sounded straightforward and logical, but something nagged at the back of his mind. Munro had courted sisters before—Bethia and Flora Peterkin were only the latest—but if he truly meant to wed Elizabeth MacColl he bloody well couldn't remain in an abandoned house with Catriona MacColl. That was *not* how the MacLawrys handled themselves. If the redhead had dug her claws into him for money and protection then Arran would have quite the conversation tomorrow.

But the lass had held a shovel on him. And she'd all but ordered Bear to behave himself . . . and his brother had listened to her. Ranulf shook himself. Whatever this was, it would end tomorrow. It had to, for all their sakes.

Catriona sat cross-legged before the kitchen hearth and watched Bear pace. With his head lowered, his thoughts clearly far from Haldane Abbey, and his long, athletic stride, he looked more like his namesake than ever. That black, shaggy hair hanging nearly to his shoulders, those bright green eyes—he could have anyone, be with anyone, marry anyone. Why in the world had he decided she should be the one for whom he fell? For God's sake, she didn't even know how to curtsy.

And yet for her he'd punched the chief of clan Mac-Lawry. He'd accepted—practically demanded, really—exile from the home he'd known his entire life. He'd separated himself from his siblings, when everyone knew that nothing came between the MacLawrys.

"What's troubling ye?" she made herself ask, though she was fairly certain she knew the answer.

"Peter should be here by now," he replied, stopping to take a swallow of tepid tea and then resuming his pacing.

She narrowed her eyes. "*That's* what's troubling ye? That Peter Gilling is tardy? Dunnae ye ken ye have larger worries than that?"

Altering course, he seated himself beside her. "I do, as a matter of fact," he drawled. "I forgot to ask fer pretty gloves, and I doubt Peter will think to bring 'em along."

"'Pretty gloves'?" she repeated.

"Ye'll see. Ye asked fer my help, and I'll do my best fer ye." He reached over to tug on her hair, bringing her closer and kissing her softly on the mouth.

"With wee delicate gloves."

"Dunnae sass me, woman."

She chuckled. "Ye can try to stop me."

A knock sounded at the door. Releasing her, Munro stood again and lifted the bar. "It's aboot damned . . ."

As he trailed off, Catriona looked up. And couldn't quite stifle her gasp. The tall, black-haired Adonis in the doorway had to be his other brother, Arran. The middle MacLawry brother. She shoved to her feet, more because she didn't want anyone towering over her than because she was frightened. *Damnation.* So Lord

Glengask had decided to send someone else to gawk at her and order her to either marry Torriden or go far away. Why couldn't they simply leave things be? Why couldn't they just go away?

"What do ye want, Arran?" Munro asked, keeping a hand on the door, presumably so he could shut it on his brother if need be.

"Cannae a lad call on his brother if he wants to?" Light blue eyes caught hers. "And the sister of the lass his brother's decided to marry?"

Something . . . unpleasant thudded through her. And not because she'd hardly spared her sister more than a half-dozen thoughts in over a week. The MacLawrys still thought Bear wanted to marry Elizabeth. He hadn't said or done anything to dispose them of that belief. Of course he would say that he'd done it for her, to keep attention on Elizabeth, who was safe at Glengask and only being pursued by an Englishman. And he *had* done it for her; she was certain of that. All the same, she still didn't like even hearing that Bear was meant for someone else.

"That depends," Bear returned, still blocking most of the doorway, "on what the lad means to say to his brother and the lass."

Lord Arran frowned. "So ye've a mind to stay barricaded in here until Torriden goes away? Ye ken that snow is coming. Planks and a tarp willnae keep the winter oot of this room. Nor will one fire amid broken walls keep ye warm."

"Ye arenae saying anything I dunnae already know. If Glengask wants ye to frighten me, well, he cannae. And neither can ye. I gave my word to keep this lass safe."

"Then let me speak to her fer a moment, ye big ox.

I'll nae try to drag her away, or say anything against either of ye."

"Ye'll say naught to her that ye cannae say in front of me. We dunnae need yer clever tongue here."

The middle MacLawry brother blew out his breath. "There are plenty of things I cannae say in front of ye, because ye're so damned determined to make this into a fight. I'm nae here to fight. I'm bloody well nae here to get my nose broken. So ye go and sit in the corner, and let me have a word with the lass. Unless ye're scared of what she might say to me."

It made sense. The MacLawrys wanted to know her intentions, how much trouble she was willing to cause, and perhaps even if she had grounds for her dislike of Lord Torriden. They wanted their brother back, and she happened to be the stumbling block. Swallowing, Catriona stepped forward. Arran was the cleverest of them, Bear had said, though her giant had far more wits about him than she'd first expected. She didn't feel at all clever, herself, but she could be honest. "I'll go fer a stroll with ye, Laird Arran," she said, rather pleased that her voice remained steady.

"Nae," Bear cut in. "Ye willnae."

She shoved at his hip, trying to make room for herself to get through the doorway. "I'm nae certain I heard ye, there. Did ye just say ye werenae going to let me talk?"

With a grumble that sounded more like a growl, he shifted sideways. "Do as ye will, then. But I'm nae standing here in the corner. Ye have yer chat, and I'll be keeping an eye on the two of ye, just to be certain things stay civilized."

Arran offered his arm as she left the kitchen for the hallway, but she pretended not to notice and instead led the way toward the broken front doors. "What do ye have to say to me, then?" she prompted, as they reached the front drive.

"Nae pleasant talk aboot the weather?" he returned, lifting an eyebrow. "Or a question aboot how yer own sister is faring withoot her betrothed?"

"If that's what ye wish to talk aboot, I suppose I can follow along. But ye might have said all that in front of Bear."

A brief smile touched his mouth. "So I might've. Very well, then. To the point, it is. My brother Ranulf and I reckon that Bear's nae one to abandon ye in a predicament, so I can help ye get to wherever it is ye wish to go. Aberdeen, Edinburgh, even to the Continent or the Americas. Glengask said he offered ye a thousand pounds. In my view, ye want to stay hidden, so I'll triple that fer ye."

"That's very generous of ye." And considering that they seemed to have no idea that she and Munro were . . . together, she had to wonder if a subsequent offer would be more or less generous.

"Aye. We've nae quarrel with the MacDonalds, but by virtue of the fact that we're MacLawrys, we get noticed. Glengask reckons he was a wee bit too forceful yesterday, so I'm here to make certain ye ken that we've no wish to harm ye. It's clear that ye dunnae want to be married to Lord Torriden, and because ye're to be my brother's in-law, we'll nae force that on ye, either. But ye need to go away from here. If ye're discovered, ye'll be putting us, and Bear, into the middle of the MacDonald squabble."

Oh, it all made sense. A great deal of sense. And a few weeks ago she might have jumped at the chance to fund herself well away from the MacDonalds. She couldn't leave the Highlands, though, when it was the only place she felt comfortable. A house without a roof looking to join the floor, though, and a cow for milk— she could see herself with that. Or she could have.

He was right about something else she'd never truly considered, either. Bear was very noticeable. Even if he hadn't been one of the infamous MacLawry siblings, he was tall, broad-shouldered, and striking. Being with him anywhere made the odds of her staying hidden much worse.

And yet neither was it all so straightforward. Everything had become more complicated. Now someone else owned her heart, and even if he garnered more attention sent in her direction, she couldn't imagine being somewhere he was not. "I understand yer predicament," she said slowly, trying to find the most correct and least offensive words, "and I'm sorry to have caused it. That wasnae why I brought Elizabeth here."

"Why did ye bring her here?"

"I couldnae bring her to Islay, because of—"

"Because of Torriden," he finished for her. "There are other places outside of Islay and London."

She nodded. "Aye. I reckon I might have taken her to another city. She likely would've been happier with people aboot. But we didnae have any money, so I couldnae have seen her with a nice place to stay in a town, anyway. It's easier to be poor in the countryside, I reckon."

"*She* would have been happier," he repeated, setting upon that tiny portion of her comments like a hound on a rabbit. "Ye prefer to nae have people aboot?"

Catriona glanced over her shoulder for Bear, but he stalked just out of earshot, evidently waiting for her signal before he charged into battle. She stifled a sigh.

Lord Arran had to know how out of place she would be in any town just by looking at her. "I've nae illusions about myself, if that's yer meaning."

"I'm just curious," Arran returned. "Bear seems very determined to protect ye."

With a shrug she stopped by the low front wall. "I've told him over and over that I dunnae need protection. I can look after myself."

"And yet he put a fist into our *bràthair*'s face when Ranulf said ye needed to leave." He favored her with another sideways glance. "Ye ken why we cannae have ye staying here, aye?"

Oh, she understood. Her presence meant nothing but trouble for all the MacLawrys, and for Bear especially. And yet the idea of leaving, of being without him in her life . . . She'd never felt selfish before. But she did now. She wanted Munro. She wanted to stay in the Highlands. "I ken that I came here to keep my sister safe, and to hide myself. I dunnae quite feel like that lass any longer—or I didn't, until ye and yer big brother came to stare at me like I was a king's jester."

"Ye speak yer mind, I see."

"I'm nae dressed fer subtlety."

He tilted his head, light green eyes assessing, and very different from the warm, direct gaze of his younger brother. "Then I'll be direct, as well. I think ye've been stared at before, Lady Catriona. And I think ye didnae want to be stared at by the man promised to marry ye. Unless ye've been sewn into those clothes, ye dunnae have to wear 'em, so I reckon ye didnae want to be fit fer Lord Torriden. My question is, why are ye claiming ye dunnae need Bear aboot, and then keeping him close by yer side?"

Just like that, he'd read her character, assessed her

thoughts, and declared her a coward. And he wasn't too far off, either. "Ask yer brother, m'laird. He's nae in chains."

"I married a Campbell lass," he said unexpectedly. "Did ye know that? The granddaughter of the Campbell."

"Bear told me. And I've heard tales."

"I nearly began a war to keep her by my side. And I'd do it again, in a heartbeat. Mary's the air in my lungs, and the blood in my veins."

"That's a lovely sentiment. I dunnae quite see the p—"

"My point is," he broke in, his voice still low and steady and cool, as if they were discussing cattle or the wheat harvest and not her entire future, "if ye came here to escape a marriage ye didnae want, I've three thousands pounds that'll see ye where ye want to go. Ye can make yerself safe, and if ye live frugally ye'll nae have to find employment anywhere. If ye're here fer another reason, ye'd best be ready to fight. Fight the MacLawrys fer it. Do ye ken?"

"Aye."

With that he pulled a billfold from his pocket and handed it to her. "Dunnae do what ye *think* is right. Do what ye *know* is right. My brother's put his arse in the middle of this, and he doesnae know how to change his course once he's settled on someaught. Dunnae make him regret his loyalty."

As Arran MacLawry nodded and turned toward his younger brother, Catriona closed her fingers around the billfold. Three thousand pounds *would* see her to Aberdeen and into a small house, with more than enough left over to give her time to find . . . something she could do to make a living. Or perhaps a cottage in the country, where she could keep to herself. She would still *be* herself, of course—whatever she did, she couldn't seem to be rid of that.

She turned to watch as the brothers spoke for a moment and then shook hands, suspicion in the hard, straight line of Bear's shoulders, and caution in the way Arran set his feet, ready to dodge a blow. That was wrong; the MacLawrys were united. Always. And two of the three brothers now had made it very clear that they didn't consider her worthy of being part of the clan—even as the sister to the lady they both seemed to think Bear should and would be marrying.

As Arran swung up onto his black Thoroughbred, the cart and Peter Gilling bumped into view along the drive. The back of the wagon rose in an irregularly shaped mound, the load covered with a heavy tarp. Whatever Bear had sent for, evidently he'd meant it to last him for some time.

"What are ye carrying, Peter?" Arran asked, reining in beside the cart.

The footman flushed. "I couldnae say, Laird Arran. I cannae read, as ye know, so I didnae see the list. I was put in charge of gathering Laird Bear's clothes and boots."

The middle MacLawry brother twisted in the saddle to face the abbey. "The back half of this building fell beneath the weight of winter snow, Bear. I dunnae want to come oot and find the front half gone with ye inside it."

"Mind yer own hoose, Arran, and I'll mind mine," Bear returned, his fingers brushing against hers.

"So be it." With a nudge of his heels Arran MacLawry sent his mount into a trot. In a moment he was gone behind the overgrown weeds and foliage.

Bear immediately caught hold of her hand. "He did-nae frighten ye away, I hope."

"He was very polite," she returned, taking in his large fingers wrapped around her smaller ones. "He gave me three thousand pounds to settle myself elsewhere, and said the MacLawrys didnae want trouble with the Mac-Donalds."

His gaze held hers. "The rest of the MacLawrys might be happy with letting things happen that should-nae. They have bairns and tea parties and go shopping and chat aboot London, now. This MacLawry likes a bit of a brawl, and I'm looking forward to one. But keep the money; I've said my piece, and whatever I may want of ye, the decision is yers."

That was circumspect of him. "I will keep it, then."

Tugging her forward, he walked them up to the cart as Peter hopped to the ground. "Did ye get what I asked fer?"

"Aye, m'laird. Every bit of it. And a note from yer . . . other party," the servant said, digging into his sporran and pulling out a well-folded missive.

Munro unfolded it, running his gaze along several lines. A smile touched his mouth, and he handed the letter to her. "My sister sends her kind regards, and a few things we might find useful," he said, and pulled back the tarp to reveal a large trunk, several boxes, and the unmistakable shape of a full-length mirror beneath a heavy blanket.

"What's all this for?" Catriona asked, hopping onto the cart and unlatching the trunk. Silk spilled out into her hands. Yards and yards of silk and muslin and cotton, all formed into what looked like a dozen lovely gowns. "Oh, dear."

"Aye." His grin deepened, and he leaned in for a kiss.

"This MacLawry and this MacDonald are aboot to gear up fer war. Are ye ready?"

She couldn't help meeting his smile with one of her own. No one made her feel as he did, and she had the distinct feeling that no one ever would again. "This is what ye want, Munro? Truly? Very truly?"

His slow, wicked smile made her heart flip-flop. "Ask me as many times as ye wish, my lass. I want to be with ye. I want to tell Glengask that he doesnae get to dictate to me any more than he could to Arran or Rowena." He sighed. "They find me useful to have aboot because I'm a big, intimidating lad. I want to know what they'll do now that I've decided to be big and intimidating fer myself."

This *was* for him, as well as for her. And that made it . . . easier. As he'd said before, he didn't seem to be a man who could be forced to do something against his own will. Which meant he did want all of this. And her. Wordlessly she handed the billfold over to him. "Then I'm nae going anywhere. Aye. I'm ready."

Chapter Sixteen

"Can I open my eyes yet?" Munro asked, trying to decide whether Cat was being missish, or coy. He'd seen her naked and he'd touched her bare skin enough that he could say she was teasing him now on purpose, except that where dresses were concerned, he could damned well believe Catriona was genuinely nervous. As for him, just the thought of seeing her in proper lass's clothes made his kilt tent up again. Apparently thinking of her at all aroused him.

"Wait a bloody minute," she grumbled, her voice strained.

"What's amiss? I told ye I could help ye with the buttons."

"But then ye'll see me before I'm ready."

He stifled a grin that would likely have gained him a black eye. "I can button ye with my eyes closed. Just come over here and guide me."

She sighed audibly. "Open yer damned eyes, then. Ye're supposed to be showing me how to do this, anyway."

"Ye'd have a maid to help ye, lass. Did ye nae have one growing up?"

"Nae. I almost had a valet, but I think my father realized that would be going too far."

After giving her a moment or two to change her mind about whether he could look at her or not, he opened his eyes. And stopped breathing. Catriona and his sister were of a size, though Cat's bosom was more generous. And the way she filled out the soft green silk with its lace sleeves and neckline stunned him. "Well, now," he breathed.

The already high color in her cheeks darkened. "Stop that. It isnae helpful." She stomped her foot. "And I thought ye said ye liked me in trousers."

"I do like ye in trousers. And I like ye in a dress, and I like ye in naught but what God gave ye." He shrugged, resisting the urge to touch her. If he pulled her out of the dress now, she'd likely never put one on again. "Ye look different, is all. And splendid."

The corners of her mouth dimpled. "Fine, then. Help me button this thing up. Why they dunnae put the buttons in the front, I have nae idea."

Standing, he stepped forward to tug the edges of the gown together across her back. "Because this dress is aboot showing off. If ye can afford to wear it, ye can afford a maid."

"That doesnae take into account the option of borrowing the clothes." She'd pinned her hair up in a messy tangle of scarlet, the sight of which didn't help his concentration at all. He'd fastened—and unfastened—a lass's gown before, but he couldn't remember ever feeling so mesmerized by such a simple, ordinary task. When he'd made her his once and for all, he wasn't certain he wanted her to have a maid. He wouldn't mind doing this every day for the rest of his life.

Three buttons from the bottom, Munro leaned down and kissed the nape of her neck. The delicate shiver that went through her made him hard. Perhaps a wee bit of undressing wouldn't do any harm.

"Stop that, giant," she grumbled, before he could undo the progress he'd made. "Yer family's already seen me and decided I'm a mannish clod. I want to make a better second impression. And I dunnae want them to think ye're the fool for choosing me over Elizabeth."

Well, he couldn't argue with that, even if he didn't see anything mannish about her. Whatever she said, this wasn't about him and whether his family thought him foolish. This was about her, and how she saw herself. He meant to do whatever it took to help her see the lass she wanted to be when she looked in the mirror. Not one she was embarrassed by and ashamed of.

Clenching his jaw against his lust, he finished buttoning the wee, delicate ivory buttons that trailed down her back to her waist. "All secured," he announced when he'd finished, and stepped back again. "Turn around and let's see ye."

Blowing out her breath, she did so. With her chin in the air and her hands on her hips she was clearly daring him to comment, but he didn't know which would get him in more trouble—admiring her, or saying he preferred her more accustomed attire. "Ye look like a lass stepping oot fer a soiree," he said after a moment, mentally crossing his fingers. "Ye've nae grown an extra arm, and ye havenae fallen doon. How do ye feel?"

"Naked. And with a cold breeze going up my legs." Munro risked a grin. "As ye're talking to a lad wearing a kilt, ye'll get no sympathy from me on that account, wildcat. Take a walk aboot the room. And dunnae stomp; ye're in slippers, and ye'll hurt yer feet."

The glare she sent him at least had a touch of exasperated humor in it, and that was more than he'd expected. Neither had she tried to justify her man's attire as being more practical or comfortable, though he knew that it at least was warmer. All in all, standing there she looked like a lovely lass in a dress that hugged her curves like firelight.

"Walk," he repeated, gesturing her toward the doorway.

She walked, moving to the door and back to the table, then stopping to face him again. "Well?"

"Yer steps are too long." He eyed her for a moment. "Pretend ye're walking through a puddle and trying nae to make a splash."

"This is ridiculous."

"And look in the mirror," he pressed, ignoring her protest.

She shook her head. "I dunnae want to."

"Then walk into Glengask as ye prefer; it doesnae make any difference to me."

That made her grimace, but she walked the path again, this time taking more care to place her feet. "I feel like I'm about to fall over," she muttered, digging her hands into her skirt and lifting so she could see her shoes. "And aye, I know I cannae walk with my gown hiked up to my knees. I'm practicing."

"Ye'd see me doing the same thing if I was to wear those wee bits of scrap. Aside from that, I like looking at yer legs."

Finally she meandered over to the corner where he'd

set the mirror. For a long moment she stood glaring at him, as if it were his fault that she wanted to wear a gown, then with an audible breath she turned around. "Oh."

"Ye see? Ye look like a lass in a gown."

Reaching up, she tugged the neckline up a bit, then scowled at the reflection of her hair. "This doesnae look like me."

"It *is* ye, so argue with yer own reflection if ye want to."

She turned this way and that, swishing the gown about her legs. However many lessons she still needed in etiquette and propriety, the view kept his attention well enough that the roof could have caved in without him noticing. His family would laugh if they knew he'd taken on the task of teaching a lass how to act like a lass, but for God's sake, someone needed to do it—and he didn't want anyone else looking at her askance.

Then she tried a curtsy, and nearly fell into the mirror. "Damnation," she muttered, holding on to the wood frame to right herself. "I cannae do this, Bear."

Munro straightened, walking over to take her hand and stand facing the mirror beside her. There he was, unruly hair that badly needed a barber's attention, a clean white shirt and waistcoat with a faded kilt starting to unravel along the bottom edge, a giant famous for his muscles and his fists. What a pair they were.

"Try it again," he said aloud, holding her fingers firmly. "I'll nae let ye fall. And move yer hind leg back a bit, so ye've a sturdier base."

With a frown she sank down again, wobbling on the shoes' low heels. Once she became his wife there would be very few people to whom she would ever need curtsy, but if she wanted to learn how to do it, he would do his damnedest to show her.

"That was better," she said, watching herself assessingly as she tried it a third time. "All I need is for ye to hold my hand so I dunnae topple over."

"Then I'll hold yer hand," he returned. "Whether or nae ye decide to curtsy." When that only made her smile, he ran the forefinger of his free hand along her skin just above the low neckline. Soft and warm, she was, and his in everything but name—whether she was ready to admit it yet or not.

Someone rapped at the door. Immediately Cat clutched onto her skirt and went to hide behind the corner of the fireplace. Interesting, that. In her trousers she was fearless. Whether she didn't feel as . . . strong in a gown or if she truly thought she looked hideous, the change in her character was obvious. And in his, as well. After Ranulf and then Arran had come calling, he'd found that his willingness to do anything to protect his lass, even if she might claim she didn't need him, had grown by leaps and bounds.

"Who is it?" he asked, moving up to the door.

"It's Peter, m'laird. I've brought 'em."

Munro lifted the bar and pulled open the door. "How many?"

"Once they realized they'd be laboring fer a Mac-Lawry, I couldnae keep 'em away," the servant returned. "A dozen fer today. I could double that tomorrow, if ye wanted."

"Let's see how the twelve do," Murno returned. "Cat, I'll be back in a moment. Keep practicing."

Peter managed a glance past him, a swift grin touching his craggy face. "I had occasion t'wear a gown once, lass. Laird Arran said I needed to move my hips more."

"Shut yer gobber, ye heathen," Munro countered,

grabbing the footman by the jacket and towing him up the hallway. "Cannae ye see she's nervous?"

"I'd be nervous, too, if I had to put on proper attire fer the first time and act like a blue-blooded Sassannach or someaught." Peter narrowed his eyes. "Ye mean to bring her to Glengask, then? But nae to hand her over to the viscount?"

"I'm nae handing her over to anyone. She's mine, Peter."

"That isnae going to make Laird Glengask or the MacDonald happy." The servant sighed. "Why is it when ye and yer brothers decide to wreak havoc, ye always throw me into the middle of it with ye?"

"Because we trust ye, Peter Gilling."

"Aye, I ken that. Sometimes I think I should be a shiftier fellow, though. Someone nae fit fer mad adventures and beginning wars."

Hiding his grin, Munro clapped the servant on the shoulder. "Ah, ye're too steadfast and trustworthy. A MacLawry, through and through."

"I suppose so. It's a burden I have to carry."

The dozen men outside were already pulling down the rubble at the rear of Haldane Abbey, separating stones that could be used again from the ones that would need to be carted away. They were polite enough to him, though he didn't have to be clairvoyant to catch the sideways glances and crossed fingers they sent toward the abbey every so often. The place had been rumored to be haunted for over a hundred years, after all, though neither he nor Cat had seen or heard anything they couldn't put to shifting timber and tumbled bits of stone.

"I reckon ye should put old Sholto Landers in charge, being that he and his *athair* were in the crew that built that pottery works fer yer brother. But then again ye may nae want him aboot, since his boy Sorley is set to marry Miss Bethia."

Munro slowed. "Bethia Peterkin?"

"Aye. Owen said Sir Alpin called on Glengask a few days ago to announce the betrothal. Apparently he was worried, Sir Alpin was, that ye'd be angry aboot it."

The image that came to his mind was a wicked tongue and a great deal of yowling. An evening's entertainment when he had nothing better to do. Those evenings, though, were gone now. And surprisingly enough, he hadn't even given them a second thought until this moment. Apparently he'd grown up without even realizing it. Only one lass kept his interest now, and he enjoyed her as much for the way she kept him on his toes as for the way she made him feel in bed.

"Are ye? Angry, I mean."

Shaking himself, he gestured Peter to continue toward the tall, white-haired Scot currently jotting down notes on a much-folded piece of paper. "Sholto," he said, offering his hand.

The older man stood up, wiped his palm on his jacket, and shook hands. "Laird Bear. It's aboot time someone made use of this old place."

"Do ye think ye might be willing to meet with an architect and take charge of putting the abbey back together?"

Color touched pale cheeks. "Aye? Aye, I mean. I'd be honored." He cleared his throat. "I thought ye might be a wee bit . . . angry over my Sorley winning Bethia Peterkin. He's made a good life fer himself, though. He went to school, and now he's a physician. He's—"

"I'm nae angry, Sholto. I reckon yer Sorley will be a good husband to Bethia. I lost her to the better man."

Sholto seemed to grow an inch or two. "That's very

kind of ye, m'laird. And I'd be pleased to meet with yer architect."

"Thank ye. In the meantime, I'll be relying on ye to get this ruin ready fer restoration."

"I'll see to it, m'laird."

As Munro turned back for the front of the house, he caught one of the other workers making the sign against the evil eye and spitting, while several others had stopped working to stare up toward the second floor of the abbey. "What's amiss, lads?" he asked.

Immediately they went back to work amid a chorus of, "Good day, Laird Bear," and "There's a chill in the air today. I reckon we'll have snow by the end of the week."

Given the reputation of the place, he couldn't blame some of the lads for being nervous around it. He didn't feel it, of course; Haldane Abbey had been nothing but a place of blessings and surprises since he'd stumbled across Catriona MacColl. Even so, he sent a quick glance up toward the roofless second story as he left the garden. Nothing caught his gaze but the stack of lumber they'd left up there to keep the tarp in place.

When he returned to the kitchen, Cat was walking in a large circle, her steps overly cautious but better than the stomping she'd done when she'd first donned the walking shoes. Leaning back against the door frame, he took a moment to just look at her. Perhaps it was her sister who had the finer, more delicate features, the soft, honey-colored hair, and the trimmer waist that a man's two hands could span. But Cat . . . that flaming hair, those delicious curves, the stubborn determination to have the life she wanted—she shone brighter than fire-light in his eyes, and he never wanted to look away.

For the first time, though, he wondered if he was the

best choice for her. She wanted to learn how to be more refined, more of a lady, and he barely warranted the title gentleman. Perhaps Bethia Peterkin was the sort of lass he'd earned for himself, good for a tumble and not much caring about anything else. The thought of a life-time of that made him shudder, but a few months ago that was the trail he'd been pursuing.

Even the idea that Torriden could help his wildcat better than he could made his jaw clench and sent ice through his chest, but God help him, he wanted her to be happy. "Cat," he said, hearing the growl in his voice and trying to shove it back. "I need to ask ye a question."

She lifted her head, the slight, amused smile at the corners of her mouth dropping as she looked at him. "What is it?"

"I keep . . . bringing ye things ye say ye dunnae need, making changes to the abbey ye say ye dunnae require, and now I reckon it's because of me that ye're wearing a gown and learning to walk in dainty shoes when I ken ye're happier in boots and trousers. I'm loud, I like brawls and punching things, and I only started reading Shakespeare's sonnets because ye said ye enjoyed them." He swallowed. "Is this—am I—what ye want? Truly? Because if I'm nae the one fer ye, ye need to tell m—"

Halfway through his rambling she dropped the hair-brush she'd been carrying and strode toward him. She didn't stop until she yanked his face down for a hard, fierce kiss, tangling one hand into his rough coat and sliding the other around his neck. He wrapped his arms around her, lifting her off her feet and pulling her close against his chest.

"All this time," she muttered, in between kisses, "I've been thinking I'm only trouble fer ye, that ye felt obligated to take me in because ye were the one to find me. Ye're the only . . . person I've ever met who makes me feel like me, and be happy aboot it. Even my *athair*—he wanted to see a lad. I'm a poor excuse fer a lass, and I dunnae want to cause so much trouble fer ye, Bear."

"Didnae ye hear me a moment ago?" he returned, setting her back on her feet but not releasing his grip on her waist. "I like trouble. I'm a damned Highlander when we seem to be a dying breed, and ye're a damned Highlands lass. Nae an excuse fer one."

"We are a couple of misfits, I reckon," she said, her dark brown eyes shining with unshed tears.

"Aye. And I want ye with me. If that's where ye want to be."

Catriona nodded. "With ye is precisely where I want to be, Munro."

He held her gaze. "Whatever happens."

Her deep breath pushed at the already tight bosom of her gown. "Whatever happens. We stay together. And ye're nae making me wear this gown. I chose to try it oot. I've naught against dressing like a lass. I just never had a reason to risk embarrassing myself by attempting it, before."

There. That was what he wanted. Her. As for the rest—his family, her family, her betrothed—they could stomp their feet and make threats and even expel them from the clan. If he had Catriona MacColl, he had everything he needed.

Finally he let her go. "Very well, then. Do ye still want to be in a gown, or shall we burn it?"

The grin touched her mouth again. "I want to be able to wear it withoot looking like a half-wit. Ye may like me as I am, but ye'd be the only one." She put a hand over his mouth before he could protest that. "Ye cannae deny, both yer brothers have a notion of what sort of lass I am. If we're to stand before them—whether ye mean to cast them aside or nae—I'd like to be able to show them I'm nae some madwoman."

For Saint Andrew's sake, he could understand wanting to be like everyone else. To not be noted for his size or the nickname he'd had since he was eight years old, to be able to walk into a proper soiree and not have every eye turn to look at him and wonder if he'd be tromping on everyone's toes. Oddly enough, the only time he didn't mind being called a giant was when she said it to him. "Then get back to gliding aboot the room, woman," he said, with a grin of his own.

"I'd like to see ye look graceful in these things," she returned, but resumed walking.

"I can ask yer sister to come teach ye," he ventured after a moment. "I reckon she knows how to do all these lady things."

She shook her head. "Nae. I . . . I'd like to surprise her, too."

"Or *my* sister."

"Stop it, Bear. I'll be happy to figure oot how to be yer version of a proper lass. Anything more is just looking for disaster to strike."

Munro laughed. "Ye're already my version of a proper lass, lass." He tilted his head, continuing to watch her appreciatively as she minced now from the table to the hearth. "I dunnae suppose ye ken how to waltz, do ye?"

"Nae." She shook her head, shuddering. "Papa wanted to teach me, but I refused to learn the man's steps. I could imagine the sight I would be, asking some other lass onto the floor." Her cheeks paled as she eyed him. "Why are ye asking me?"

He took a step forward. "Because I happen to be a fine dancer. At the Highlands fling, at least. But I'll teach ye to waltz, if ye dunnae mind me tripping all over ye."

With a sigh that didn't quite disguise the abrupt shaking of her hands, she walked up to him and held out her arms. "Shoulder and hand, aye?"

"Aye." He took her left hand and placed her right on his shoulder. "And I take yer waist, like so. Then we move clockwise and dunnae fall over."

"Oh, as simple as that, is it?"

"I reckon so."

If he'd ever doubted that she trusted him, the way she threw herself into learning both the waltz and how to walk like a lass in fine shoes proved that she trusted him now. And aye, he was proficient at the waltz, because when Winnie had begun complaining about her heathen big brothers not knowing anything civilized, Ranulf had hired a dance master to teach the lot of them. At the time he'd done all he could to balk, but at this moment, with this woman in his arms, he was grateful for the lessons. He loved Cat as she was, but that also meant he wouldn't embarrass her when she wanted to try something new.

And this, being with one woman, allowing himself to simply enjoy chatting and dining with and reading or listening to her read—it was all new to him, as well. He'd never thought an old kitchen could be home, but she'd made it so. She'd become his home, his peace, and his excitement with an ease he'd never looked for, and never expected. And now, he would never give her up. Even if keeping her meant giving up clan MacLawry and his brothers and sister and their spouses and bairns. If there was any way to avoid that, though, he might be willing to listen. If being a little less . . . himself would get him what he wanted, well, he'd begun to realize some things were worth changing for. Some lasses. One lass.

"Where did ye learn to braid hair?" Catriona asked, trying not to shiver in delight as Bear ran a brush through another section of her hair and began neatly plaiting it into a braid.

"Winnie. All three of us had to learn how to pin up hair fer her. I do a fair twisting bun, as well, if ye'd like to try that tomorrow."

She sent a glance at the mirror, trying not to move her head as she did so. After two days the sight of herself in a gown still surprised her, but the original shock, the sense that she was doing something wrong, had subsided. With half her hair back in looping braids she actually looked . . . ladylike. The sensation was only surface deep, because on the inside she remained much less certain, but both for Bear's and her sake she meant to give it a try.

"Did ye see the snow on the mountains this morning?" she asked, twirling a green ribbon in her fingers.

"I did. It'll nae be long, now. I reckon I'll ask some of the lads to join me up on the roof here and see what we can do with that grand hole in the ceiling. Five pounds of snow will have the tarp doon here in the kitchen with us."

That amount of snow would also have the lads giving up on construction for the winter, but she didn't say that aloud. Bear knew it as well as she did, if not better, since he'd grown up here. For the past two days, something else had been pressing at her more closely even than the weather, anyway. "Are ye surprised they've let ye be?" she asked.

"Nae," he returned, not bothering to ask to whom "they" referred. "I reckon they're waiting fer first snow, figuring I'll surrender then." Reaching around her shoulder, he took the ribbon from her fingers. "I'll be seeing 'em then, but it willnae be to surrender."

She grinned, excitement beginning to mingle with the nervousness that fluttered through her every time she thought of meeting the MacLawry face-to-face for a second time. Three days of wearing dresses hardly made her a lady, but she felt closer to being one than she had four days ago. They still wouldn't approve of her, of course. In fact, if they figured she was playing at being proper they'd dislike her even more. *That* continued to trouble her, mostly because of how the big man currently playing with her hair would react.

"Well, what do ye think?" he asked a moment later, stepping back. "Dunnae laugh, but I think I may go oot to find work as a lady's maid."

Catriona stood to face the full-length reflection of herself. "I think I look very fine," she said after a moment, turning a slow circle. "I'd hire ye to put up my hair."

It continued to surprise her how much more Munro was than the big, handsome oaf she'd first caught sight of a month ago. Aye, he jested about using his fists and his manly muscles, but he was also clever—more clever than he likely realized—and skilled with his hands in a way most men of his station wouldn't even dream. Affectionate, surprisingly tender, and for Saint Andrew's sake, he didn't mind putting her hair up for her.

"What's going on in that mind of yers, wildcat?" he asked, moving up behind her and sliding his arms about her waist.

"I want to ask ye to promise me someaught," she returned, gazing at the reflection of his pretty green eyes.

"Promise ye what, then? I'll nae agree withoot hearing, because ye're sneaky and I've nae intention of—"

"Promise me that ye'll give yer brothers a chance to talk to ye," she cut in. "Dunnae stomp yer feet and bellow and declare they've wronged ye and ye'll nae set eyes on 'em again."

"I promise ye this, Cat. I'll let my brothers say their piece. I'll listen to 'em. I'll give 'em a moment to see that they had me paired with the wrong sister, even. But if they try to insult ye, if they let Torriden anywhere near either of us, I'm going to get angry." The slow smile that curved his mouth looked anything but amused, and she was glad it wasn't directed at her. "Very angry."

"Bear, they're yer fam—"

"I ken who they are. I agreed to listen. I'll nae promise to give an inch if they suggest I part from ye."

Letting out her breath, she turned in his arms to face him. "Ye're a damned stubborn man, Munro MacLawry." Lifting up on her toes, she kissed him softly.

He kissed her back, tightening his grip around her waist. "That I am," he agreed. "And ye're a damned stubborn woman, Catriona MacColl. I almost feel sorry fer anyone who tries to step between us. Almost."

"Three damned days," Ranulf muttered, lowering his voice as Lord Torriden and Lady Elizabeth passed down the hallway headed for the billiards room. "What the devil is Bear waiting fer? She took the money, ye said."

"I put it in her hand, and she didnae throw it back at me," Arran returned. "And Bear didnae run after me and pull me oot of the saddle."

Ranulf nodded. "She seemed a bright lass. Hopefully she realized that three thousand pounds is likely to last her longer than Bear's sympathy once the weather turns cold." He reached down to scratch Fergus's head as the big hound lay beside the chair in his office. "I only hope our *bràthair*'s nae so stubborn he stays on at Haldane oot of principle."

"Peter Gilling says she's still there. Of course the mail coach isnae due in An Soadh fer another two days; mayhap he means to wait there with her until then."

"Or mayhap he means to wait until Torriden gives up and goes away. We could encourage that, I suppose, but if she gets found later it could be held against us." He smacked his fist against the surface of his desk. "I dunnae like the idea of him being that far from here, with nae a man to walk the halls at night."

"The only livable room is the kitchen, and they've patched that grand hole in the corner with tarps and planks. The first good snow will have him oot of there, even if naught else does it." Arran shifted, his gaze drifting toward the window.

"Then what has ye troubled?" Ranulf prompted.

"I just have a tickle at the back of my scalp," the middle MacLawry brother returned after a moment. "Bear has a lass here, but he's there."

"Elizabeth doesnae need his protection, because she has ours. The other one's hiding from clan. He knows I'll nae be involved with that. If Bear's one thing, it's stubborn. He doesnae want to admit that he's wrong in all this."

"Aye, I suppose ye have the right of it."

Of course he had the right of it. Bear had all but proposed to Elizabeth MacColl. He therefore felt obligated to look after the lass's odd sister. Distantly he heard the girl laughing about something or other, and he frowned. That tickle Arran talked about bothered him, as well. It was if he had a puzzle with all the pieces, but the last one didn't fit. "Cooper," he called, summoning the butler.

The servant must have been waiting just outside the door, because he appeared while his name still echoed up the hallway. "Aye, m'laird?"

"Will ye fetch me Lady Elizabeth? Tell her . . . I've a question about a name on the Society page."

"Aye, m'laird."

"What's on yer mind now?" his brother asked.

"Go along with me. And dunnae scare the lass."

Arran snorted. "I should be saying that to ye, Glengask."

With a soft rap at the door, Elizabeth peeked into the office. "Did you need to see me, my lord?" she asked in her prim Sassannach accent.

"Aye. Have a seat, if ye dunnae mind."

They'd already determined that Elizabeth MacColl was nineteen years old, that she and her mother did not get along well, and that she absolutely did not want to wed the old Duke of Visford. She hadn't denied that she had an older sister, but she had declared on several occasions that she had no idea where Catriona could be. Given what he'd discovered over the past few days, that made the young lass somewhat more devious than he'd expected. And as far as he was concerned, that in return gave him leave to be as devious as he wished.

"I didn't see Lady Mary this morning, Lord Arran," she said conversationally, smiling. "Did she come with you?"

Arran shook his head. "Nae. She and my sister are

planning a soiree or someaught. I fled here straight-away."

"Oh, a soiree! That would be delightful!"

"I was wondering, lass," Ranulf took up, "if ye could describe yer sister for me. So I can give my men some-aught to look fer when they go aboot the country-side."

"Oh. Well, as I said before, I haven't seen her in eleven years. The last I knew she had short red hair and brown eyes." She chuckled, the sound not nearly as amused as it had been before. "I suppose the brown eyes would be the same, and her hair color, but as for the rest I'm afraid I can't be of much assistance."

"And what would ye say if I mentioned that I rode to Haldane Abbey yesterday and caught sight of a red-haired lass in men's clothing?"

All the color left her face. "I—I'm certain I have no idea what you're talking about, Lord Glengask," she stammered. "By the by, is Bear about?"

"Why does she dress like that?" he persisted. "I once heard of a duke's boy who pranced aboot in gowns, but he had to go live in the country with an aunt and was-nae allowed to have pets."

"It isn't like that," she retorted forcefully, then sub-sided again. "I mean—"

"We're listening, lass. I dunnae think Lord Torriden will be as patient."

"He knows. I mean, everyone in the clan knows my sister is . . . eccentric. But it isn't her fault, and she really isn't."

"Perhaps from the beginning, Lady Elizabeth," Arran suggested, in his usual diplomatic tones.

"Yes. Very well." She sighed heavily. "My father wanted a son. Only a son. And after his wife—his first wife—died, he cut Cat's hair, put her in breeches, and raised her to be a boy. That was before she could even walk."

"He didnae do her any favors, then."

"No, he didn't," she returned, nodding at Ranulf. "He refused to let my mother teach her to be otherwise, and then tried to do the same thing to me. That's why we left Islay." The lass sat forward, putting her palms flat on his desk. "As soon as she was old enough to stand up to Father she stopped cutting her hair, but he wouldn't let her have a maid or a governess or anyone to teach her how to be . . . a girl. She knows how people view her, and she's very shy about how she looks. I tried to get her to wear one of my dresses, but I don't think she wanted her younger sister showing her how to be a lady."

"Why's she against marrying Lord Torriden?" Ranulf pursued. "He seems pleasant enough, even if he does wear his shirt points too high."

"Charles is very fashionable," she countered, then subsided again. "I didn't know she was supposed to marry him. She never said anything about it. If I were to hazard a guess, I would say that she would be too embarrassed to wed such a paragon of the *haute ton*. I would be, anyway, if I'd never worn a gown before."

"Do ye have any idea who arranged the match?"

"As Charles said, it would have been my uncle, the present Lord Islay, and the MacDonald. I know that the Islay MacDonalds don't think much of the Sutherland MacDonalds." She frowned. "Do you think she was meant as an insult?" Elizabeth put her hands over her mouth. "Oh, that would be horrid for her. And she would realize it, too. She's very smart."

Several things were beginning to make sense, and Ranulf wasn't certain he liked the painting that was emerging. "If everyone knows aboot yer sister, why would Lord Torriden come all the way here to find her?"

"Ye cannae be insulted unless ye let the scenario play oot," Arran commented, his expression hardening. "I'd guess the MacDonald wants this conflict settled, and until Lady Catriona is presented officially to Torriden, all either side can do is circle aboot and snort at each other."

"Oh, no," Elizabeth breathed, tears overflowing her eyes. "Poor Cat. And poor Charles."

"Aye, poor Charles," Ranulf repeated dryly. "His task is to find yer sister and then turn his back on her so clan MacDonald can get on with starting an oot-and-oot war." On his doorstep, apparently.

"But what if he means to marry her?" the lass insisted, wiping at her cheeks. "Wouldn't that heal the rift between Islay and Sutherland?"

"That would depend on whether the MacDonald decided to be insulted or nae, regardless." For a moment Ranulf considered what he knew of old Eachann MacDonald, the Earl of Gorrie. The man was proud to a fault, and stubborn as the weather. "I'd put my blunt on insulted, I reckon," he decided.

Arran stirred, then climbed to his feet. "Thank ye fer being honest with us, Elizabeth," he said, offering his hand to help her out of the chair. "I'll ask ye nae to say anything to Torriden, though I wager ye'd no intention of doing that, anyway."

She shook her head. "I won't say a word. And . . . I'm glad you know, Lord Glengask. You've been so kind to me, and lying about my sister's whereabouts has been twisting me up inside."

He nodded at her, sitting still until Arran ushered her out of the office and shut the door again. Then he let loose with a string of Gaelic curses that would have made his grandfather blush. "The MacDonald wants to control Islay again, and he sent Torriden here, to *my* house, hoping to begin his war."

"I gave her the money," his brother stated, scowling. "If she—when she—leaves, we're still oot of it."

"I'm nae certain it'll be that simple, any longer." Ranulf slammed his fist against the desktop once more. "Did ye happen to notice whose name came up the most in that conversation?"

"What?" Arran's gaze roamed the floor as he considered. "Torriden's."

"Aye. Elizabeth referred to poor Charles a handful of times, but barely mentioned the man who's been watching over her sister. Nae the man she's supposedly aboot to wed."

"But—"

"And who's nae spent any breath asking after the woman he's finally fallen for, after nearly ten years spent gaining the favor of half the lasses for a hundred miles around?"

Silence, then Arran began swearing, as well. "We have the wrong damned sister."

Chapter Seventeen

P eter had brought more blankets, but warm as they were, they were no substitute for a nice, soft bed. Wherever he and Cat ended up, Munro decided, the first thing he meant to do for her was purchase her the largest, softest bed ever made.

A lass shouldn't have to worry about her backside being bruised during sex. Of course as he looked down at her, as he slid deep inside her again and again, she looked anything but concerned about her arse being bruised. Instead she grinned up at him, her fingers dug into his shoulders and her ankles locked around his thighs.

Settling lower, he kissed her hot and openmouthed, timing the motion of his tongue to match that of his cock. She moaned, arching her back and then coming around him. His lass, she was. No one else's. Ever.

Lowering his head against her neck, her red hair mixing with his black mop, he let himself go, pushing into her harder and faster until he climaxed, spilling into her. Anyone who said she was mannish, or less a lass because she wore trousers, deserved a punch in the nose.

And he would be happy to personally deliver every one of them.

The moment he regained control of his muscles, he turned them sideways, wrapping her into his arms for another kiss. This time he wanted it to last, slow and soft and endless. "I love ye, wildcat," he murmured. "Ye ken that, aye?"

"I do. *Tha gaol agam ort-fhèin, leannan.*"

She'd said it before, but hearing her say she loved him in Gaelic somehow meant . . . more. Deeper. Older. After all, for years the Sassannach had tried to kill the language of the Highlanders, the same way they'd tried to kill the culture by forbidding kilts and weapons and bagpipes. And yet they survived, in ways that sometimes felt almost as miraculous as the way he'd met her.

The low fire hissed, sputtering, and blazed again. "Rain?" he guessed. "Or do ye think we have snow?"

Cat pulled the blankets up closer around them. "It's cold enough for snow."

"Arran was right, ye know. We cannae stay here through the winter."

With a soft sigh she ran her fingers through his hair. "I cannae help feeling that once I leave here, this will all turn oot to be a faerie dream. I'll arrive on Glengask's doorstep to find I'm alone, wearing trousers, and Lord Torriden will laugh at me before he turns his back."

"I can swear to ye, lass, ye'll nae be alone. Ye'll be wearing a gown, and I hope Lord Torriden tries laughing at someaught, because I've been wanting to throttle him since he rode up in his grand, fancy carriage." He kissed her again. "But if he laughs at *ye,* my lass, then he's even more a fool than I already thought him. Ye . . . Ye stop my heart, Catriona. Every time I look at ye, or hear yer voice."

She smiled. "For a big, brawny man, ye have quite a way with words."

He laughed. "Ye're the first person ever to say that, I reckon." Cat was also the first person to ever see him as more than . . . Bear.

Grinning back at him, she reached beneath the corner of the blanket and produced the pocket watch he'd given her. Snuggling against him in a way that left him feeling both protective and aroused, she clicked it open. "Nearly seven o'clock. It'll be light soon. Do we wait and see how heavy the snow is, or head to Glengask regardless?"

His heart stuttered. The desire to keep her safe, both from harm and from ridicule and embarrassment, made him loath to expose her to anyone who called themselves civilized. As they'd already decided, though, remaining at Haldane was simply impossible. If he hadn't been so close to his siblings, so connected to the MacLawrys, he would have suggested they take the money Arran had given her, together with the funds he had saved up, and simply leave. But that would mean leaving the Highlands, and neither of them wanted to do that.

"Ye have the final word," he said slowly, "but I dunnae think we'll have a better moment than today."

She nodded. "I agree. The last thing I want is for Torriden to decide he needs to send for more MacDonalds to look for me."

Damn, she was a brave lass. Telling her so would only make her more self-conscious about it, though, and so he settled for rolling onto his back and pulling her over on top of him. "It's nae daylight yet."

With a quick grin she slipped beneath the blanket and down his chest. "I noticed that," she said, her voice muffled.

Whether she felt more easy about what was to come or if she was merely trying to distract herself, he wasn't about to complain. However shy she was about her appearance, in bed she was damned fearless. And very inventive.

Finally he couldn't conjure another reason for them to remain in the warm, rumpled blankets, and he slid out from under them to dress and bank the fire. If his plan went poorly, and he had a good idea that it might, he and Cat might be returning here tonight. Afterward, they would head to Aberdeen where he could claim his blunt from the bank there, and then they could go wherever they pleased.

If it went well . . . He turned around to watch Catriona pull a shift over her head and then step into the soft green and silver gown they'd decided best fit her. It was a bit fancy, but as far as he was concerned this was one hell of an occasion. For both their sakes he hoped his brothers would understand what she meant to him and just how determined he was to remain with her. If not, though, he meant to be ready to act.

"I dunnae need ye looking worried, giant," she said, turning her back on him. "Buttons, if ye please."

"Aye." Being careful not to pull off any buttons or wrinkle the delicate lace overlaying the silk neckline, he fastened the gown for her. "I'm still happy to go in before ye and state my demands, ye know."

"I know. But they arenae just yer demands, Munro. And I've been hiding long enough." She shook out her fingers. "Ye made my hair look nice."

"I even brushed oot my own hair."

"Well, ye're full of surprises," Catriona said, forcing a smile despite the shivering nerves plucking at her insides like crows. The one thing she didn't doubt was his promise to protect her. She would be safe. But what about him? What about his relationship with his siblings? She did not want to be responsible for destroying that.

The only thing she could do to protect *him* at this point was to run. And she wasn't about to do that. Perhaps she was only being selfish, but she didn't wish to be anywhere without him. She'd spent so much of her life feeling alone, and the idea of going back to that life filled her with icy dread. She'd found someone, finally and well after she'd given up looking, who seemed able to look past the odd clothes and mad tangle of hair and see . . . her. And he loved her.

His muscular arms slipped around her waist from behind. "Dunnae ye fret, Cat. I ken what might happen, and I'm where I want to be."

"And now ye're a witch who can read my thoughts, are ye?" she returned, twisting to face him and kissing his half-smiling mouth. His eyes were much more serious, but then so were hers.

"I dunnae see the need to pack all our things, one way or the other," he said instead of answering. "Are ye ready?"

She tried to stifle the resulting shiver down her spine, but he had to know how nervous she was. "Aye. Ready as I'll ever be."

Munro shrugged into his heavy coat, then helped her into the oversized one he'd liberated from his oldest brother. It wasn't at all feminine, but with a two-mile ride ahead of them, she preferred to be warm.

While he went to fetch his horse, she took a last look around the large room that had become her home over the past weeks. When she next saw it, everything would have changed. And regardless of what happened, she'd likely spend no more than another night here. Haunted or not, wrecked or not, Haldane Abbey had saved her life, both literally and figuratively.

"It's definitely snowing," Bear said, stomping back into the kitchen to shake white from his hair and shoulders. "Trousers would be warmer fer ye."

She shook her head. "Nae. I may have met yer brothers, but this is my—our declaration. I mean to do it withoot giving either of us cause to be embarrassed."

For a moment his expression became exasperated. "Ye dunnae embarrass me, wildcat. But I do understand. Let's get to it, then."

This was her last chance to change her mind. As she watched him making a last check of the fire and pausing to slip his dagger into his boot, then pull gloves out of his coat pocket and hand them to her, though, she knew already that she would stay in this until the end. When she'd first fled Islay to collect Elizabeth and then turned north again to hide in her beloved Highlands, she'd imagined a life for herself. It had been solitary and isolated, and she'd told herself that would make her happy.

In the weeks since then, however, she'd learned the difference between surviving and being happy. Bear made her happy, both with her life and with herself. In his company she wasn't some oddity. The challenge today was to see if his family would view her as anything *but* that odd, mannish lass. And so even if she froze her legs off, she would not be wearing trousers.

He tied their satchel of necessaries to the saddle, then swung up and held down his hand. Mindful that she was wearing something that constricted the movement of her legs, she stepped into the stirrup he left open and then let him lift her up before him. Bear opened the blanket he'd slung over his shoulder and wrapped it around the two of them. "Comfortable?"

"Aye," she returned, and kissed him on the cheek.

"Stop that, or ye'll have me sending Saturn into the nettles." With a grin he kissed her back, then clucked at the gelding.

In the space of one night the land had gone from deep greens and earthy browns to white. Even Haldane Abbey looked romantic, in a ghostly, haunted way, as snow covered the tops of broken walls and blanketed tumbled stone. A deer spooked in front of them, his breath fogging in the air.

Bear's chest against her side felt warm and solid, and she pressed herself closer against him and held the blanket closed against the chill. "Perhaps *ye* should have worn trousers today," she suggested, pushing one corner of the blanket out so it covered his thigh.

"Nae. Fer me it's a kilt or naught."

That made her smile. "Well, ye look very fine either way."

"As do ye, my lass."

He kept Saturn to a walk as they navigated along the disused road leading away from the abbey, but she wasn't certain it was out of concern for her comfort, or to delay their arrival at Glengask for as long as possible. However boldly he spoke, however strong and capable he was, he had to be concerned over how his family would react to the news that it wasn't Elizabeth he meant to claim, but her older half sister.

At least they would have the advantage of surprise. The rest of the MacLawry siblings seemed to think Bear meant to hold out at the abbey until the roof caved in from the weight of the snow. And yet there they were, the first day of snowfall. It all felt like some kind of chess game—even though neither of them particularly enjoyed chess. It wasn't nearly straightforward enough.

She wanted so much for this—for him—that it was difficult not to think ahead, to imagine all the possible trails the next few hours might take. At least she knew one thing for certain; they would be together, whatever happened.

Ranulf squatted down to pick up his son. "Nae much of a fan of snow, are ye, William?" he drawled, brushing the cold white stuff from his son's face and front.

"I don't think he expected it to be cold," Charlotte commented, laughing as the seven-month-old scowled at the white blanket now covering the Glengask garden.

A few feet away the two deerhounds bounded through the white powder, barking and rolling as snow flung through the air. "I think Fergus and Una led him astray," he said aloud, brushing off the bench to sit beside his wife.

She hugged his arm, leaning over to kiss their bairn on the cheek. "Oh, he's cold. I should bring him inside."

"He crawled face-first into a wee snowbank. We Highlanders dunnae back away from a bit of cold."

"Mm-hm." Reaching over, Charlotte pulled her husband's coat around the little one, then sank against his shoulder again. "Have you decided what to do?"

Of course he knew to what she was referring. They'd talked about almost nothing else since yesterday after dinner, once they'd managed to send Torriden off to read poetry with Elizabeth. The lass was clearly worried about her sister, but she'd been willing enough to play her part and distract the viscount while the rest of them tried to come up with a way to avoid war with the Mac-Donalds.

Unfortunately every scenario ended with Bear bidding Catriona farewell. From the way the youngest MacLawry brother had been acting, however, that didn't seem a likely outcome. "I'll have to talk to him, and explain what's at stake fer both the MacLawrys and the MacDonalds. If the lass doesnae wish to wed Torriden I won't force it, but she does need to be elsewhere. We're pulled partway into this mess already just by having her half sister under our roof."

"The longer you wait, the harder this will be," Charlotte murmured, in the midst of a game of peekaboo with her son. "And if he truly cares for her, I'm not certain anyone should be attempting to separate them."

"I do understand that, ye know," Ranulf returned. "I married ye, and Arran wed Mary, and I turned aside clan Buchanan so Rowena could have Lachlan. This is stepping into another clan's business, though. A pivotal part of it."

From her expression she wasn't convinced. Already she'd reminded him, twice, that Mary Campbell had been set to wed a MacAllister and that Arran marrying her hadn't caused much additional trouble. It had caused a great deal of trouble, actually, and had forced an alliance with the Campbell that likely had Ranulf's father and grandfather rolling in their graves. In that instance, at least the result had been greater stability, which with the birth of his son and nephew and niece had become increasingly necessary.

The MacDonald was a spiteful old man, though, and one clearly looking for a reason to battle half his own clan. In addition, Lord Gorrie had already given his permission for Munro to wed Elizabeth. Announcing that Elizabeth was being cast aside in favor of Catriona would be insult enough. But coupling that with denying the MacDonald the lass he more than likely meant to use to begin his war . . .

Arran came into view around the side of the house, Mary walking beside him and young Mòrag swinging between them and shrieking with laughter. "Mòrag likes the snow, I assume?" he asked dryly.

"Aye. She thinks we made it all fer her. She wanted it in her bedchamber this morning, and pushed all the windows open." Arran's fond, amused expression faded. "Ye still reckon we should go today?"

"I dunnae think we'll be getting rid of Torriden anytime soon as long as I have to be pleasant to him, so aye, we'd best see to this before Bear decides to kill him."

"This is all horrid," Mary said, scooping up her daughter. "And we still don't know for certain what Bear might be thinking. Or planning."

"Half the time Bear doesnae even ken what he's thinking," Arran put in. "Did ye send fer Lachlan?"

"I'm here" came from behind them, as their brother-in-law trotted up from the direction of the house. "Rowena's inside the coach, trying to coax Colin oot from under a blanket. What's amiss?"

Ranulf stood, helping Charlotte to her feet. "I only want to say this once more, so if ye'll fetch Rowena we'll meet in the morning room."

"Aye."

Lachlan headed back to the drive, while Ranulf led the rest of his family into the house. Before all the marriages and bairns, he'd made his decisions alone, sometimes asking Arran's advice, but with the understanding that what he said was the law. As the size of the family increased, he'd discovered that his decisions affected them in ways he couldn't previously have conceived, and these family meetings had become more frequent. The final decision was still his, as was the responsibility and weight of the consequences, but the MacLawrys had never been closer. And to his surprise, he liked it that way.

As they gathered in the warm, bright morning room, he didn't like the fact that Bear wasn't there. A literally large part of the family was absent, and since this concerned Munro, he should have been present. On the other hand, having a strategy before they confronted Bear was likely a very wise idea. Once everyone was settled with tea or coffee or a large stack of wooden blocks, he sat on the deep windowsill and told them what he'd learned about Catriona, Elizabeth, Torriden, and clan MacDonald.

Mary and Charlotte had both heard most of it already, but as he spoke Lachlan's expression became more and more grim, and the color left Rowena's face to the point that he stopped talking, alarmed that she might faint. *"Piuthar,"* he said, rising to walk over to her, "we'll figure this oot. Ye needn't fret."

"That's isnae it," she muttered, sending a look at her husband. A moment later he nodded, swearing under his breath, and handed her a folded note from his pocket. She opened it, read through it, and then handed it to Ranulf. "I received this four days ago."

With a frown he unfolded it. The writing was couched in Bear's confident scrawl. As he read through it, a chill went down his spine. "Sweet Saint Andrew," he murmured.

"What is it?" Arran asked.

Ranulf blew out his breath. "The first part's just a list of what Bear wanted from Glengask after I banished him from the hoose. He put a note at the bottom, though. 'Winnie,'" he read aloud, "'I've a lass with me who's never had the chance to be a lady. Will you help me give her one? I need a few gowns with whatever goes beneath them, some proper walking shoes, hair clips, and lip rouge. And whatever else you deem important. She has my heart, Rowena. Mine. I think I teased Lach too much when he fell for you. I'll tell you more when I can. Bear.' The word 'mine' is underlined. Twice."

For a moment the only sound in the room was the giggling of bairns pushing wooden blocks across the floor. They'd already done the arithmetic, but the idea of Bear losing his heart didn't compare to actually seeing it. Up until two days ago Ranulf—and the rest of them—had thought their youngest brother meant to wed Elizabeth MacColl. As he considered it, though, Munro had never said a word to encourage that rumor, had never shown any particular affection for the proper lass, and most tellingly, he *had* left Glengask to protect someone else nearly the moment a potential rival had arrived. They should have realized it much damned sooner.

"What do we do?" Arran finally asked, his voice low and unhappy.

"What do ye mean?" Rowena countered, sitting forward. "We help Bear. Why is that a question?"

"For all the reasons we just discussed," Arran retorted, scowling. "Ye have a five-month-old bairn, Winnie. Do ye want to see us back to posting men all aboot the hoose and nae going anywhere withoot an armed escort?"

"Nae. Of course not. But why does that mean Bear is the only one of us to nae have who he wants?"

Ranulf shook himself. "Bear is a very changeable lad," he said. "All we have to judge his feelings is one short note and me getting punched in the eye. I'd wager he doesnae ken exactly what's at stake here. If we can make him see that we'll nae be abandoning the lass, but sending her someplace safe and with enough blunt to live well, then he'll nae have to feel so protective. He'll see reason." It hadn't worked the two previous times he and then Arran had attempted it, but they hadn't had all the facts, then. They did now. Hopefully.

"So ye think Catriona MacColl is a lost kitten or someaught to him?" Rowena asked, clearly not yet convinced. She'd always been the most romantic of them, though, so he wasn't surprised. "That when we find her a good home he'll pat her on the head and send her away?"

"Ye'd best hope that's what happens." Ranulf resumed his seat in the window. Standing and dictating terms might have worked a few years ago, but he'd learned more subtle ways to lead his family where he thought they needed to go. "At this moment the Mac-Lawrys are in the enviable position of being feared and respected fer our past willingness to take action. If we're pressed into doing someaught now, we'll have to crush the MacDonalds. If we dunnae, we'll have every other clan who's ever had a disagreement with us begin chipping away."

"Cannae we . . . compensate them fer Catriona?" Rowena insisted, her stubborn expression softening into one of sadness.

"Aye, we could. And then we'll have the reputation fer throwing money at threats and troubles. And more threats and troubles will come, believe me."

"It isn't fai—"

The morning room door flew open. "I beg your pardon," Lord Torriden said, panting and red-faced, "but I've been in the village, and some of the lads at the blacksmith were chatting about a red-haired ghost at someplace called Haldane Abbey. I think that may be Lady Catriona. And I must ask for your assistance in guiding me there, at once."

Elizabeth entered the room behind him, as out of breath as the viscount. "I told him it was silly, that Lady Glengask told me all about Haldane Abbey, and that everyone has been saying for ages that it's haunted."

Well, the lass had tried to help, anyway. Now, though, whatever plans they'd been about to lay, however carefully he meant to plot what he wanted—needed—to say to Bear to convince him that his feelings for the lass were out of a need to protect her rather than love, the time seemed to be gone.

"It's still snowing," he said aloud, feeling his way as he went. "The path doon to the valley is rough enough in good weather. I'll take ye tomorrow myself, if the weather clears."

"That is not—"

Cooper skidded into the room. "M'laird," he stammered, jerking his neck sideways like a drunken chicken.

"What the devil are ye up to, Cooper?" he demanded of the butler, out of patience. "Are ye having a spasm?"

The servant sighed. "Oot the window, m'laird," he muttered, jabbing a forefinger toward the front drive.

Ranulf twisted around to look outside. For a moment all he could make out was the light fall of snow. Then the distinctive shape of Munro and his big gelding, Saturn, came into view. Thank God. He'd sent her away, and none of the scenarios that had been giving him sleeping and waking nightmares for the past two nights would come to pass.

As Bear drew closer, though, Ranulf's heart thudded. She was with him. Sitting across the front of the saddle, a heavy blanket around the two of them. So Bear had decided on his own course of action—the worst possible decision Ranulf could imagine. He'd brought Catriona MacColl home, while her fiancé remained, and before anyone could make any plans to minimize the impending disaster. He didn't even waste a moment trying to convince himself that they'd come to Glengask to hand her over to the MacDonalds.

"*Chac,*" he muttered, glancing away as he felt Arran come up behind him.

"This isnae going to end well," his brother breathed. "Do ye think we can turn him away before—"

"That's her, isn't it?" Torriden exclaimed from beside the room's second window. "Your brother has found her!"

He and Arran glanced at each other. The viscount had come up with a storyline for them. Evidently they had a very slim chance to avoid a war with the MacDonalds, after all. If Bear was willing to cooperate.

Glengask always had at least two men up on the widow's walk, keeping watch over all approaches to the castle. Munro therefore knew he and Cat had been seen the moment they turned up the road that ran along the north edge of the loch. He wasn't surprised, either, that no one emerged from the house until they were nearly to the front door. Ranulf would want time to assess whether they meant to cooperate and hand over Cat, or if his explicit orders had been ignored.

Drawing Saturn to a halt, he handed Catriona to the ground, then swung down after her. She shivered visibly, though he wasn't certain whether it was from the cold, or from the idea that she was about to confront both the most powerful family in the Highlands, and the man her own family was trying to force her to marry. He wrapped the blanket around her shoulders, tugging her closer as he did so. "Are ye ready, my lass?"

She nodded. "At least we'll know what happens. I willnae be conjuring all the horrors I can imagine."

"I told ye what happens next. We stay together." Deliberately keeping an arm across her shoulder, he headed them toward the shallow granite steps of Glengask.

For a few moments he wondered whether anyone would open the front doors at all, or if they'd barred the entrance against him. As he was beginning to wonder if there were horrors he and Cat hadn't yet imagined, though, the left door swung open and Ranulf emerged, Arran on his heels. Munro hoped they were ready for a fight, because he damned well was. Both of them had tried to separate him from Cat, and that would not stand.

"Ye ken Torriden is here," Ranulf said in a low voice, stopping between them and the door. "And he's seen ye through the window."

Munro tightened his grip on Cat's shoulder. "Good," he rumbled. "I'm finished with hiding."

"Dammit, Bear, ye're going to shove us into a war."

"Then dunnae stand with me. I reckon I can manage on my own."

Ranulf took a hard breath. "We need a word with ye. Now."

"I'm standing right here."

"Alone, Bear," his oldest brother stated, finally sending a glance at the blanket-wrapped Catriona.

He shook his head. "I ken what ye want. Ye'd have me give over Cat to Torriden so the MacDonalds can go aboot their feuding and leave the MacLawrys oot of it."

Ranulf opened and shut his mouth. "Aye, that's what

I want. If ye'd listen fer a minute, I'll explain why. We have young ones n—"

"Here's what *I* want," Munro interrupted. For God's sake, did his brothers think he hadn't considered them and their wives and their bairns in all this? "I want to have luncheon with my family and Elizabeth and Lord Torriden. At the end of it, Cat and I will either stay, together, or we'll leave, together. The rest of the mess, the lot of ye can wrestle with. I'm done."

"Bear, ye—"

"And there's one thing ye'd best keep in mind," he continued. "Catriona MacColl is mine. Ye'll nae pay her to go away," and he tossed the bundle of money back at Arran's chest, "and ye'll nae insult her." With that he sent Ranulf a pointed glance. "Nor do ye get to decide her fate. The lot of ye dunnae even know her."

She lifted her hand to place over his where it rested on her shoulder. "We dunnae want trouble," she said, her voice admirably steady. "I didnae plan for any of this. But I'm finished with running, and I reckon it's time to make a stand. I'm sorry it has to be here and now."

"Dunnae apologize," Munro countered. "If they'd booted Torriden oot on his arse when he arrived in his fancy coach, none of this would be happening now."

Cat tapped her fingers against his knuckles. "They didnae know I was here then, Bear. We are partly to blame."

Her sympathizing with his brothers wasn't helping anything, but she did have a point. He hadn't precisely been honest with them. "I'll concede that point, then. Now, are ye going to invite us in, or should we turn aboot now?"

"Dammit, Bear," Ranulf persisted, below his breath, "we could have managed this better."

"I dunnae believe that, since ye began it badly. Is Winnie here? And Lach?"

"Everyone's here. And I'm asking ye nae to do this."

Ranulf rarely *asked* for anything. They both knew that, too, but Munro wasn't in the mood to be persuaded. They thought him a rampaging bull, and for the moment it suited him to be one. So he shifted his grip to Cat's chilled hand and stomped between his brothers for the door. The sooner they began, the sooner he'd know what he needed to do next.

"Slow doon, ye giant," Cat whispered at him. "I'm in a damned gown."

He immediately shortened his strides as he stepped into the foyer with her. They'd barely entered the house, though, when pretty, perfect Viscount Torriden marched up to them. "My lady," he said, sketching a deep bow. "I'm so grateful that you've been found safely. After those workers said they saw you on the roof of this Haldane Abbey, I hardly dared to hope, but may I say that you and I will—"

"Shut up, Torriden," Munro interrupted. "This lass is mine. Nae yers."

The light-brown-haired MacDonald straightened, blinking. "I beg your pardon? I believe I told you when I arrived that Lady Catriona was promised to me by both the MacDonald and her uncle, Lord Islay."

Her grip on Munro's fingers tightened, and then she let him go. "Mayhap they did promise me to ye," she said, this time her voice shaking, "but I didnae agree to anything. I ken what part I'm supposed to play, and I refuse."

"You . . . refuse?"

"Ye heard the lass. Step aside, wee man."

To his credit, Torriden moved out of the way, though

Munro would have preferred that he'd stood his ground. He'd been coiled for a fight for days. A charging bull— or bear, rather—needed a target. This would go the way he envisioned, because any twist or turn could cost him Catriona. And that . . . He took a hard breath, his years of playing about, of breaking hearts, of looking for someone, anyone, with whom to spend the night, crashing against him like a cold, relentless wave. Losing Catriona was not allowed to happen.

"Cooper, set two more places fer luncheon," he said, spotting the butler hiding at the base of the stairs.

"Um, aye, m'laird." Seeming grateful to escape, the servant practically sprinted for the kitchen.

With the butler gone, it was Peter Gilling who stepped in to take the blanket and then the coat from Cat. Knowing how uncertain she was about her new attire, Munro kept a close eye on her. True to her stubborn, brave self, she kept her chin up and her gaze on the hallway as the pretty green and silver silk came into view, shifting and shimmering around her. Even with a rival and the hostility of his own brothers all around him, lust tugged at his gut. Perhaps she wasn't a delicate, breakable flower, but she was beautiful in a fierce Highlands way that stole his breath.

"This is not—I don't believe— How—I will contact my uncle at once!" Torriden blustered, as he eyed Cat in a way that had Munro coiling his fist all over again. The need to protect, to beat the astonished indignation off the pretty man's face, nearly overwhelmed him.

Of course the viscount was surprised. He'd expected a freakish lass in trousers, not a dark-eyed, well-curved vision. And since she'd been meant as an insult that the northern MacDonalds were more than ready to act upon, Torriden likely had no idea which way to turn.

As Munro took Cat's hand again to lead her to the morning room where they'd have a bit more space around them, a petite, dark-haired sprite practically flung herself against his chest. "Bear!" Winnie said fiercely, hugging him. "I'm so glad ye're home."

He hugged her back with his free hand. "It's good to be back," he answered, though he wasn't entirely certain yet that that was true.

"They know aboot the note ye sent me," she whispered in his ear just before she released him again. "And I'm on yer side."

With an appreciative nod he gestured at Cat. "Catriona, my sister, Rowena, Lady Gray. Winnie, Lady Catriona MacColl."

Rather than curtsying or offering her hand, Winnie hugged Cat much as she had him. He would be forever grateful for that gesture of acceptance. "Welcome to Glengask, Lady Catriona," she said, smiling.

"Thank ye, my lady. Bear's told me a great deal about ye." Cat glanced about the room, seeming to notice the other ladies and the bairns for the first time. "He's told me about all of ye. It made me wish my sister hadn't lived so far away for so long."

"But we're together now," Elizabeth said, hugging her as Winnie had. "You should have told me, Cat," she murmured, almost too quietly for him to overhear. "I might've helped . . . somehow."

"It was my burden, Elizabeth. Ye had yer own."

"If you say so." Elizabeth squeezed her hand. "You look very fine in that gown, by the way. I've never seen it before. Where in the world did you get it?"

So Elizabeth and more than likely Torriden didn't know the details of their return. That was something, anyway. Before Cat could answer, he stepped in to introduce her to his in-laws and nephews and niece. They were all polite, if a little cool—which didn't surprise him, considering the position she was in. That didn't mean he liked it, though. This was a lass who'd had very little in the way of a family, while the one person who had seemed to care for her had put some very stiff conditions on that affection and had tried to turn her into something she wasn't.

Behind him Ranulf and Arran continued to whisper together. Whatever they might be planning, he supposed he would have to meet with them in private. This was one time where the needs of the MacLawrys were outweighed by the needs of a precious lass, whether they agreed with him or not.

"Lord Glengask, lords and ladies," Cooper announced after twenty or so minutes, leaning into the room, "luncheon is served."

It wasn't even noon yet. No doubt Ranulf had had a hand in rushing things along, though, so he could get to the crux of what he saw as the problem. That suspicion was confirmed when the marquis began ushering everyone to the door while the nanny and a pair of maids came to collect the bairns.

"Bear?" the marquis prompted, lifting an eyebrow when his youngest brother didn't move.

"We'll be along in a moment," Munro returned, realizing that once he'd decided to defy the MacLawry, the more he did it, the easier it got.

"Ye'd best be. This is yer doing."

Once Ranulf had left them alone in the morning room, Munro shut the door and leaned back against it. "How are ye, my lass?"

Sighing, Catriona sank down on the couch. "They all want me gone, Bear. They're polite about it, but nae a one of 'em wants me here. This was a mistake. And yer brother is correct; I'm meant to cause a war. If I stay with ye, the war will come here."

He stalked over to sit beside her, anger tightening the muscles across his shoulders. They all had no idea how damned reasonable he'd been through all of this. And they had no idea how very near he was to deciding this with his fists. "The war willnae come here, because I willnae allow that. If it comes to that, we willnae be here, and I'll make it known that I've gone against my clan chief's orders." He tucked a strand of her scarlet hair back behind her ear. "Would ye still want me if we had to leave the Highlands?"

A tear ran down her cheek, but she brushed it away before he could do so. "I'm causing ye more and more trouble. I didnae want that."

"None of it is yer fault, Cat," he returned. "I asked ye a question."

"Ye know I want ye, wherever we are."

Slowly he leaned closer and kissed her. "I know. I wanted to hear ye say it again."

"What's next, then?"

He glanced toward the closed door. "I reckon ye need to be honest and tell the tale of how ye grew up. I think my family needs to hear it, and mayhap it'll either help Torriden see reason, or at least he'll know what's coming when I beat him to a pulp."

"Munro, ye say the sweetest things."

That made him laugh. However nervous she was, she remained his wildcat, thank God. "Here we go, then."

" 'Once more unto the breach,' " she quoted, rising beside him.

It occurred to him again that he needed to ask her to marry him. Unconventional as she was, there was no sense making things even more difficult than they were likely to be. He nearly said it right then, in the Glengask morning room, but part of him, the part that was still a bit too prideful, perhaps, didn't want the question to be a crutch for her. If they were to marry, he would be *obligated* to protect her. This way, he could make it clear that he made his stand against his own because he *chose* to do so. Then, when they'd decided their own fate, he would ask her.

Chapter Eighteen

He was willing both to fight and to walk away from his own family. Catriona might have tried to talk him out of both, but clearly she wasn't going to change his mind. The hardest part of the equation to grasp, for her, at least, was that he was willing to do that for her. But even if she didn't quite see *why,* she had to accept that he was. And she, therefore, could do no less.

She reached the door first, and pulled it open. Then, of course, she had no idea where the MacLawrys were taking luncheon, so she had to wait for him to offer an arm. "I'm nae scared, ye know," she commented, as they turned down the hallway. "Nae for myself."

"I dunnae want ye to be scared fer me, either. I've argued with my family before. They've argued with each other. Arran and Ranulf—fer a time after Arran decided he wanted Mary, they didn't even speak. Ranulf banished him from London, where they were staying. Today, though, they look thick as thieves again, ye may have noticed." He shrugged. "So aye, we may fight. We may throw a few punches. But they remain my family.

Wherever I go. Ye're the one I cannae live apart from. This is fer my life, as much as it is yers."

She squared her shoulders. If he was willing to risk so much, then by Saint Andrew she would do her damnedest to see this luncheon end to their advantage. Because whether he was willing to leave behind his family or not, she didn't want him to have to do so.

When he pushed open the dining room door—the small dining room, as he called it—they both stopped in the doorway. Two seats remained open, the first between Lady Gray and Lady Mary, and the second between Torriden and Glengask. As the rest of the party had sat man-woman, clearly she was meant to sit between the two men. "Bear," she whispered, feeling the color leave her face. This was where she felt most out of water; in the face of proper Society. Or as close as anyone came to that in the Highlands.

Abruptly Munro left her side to stride deeper into the room. Before anyone could move he'd pulled out the empty chair between the lords and then lifted his sister, chair and all, to set her in the empty space. Then he returned to hand Catriona into the seat beside Lady Mary, scooted the remaining chair into the empty spot beside her, and sat down there himself. "There," he said with a slight grin that didn't touch his eyes. "Much better."

If the rest of the party needed a reminder of his strength and formidability, that provided it. Stifling an abrupt smile of her own, she gave Lady Mary a polite nod. From what Bear had said, Mary was just twenty-three, a year younger than herself. And they had more than their age in common. "Ye're the Campbell's granddaughter, I hear. Did ye worry about upending yer clan when ye fell for Lord Arran?"

"Yes, I did," she returned. "I worried a great deal about what I was doing to my own life and to his."

"What convinced ye to take the chance?"

Light green eyes glanced across the table at light blue ones. "I've found the MacLawry men to be very nearly irresistible," she said after a moment, smiling. "I suppose I would have to call it a leap of faith."

"I like that," Catriona returned. "A leap of faith. I've been told that my father married my mother because she was the one sister in a family with eight brothers. He figured the odds were good that she would give him a boy. He grew up with two brothers, but from what I've been able to decipher they never got along. I dunnae ken if he wanted another chance at making a happy family, or if he wanted to make certain that neither of them or their heirs ever inherited his title, but he was determined that his child—all his children—would be sons."

"Your sister mentioned something about that," Mary said.

"Did ye, Elizabeth?"

Her sister looked dismayed. "I had to, Cat. When they found you, they didn't . . . I had to explain things."

Of course she had. Elizabeth would have been embarrassed for her. And for herself, for having such an odd sister, most likely. "Dunnae worry yerself, Elizabeth." She deliberately faced Glengask, who, unlike the others, wasn't even pretending to eat his luncheon. "I liked growing up the way I did. I learned to ride, to hunt, to trap, to fish. The first time I realized I was different was when my father wouldnae let me go swimming with the boys from the village.

"When my father remarried, his new wife, Elizabeth's mother, took one look at me and announced that he must hire a governess and civilize me. He refused, and so she sent to London for a gown she thought would fit me. I thought it was grand fun to dress up like that, but when my father caught me, he ripped off the gown and burned it, and made me swear nae to dress so outlandishly ever again. I dunnae know exactly what he said to Anne, but she barely spoke a word to me after that. Nae a kind word, at the least."

"I didn't know that, Cat," Elizabeth said, reaching across the table.

Catriona squeezed her fingers, then released her again. "I got used to hearing whispers, to having the daughters of other lords laugh behind their hands at me, to being made fun of by everyone from stable boys to my uncles. I expected it, really."

Beneath the table, Bear's fingers brushed her knee. He knew all this, of course. While she doubted it would make any difference in the world, in a way it felt good to explain herself. It felt freeing, almost.

"By the time my father died, I was twenty-two. I'd stopped cutting my hair, but I didn't know how to fashion it in anything other than a ponytail. I wore trousers and shirts and coats, because I'd been forbidden to wear anything else, and because I didnae ken how to find a gown that would fit me properly, or the bits that go beneath it. And by then I'd realized that . . . I wouldn't be marrying. That suited me, because, well, I knew how I appeared, and I had no idea how to change it.

"Then my uncle announced that I was to be offered to the Sutherland MacDonalds, because the MacDonald had ordered the feud to end. That . . . troubled me. But then I overheard him talking to his brother about what they hoped sending me away would accomplish. He knew I would be an insult, and he knew the likely result. And he was happy to be rid of me."

"I must protest," Lord Torriden said, his color high. "This is MacDonald business."

She scowled at him. "I know ye're here to collect me so you can publicly turn yer back on me in front of the MacDonald. My uncle wants to start a war, and yer uncle won't allow the insult to pass. And the fact that ye came to find me, knowing ye'd be expected to scoff at me as much as the rest of 'em, doesnae make me look on ye any more kindly. What are ye, the MacDonald's dog?"

Bear snorted. "A prissy poodle dog."

"That's enough of that," Ranulf cut in. "The fact remains, ye are a vital part of MacDonald politics. Yer absence will cause as much trouble as yer presence. The only thing worse would be ye showing up where ye shouldnae be. As ye appeared here, ye bring trouble to our doorstep."

That hurt. The man Bear most respected essentially dismissing her. Reducing her to a pawn in a game she didn't even want to play. She held his gaze. "Yer brother told me that ye enjoy trouble, Lord Glengask. That ye've managed to turn trouble to yer advantage so often that most dunnae dare bring ye trouble any longer."

"Does the MacDonald want a war?" Elizabeth broke in, a little sharply. "Because Cat doesn't look so terrible any longer. Why would he be insulted?"

Torriden stirred again. "Of course he doesn't want a war. War costs money and resources. But neither can he allow himself, his immediate family, to be insulted and not answer it. That weakens him." He leaned forward, banging his knife handle against the table. "You running off rather than agreeing to marry his nephew weakens him. I'm trying to *prevent* a war."

That surprised her. "So ye would marry me?" she

answered, lifting both eyebrows. "Ye wouldnae find me insulting and mannish and send me back to Islay along with a threat to my uncle?"

"I don't know how I would find you," he retorted, "as this is the first time we've met. You seem . . . tolerable enough, except for your manners. I daresay there are ways to manage a marriage made for an alliance, however the spouses feel about each other."

"Nae!" Bear broke in, shoving to his feet. "Ye dunnae get to say that ye'd take her because ye have to. Ye dunnae get to insult a lass who's managed to make a life fer herself despite what those who are supposed to care aboot her throw in her way. And ye dunnae get to assume ye'll be marrying her, because that willnae happen."

"Munro, sit down," the marquis ordered.

"I willnae," he retorted. "Ye're a damned bunch of hypocrites. Ye marry a lass ye want, and try to make Arran wed to make the alliance ye missed. Then Arran marries who he wants, and ye try to get Winnie to make the alliance *he* missed. And now ye want me to marry someone ye choose fer me, even knowing what a damned poor excuse fer a husband I would be, and how little I wanted the responsibility. Well, I've found my own way. I've found my lass, and I willnae let her go. Make yer alliance around that."

Lord Glengask stood, as well. "Do ye think I'm trying to be cruel?" he demanded, his eyes narrowed and his jaw clenched. "Ye're my brother, and I love ye dearly. But ye arenae my only responsibility."

"I'm nae yer responsibility at all. Ye told me to send her away or give her up. I came here because Cat said ye had yer reasons, and she didnae want to run. Well, now I know yer reasons, and I dunnae agree with them.

So drink a damned toast. I'm sending her away. But I'm going with her. We'll nae bring ye trouble, Ranulf."

Catriona shut her eyes for a moment, wishing they could begin the day again, and that she might have convinced Munro simply to stay beneath the blankets with her. "I dunnae want ye to be separated from yer family, Munro," she said quietly.

He looked down at her. "And I willnae be separated from ye, wildcat," he said, his voice more controlled. "I told ye that. And after what I'm hearing today, do ye think I'm so eager to spend my days here? He wants what's easiest. That's nae my brother. I dunnae know who that is."

"That's enough!" Ranulf roared. "I have tried to be reasonable, but ye clearly want a fight. Go, then! I'll nae have ye putting my son in danger because ye cannae do what's best fer yer own clan!"

Lord Torriden had the bad sense to stand up at that moment. "Lady Catriona bears just as much blame for the harm she's doing to clan MacDonald. And for less reason, given that she is clearly poised to gain far more than she can possibly offer."

Bear went over the table at him. Before the viscount could do more than emit a high-pitched squeak he went backward over his chair with Munro's fist imbedded in his chin. It seemed to happen in slow motion, but a heartbeat later the room exploded into action.

Catriona grabbed the very pregnant Lady Mary's arm and pulled her away from the table while Lady Glengask caught hold of both Elizabeth and Bear's sister and dragged them around to the far corner of the room, as well. The men, though, all moved forward. And every one of them went after Munro.

He'd done it wrong, Munro knew. He'd decided to be calm and patient and logical, and then the MacDonald bastard had insulted Cat—again. If he'd had any hope that anyone here meant to listen to him he might have reacted differently, but they'd clearly already made up their minds that he was both wrong and an idiot.

Grabbing Torriden by his high shirt points, Munro hefted him into the air and slammed him down onto the table. Wine glasses and bread went flying. To his left Arran was trying to haul backward on his arm, with Lachlan on the right, and the hand in the back of his jacket more than likely Ranulf. As far as he was concerned they all deserved a pummeling. Not one of them had even tried to see Cat through his eyes. Ignoring the men hauling on him, he lifted the squealing Torriden and shoved him back down again. "Apologize!" he growled, dragging the viscount across the length of the table while dishes clattered to the floor around them.

Arran jumped on his back and wrapped an arm around his neck. Before his older brother could firm up his grip, Munro ducked forward, reaching back, and flung his brother over his shoulder, using Torriden to cushion his fall. Twisting, he turned just in time to see Lachlan's fist aimed at his head.

The blow, though, didn't land. Instead Viscount Gray stumbled as Catriona leaped onto his back and grabbed hold of his arm. "Ye willnae hurt him!" she yelled, covering his eyes with her hands.

Out of the corner of his eye Munro noted the servants pouring into the small dining room. A moment later the sheer weight of men hanging on to his arms and his back and his legs drove him to his knees. Losing here, though, meant losing . . . everything. With a roar he shoved back to his feet, then stumbled again.

A shot rang out. "*Enough!*" Charlotte yelled, as wood and plaster from above the far window splintered.

With a last grunt Munro shoved to his feet again. Warm wet trickled from his nose, but he barely noted it as he took Cat around the waist and bodily lifted her off Lachlan. "It's me," he grunted, when she sent an elbow into his rib cage.

"Put me down, giant," she ordered, clearly out of breath. "I'll nae have ye throwing me about."

He set her on her feet. Her pretty scarlet hair had come out of its pins, one of her braids hanging crazily sideways, and the left shoulder of her gown was torn. Scowling, he tugged the material back up over her shoulder. "Ye shouldnae have jumped in like that."

"Ye were outnumbered," she returned, still panting. Then she slapped him on the arm. "Ye didnae help anything. And ye fought yer own brothers." Taking a napkin off the floor, she dabbed it against his nose. "Ye shouldnae have done that."

"I'd do it again," he returned, finally lifting his head to send a glare at Ranulf. "Ye've a Sassannach bride who shoots pistols in yer dining room."

"I—"

"And ye," he interrupted, turning his gaze on Arran, "married a damned Campbell and got shot fer it."

"I ken what—"

"Shut up," he countered. "I'm nae finished with ye. And I'll say my piece before I go. Winnie got herself promised to the Buchanans and dragged off by a Campbell, and still won the man she wanted. What the devil makes ye think I'll nae have this MacDonald lass just because it's nae convenient fer ye?"

The black bruise around his eye beginning to fade, Ranulf gazed at him levelly. "If it was a matter of convenience, we'd figure someaught oot, Bear, and ye know that."

That was that, then. He and Cat weren't welcome. They weren't safe, with all the bairns about. He did understand that, whether his family realized it or not. With a slow nod, he turned around to reach for Catriona's hand—then stopped.

On the far side of the table Elizabeth MacColl sat on a chair beside Torriden, who wasn't as pretty now with his bloody nose and torn coat. The lass pressed a napkin to his face, tears in her eyes. Saint Andrew forgive him for his lack of compassion, but it might well have been the loveliest sight he'd ever seen.

"Elizabeth," he said, keeping his distance from the pair on the chance he'd spook one or the other of them into flight. "Are ye ready to see yer sister vanish into the wilderness after finding her again? Ye spent eleven years apart, ye said."

"This has naught to do with Elizabeth," Cat broke in with a scowl of her own. "Dunnae try to blame any of this on her."

"I amnae," he returned. "I'm only saying that ye willnae be marrying Torriden, and because his clan chief demands an alliance between Lord Islay and himself, ye and I have to flee the Highlands."

A tear ran down Cat's soft cheek. "Dunnae be so cruel, ye big oaf."

At that he did take her hand, drawing her against his side and brushing the tear away with his fingers. "Do ye nae see what I see?" he whispered, gesturing with his chin toward her sister.

"What?"

His family considered him the dim-witted one, but

at this moment he was fairly certain he was the only one in the room seeing clearly. "Elizabeth. Are ye nae a daughter of the former Lord Islay, and the niece of the present earl?"

"Of course I am."

"Aye. And that's exactly the same relationship Catriona has—had—to them."

Elizabeth stared at him, the color leaving her face, then flooding it again. "Say that again, Bear?" she prompted.

"I'll only point oot that ye came here to avoid marriage to a man forty-two years yer senior and with a reputation for killing off his own wives. Ye fled a duke. Do ye think ye'll ever be welcome back in London? Or find yerself a different husband there?"

"Oh," Cat breathed, her hand tightening convulsively in his.

"I'll also point oot," Munro continued, "that this Torriden lad is pretty, and he's but seven years yer elder, and with those clothes he wears I'd wager he has a bit more culture than most any other man ye'd find in the Highlands."

"I think we've all just been insulted," Lady Glengask murmured, a fair degree of humor in her tone, as Ranulf made his way over and relieved her of the spent pistol.

Beside Munro, Cat took a deep breath. "Ye cannae make her do this," she murmured, then continued in a louder voice. "Elizabeth, ye need nae do this to—"

"You told me I should never let other people dictate my life for me, Cat," her sister returned, her gaze on Lord Torriden rather than her sister. "I envied you for the freedom you had. But then you never told me that you were fleeing for the same reason I was. So if you don't mind, I would like to think about what Bear said for a moment. For my own sake."

Lord Torriden looked confused. Glengask, on the other hand, stood beside Charlotte to watch the play unfold with an expression of keen interest on his face. Munro didn't expect him to argue; if it kept trouble from clan MacLawry, Ranulf would consider it.

"My lady, Elizabeth, I'm . . . What the devil are the lot of you talking about?" the viscount blustered, standing in an attempt to tug his disheveled clothes back into some semblance of order.

"About you," Elizabeth answered. "And me."

"But I . . . I am promised to your sister. However we—I—may feel, I am obligated to—"

"Ye arenae," Bear broke in, deciding that while it might be a positive happenstance that he hadn't knocked the man out cold, he didn't want to listen to him any longer. "Fer the last damned time, ye cannae have her. She is mine."

"Ye cannae have me," Catriona echoed, moving still closer against Bear's side. Clever, clever Bear. Could this be happening? Could she have what—who—she truly wanted? The only thing she'd ever allowed her heart to desire?

"I . . ." Torriden looked about the room. "Perhaps you and I might have a word in private, Elizabeth," he said. "I will not make my decisions based on the convenience of other people. Particularly not those of another clan." He sent a pointed glance at Bear. "Or those who prefer punching to dialogue."

"Certainly." With one of her charming smiles Elizabeth wrapped her hand around his arm, and the two of them made their way out of the room.

For a moment the remaining diners sat or stood where they were, looking at each other. "Well, that was a surprise," Arran finally commented.

The marquis cleared his throat. "Bear. Munro, if ye would, take Lady Catriona up to the library before ye stomp oot of the house. Wait fer a few minutes while we figure things oot."

"I dunnae think ye'll be figuring anything oot," Bear returned. "*I* figured it oot, when it was there right in front of ye the entire time. Fer once none of this is up to ye, is it?"

"Nae, it isnae," Glengask retorted. "And nae, I dunnae like the way ye decided to risk the safety of this family fer yer own sake. But as I *do* want what makes ye happy, give me a damned minute to see what happens and then have a word with Torriden."

Bear looked as though he preferred to stay and argue, so Catriona yanked on his hand. "The library, Munro. Show it to me."

As they passed the closed door of the morning room on the way to the stairs she was certain she heard the low murmur of voices. Resisting the temptation to stay and eavesdrop, she and Munro headed upstairs and then into a room with large, tall windows and a roaring fire in the hearth. Outside snow continued to fall, heavier now.

Behind her the door closed, and then warm, strong arms wrapped around her waist. "Ye jumped on Lachlan, ye wildcat," Bear murmured into her hair, chuckling.

"Of course I did," she returned stoutly, turning to face him and lifting up on her toes to catch his mouth in a kiss. "I couldnae see ye outnumbered, even though ye shouldnae have punched Torriden. He's nae the first man to insult me."

"He'll be the last one to try it."

She smiled. "Yer sister hugged me, Bear. Most women won't even look at me straight on. We had a chance."

"Nae. We *have* a chance, if pretty Torriden has any brains in his head. If he wants to keep breathing."

"Stop threatening people, giant. Ye were lucky that ye bloodying Torriden's beak made Elizabeth want to go tend him. If she hadnae . . ."

"But she did." He held her a little away from him. "Did I mention that there's nae a man or a woman in the world who can order me aboot, except fer ye?"

"I'm beginning to realize that some people might find ye difficult to manage," she returned.

He sighed. "Aye. And I suppose that MacDonald fool could refuse the idea. If he's here to begin a war with yer side of the clan, he'll nae take yer sister. Whatever happened, I should at least have demanded we spend the night here. I want ye in a proper bed. I want ye beneath me in soft sheets, with goose down to cushion ye."

Catriona laughed. She couldn't help herself. "In all of this mess, that's what concerns ye?" she asked, trying to catch her breath. "Ye want me to have a cushion for my arse?"

"I want ye to have the life ye want, where ye can wear trousers or a gown, sew or hunt, and have a damned soft bed to lie in. Is that so mad?" he demanded, frowning.

She kissed him again. "Nae. It isnae mad. It's wonderful. Ye're wonderful." Another kiss, softer and slower as his temper cooled. "Ye said I have yer heart, my giant. Ye have mine, ye ken."

His springtime-colored eyes held hers, and then he took both her hands in his and sank to one knee.

Good heavens. She'd known they would be together, but to see . . . this. And now, when for the first time she felt some optimism about her future . . . It was almost too much. Almost.

"I told ye I'd keep ye safe," he said quietly. "That isnae enough. What I should have said is that I'd do everything in my power to see ye happy. That I will love ye from my first breath in the morning to my last breath at night, and all through my dreams. That ye've made me a better man than I thought I was. Wherever we end up, Catriona MacColl, I want to be with ye there. Forever. Will ye marry me, my lass?"

She sighed, slowly and happily. "Ye're a brave, stubborn man, Munro MacLawry. Ye're the first man ever to see . . . me. I never thought I'd fall in love at all, and I tried nae to fall in love with ye, but I couldnae help myself. Ye've already seen me happy. Aye, I'll marry ye. I'd marry ye twice, if I could."

He pulled her down onto his knee and kissed her, wrapping his large hands around her and holding her hard against him. She couldn't even breathe, but she didn't care. It wasn't a dream any longer. Munro had said he was hers, and she his, but now it was real. They were real. Their future was real. She had no idea where they might find themselves, but they would be together. After she'd thought she would always be alone.

"Well, ye dunnae mean to make anything easy fer me, do ye?" Ranulf MacLawry said from the direction of the doorway.

She hadn't even heard the door open. When she tried to rise, though, Bear only scooped her into his arms and off her feet completely as he stood. "Just so ye realize that this is how it will be," he said, the humor leaving his eyes. "Cat and me. Together."

"Ye made that fairly clear, Bear." The marquis turned his gaze to her. "Yer sister saved ye, ye ken."

She tried to gain her feet, knocking Bear in the shoulder until he relented and set her down. "She and Lord Torriden . . . Goodness, I cannae even say it."

"I'll say it, then," Glengask returned. "They came to an agreement. I thought she was helping ye oot all this time, keeping the viscount distracted. Now I'm nae so certain she didnae have someaught in mind all along."

"I never gave her enough credit," Catriona said, wondering if the smile she felt pulling at her mouth was at all proper, under the circumstances.

"Neither did I," he said. "She may have just caught on quickly to Bear's plan, or she may have been playing a game, but she's nae a woman to cross." He paused. "May I have a private word with ye, lass?"

"Nae," Bear uttered.

"Aye," she said, glaring up at him and then walking across the room to his brother. "I'm listening."

"I've been trying since he was eight years old to get him to do as I say," the marquis commented, keeping his voice low. "He listens to ye, though. Ye calm him, I think."

"I love him," she returned.

"This isnae at all what I expected, ye know. At first I thought Bear had found some English-bred lass he wanted to rescue. We all assumed he meant to marry yer sister."

"I tried to get him to do that, to save her from Visford," she admitted. "He was surprised. And then he got mad at me."

"I should have paid closer attention. I knew he'd been restless, but I thought all I needed to do was send a likely lass in his direction." The marquis looked past her shoulder. "Before he comes over here to knock me on my arse again, I want to apologize to ye. I've become accustomed to seeing things my own way. Ye made me see through yer eyes fer a moment there, in the dining room. I misjudged ye."

Catriona imagined that Lord Glengask was not a man who apologized often. She nodded. "My father either never realized, or at least never admitted, that he'd made a mistake, and he had far more cause to apologize to me than ye do. I . . . The idea of being a part of a family that's willing to go to such extremes for each other warms me to my toes, m'laird. I hope I *can* be a part of it."

"Ye already are." He took a step backward. "I was apologizing, Bear. Dunnae pummel me."

"It's settled, then? Torriden has the MacColl he wants, and he'll leave us be? *Ye'll* leave us be?"

"Aye, and nae. Aye, Torriden has said he wishes to marry Elizabeth. And nae, I'll nae leave ye be, because ye're a part of this family. As is the lass to whom ye've just proposed. So kiss her, and then come doon to the dining room so we can find some clean plates and finish eating whatever ye didnae smash."

"I'll kiss her after ye leave the damned room, Glengask."

Despite his words, Bear offered his hand to his brother, who shook it promptly. *Thank heavens.* With another glance at her, the marquis turned on his heel and left the room, closing the door quietly behind him.

"And now fer ye, wildcat." Bear swung her up in the air, twirling her about and kissing her.

"Stop flinging me aboot like a sack of potatoes, ye heathen," she ordered, laughing. She felt so light inside she wouldn't have been the least bit surprised if she could fly through the air. This was joy, she realized. The first of many moments of joy.

"Very well," he said, setting her back on her feet again, but not releasing her. "Did ye know those workers saw ye the other day? I saw them looking up at the roof, but ye were gone by then. They must've been the ones gossiping to Torriden."

She frowned. "I didn't go outside. I havenae yet, with the workers there and me trying to look like a lady. I dunnae know what they were talking about."

"But . . ." He trailed off. "It doesnae matter, I suppose. I have ye, and if ye wish it, we'll have Haldane fer ourselves."

She already fallen half in love with the old ruin, even with only one livable room inside. Even if it was haunted. After all, that was where she'd met Munro. And where she'd realized that a man like him could love a lass like her. "I do wish it," she said. "As long as ye give me a big, soft bed."

He roared with laughter. "I'll give ye a big, soft bed, my wildcat. As long as ye share it with me."

"Then we have an accord, giant. Now kiss me again."